Three

in the Snow

Annie Groves was originally created by the much-loved writer Penny Halsall, who died in 2011. The stories drew on her own family's history, picked up from listening to her grandmother's stories when she was a child.

Linda Finlay is the author of many historical novels, and she has always loved crafting stories about brave women who have broken the mould. She is delighted to continue the Annie Groves legacy and to create new stories to inspire the next generation of heroines.

Also by Annie Groves

The Pride Family series
Ellie Pride
Connie's Courage
Hettie of Hope Street

The WWII series
Goodnight Sweetheart
Some Sunny Day
The Grafton Girls
As Time Goes By

The Campion series
Across the Mersey
Daughters of Liverpool
The Heart of the Family
Where the Heart Is
When the Lights Go On Again

The Article Row series
London Belles
Home for Christmas
My Sweet Valentine
Only a Mother Knows
A Christmas Promise

The Empire Street series
Child of the Mersey
Christmas on the Mersey
The Mersey Daughter
Winter on the Mersey

The District Nurses series
The District Nurses of Victory Walk
Christmas for the District Nurses
Wartime for the District Nurses
A Gift for the District Nurses
The District Nurses Make a Wish

The Three Sisters series
The Three Sisters of Victory Walk
Secrets for the Three Sisters

ANNIE GROVES

Three Sisters *in the* Snow

HarperCollins*Publishers*

HarperCollins*Publishers* Ltd
1 London Bridge Street
London SE1 9GF

www.harpercollins.co.uk

HarperCollins*Publishers*
Macken House,
39/40 Mayor Street Upper,
Dublin 1
D01 C9W8
Ireland

First published by HarperCollins*Publishers* Ltd 2025
1

A catalogue record for this book is available from the British Library.

ISBN: 978-0-00-875481-5 (PB)

This novel is entirely a work of fiction.
The names, characters and incidents portrayed in it are
the work of the author's imagination. Any resemblance to
actual persons, living or dead, events or localities is
entirely coincidental.

Set in Sabon LT Std by Palimpsest Book Production Ltd, Falkirk, Stirlingshire

Printed and bound in the UK using 100% Renewable Electricity
by CPI Group (UK) Ltd

MIX
Paper | Supporting
responsible forestry
FSC™ C007454

For my wonderful family & all those who bravely gave their lives that we may enjoy the freedom we have today.

CHAPTER ONE

January 1942

'There you go, Snuffles,' Patty Harrison murmured, carefully placing an old rug over the rabbit's hutch to keep out the worst of the winter weather. Catching sight of the Anderson shelter at the bottom of the garden, she shuddered as she recalled that terrible night the previous year when the area around Dalston had been bombed. Although their house had only suffered minimal damage to the windows, her poor sister Vera, who'd lived only a few streets away hadn't been so fortunate. How her heart went out to her. Of course, they'd been fortunate to have use of the flat above her husband's work premises, but it was only large enough to house one of their three daughters.

Which was why the middle girl, Hope, was now living here in Victory Walk with Patty and Bert whilst her older sister Faith and her young son Artie had been taken in by Faith's mother-in-law. She knew her sister hated having her family split, but at least they were all safe, which was more than those poor unfortunate families living closer to London, like Bermondsey, Lambeth and the docks which had suffered terribly.

Now, thankfully, it seemed Hitler had decided to

turn his back on London, but it didn't do to be complacent, and Patty made a note to take extra blankets to the shelter, just in case the situation changed.

Mindful of the frost glistening beneath her, she made her way back along the path, thanking her lucky stars that her own family was safe, although she prayed each night that their eldest son, Peter, who was away serving in the army, would return home safely. With her breath rising like mist before her, she reached the door of their little terraced home, shutting the door firmly behind her.

'What I wouldn't give for a nice fur coat like Snuffles,' she announced. 'It's that perishing outside, I've had to put another rug over his hutch. Robbie would never forgive me if he found his rabbit frozen stiff.' She stood in front of the range, rubbing her hands together, then sank gratefully into a chair. 'At least the frost's keeping the dirt from those bombed-out houses down a bit. Oh, sorry, that was thoughtless, Hope.'

'Not at all, Auntie Patty – and I'm grateful to you and Uncle Bert for letting me have Peter's room. Anyway, you should see the state the ambulances get in when we drive through all those derelict streets. We spend as much time cleaning them as answering emergencies these days. If it's not blood on the inside, it's muck on the outside.'

'Well, at least we've had another uninterrupted night.'

'Do you think Hitler's forgotten about London now everything's gone quiet, only they were saying at the depot that it's the beginning of the end,' Hope said, placing a steaming cup of tea on the big table before her.

Bert looked up from his newspaper. 'I wouldn't bank on that, Hope. According to the headlines, the Germans are still attacking the Russians but the snow's stopping their tanks. However, there's still fighting in North Africa, and Winston Churchill announced on the news last night that the Malay peninsula has been overrun by the Japanese.'

'All this fighting! I wish they'd just stop,' Hope declared, placing the blue woollen beret Patty had knitted her on her golden hair, then tucking the loose ends inside.

'Poor Peter, he could be fighting anywhere. I do wish he'd write and let us know he's safe,' Patty sighed, exchanging a knowing look with Bert. 'All I want is life to be back to normal and my family together again.'

Snatching up her gas mask, Hope kissed her aunt's cheek. 'I'm on the early shift so should be home by mid-afternoon. Shall I make a start on the potatoes then?'

'Yes, please, love. Don't forget, cut them small to save fuel, then I'll mash them up with those leftover vegetables and make rissoles. If we're lucky, I might be able to get some corned beef to go with them. That's if the queue's not snaking all the way down the high street. Honestly, it's taking longer and longer to buy anything these days and even then, choice is becoming so limited you wonder whether it's worth it.'

As the door closed behind her niece, Patty turned to her husband. 'She's a joy to have here, that one, it's like she's always lived with us. I was thinking earlier how proud I feel with the way our children are coping with this war, Bert, although I wish we'd hear from Peter, of course. There's our Rose putting in long hours at Homerton Hospital, Clover serving with the ATS, Daisy keeping things running at Manor House tube station . . .'

'Not single-handedly,' Bert smiled indulgently. 'But I take your point. And here she comes now,' he added, as their middle daughter, Daisy entered the kitchen yawning widely.

'Gosh, I hate these cold mornings. You should see the frost patterns on the inside of my bedroom window. I've given Robbie a shout – that lazy toerag of a brother of mine was pretending to still be asleep. Any tea left in the pot, Ma?'

'Yes, and if you're lucky, them used leaves might have taken on a bit of colour by now. You'd best get some porridge down you too, it'll warm your insides before you go out,' Patty added, nodding towards the pan on top of the range. The sudden rat-a-tat of the letterbox made them jump.

'I'll get it,' said Bert. 'Time I was leaving for the factory anyway. Mr Sutherland wants to see me first thing to discuss our meeting tomorrow – that article in the paper before Christmas calling unmarried women over twenty to enlist by spring means yet more shuffling around of the workers. Don't know how we're meant to keep up production, let alone increase it,' he muttered, reappearing moments later with a clutch of letters. 'Seems we've got a week's worth in one go, nothing from Peter though, I'm afraid.' He kissed Patty's cheek and, as the door closed behind him, she began sifting through the envelopes.

'I wonder who this one's from? It's typewritten and postmarked Ministry of Defence.' Quickly she tore open the envelope, frowning as she scanned the contents.

'Whatever's wrong, Ma?' Daisy asked. 'You've gone as white as the tablecloth,'

'Seems our Clover was struck down with influenza which turned to pneumonia.'

'Oh, poor thing. How bad is she?'

'It says she's recovering but has been moved to a defence convalescent home in the country called Beechwood, in Buckinghamshire. They've enclosed two train passes for us to visit. Oh, why didn't they bring her home so I could look after her? And why send her all the way to Buckinghamshire from North Wales? I don't even know where that is. Heavens, Daisy, these seats are reserved for tomorrow and Bert's got that important meeting. I'll have to see if we can move them on a day or so.'

'I doubt you'll be able to do that. The trains are jam-packed with service personnel moving from one place to another and reserved places are like gold dust. Don't worry, Ma, we'll visit her together,' Daisy said, patting her mother's hand. 'Under the circumstances, I'm sure Mr Rathbone will give me the day off. Pass me the letter and tickets and I'll check where exactly this home is and how to get there.'

Patty's thoughts were spinning like a top. How could she not have known her second eldest daughter was ill? And just how bad was she? She'd heard such dreadful things about influenza, let alone the pneumonia, and knew she wouldn't rest until she'd seen Clover for herself.

In the drawing room of Beechwood convalescent home, Clover was sitting beside the fire, trying to pen a letter to her parents. However, the walk from the dining room had left her feeling weak and she sat back in the chair and closed her eyes. She was still bemused as to why she'd been sent all the way here from the base in North Wales. Was it really only the previous day she'd been collected from the sick bay by an ATS driver? And in a sleek black car instead of the usual drab olive-coloured one as well. She'd been instructed to sit beside the driver in the front whilst an officer occupied the back. He'd been so preoccupied with his file of papers he hadn't even acknowledged her presence.

That bout of influenza had been bad enough but then it had turned to pneumonia, knocking her for six. The slightest exertion fatigued her and there was no way she'd be able to operate the heavy anti-aircraft searchlights back at base. Surely, she wasn't being discharged for failure to carry out her duties? Well, as her old gran used to say, there's no use dwelling on things you can't change; she'd find out in due course.

Meanwhile, the staff here were kind, the food tasty and plentiful, and a bedroom to herself was pure luxury after the privations of the Nissen hut she'd been sharing with five others. This elegant Edwardian house, with its red velvet drapes and wide bay windows that over-looked the manicured gardens, was luxury of a kind she'd only ever dreamed of. Clover smiled, picturing her mother's face if she saw where she was staying. Feeling stronger, she resumed her letter writing, assuring her family she was feeling better and would visit soon. As she sealed the envelope, a longing to see them shot through her and she vowed to visit Victory Walk on the way back to North Wales. London wasn't that far away, after all. Feeling unsettled, she picked up the newspaper from the table. Turning to the crossword, she noticed the cryptic clues were only partly completed and smiled. She loved a challenge and was soon absorbed.

'Excuse me, Miss Harrison.' Jolted back to the present, Clover looked up to find the day nurse standing over her. 'You have a visitor.'

'Apologies for intruding when you have yet to fully recover, but it's vital I speak with you.'

Clover stared up in surprise at the stern-looking man who was towering over her. He was dressed in a crisp green uniform, cap under his arm, and sporting gold-rimmed spectacles that magnified piercing grey eyes. Dapper, her pa would call him with his hair slicked back with pomade. Hastily, she put her paper on the table beside her and made to stand.

'Don't get up. Major Westwood. Best if we conduct this interview sitting,' he said in clipped tones, taking the chair opposite her and placing an official-looking folder on his lap. Interview? What had she done? She looked around for the nurse, but the room was now empty save for her and this army officer who clearly meant business. She swallowed and pulled her cardigan tighter round her.

'I trust you're recovering and in better health now?' he enquired.

'Thank you, yes. In fact, I—'

'Good, good,' he interrupted, not waiting for her to finish. 'I understand that you have been trained to use the latest anti-aircraft searchlights and clearly you enjoy completing puzzles,' he continued, picking up the newspaper and studying it.

'Well yes, I presumed whoever started it h—'

'Back at base you played scrabble, completed jigsaw puzzles and have been heard conversing in both French and German,' he interjected. Clover swallowed. Heavens, this sounded really serious. Was it against army rules? Had someone been spying on her? Or worse still, did they think she was a spy?

'My friend's mother is French and Marigold's been teaching me the language so that I can converse when we visit after the war. I've always wanted to travel.'

'That would be Marigold Pewsey, telephonist?' he asked, glancing at the file on his lap.

'Why yes,' she replied, staring at him in astonishment.

'Stationed in Paris before being transferred to North Wales,' he continued as if she hadn't spoken. 'And I presume it's because of this desire to travel you have also been learning German from Nele Weber?' His grey eyes were hard as flint. She returned his stare, refusing to be intimidated. After all, she'd done nothing wrong.

'She was schooled in Berlin so . . .'

'Indeed?' He gave her a level look, as if evaluating what she was saying.

'Indeed yes. And as our base is miles from anywhere, we make our own recreation whilst on standby. As I've already said, I wish to . . .'

'Travel,' he finished for her. 'Presumably, then, Miss Harrison, being the logical, rational and clear-thinking person you obviously are, you would be prepared to learn more?'

'Well, yes, of course, I would,' she began, wondering where this was leading. He seemed remarkably well-informed about her.

'Are you afraid of hard work and long hours?'

'Of course not,' she spluttered, indignant that he should suggest such a thing.

To her surprise, his lips twitched. 'Sorry, had to make sure. We need people with a certain kind of mind for a particular type of work to further the war effort. We think you have the skills, although you will need additional training. Instead of returning to Wales, Miss Harrison, you are being transferred – you could even say promoted – to somewhere near here.'

'But . . .' she began.

'Come now, Miss Harrison, you really don't think you were brought all the way here in a smart military limousine, merely to recover, did you? You could have been admitted to a convalescent home much nearer your base. The Red Cross have taken over many suitable houses and are doing a splendid job nursing our defence staff back to health.'

'I did wonder why . . .' she began but he was in full flow.

'We understand you still need time to fully recover and will grant you another three weeks' leave.'

'I won't need that long,' she protested.

'Believe me when I say you will need to have regained your stamina, both mentally and physically. I suggest you use the time to study this copy of Hugo's *German in 3 Months*.' He held up a small book. 'As well as the language and grammar, there are various exercises to see how much you've absorbed, then you can check the answers in the back. At the end of your stay here a driver will be sent to take you to your next post just a few miles away in Bletchley. There you will be given further instructions.'

Clover frowned. 'But I was going home to visit my parents.'

'Not possible. You must spend the time here brushing up your language skills in the privacy of your room, oh and continue solving the cryptic clues in the crossword, of course.' His eyes twinkled. 'Your parents have been sent train tickets and should be arriving any day now,' he told her. 'You may tell them you're being transferred to a place referred to as BP, to do clerical work.'

'Clerical work? But . . .' she spluttered.

'Make it *special* clerical work if you wish, but that is all you may say. You'll be given a box number where they can write to you, and of course you'll get leave to visit them after you've completed your training. Now, it wasn't obligatory before for you to sign the

OSA, the Official Secrets Act, but it is now. Do you have any questions?' He deftly removed papers from the folder and looked expectantly at her.

'Er, well, this has come as a shock, although of course like everyone else I want to do anything I can to help the war effort. What exactly am I signing?'

'You are signing to say you will never breathe a word about anything you are told or learn. I cannot stress the importance of this. Disobedience is classed as treason with a penalty of prison or worse, it is that serious. As you say, we must all do our bit to help win this war.' He handed her the papers along with a smart-looking fountain pen. Looking down at his folder, he waited whilst she read and signed, then promptly placed them back in his case before rising.

'Good luck, Miss Harrison. Remember, you must tell no one here, or anywhere, what you will be doing.' Then, before she could reply, he was striding from the room.

Wait until Marigold heard about the major's visit, she thought before remembering she couldn't mention it. Even if she could, how could she tell anyone what she was going to be doing when she didn't know herself? And a tingle of excitement shivered down her spine.

CHAPTER TWO

In her temporary home above Arthur's business, Vera was presiding over afternoon tea. Unfortunately, the effects of her beautifully laid table with snowy cloth and napkins were not appreciated by her three daughters, squeezed uncomfortably together, knee touching knee. Only Artie was having fun, gleefully tugging at the tassels that swung temptingly in front of him, then squealing as the cloth moved, making the crockery chink together.

'For heaven's sake, can't you control him?' Vera complained.

'It would be more sensible to use mugs,' Faith told her as pulling her son onto her lap elicited wails of protest.

'I couldn't possibly serve tea in mugs!' Vera looked outraged. 'This is Hackney, you know. Whatever would Arthur's colleagues and their wives say when they visit?'

'They haven't yet, Ma,' Joy reminded her.

'It's only a matter of time,' Vera insisted. 'Now, who's for another paste sandwich?'

'No, thanks, Ma, it's time I took Artie home for his nap,' Faith said, getting to her feet. 'Martin's mother is cooking chicken for our meal tonight.'

'I don't know how that woman manages to get so

many luxuries, I'm sure,' Vera told her, looking put out. 'Hopefully they'll do the repairs to our house soon then we'll all be able to live together again. It's not right our family being split like this.'

'I know, Ma,' Hope soothed. 'I don't think our house will be repaired anytime soon, though. Materials are hard to come by and more families are being made homeless all the time. Still, at least we've all got a roof over our head and Auntie Patty's looking after me really well.'

'And when our house is liveable again, you'll have to move back to Dalston,' Faith told her.

'There is that, ' Vera agreed. 'But living like this is hopeless,' she sighed, gesturing around the room and knocking over her cup in the process. 'Oh, damn!' she cried, watching as the brown liquid spread over her pristine cloth.

'Not in front of Artie, please,' Faith cried, jumping to her feet. 'Come on, young man, time we were gone. Bye all.'

Joy tried to mop up the spilt tea but there was no room to move, and she knocked the plate of sandwiches onto the floor.

'Oops,' she giggled. 'Never mind, the mice will enjoy a party tonight,'

'We do not have mice,' Vera declared hotly, taking herself off to the bedroom in a huff.

'Oh dear,' Hope murmured. 'I think we'll have to meet up at Auntie's next time. Come on, let's get this lot cleared away then we'll go and see what they've got at the market. Give Ma time to cool down.'

'Yes, let's. Father will be home soon, and I'd rather not be here. Their arguments are getting worse, Hope.'

'It must be hard, all being on top of one another like this.'

'Yes, if only I was old enough to join up then I could move out,' Joy sighed.

It was just getting light as Rose carefully made her way towards Homerton Hospital along pavements glistening with frost. Although everywhere looked pretty, she shuddered to think how easy it would be for people to slip and fall during the blackout and the last thing the hospital needed was people breaking limbs or worse. Hitler may have been quiet, with no bombs falling on London for some months now, but there had been an influx of patients suffering the usual winter ailments.

As they so often did of late, her thoughts turned to Philip, her tall, broad-shouldered boyfriend who was serving as a pilot in the RAF. The idyllic few days they had spent together in Canterbury the previous year felt like ages ago now. It had been a carefree time away from the stresses of war, culminating in his proposal, if not for marriage exactly, then an intent for the future. Of course, his mother hadn't approved of Rose, making it clear she was not the right class of person for her darling son. However, Rose was sure when she saw how happy they were together, she'd come round. Not that she'd had a letter from Philip recently, but with all the fighting going on in the world, he could have been posted anywhere.

'Sister Harrison, a word if you please.' Rose had

barely stepped through the hospital doors before she was accosted.

'Yes, of course, Matron. Is something wrong?' she asked, noting the older woman's serious demeanour as she stepped into her office.

'I went to see Katherine yesterday. As you know, baby Jean was born prematurely and although mother and daughter are making good progress, they're still not out of the woods. She is a frail, sickly infant and Katherine is desperately trying to get her to keep her feeds down. Luckily, Richard has another week's leave, but with Katherine being an older mother it's taking her longer to regain her strength. The upshot is that she's decided her family must come first and won't be returning to work in the foreseeable future.'

'Poor Katherine, I'll call and see her on my next day off,' Rose replied, pleased that she had at last finished the little Angel top she'd been painstakingly knitting these past months. All it needed were some tiny pearl buttons to sew on the back and she could take it with her.

'Better make it today or tomorrow, then.' The woman sighed and Rose noticed just how tired she was looking. 'However, first things first. You've done an admirable job these past months acting as sister on men's general, but I'm conscious that these are not normal times, and you're still very young.' Here it comes, Rose thought, she's going to bring in someone more senior from another hospital and I'll be back to being plain old Nurse Harrison.

'As I said earlier, we're going to be very busy – no,

extremely busy. Even as we speak, injured servicemen are being returned home via the train transport network and will be arriving within the next few days. Exact details will be relayed shortly. That means we'll be packed to, or even beyond, capacity, which will require extra reserves of strength and organizational skills, as well as dedicated nursing. Some of these men have been horrifically burned, lost limbs or are suffering from fever or trauma. So, what do you think, Sister Harrison. Are you up to the task?'

'Well, of course, I will do my best to see these poor men get the very best treatment we can provide.'

'Of that I have no doubt. What I mean is, are you prepared for your role as sister to be made permanent?'

'Yes, indeed, Matron,' Rose replied, her heart leaping.

'Good. In that case, I suggest you check on your stock of supplies, especially morphine, which as you know, must be kept under lock and key at all times. There really is no telling what state these poor men will be in. We can't begin to imagine what they've been through. Now, you'd better make haste to your ward and relieve the night staff. Tell them to get all the rest they can as they're going to need it.'

Hurrying along the corridor where the usual smells of disinfectant and cooking permeated the air, her mind was so full of what Matron had told her that she almost bumped into Dr Edwards.

'Oops, careful,' he said, putting out his hand to steady her.

'Sorry, doctor, I was miles away.'

'Hmm, probably with that handsome pilot, lucky

16

chap,' he said with a rueful grin. 'Actually, I'm glad I've bumped into you.' Another grin before his look turned serious. 'I've just come from your ward. Had to sedate old Mr Parsons – thought he was riding a horse back in the Great War, poor chap. Anyway, just giving you advance notice. Can't stop, emergency downstairs,' he said, disappearing in a flurry of white coat tails.

This has all the makings of an eventful day, Rose mused, glancing down the ward at Mr Parsons as she made her way to her station where two weary nurses waited, anxious to be relieved.

'Good morning,' she greeted them brightly. 'I hear from Dr Edwards that you had some excitement with Mr Parsons.'

'He thought the iron posts on his bed were his horse and he were trying to muster his troops. Made a right old racket, he did,' Susan, the new trainee explained, her green eyes wide.

'Woke most of the others too. Had a right old job settling them all down but I held his hand whilst Dr Edwards gave him his injection,' Effie added, and Rose couldn't help but notice how mature she'd become since returning to the ward.

'Well, he seems to be sleeping now,' she replied, glancing again at the end bed. 'Might be an idea to move him nearer the station so we can keep an eye on him; but don't worry I'll get the day nurses to see to that,' she added quickly, seeing the look of dismay on their faces. 'Right, pass me the patients' notes, and we'll do the handover. Then I have something important to convey before you go.'

It was sometime later, having briefed the day staff, carried out the morning TPR's – temperature, pulse and respiration checks – then accompanied the day duty doctor on his rounds, before Rose was able to inspect her stock of supplies as Matron had instructed. She made a list of what needed replenishing, adding additional antiseptic, bandages, lint and ointments for burns, all the while hoping there would be sufficient in the stores for supplies were becoming more difficult to get hold of these days, despite Ministry reassurances. Finally, noticing it was way past lunchtime, and desperate for a breath of fresh air, she handed over responsibility for the ward to the staff nurse, donned her outdoor attire and then, fingers crossed, checked her post. However, there was still no letter from Philip. It had been so long since she'd heard from him. Surely he hadn't changed his mind? This war made everything uncertain. Shaking her head to banish these unwanted thoughts, she stepped outside into the fresh air. Although the frost had cleared, it was still desperately cold, but she was determined to get the buttons she needed to finish the top for baby Jean. However, with no time to make it to Ridley Road Market, she headed to the haberdashery shop off More Street.

'Only got four left, I'm afraid, ducks. Difficult to get hold of any more with this blinkin' war,' the shopkeeper grumbled.

'That will be fine,' Rose replied, thinking how lucky it was her mother had found the pink wool left over from when Daisy had been a baby. Didn't do to get rid of anything, specially now, she'd told Rose.

Making her way back to the hospital, she was just debating whether she had time to nip into the canteen for a sandwich when she saw Philip's mother, smartly dressed in fox fur hat and coat, approaching on the other side of the road. Although she'd tried to be friendly to the woman, Mrs Sutherland had made it clear she thought Philip could do better for himself, and Rose steeled herself to either be ignored, or politely acknowledged. However, to Rose's astonishment, the woman held up a kid-gloved hand, stopped a passing delivery van, then hurried across to join her.

'Ah, Miss Harrison, how are you?' she greeted Rose.

'I'm fine, thank you, Mrs Sutherland. Busy at the hospital, as usual,' she added, hoping to prompt the woman to remember she was Sister Harrison now, but as her mother was fond of saying, some seed falls on stony ground, for the woman merely nodded. 'I hope you're keeping well too. And Charlotte.'

'Thank you, yes. Charlotte is making such good progress in the WAAF, she's already on her way to receiving a promotion. We're extremely proud of her as you can imagine. Nice class of person there, you see. More suited to our own.'

'That's good to hear,' Rose replied, politely.

'Has Philip written with his news?' she asked quirking a pencilled brow.

'I haven't heard from him for a few weeks now. I expect he's busy.'

'Oh, indeed he is.' The woman paused then gave a condescending smile. 'He's become affianced to the most charming young lady, the Earl of Edmonton's daughter.

Oh, you didn't know?' she added, her lips curling in another smile, this time triumphant, as Rose let out an involuntary gasp. So, her suspicions were correct.

'I thought he might have let you know. Well, I must get on. There is so much to arrange as I'm sure you can imagine. Good day to you, Miss Harrison,' she added, all but gliding on her way, leaving a trail of Chanel perfume in her wake.

'Are you all right?' an elderly gentleman asked, stopping and frowning worriedly as Rose stood rooted to the pavement, staring after the woman.

'Er yes, thank you,' she replied, and in a daze, began walking again. To think she'd been worrying about Philip when all the time he'd been seeing – no, *courting* – someone else. And after all he'd said about their future on that wonderful weekend away! Obviously, he'd been playing her for a fool. Thank goodness she'd insisted on separate bedrooms. Anger quickened her pace so that by the time she arrived at the hospital she'd worked herself into a frenzy.

CHAPTER THREE

'Clover, dear girl, it's so good to see you,' Patty exclaimed hurrying across the room and hugging her daughter tightly to her. 'Why, you're all skin and bones. Let me look at you,' she added, drawing away and narrowing her eyes.

'I'm fine, Ma, really. In fact, I've just written you a letter,' she added, indicating the envelope on the table.

'Hmm, you look very pale to me,' Patty replied. 'Oh, you wouldn't believe the journey we had getting here. We got to Euston only to find the train was late and then it was packed with servicemen. We even had difficulty getting to our seats. Then we had to walk from the station and all the way up the long driveway leading to this house. Those beech trees might be beautiful but it's freezing and—'

'All right, Ma, let poor Clover breathe,' Daisy laughed. 'It's good to see you, sis,' she grinned. 'Are you coming back with us? 'Cos if so, I'll have to tidy my clothes off your bed.'

'No, you're safe for a while,' Clover replied quickly, not wanting to discuss her future plans. 'Why don't we sit down,' she added, feeling weak after such an exuberant greeting.

'I've brought you a little something,' Patty said, fishing

in her bag. 'It's not much but all I could manage at short notice. Still, it's the thought that counts.'

'Thanks, Ma,' Clover smiled, staring at the red apple and remembering the last time she'd eaten one. She'd been out walking with Marigold and they'd really got to know each other for the first time.

'Well, this is a right grand house and everywhere smells lovely too,' Patty murmured, sinking into one of the comfy armchairs beside the fire and gazing around the elegant room with its high ceilings and plush, if faded, décor.

'Think I'll get flu if this is where you get sent,' Daisy grinned.

'Daisy, how could you when your sister's been so poorly?' Patty scolded but was interrupted by the arrival of a dark-haired orderly in white overalls carrying a tray of refreshments. 'Ooh, thank you, dear,' she said, her eyes lighting up at the sight of the teacakes glistening with what looked like real butter instead of the scrape of pale margarine they'd become used to.

'Matron thought you'd welcome something hot after your travels,' the woman replied. 'Would you like me to pour, Miss Harrison.'

'That's fine, thank you, Doreen, you've got enough to do,' Clover told her, reaching for the pot.

'Shall I take your outdoor things?' the woman offered. 'Although I'm afraid the fire is somewhat sparse, what with rationing biting harder now.'

'Thank you,' Patty said, slipping the gas mask from her shoulder then shrugging out of her faded coat and scarf. 'You too, Daisy, or you won't feel the benefit

22

when you leave. Goodness, that tea looks strong,' She frowned at the dark liquid in the cup Clover handed her.

'That's because it's coffee, Ma. They have tea in the afternoons here. Don't worry, it's quite tasty, unlike that beastly chicory stuff we get served back at base. Now, tell me how things are in Victory Walk?'

'Your pa sends his love and says he's sorry he couldn't come today but he has an important meeting with Mr Sutherland. They're having to rearrange everything now more women are signing up. And we haven't had a letter from Peter in a while,' she sighed, a shadow clouding her eyes as she thought of her eldest son fighting who knew where. 'Robbie's still besotted with his blinkin' rabbit and I'm not keen on him playing with those older boys but his friends haven't returned from the country yet.'

'Hope has settled in well,' Daisy told her, 'although she's going to be busy driving returning injured servicemen to hospitals in the area. Apparently so many are being repatriated, the military ambulances can't accommodate them all.'

'I expect Rose will be hectic too then,' Clover sighed. 'Don't look so worried, Mum – Peter survived Dunkirk so I'm sure he's not going to let the enemy get him now. Come on, eat up. It's not every day we get a treat like this.'

'You're right,' Patty agreed, taking another bite of her teacake then eagerly licking the butter from her lips and savouring the taste. 'Now, tell me, Clover. How come you've been sent all the way here to

Buckinghamshire to recover when you've got a perfectly good home waiting an hour or so away?'

'When the trains are running to schedule,' Daisy interjected, raising her brows. 'What I'd like to know is why most people here are in uniform, if they're recuperating?' She frowned, peering around the room which had filled with servicemen and a couple of women in day clothes since they had arrived. 'Not that I'm complaining. I mean, just look at those dashing hunks at the table by the window. It's a rare sight with most of the young men away now.'

'Really, Daisy,' Clover rebuked. 'Being a defence convalescent home, it's expected here.' She ignored the reference to the men. 'Saves on clothing coupons too.'

'Hmm, maybe I should get a uniform then,' Daisy mused, recalling the recruitment posters she'd seen on the way here for the Land Army. Being out in the country, growing food for the nation sounded far more exciting than being stuck underground all day.

'Do you have a special friend of your own back in Wales?' Patty asked, looking quizzically at Clover.

'I have lots of friends,' she smiled, knowing full well what her mother meant and refusing to be drawn.

'That's good,' replied Patty. Then, realizing nothing more was forthcoming, she jumped to her feet. 'All this coffee is going through me. I need the cloakroom.'

'It's through the archway and on the left,' Clover told her.

'Well, come on, spill the beans,' Daisy urged as soon as her mother had disappeared. 'What's it like back at base with all those lovely men?'

'Actually, Daisy, if you must know we're referred to as officers' groundsheets,' Clover said stiffly. 'Anyway, how's that young fellow of yours, Freddy? Have you heard from him?'

Daisy shook her head. 'All seems to have gone quiet.' She let out a sigh. It had been an age since she'd last seen Freddy and she really missed him.

'It's not surprising. Most of them have either been sent abroad or, like your Freddy, are busy patrolling our seas so that provisions can get through. Don't worry, sis, I'm sure you'll hear soon. So, how's life at Manor House tube station? Mr Rathbone still cracking the whip?'

'He's a poppet as well you know. In fact, he totally supported me taking time off to come here today, even helped me work out the best route. It's all gone rather quiet now Hitler's stopped bombing London. Not so many people are sheltering at night and actually I—' She stopped as their mother came bustling back. It wouldn't do to let her know what she was thinking.

'Lovely facilities, you really must go before we leave, Daisy. There's Izal paper, proper soap that doesn't smell like antiseptic and—'

'Ma!' Daisy exclaimed, glancing anxiously towards the men sitting around the big, polished table.

'Sorry, it's just so nice to experience a bit of luxury. If it wasn't for Bert's newspapers . . .' Noting Daisy's frown she stuttered to a halt. 'Now, our Clover, you haven't told us how you're really feeling? When are they letting you come home so I can look after you and feed you up best as I can?'

'Well, Ma, that's the thing. I can't come home because

I'm being transferred to somewhere near here that's referred to as BP.'

'BP? What kind of name is that? What will you be doing exactly? I trust they're not sending you to fight,' Patty cried, clutching at her heart.

'No, Ma, you know the ATS won't let women see active service. I'll be quite safe doing clerical work.'

'Clerical work!' Patty exclaimed. 'But you—'

'Special clerical work,' Clover added quickly. 'My orders are to spend the next three weeks recuperating here before reporting for duty, when I'll find out more about what I'll be doing. Meanwhile, I have things to read and learn,' she added quickly as Patty opened her mouth to protest.

'I suppose you aren't able to operate those heavy searchlights until you're back to strength,' Patty replied.

'Exactly,' Clover nodded, ignoring the look her sister was giving her. 'I'll send you my new address as soon as I know it, but I'm afraid I really can't tell you any more at the moment.'

'Excuse me, Mrs Harrison, but it's time for your daughter's luncheon before her afternoon nap,' the orderly said, reappearing with their things. 'I'm sorry we can't invite you to stay but well, rations, you know.'

'Yes, of course. Blooming rations, eh?' Patty said, taking her coat from the woman. 'It was kind of you to offer us refreshments though, thank you; them teacakes were a rare treat.'

'You're welcome, Mrs Harrison. No, don't get up,' she added, turning as Clover began to rise. 'I'll see your family out.'

Patty leaned forward and kissed Clover's cheek. 'You take care of yourself, our Clover, and see that you write soon.'

'Well!' cried Patty when moments later they found themselves walking back down the long driveway. 'What do you make of that, our Daisy?'

'I don't know, but I'd definitely be taking more notice of those handsome men than our Clover was.' And while Daisy laughed, she couldn't help her thoughts turning to Freddy, her own handsome serviceman. My, how she missed him.

Meanwhile Patty was busy with her own thoughts. Her gut was telling her that Clover knew more about this new job than she was letting on. The question was: why wasn't she telling?

She'd have to run it past Bert when they got home. He knew more about these things.

However, when they arrived back at Victory Walk, Bert was frowning when he looked up from the news bulletin on the wireless.

'They've just announced that the repatriation of our injured boys from North Africa is underway, Patty. Seems some are pretty badly injured and there are many more of them than they originally thought,' he added quietly as they exchanged a look of tacit understanding.

Please don't let our Peter be amongst them, she prayed.

'Right, everyone, inside please, I have important news to impart!' The new station officer's strident voice rang out from the depot's doors.

Hope looked up from the front of the ambulance she'd been cleaning and threw her cloth into the bucket. Despite her heavy ambulance service coat, she was freezing cold, her hands red and wrinkled from the icy water.

'My fingers are shrivelled like chitterlings,' Hope moaned as she and Kitty, the girl she was rostered with that day, gratefully made their way into the comparative warmth of the depot, surprised to see it already half-filled with staff from other shifts.

'You mean you can remember what they're like?' the girl scoffed. 'When I think of the nice thick broth me ma used to cook with them in, well, it fair makes me mouth water. Lucky to find more than a bit of carrot and barley in it now. Must have lost at least a stone since this wretched war started.' Hope stared at the plump girl in surprise but refrained from answering.

'Come along, Potter, Hendy, we haven't got all day,' Station Officer Strang urged.

'Yes, ma'am,' Kitty muttered, tucking a wayward auburn lock behind her ear. 'Hope this promotion ain't gone to her head. Come up from South of the Thames, she has.'

'Right, crew, listen up, please. I've called a meeting of the entire station as this is important and involves each and every one of you.' Sonia Strang waited until they were all paying attention. Hope took a quick look around, hoping to catch a glimpse of her friend Ian MacLeod. If this briefing was so important, then surely he should be here too? However, as the station officer continued, she found herself paying close attention to what she was saying.

'I have been informed that an ambulance train ferrying wounded men returning from North Africa will be arriving at Liverpool Street Station within the next day or so – exact date and time of arrival to be confirmed shortly. Our job, along with other ambulance crews in the district will be to ferry them to military and local hospitals, including our own. Again, exact details will be relayed when numbers are known. We have been put on high alert so until then those on duty will remain here until 7.00 p.m. when the night shift will take over. This will be an arduous task, but I know you will want to do your duty by those servicemen who have put their lives on the line for us.' There was a general murmur of agreement.

'Now, I suggest those not on duty go home, have a hearty supper and good night's sleep . . .' This last statement was met with a mix of laughter and ribald remarks.

'Can't remember when I last had a good hearty supper, miss.'

'Fair enough Simpson, I take your point. However, your wife is a resourceful woman so I'm sure she'll have something hot ready for you.' More laughter echoed round the room, which she chose to ignore. 'Obviously, all leave is cancelled for the foreseeable.'

'When did we last get leave?' Kitty muttered.

'Please see your vehicles are properly parked and ready for action and pray Hitler will still be too busy to bomb London tonight. Now scoot.'

With a clattering of boots and much mumbling and muttering, the assembled group dispersed.

'Well, that's us off home then,' Hope said. 'I serviced our vehicle earlier, so I'll park it up then see you tomorrow, Kitty.'

'Before you do, I think someone's looking for you,' Kitty smirked, giving her a nudge. Hope looked up to see Ian MacLeod making his way towards her. Her heart flipped and she was about to ask him where he'd been then saw the look of utter despair on his face.

'Ian, what's happened?'

'It's my sister and kids. An unexploded bomb went off in her street. Bomb disposal chaps reckon it could have lain dormant for months until vibration from the traffic finally set it off. Three houses in the terrace demolished, fifteen people killed.'

'That's terrible!' Hope gasped. 'Y-your sister and children?'

'They're fine, thank God, but it has shaken her up something rotten. As you know, she's helped me look after them since my wife died. Now she thinks they'll all be safer in the country and I agree so she's taking them to stay with her sister-in-law in Dorset. But with the use of private vehicles banned, it'll be challenging trying to visit, to say the least so I won't see much of them.' His voice broke slightly then it steadied. 'However, their safety is paramount. I was going to go with them, see them settled, but in view of the briefing just now I'll have to make do with seeing them onto the train.'

Hope squeezed his arm in sympathy. 'Surely if you explain, Strang will understand?'

He shook his head. 'It's important I'm there to assist the soldiers.'

'But surely . . .' she began.

'Look, Hope, you don't understand so leave it be, eh?'

His bright blue eyes hardened to navy, sending a shiver down her spine. She couldn't begin to understand his reasoning as there were plenty of them to attend to the incoming men. All she knew was that, one way or another, Hitler and his bombs were hellbent on disrupting all their lives.

CHAPTER FOUR

'Sister Harrison, your ward is already to receive our guests, I take it?' Matron asked, appearing in the doorway, her keen eyes taking in the whole ward at a glance.

'Yes, Matron. I've been able to discharge two of our existing patients into the care of the district nurses, and one has been placed in our local residential home. I've moved the rest down towards the end so we can give the servicemen our immediate attention, although I'm afraid Mr Parsons is still somewhat disturbed.'

'Ah yes, Dr Edwards did mention him. It's a crying shame that someone who served our country so well in the Great War should end up like that,' she sighed. 'Still, we must treat him with the dignity he deserves, even if we do have to sedate him from time to time.' She ran her fingers across the iron bedstead beside her and nodded. 'Some of these servicemen will have open wounds so cleanliness at all times is more imperative than ever. Others will be in torment – and I do not say that word lightly. I take it you've briefed your staff?'

'Of course, Matron,' Rose replied, hoping her younger nurses wouldn't find the situation too distressing. 'We've checked our supplies and are stocked as best we can.' She didn't add that they'd spent the morning disinfecting all the work surfaces for surely the strong smell spoke for itself.

'And what about you, Sister Harrison? You're looking quite peaky yourself, if I may say.'

'I'm fine, thank you,' she said quickly, wondering why she should be so surprised the woman had noticed. Since meeting Mrs Sutherland the other day, Rose had been anything but fine.

'Remember, no matter how busy we get, it is paramount that you look after yourself for you cannot nurse others if you yourself are out of sorts. Should you wish to discuss anything at any time, my door is always open.'

'Thank you, Matron,' Rose replied, but the woman had gone, and she was talking to thin air. How had Matron known she was unhappy? She'd tried so hard to appear her normal self, but there was no time to dwell on her own feelings for the first ambulances were pulling up.

* * *

'Everyone, listen up, please,' Station Officer Strang called, her firm and decisive tone drawing immediate attention. 'Following on from yesterday's briefing, I reiterate: today is going to be challenging, but hopefully you'll be happy doing your bit to help the brave servicemen who are being repatriated from North Africa.'

'Hear, hear,' the group murmured.

'As I've already said, along with other ambulance station crews in the area, we're to assemble at Liverpool Street Station ready to transport the men to Queen Alexandra's Military Hospital. When Alexandra's has reached capacity, you'll be directed to other hospitals which are on standby, ready to receive your patients. As you can imagine, this operation must be carried out with military precision, and I expect you to obey orders immediately and without argument. I know I can rely on you.' She paused and looked at them each in turn.

'Blimey, it sounds like she's the blinkin' military,' Kitty whispered.

Sonia Strang had superb hearing. 'Then you'll know to obey, Hendy,' she retorted. 'Their train is due to arrive at 2.00 p.m. – however, there could of course be delays. Geraldine, you're rostered with MacLeod and will stay here in case of any local emergency.' Hope's heart sank and she glanced covertly around hoping to catch sight of Ian. After their cool parting yesterday, she'd hoped they would be working together today. She wanted to clear the air between them and check that his family had boarded their train safely. However, there was no time to dwell on her thoughts, as the station officer continued issuing orders.

'I shall be driving with you, Hope, and we'll lead the convoy. The rest of you will pair up as per the roster.'

'Lucky you, eh?' Kitty whispered, nudging her side. 'Teacher's pet, what?'

Hope felt a momentary pang that she wouldn't be driving, then chided herself for being petty. Undoubtedly, some of the servicemen would require medical assistance on the journey so as soon as they were dismissed she'd make another thorough check of their supplies. It wouldn't do to be found lacking.

'One last thing: these poor boys have had a rough time of it and your brief is to be cheerful and welcoming. The last thing they'll want to see are long faces or to receive meaningless words of platitude. And please make sure your hands are clean before you leave.' Hope glanced down at hers, noting the oil streaks that were an occupational hazard these days. 'Now, it's going to be a long and arduous afternoon, so I suggest you all have a hot drink then check your vehicles are ready. We will leave in precisely thirty minutes. Any questions?'

As the hall rang with silence, everyone focused on the task ahead, Hope spotted Ian arriving, and her heart flipped. Thank heavens, she'd be able to speak with him before they left. 'Good luck, everyone,' Sonia Strang cried. 'Ah, MacLeod, good of you to join us. In my office now, please.'

As Ian crossed the hall, he smiled in Hope's direction, but didn't stop. Stifling a sigh, she ignored the queue lining up for hot drinks, went to the cloakroom to wash her hands then made her way outside to her vehicle. She would have to try to catch him later.

'Right, ready for off,' Sonia Strang said, jumping into the driving seat some minutes later. 'MacLeod will man the depot in our absence and telephone if there is any emergency he can't handle, which I'm sure there won't be. Now hold on, it's a little while since I've driven one of these,' she said, releasing the ambulance's brake and double declutching. 'Ah, just like riding a bicycle,' she grinned as they lurched out of the depot yard, the rest of the fleet following behind.

'I'm surprised you chose Ian MacLeod to man the depot,' Hope ventured, hanging on for dear life as Sonia Strang led the convoy of ambulances through the streets, ignoring potholes and swerving around debris without slowing.

'Why? Don't you think he's capable?' The station officer frowned. 'I know the gossip has followed him, but I thought that's all it was, gossip.'

'What do you mean?' Hope asked, puzzled.

'Perhaps you should ask him. I mean, I'm new here and you know how people like to talk. Well . . .' she sighed seeing Hope frown. 'Rumour hath it he's a conchie; you know, a conscientious objector. But like I say, it's probably just gossip. Still, I should ask him.

'Now, hold on, Potter, we need to step on it, can't let the station down.' The ambulance sped forward, throwing Hope back against her seat and she couldn't have spoken even if she wanted. Even her thoughts were being tossed around as the streets passed by in a blur.

Was that why he'd wanted to help the soldiers, to ease his conscience?

'Just look at it all!' Sonia snorted, gesturing at the devastation they were passing. Bombed-out buildings, heaps of rubble and hardly a tree left standing. 'Ruddy

Hitler, I guess the landscape will never be the same again.'

It was a sobering thought, but there was little time to reflect as before long they were pulling up at the approach to Liverpool Street Station, where they were directed to join the queue of medical vehicles already waiting.

'Right, we'll park here then see what's what. Bring the stretcher.' Sonia Strang's bark would have done any military officer proud.

The activity inside the station was phenomenal. Organized chaos reigned with people scurrying this way and that, whistles blowing, steam hissing from the trains' brakes and clouds of smoke tainting the air. Medical orderlies marched by carrying the casualties of war on stretchers, laying them side by side along the concourse. An officer then meticulously consulted his clipboard and allocated each waiting ambulance crew a patient, telling them where they were to be taken.

'Wait right there,' they were instructed, and duly stood in line. Hope looked round for her colleagues but couldn't make them out in the melee. What she did notice was how smart everyone else from other services looked in their various uniforms. Quite different from the ambulance crews with their heavy issue coats over their cotton drill overalls.

She watched as the walking wounded were led towards a waiting WRVS wagon where cheerful ladies dispensed mugs of tea to the eager men. Some were on crutches, others had arms in slings or bandages covering their heads. Yet despite their injuries and all they'd been through, the sense of camaraderie was tangible.

'Thanks, love, I've been waiting for this ever since we left Blighty,' she heard one soldier say and seeing one sleeve of his jacket pinned up where his arm should be, wondered how he could be so cheerful. As if he sensed Hope looking, he shot her a saucy wink and she couldn't help smiling back.

'Careful, Potter,' Sonia cautioned but although her tone was sharp, there was a smile playing on her lips. 'Right, this is us,' she added, and they bent to lift a stretcher, leaving theirs to be used in its place. Their patient was unconscious, and Hope could tell from his pallor that he was in a bad way.

'We need to hurry,' she cried.

'Keep calm, Potter. I understand your concern, but we can only go as fast as this queue allows.'

It seemed an age before they reached their vehicle.

'Right,' Sonia instructed, 'in the back with the patient and keep an eye on him but don't give him anything if he wakes. We don't know what or if he's already been prescribed. I'll get us out of here as quickly as possible.'

Hope climbed up beside the man as they were directed back onto the road and although the station officer drove quickly, she was careful so the ride to the Queen Alexandra's Military Hospital was smoother than before. There, staff were waiting to relieve them of their patient, who hadn't regained consciousness during their journey. 'All love and good luck,' she murmured to him before jumping up beside the station officer.

'Well done, girl,' Sonia said and to Hope's surprise she patted her hand before starting up the engine. 'Here we go again,' the station officer murmured, turning back towards the train station where they collected four of the walking wounded who, despite their injuries were so relieved to be back on home ground, they laughed and joked in the back of the ambulance for the entire journey.

And so the afternoon wore on into the evening – same routine, different patients, different hospital. With the partially covered lights barely illuminating their way, Sonia sighed as she tried to miss the inevitable potholes or worse but even in this poor light there was no missing the decaying parts of dead bodies still dangling from the trees. Sometimes they passed an ambulance crew from their own depot, but everyone was too focused on their duties to do anything other than raise their hand in acknowledgement. However, even in the dim light the devastation all around them was horrifying, damaged buildings with their blown-out windows gaping like toothless monsters, remnants of clothes and curtains caught in the trees and flapping like skeletons in the breeze.

'Won't be anywhere left for Hitler's grand invasion if he doesn't hurry up,' Sonia cried, gesturing to the ruined properties in Chatsworth Road.

'You don't think he will really invade?' Hope asked, her voice coming out in a squeak.

'Who knows what goes through that maniac's mind.'

In the back of the ambulance, Hope swallowed and found herself gripping the patient's hand harder. It didn't bear thinking about.

'Don't you worry, lass, me and the lads are fighting to the death to save our country and families,' the soldier wheezed before closing his eyes again.

Finally, they drew up alongside other medical vehicles beside the hospital at Homerton. 'Last one for us,' Sonia murmured, opening the doors and helping her clamber down, looking as exhausted as Hope felt. She turned to her patient. 'Thanks, girl, you're an angel,' he murmured, and she just had time to smile before he was whisked away by the efficient staff who'd been waiting.

'Right, girl, I'm driving you home now,' Sonia said as she once again clambered up beside her.

'But I thought that was against orders?' Hope murmured, hardly able to keep her eyes open.

'Lucky for you *I* give the orders around here then,' her station officer quipped.

Although she was exhausted and went straight to bed, Hope couldn't sleep, the events of the day going round and round in her head like horses on a carousel. How many of the soldiers had they managed to help save, she wondered. They'd all been injured, yet those that were conscious had been quite jovial, happy to be back home in England, although some couldn't help moaning and wincing when they hit the numerous bumps and potholes in the road. However, none of them had ever once complained. Then there had been those who were unconscious and in a really bad way. She sent up a prayer they would all recover.

It was only then that she remembered Sonia's words about the gossip that had followed Ian MacLeod. Was it true? And if it was, would it change how she felt about him? She'd have to ask him next time she saw him, she thought, as she finally drifted into a restless sleep.

CHAPTER FIVE

Patty looked up as the door of the greengrocer's opened letting in a blast of ice-cold air.

'Hurry up and shut that! Oh, it's you, Vera,' she said, wrapping her cardigan tighter round herself as her sister manoeuvred her bulk through the door. She was wearing what Patty thought of as her Windolene coat because of its vivid pinky-purple shade.

'It's brass-monkey weather and no mistake,' her sister greeted her.

'Or even brassicas, looking at these poor specimens,' Patty sighed, indicating the withered Brussels sprouts and cabbages she'd been stacking on the shelves, spreading them out to look as though there was more on offer. 'Hardly enough to feed a family, let alone the good folk of Dalston.'

'This cold's no laughing matter, what with them cutting the fuel ration,' Vera moaned, lowering herself onto the stool and setting it rocking.

'At least I've some tea leaves out the back to make a brew. That'll warm us.'

However, Vera was in no mood to be placated.

'There's not much left in the butcher's either and it's only halfway through the morning. Talking of cutting rations, there's hardly any decent clothing anywhere and you should see the cost of what little there is! Not a frill or trimming to be seen, it's all plain material pared back to the minimum. Honestly, you can keep your utility clothing. John Lewis would have had better stock if they hadn't been bombed,' Vera huffed, as if the department store itself had been responsible for its devastation the previous year.

'As for "Beauty is your duty", well, there's no rouge to be had for love nor money, and do you know they're making powder for feet now instead of for the face? How am I meant to keep up with the wives of Arthur's business colleagues, that's what I want to know? He mixes with councillors and businessmen, you know.'

'It can't be easy,' Patty sympathized, suppressing a sigh, for she'd heard it all countless times before.

The door being kicked open made her look up sharply, but it was only a gangly youth bent double under the weight of a sack. Gone were the days when burly Stan would wheel his cart round to the side entrance and help her unload the deliveries. 'Thanks, love. Just put it down there,' she told him, jumping out of the way as it landed on the floor, narrowly missing her feet.

'Sorry, missus, 'tis right heavy that,' he gasped.

Poor thing, she thought, for the lad was just skin and bones in a threadbare jacket despite the wintry weather. Picking up an apple, she rolled it across the floor in front of him. He eyed the fruit hungrily but duly retrieved it and held it out to her.

'Oops, butterfingers,' she tutted. 'Won't be able to sell that now so you'd better have it.'

'Cor, ta, missus,' he muttered, biting into it then making off in case she should change her mind.

'You always was soft in the head,' Vera told her.

'Well, at least we'll have some spuds to go with the greens now,' Patty said. tearing open the sack and releasing their earthy aroma. 'Bubble and squeak tonight, I think. Although it might be more bubble than squeak,' she laughed. 'Still, as it's quiet, I'll go out the back and get us that brew.'

Moments later they were sipping the reused leaves that passed as tea these days. Vera turned to Patty.

'It is quiet in here. Where are your customers?'

'They come in early, hoping to get the best pick.'

'Pick of what, though?' Vera snorted, eyeing the shrivelled greens with distaste. 'Any news of Peter?'

'No,' Patty sighed. 'Bert reckons the way the fighting's going they'll not have time to write home. It's hard not knowing he's all right, though.'

'Oh well, they say it's the bad news that travels the quickest,' Vera replied.

'Thanks – I think.'

'Anyhow, you were out when I called by your house to see Hope yesterday. She said Clover has been poorly and you'd gone to visit her in some home near Buckinghamshire. Seems funny transferring her from North Wales. I hope everything's all right?'

Patty suppressed a smile. That explained her sister's visit – she couldn't abide not knowing what was going on. Briefly, Patty filled her in.

'And apparently she's being transferred to a clerical job in somewhere known as BP, so hopefully we'll be seeing more of her,' she finished.

'Clerical? Your Clover? Bit different from manning the searchlights, isn't it?'

'That's probably because she's been so poorly,' Patty said quickly, putting her mug down on the ledge as Vera opened her mouth to question her further. The truth was, the more she thought about it, the more she felt Clover was hiding something from her. 'Anyhow, I'd best carry on while we talk,' she said, bending to empty the potatoes from the sack onto the wooden shelves.

'Well, I thought she'd have been sent home to recuperate. Still, it will be nice for you to see more of your girl when she's better. It's difficult for me to have my lot round, the flat being so pokey.'

'Any news on the repairs to your home?'

Vera shook her head. 'I went to see the council again yesterday. They've secured the chimney stack, but apparently making properties safe is all they can manage at the moment. They've not got the materials nor the manpower to do any more, so goodness only knows when we'll be able to move back in. I tell you, Patty, we're squashed together like blinkin' sardines – poor Joy has to make her bed up each night and there's nowhere for her things. Living over the business premises isn't the same as having your own house. Mind you, we're right thankful you've taken in our Hope.'

'We love having her and she's fitted in well. And at least you all have a roof over your head,' Patty pointed out. 'So many families have been made homeless and now some of our soldiers are returning.'

'That's what the man at the council said. Hope reckons she's going to be very busy helping to ferry the badly injured to all the hospitals in the area that can accommodate them. Let's hope Hitler keeps his blinkin' nose out.'

'Golly, yes, another actual raid doesn't bear thinking about,' Patty shuddered. 'It's bad enough with all these false alarms. Obviously, Rose will be busy at the hospital too. Funny to think they might be working together, isn't it?'

'Who'd have thought it?' Vera mused, taking another sip of her tea.

'Talking of being together, I was thinking . . .' Patty began

'Anyway, at least Hackney is a better area to live in,' Vera continued, ignoring her.

Well, thought Patty, *I'm blowed if I'll issue my invite now, for she'd been about to say it was time the family all got together and why didn't they come over for a pot-luck meal.*

'Joy has some nice friends to go out with when she's not helping dispense teas with the WRVS,' Vera continued blithely. Then she let out another long sigh. 'The trouble is all the women there look so smart. Oh, if only they had decent things in the shops.'

'Perhaps it's more about joining in with their activities?' Patty suggested.

'Got to look the part first. It's so true what they say about appearances.'

46

'Tell you what, Vera. I've just read an interesting feature in *Woman's Own* about revamping existing outfits. Bert will be on fire duty this weekend and the girls are going to be busy, so why not bring over some of your clothes and we'll go through my sewing box, see what we can find?'

'Do you mean that?' Vera asked, brightening.

'Certainly. We can put our own spin on "make do and mend". I'll see what bits and bobs I can get hold of and rustle up a stew. It can be simmering on the range while we work,' she told her sister, straightening up and rubbing the dirt from her hands. 'What do you think?'

'I think you need to look after those hands of yours. They look like an old woman's. Bloomin' war or not, you should rub in some cream to soften them,' Vera retorted. 'Remember, beauty is your duty!' was her sister's parting shot.

It was all right for Vera, Patty thought, she didn't have to handle all these dirty vegetables – and she always did as little as she could around the house at the best of times.

CHAPTER SIX

Pulling her warm red scarf tighter around her, gas mask bobbing at her side, Daisy stepped carefully along the pavements of Victory Walk, mindful of the icy coating. Having listened to poor Hope's account of her activities the day before, she was later than usual leaving for her job at Manor House tube station. Her poor cousin was still exhausted but luckily not on duty until the afternoon. Although Daisy and her mother had endured a long day travelling to see Clover, it seemed nothing by comparison. However, she was going to be late if she wasn't careful and she hoped Mr Rathbone would be in a forgiving mood. As ever, her thoughts returned to Freddy who was never far from her mind these days and she wondered when she would next hear from him. She was so lost in thought that she didn't hear the car door opening or the fall of footsteps behind her.

'Daisy, light of my life!' And there, as if she'd conjured him up, was the very man himself, smiling down at her.

'Freddy, what one earth . . .' she began, turning so quickly she would have slipped had he not caught her.

'Feel free to fall for me all over again,' he quipped, pulling her closer. As his arms tightened around her and she drank in the scent of his uniform greatcoat, and the very aroma that was him, she quite forgot she was standing in full view of any neighbours who happened to be looking out of their window. For a few moments they stood there, his chin resting on top of her head. She nestled closer to his heart, revelling in the fact they were together again. It was only when they heard raucous whistling that they broke apart.

'Who's that?' Daisy jumped, blushing as red as the hips in the bush behind.

'I cadged a lift,' Freddy replied, turning and signalling to the dark canvas-topped military vehicle that was parked on the road behind them. 'Daisy, this really is a whirlwind visit. We're on the move and you know I can't say where. But before we leave I just had to come and see you.' Hearing the unusually serious tone of his voice, she looked up at him, her heart sinking when she saw the expression in his dark eyes. 'Don't expect to hear from me for a while but you'll be in my thoughts every single day, until we next meet.'

'And you'll be in mine too,' she assured him.

The impatient blast of a horn made him grimace. 'So many flying visits I should have joined the RAF,' he quipped. Bending, he kissed her briefly but soundly; then, before she could say anything he was gone. All she could do was watch helplessly as the vehicle disappeared into the distance, leaving a cloud of smoke behind.

Her thoughts in turmoil, Daisy hurried to work, hardly noticing the businessmen in bowler hats carrying briefcases, or the harassed women with their shopping baskets determined to join the queues for what little rations they could obtain. Finally, reaching the intersection of the Seven Sisters Road and Green Lanes, she ran down the steps leading to the Manor House tube station ticket hall and the office beyond.

'I'm sorry I'm late, Mr Rathbone, but you'll never guess who . . . oh,' Daisy gasped seeing the strange man in his middle thirties, sitting at her boss' desk.

'Miss Harrison, I presume.'

'Yes, sir,' she replied, not liking the supercilious way he was staring at her. With his dark, slicked-back hair, bluish-black slit-like eyes and pointy nose, he reminded her of the weasels on Hackney Downs. However, the London Transport Management badge he was wearing alerted her to the fact he must be someone in authority. Taking a silver pocket watch from his waistcoat pocket, he made a show of checking it against the office clock.

'I suppose we should be grateful you've decided to join us, Miss Harrison, even if you are some twenty minutes late.'

'My apologies, but you see—'

'What I see, Miss Harrison, is an empty desk piled high with paperwork waiting to be attended to,' he interjected.

'But my desk was clear when I left work . . .'

'The day before yesterday,' he finished for her. 'Tell me, Miss Harrison, is it your usual practice to put in part-time hours for which you are paid a full-time wage?'

'No, of course not,' she spluttered. 'I'll have you

know I usually work longer hours than those I'm paid for. Mr Rathbone agreed . . .' she began, stuttering to a halt as he held up his hand.

'But Mr Rathbone is no longer here, as you would have known had you graced us with your presence yesterday. The fact is, Mr Rathbone tripped over the kerb on his way home from work during the blackout and sustained a fractured leg. Obviously, he's now indisposed, and, in his absence, it is I, Percy Pratt, who is in charge here. However, Miss Harrison, in the interest of maintaining the highest of standards, you will address me as Mr Pratt.'

'But of course, Mr Pratt,' she replied, thinking his name suited him. 'Poor Mr Rathbone, I do hope he'll be all right.'

'I'm sure the local hospital will take care of his requirements, although I'm led to believe they're some-what run off their feet with more important patients, soldiers who have been repatriated, no less.'

Daisy opened her mouth to say that actually she did know because her sister Rose was a nurse there. She also wanted to ask why he wasn't in the forces but seeing his scowl thought better of it.

'Well, I'll just go and check that the platforms have been cleaned and cleared ready for the trains,' she said, desperate to escape from this overbearing man.

'Stay where you are. Your place is at your desk where you'll remain until you've cleared that backlog of paper-work,' he ordered.

'Look, Mr Pratt. I don't know where all this has come from,' she said, pointing to the mound of forms and tickets. 'I've always cleared my in-tray before leaving work.'

'Then you'd better get on and clear it now. You are a clerk, are you not?' he continued before she could reply. 'Well, my understanding of a clerk's role is to attend to the administration in order that we males in management can deal with those important matters required to keep our train network running smoothly. No easy feat during these dark days of war. Now, I'm going down to the platforms to ensure everyone's doing their job correctly and, when I return, I expect to see that you've made a dent in that unforgiveable mountain of paperwork. In all my years of working for the Transport Board, I have never seen such a shambles!' With that, he snatched his cap from the peg and strode from the room, leaving Daisy seething with indignation.

What a pompous idiot, she fumed. Even when she'd been naughty as a child, her father had never spoken to her like that. And what on earth was all this paperwork? Even Mr Rathbone, who was a stickler for everything being up to date and in its place, never produced such volumes.

Looking closer at the paperwork, she saw that most of it related to other London tube stations. How on earth was she meant to deal with that?

'Having problems, Miss Harrison?' Mr Pratt asked, reappearing some time later.

'Not at all. I've collated everything relating to Manor House Station but as this pile here,' she said, pointing to the larger one in front of her, 'relates to other stations I'm not sure it has anything to do with us.'

'But it's all London Transport paperwork, is it not?'

'Well, yes, but . . .'

'No buts, Miss Harrison. Surely, it should be within the capability of one of its clerks to be able to deal with it?' he challenged, before turning on his heel and disappearing again.

Fighting down her exasperation and determined not to let him get the better of her, Daisy spent the rest of the day trying to sort out the mess of receipts, old tickets and letters from the Transport Board, but if Mr Pratt thought she wasn't going onto the platforms tomorrow, he could think again. She might be a clerk, but she was a jolly good one and she cared what happened to the staff and passengers she'd come to know.

However, no amount of sorting and filing could stop her thoughts returning to Freddy. She put her hand to her lips, remembering the sweetness of his kiss. Even for him that had been a flying visit and, although she wouldn't have swapped those few precious moments for all the world, instinct told her there had been more to it than he'd let on.

CHAPTER SEVEN

The men's ward at Homerton Hospital was buzzing with activity. Rose and her staff were rushed off their feet, dealing with the new admissions. There had been a fire in the rooms above a pub on the docks earlier that day, meaning the accident and emergency department was already overwhelmed treating casualties suffering from smoke inhalation and burns so they only had the capacity and staff to deal with those soldiers who were badly injured, leaving Rose and her staff to assess the walking wounded, allocate beds then carry out the TPRs.

'I've come to check on Mr Rathbone's leg, but I can see you're up to your eyes so let me help assess these patients beforehand, sister,' Dr Edwards said, stifling a yawn as he appeared by her side some time later. Rose smiled her thanks and took him on a tour of the ward, handing him the notes they'd already drawn up on each of the men. 'Goodness, it's certainly packed in here,' he said as they squeezed between the extra beds the orderlies had hastily brought up from the basement.

'We weren't expecting quite so many soldiers,' Rose told him.

'And some of them are quite lively,' Effie laughed,

passing by with a bedpan. 'It seems a right shame having to shut them up after all they've been though.'

'We need to separate the more badly injured from those with less serious wounds,' he murmured, seeing the man he was examining wince as the soldiers called to their colleagues across the ward. They were so pleased to be home even their injuries couldn't dampen their spirits. 'Are there no smaller rooms available?'

'Not at the moment, although I've asked to be informed as soon as any become free,' Rose told him, then hurried to the soldiers across the ward, pointing out that there were patients who were very poorly and needed peace and quiet. Instantly they lowered their voices, only for the noise level to rise again moments later.

'Me mum always says the only way to keep a man quiet is to feed him,' Susan chirped. She might be a trainee, Rose thought, but what she said made a lot of sense.

'Right, keep this closed for the time being,' Dr Edwards instructed, reappearing from behind the curtain. 'I've completed my initial examinations and those men sitting up may have food. However, those lying down must be strictly nil by mouth until I've thoroughly assessed the extent of their injuries and know if we need to operate,'

'Yes, doctor,' she said, and turned to instruct Susan, 'Please tell the orderlies to bring in the men's meals,' she said. 'Oh, and check if Mr Parsons is awake and wants anything.'

'He's having the time of his life,' the girl laughed,

pointing behind them to where the man in question was perched on the end of his bed, exchanging banter with some of the soldiers.

'He's certainly come alive! I never would have believed it,' the doctor murmured. 'Best tonic ever for the old chap.'

They were interrupted a few minutes later by the clattering of trollies, then trays being given out. This was followed by comparative silence as the men fell hungrily on their food.

'At least the gravy smells better than that disinfectant.'

'That's better, me stomach thought me throat'd been cut,' one murmured.

'Had nothing to eat since this morning,' another grunted.

'And when did you last eat?' Dr Edwards asked Rose.

'Don't worry about me, I'm not hungry. I can—'

'On the contrary, Sister Harrison, we do worry about you.' The strident tones of Matron sounded behind her. 'You'll be of no use to any of us if you don't keep your energy levels up. Dr Oswold will be along shortly. He and I will take over here whilst you and Dr Edwards go down to the staff canteen and have a hot meal and rest. No, arguments, either of you,' she added as Rose opened her mouth to say she was too busy. 'I do not expect to see either of you for at least an hour.'

'And you weren't hungry?' Dr Edwards asked, smiling as Rose attacked her plate of stew and dumplings with enthusiasm. 'It seems we picked a good day to eat in here.'

'Hmm,' she agreed. They continued eating, a comfortable silence between them, oblivious to the clank of cutlery or chatter from the others around them.

'I see they have treacle pudding and custard for afters,' Dr Edwards said, grinning like a schoolboy.

'Oh, I couldn't manage another mouthful,' Rose told him, patting her stomach. 'But you carry on.'

'Better not or I'll never finish my round. Still got Ward 2 to see to yet,' he sighed. 'It's been a long day.'

'It certainly has, and it's not over yet so we'd better get back.'

He looked at Rose and then at his watch. 'Not unless we want to incur Matron's wrath. We've another twenty minutes before she wants to see us. So, tell me, Rose, what do you do in your spare time, when you get some, that is?'

'I visit my family in Victory Walk which is only a short stroll across Hackney Downs, or I might go to the market on Ridley Road. Sometimes, I read in my room.'

'I wonder if you'd like to go to a matinee one afternoon? I see the Odeon is showing another Sherlock Holmes film.'

'Oh,' Rose frowned.

'What's the matter, not a Sherlock fan? Or perhaps you're already taken?'

'Yes, er, I mean . . .' Remembering her encounter with Mrs Sutherland, she realized her doubts had been right and she wasn't taken after all.

'Just as friends, perhaps? I enjoy your company, Rose,

but if you'd prefer not to accompany an older man like me, then I quite understand.' Although he said it cheerfully, she could see he was hurt by her rebuttal.

'It's not that. I really am very busy at the moment.' He might be nice but there was no way she was going to risk being hurt again. Men couldn't be trusted.

'Aren't we all? But you know what they say about all work and no play?' he shrugged, then with a small smile he got to his feet. 'Now it *is* time we were getting back, or Matron will have our guts for garters. See you later,' he called as he made his way towards Ward 2.

However, the mood on the men's ward was sombre when Rose returned. The soldiers who were mobile were standing with their heads bent in respect as Susan and Effie wheeled a bed towards the door, a sheet covering the patient beneath.

'A word, Sister Harrison, if you please,' Matron said. 'I'm afraid Mr Parson's heart gave out.'

'Oh, that's so sad!' Rose said, knowing she was going to miss him.

'At least the old soldier has gone to his maker having met his compatriots from this war. We can take comfort from the fact that his final hours were happy ones.'

* * *

'How did it go with the old dragon yesterday?' Kitty asked Hope as they were washing down their vehicle in the depot yard.

'Watch out, Hendy, we dragons have big ears, as well as breathing fire!' Station Officer Strang's voice

58

rang out behind them. 'Now, everyone, grab a drink and gather inside for a debrief on yesterday's operation.'

'Wish they had gin instead of tea or that Camp stuff they pass off as coffee,' Kitty murmured as they made their way inside. As they queued for their drinks, Hope looked around for Ian MacLeod but couldn't see him. Perhaps he wasn't rostered today . . .

'Right, if I can have your attention,' Sonia Strang cried. 'Firstly, I'd like to congratulate you on a job well done. You can all be proud of yourselves. You're a credit to the London Auxiliary Ambulance Service.'

'Does that mean we get extra in our pay?' someone called.

'It means you did a great service to those men who have been injured fighting for our freedom,' the station officer replied. 'However, I must remind you that despite the appalling state of the roads, it is imperative that you all always use the shields on your lights. Now, I don't want to detain you from your duties as I know you have a lot of cleaning and clearing up to do. However, I would be interested if you have any feedback on the operation, anything that might help if we're asked to assist in such an important operation again.'

There were suggestions of time off for extra hours worked or an increase in rations but in the main everyone was pleased to have been of assistance.

'Right, if anyone thinks of anything else, feel free to come and see me. Otherwise . . . back to your duties.'

Hope checked the stretchers were in place in the ambulance and was about to start checking the oil when the station officer caught up with her.

'Any ideas on how we could have improved our operation yesterday?'

'Well, I did notice how smart the other services were in their uniforms. We appeared quite shabby and unprofessional in comparison.'

'I couldn't agree more. As you know, the ambulance service has been fighting to get its own uniform for some time now. With little success, I might add. However, it appears that the powers that be have at last taken notice. There are going to be some radical changes around here, so all I can say, Hope, is: watch this space. Oh, and I presume you were looking for MacLeod earlier?'

'Yes, I was but I couldn't see him.'

'Well, I did, Sonia Strang said, 'and you know that gossip about him? Well, he explained that his job was classed as a reserved occupation – he's an aircraft engineer!'

'But the rumours . . .'

'Ignore them, Hope. You know how people like a story. What they don't know they make up. Anyhow, Ian asked for extra time off to help his sister and family settle into their new home. As he works here on a voluntary basis, I could hardly refuse.'

'Do you know when he'll be back?' she asked, her spirits plummeting.

'He just said his children had to be his priority. Now, that oil isn't going to change itself and you might get a call out.'

As the afternoon wore on and the temperatures plummeted, Hope shivered despite her heavy coat.

However, as she bent her head under the bonnet, her thoughts went into overdrive. She understood Ian's children taking priority, but where did that leave her? And what if they didn't settle in Dorset? Would he stay there? He couldn't keep travelling back and forth, especially as train passes were almost impossible for civilians to get now. Why, oh, why was life so difficult?

CHAPTER EIGHT

'They say here the war effort is accelerating, and there are reports that Singapore has fallen to the Japanese,' Bert said, throwing his newspaper down on the kitchen table where Patty was peeling vegetables for a stew. 'That's not good news for the allies! I don't know, Patty, all this fighting, when will it end?'

'And we still haven't heard from Peter,' she replied, knowing her husband was thinking about their elder son. Leaning over, he put his arms around her and pulled her close. She stood there for a few moments, taking comfort from his familiar warmth.

'Try not to worry, love. He'll turn up one of these days asking what's for dinner.' She nodded, noticing how tired he looked. His fire-watching duties along with extra shifts at the factory were taking their toll.

'I pray you're right.'

'Well, time I wasn't here,' he told her, gathering up his lunch box and helmet. 'Judging from that mound of vegetables you're preparing I'm guessing we're expecting company. Do you remember when Sundays meant roast beef and Yorkshire puddings?' he asked, licking his lips.

'I certainly do,' Patty sighed. 'And, hopefully, we'll be having it again one day soon. In the meantime, it'll be a case of hunting the scrag end in the stew. And in answer to your question, Vera's coming round. She was complaining how impossible it is to entertain in her tiny flat, so I told her to bring Faith and Artie along. Daisy's at home and Hope should be back lunchtime – and you never know when Rose might pop in. Oh, and here's Robbie, just in time to take these leaves and stalks out to his rabbit.'

'But it's freezing out there, Ma! Besides, I'm starving,' he moaned, glancing hopefully at the pot of porridge on the range.

'And Snuggles *will* starve if you don't look after him. Hurry up, then you can have your breakfast, and make sure you put on your boots – there's been a heavy frost again,' Patty told him.

'Nice to see some normality during these times,' Bert smiled, bending and kissing her cheek. 'Although remind Robbie he's to keep away from those bomb sites. They've shored up what they can but some of those ruins are still precarious.'

With the stew simmering on the hob, and Robbie outside playing with his pal Ricky, Patty cleared away the breakfast dishes and scrubbed the deal table ready for her sewing session with Vera. No doubt her sister would arrive with bags of clothes in a rainbow of colours – and knowing Faith she would get in on the act too. Then, savouring a few moments' peace and quiet, she settled herself into the chair nearest the range, picked up the latest copy of *Woman's Own*, her weekly treat, and began flicking through the knitting patterns. One for a balaclava with matching gloves caught her eye and would be nice and warm for Robbie; if she unravelled the burgundy pullover she'd bought at a jumble sale recently, there should be just enough wool and it would make a change from knitting socks.

'Anyone home?' Vera shouted from the hallway. There followed banging and clattering as Faith manoeuvred the pushchair into the room.

'Hello, Faith love, nice to see you. Goodness me, you've grown my lad,' Patty clucked at Artie who gave her a toothy grin. 'Kettle's boiled.'

'I could murder a cuppa,' Vera said, sinking into a chair.

'Me too,' Faith replied, doing the same. 'You've no idea what it's like bringing up a child,' she added, leaving a stunned Patty to deal with Artie.

'Come along, young man, let's see if Granny Patty can find you a biccie,' she said, resisting the urge to tell her niece she'd brought up five of her own, thank you very much.

'Oh, we don't go in for baby talk,' Faith told her airily as she ran her fingers through her fair hair. 'Grandma wants you to speak properly like your father, doesn't she, Artie?' she said.

Patty was tempted to ask her niece if she'd forgotten that Martin wasn't really Artie's father, when Vera began rummaging in her capacious bag.

'You don't have to worry about those home-baked efforts,' she cried, gleefully brandishing a packet of biscuits. 'Garibaldi, no less.'

'Goodness, I've not seen those in ages,' Patty exclaimed, her mouth watering.

'That's what comes of being well-connected over Hackney way.' As her sister gave a satisfied grin and Artie waved his chubby arms happily, Patty busied herself with the teapot.

'So have you heard from Martin?' Patty asked, determined to be polite.

'No,' Faith replied, then shrugged and began munching on a biscuit.

'Will this bitter weather never ease up? I thought it might be better now we're in February. Thank goodness there haven't been any night-time air raids, we'd freeze in that blooming shelter under the church hall,' Vera declared, oblivious to Patty trying to deal with Artie and make the tea at the same time.

'These are nice, aren't they,' Vera said, helping herself to another biscuit. 'Now, where is that article you wanted to show me?'

'Ooh yes, Auntie, that's what persuaded me to come. Ma said you could make me a new outfit,' Faith said, jumping up as Patty opened the magazine.

'That would smarten up my yellow frock no end,' Vera exclaimed stabbing her finger at the feature entitled, 'Five Ways to Freshen Up A Favourite Dress'.

'And that sash would show up my waist wonderfully now I've got my figure back,' Faith gushed, running her hands over her slim hips.

'I could have a belt like that as well,' Vera cried.

While Patty agreed that a sash would certainly work well for her niece and a crisp white collar would look good on Vera, adding a tight belt would surely only emphasize her sister's girth and, it had to be said, her clothes were already on the snug side. 'Surely everyone who reads this will do the same though, Vera?' she said tactfully. 'I like this idea of inserting a contrast panel into the bodice or skirt, that would smarten up an outfit and make it individual.'

'Good. I've been invited to join the Hackney Women's Institute, you know, so I'll need to look my best. Did I tell you the wives of Arthur's business colleagues are very smart?'

'I believe you did mention it, yes. Oh, Faith, Artie wants you,' Patty said, wondering how the girl could ignore the wails that had erupted.

'Well really,' she huffed. 'I came here for a rest. Martin's mother always deals with him. Here, you have him, Ma, you're always complaining you don't get to see him enough.' As she went to pass the wailing toddler to her mother, Vera shook her head and returned her attention to the article.

'Do keep the boy quiet! I need to concentrate. Now, what were you saying, Patty?'

'I was saying why don't we try adding some contrasting material to that grey skirt,' Patty continued, trying to ignore Artie's wailing and Faith's scowling. 'Worn with different blouses, it would make a more versatile outfit than adapting a dress. If you don't find anything suitable here, we can always pay a visit to Ridley Road Market.'

'Don't fancy venturing out in that bitter cold until I have to. Ooh, this pink gingham would look good,' Vera said, holding up Daisy's old school dress which Patty had hoarded.

She sighed. Still, you couldn't afford to be sentimental in wartime, she thought, taking up her scissors and carefully cutting out a panel.

'Look, it says here you can make a matching corsage, and one would look very smart on my white blouse,' Vera declared.

'And mine,' Faith cried. Patty groaned inwardly. It was going to be a long day – and if that wailing didn't stop soon, she'd end up with a headache. Perhaps she'd dish the dinner early then they'd have to clear the table . . .

'My goodness, someone's unhappy. Oh, hello, Auntie Vera,' Daisy chirped, coming into the room and taking the crying Artie from Faith. Immediately his sobs subsided and he began to chuckle as he tugged at Daisy's hair.

'Thank goodness,' Faith sighed.

'Isn't that my old dress?' Daisy asked, gesturing to the gingham.

'We're going to use that to vamp up my skirt,' Vera told her gleefully.

'And Auntie's going to make me a sash to match my dress, aren't you?' Faith said, turning her now smiling face to Patty.

'I'll see what fabric I have, but after we've eaten,' Patty said, giving Daisy a look.

'Shall I clear the table, Ma? I'm starving,' Daisy replied, gathering up the magazine and empty biscuit wrapping. 'Bet those were nice,' she said, eyeing the empty packet wistfully.

Minutes later, having mashed some potato into gravy,

Daisy pulled Artie onto her lap and the room fell silent as they ate.

'Now let's clear the table completely,' Patty said as soon as they'd finished their meal. 'We're adapting some of your auntie's clothes following the advice in this article,' she told Daisy as Vera spread her grey skirt out again.

'Some of these ideas are good. Have you got any lace?'

Patty smiled, pleased to see her daughter showing some enthusiasm, for she'd not been her cheerful self this week. 'See what you can find in my workbox.'

'And save some for me,' Vera told her. 'I'm mixing in well-connected circles, now.'

'And I need to look my best, though I never get to go out anywhere these days,' Faith sighed, fluffing up her hair. 'Oh drat,' she muttered as Artie rubbed his eyes and began sobbing.

'I'll put him down on my bed for a nap if you like?' Daisy offered but then Hope came in from work and began fussing over him, making him forget he was tired.

'Your meal's keeping hot in the warming drawer,' Patty told her.

'Thanks, Auntie, I'll have it in a moment,' she said, hoisting the boy onto her back and making him squeal with delight.

'He gets all the fun,' Faith moaned, then brightened. 'I know, let's go for a drink one night?' she suggested, looking at Daisy and Hope. 'It's ages since we've been out together and I'm sure Martin's mother will be happy to babysit,' she added, throwing her mother a triumphant look. However, the girls were so excited by the idea, they didn't notice.

'I'll see if Rose can come too,' Daisy told them. 'It'll be just like the old days, then.'

They arranged to meet up the next Saturday, and having secured a promise from Patty that her new sash would be ready by then, Faith took Artie home.

'I'll just change my clothes before I eat,' Hope announced, taking herself upstairs.

'Right, I'm off to visit Mr Rathbone at the hospital, you know how strict they are about their precious visiting hour,' Daisy announced.

'Do give him our good wishes and tell him we hope his leg will soon be better. And if you see our Rose, remind her where we live, eh?' Patty told her before she and Vera returned to their alterations.

* * *

'So, you see, Mr Rathbone, we need you to get better quickly. Manor House Station is just not the same without you,' Daisy said, leaning forward in the hard hospital chair, careful not to touch the cage that kept the bedcovers from his plastered leg.

'That's very kind of you to say, Daisy, but I'm sure my replacement is doing a good job holding the fort.'

'He's running it with military precision,' Daisy assured him, biting her tongue so as not to add what she really felt.

'Well, I know I can rely on you to assist him keeping

our Manor House tube station running efficiently, can't I, Daisy?' he asked, looking directly at her.

'Of course,' she promised, because what else could she say?

'It is kind of you to visit, Daisy,' Polly Rathbone, sitting on the other side of her husband's bed, said. 'However, it's a really bad fracture and I'm afraid it will be quite some time before he can return to work. And I'm afraid he needs to rest now.'

'Of course,' Daisy replied, getting to her feet. 'You hurry up and get better, Mr Rathbone.'

CHAPTER NINE

Hastily she left the ward, eager to be away from the ever-present smell of disinfectant. For once, she hoped she wouldn't bump into her older sister. Rose would be bound to notice there was something wrong and Daisy didn't feel up to discussing 'pompous prig Pratt' as she now considered him. She'd always loved her work, but now she was dreading having to return the next day. However, luck was not on her side for as she reached the entrance to the hospital, Rose was coming in, bringing with her a blast of cold air.

'Oh, hello, Daisy,' she murmured, blinking in surprise.

'Is everything all right, Rose? Only you look a bit peaky.'

'A bit like you, you mean,' her sister retaliated. 'Sorry, that was uncalled for. It's been a trying week.'

'Tell me about it,' Daisy replied, suddenly wanting to talk after all. Her sister gave her a searching look.

'I was just going to get some tea and toast from the canteen. Why don't you join me? We can take it up to my room and catch up in private. Or we can just talk about this frightful weather.'

'I know, this cold is making my cheeks so red, I swear I'd get through pots of Pond's Cold Cream if it wasn't so hard to come by,' Daisy laughed, feeling better already.

Upstairs, in Rose's comfortable room, they perched on her bed, plates of buttered toast balanced on their laps, pleased to be in each other's company after all.

'I really needed that,' Daisy said, letting out a sigh of contentment as she swallowed the last morsel. 'I didn't realize I was so hungry.'

'Me neither,' Rose agreed.

'You're so lucky having all this space, and with your own bathroom as well,' Daisy sighed.

'I know I am, but everything comes at a price, and I do have to work long hours. Sometimes, at the end of my shift, it's all I can do to walk up the stairs and collapse into bed. Anyway, why were you looking so glum earlier?' she asked, taking a sip of her tea whilst her sister gathered her thoughts.

'Mr Rathbone tripped over the kerb in the blackout and broke his leg. That's why I'm at the hospital.'

'Of course, Mr Rathbone's your boss! I should have put two and two together but with an intake of repatriated soldiers, we've been rushed off our feet.'

'Yes, well, his replacement is a condescending, overbearing, pompous prig!' Daisy declared hotly, making her sister laugh.

'Don't mince your words, will you, Daisy?'

'Well, he is,' she declared and then proceeded to tell her sister how she now had to stay in the office and was banned from ever going onto the platforms. 'It's the part of my job I like most, helping people, and he expects me to deal with paperwork from other stations.'

'Let's hope Mr Rathbone is back on his feet soon, although . . .' Rose broke off.

'It's a bad break, I know,' Daisy sighed, picking up her mug and gulping down her now tepid drink. 'Anyway, what were you looking so glum about?'

Rose got up and went over to the modern metal window where she stood looking out at the street below. 'As you know, I haven't heard from Philip since we came back from Canterbury. With the state of the country, I thought his letters must have had difficulty getting through.' She turned to face Daisy, and her sister was alarmed to see the anguish in her eyes. 'Then, I bumped into Mrs Sutherland, who delighted in telling me Philip was affianced, would you believe, to someone more of his standing. She was positively gloating, Daisy.'

'The old cow! Do you think she was telling the truth?'

'Why would she lie? I know she doesn't think I'm good enough for her precious son, but surely even she wouldn't make up something like that? Not having heard from Philip I was beginning to have my doubts about his intentions, but why hasn't he had the decency to write and tell me himself?'

Daisy was about to say she hadn't heard from Freddy and then he'd just appeared out of the blue but thought it would be insensitive. 'Well, there are reports of post being held up or even going missing. We did have that letter telling us about Clover, but that was from the Ministry.'

'Hope said you'd been to see her. How is she?'

'She's in clover, if you'll excuse the pun.' Daisy giggled, making Rose smile, so that despite the gravity of their situations, their mood lifted. 'You should see that convalescent home, all velvet curtains and thick carpets. She's got a room to herself, and the food's plentiful and tasty. We had butter on our teacakes and proper coffee. Mother was in her element because there was scented soap in the cloakroom. There were lots of men in uniform too, but Clover didn't seem to notice.'

'Hmm,' Rose murmured. 'How is she in herself? Hope said something about a new job.'

'She was a bit weak, if truth be told, and has to stay there for a while to fully recover, but then she's being transferred to a new job. Apparently, it's a clerical job at somewhere called Bletchley. Clover called it BP, but Mr Rathbone knew where that was. Honestly, what that man doesn't know about the rail network isn't worth knowing. Anyway, Mother's over the moon 'cos Clover will be able to come home more often, but I can't see our sister enjoying paperwork.'

'It'll be a bit of a change from searchlights but maybe they'll be too heavy for her to operate until she fully recovers her strength. Still, knowing our Clover she'll soon complain if she's not happy.'

'I must admit, seeing all those uniforms got me thinking . . .' A knock on the door stopped her mid-sentence.

'Excuse me,' Rose murmured, hurrying to open it. 'Sorry,' she said, turning back to Daisy moments later.

'There's an emergency on the ward. You can stay if you wish but I'll probably be gone a while.'

'No, I'd best be getting back. It's been lovely to see you, and try not to worry, I'm sure Mrs Sutherland's got it wrong.'

'Thank you – and you can tell that Mr Pratt he'd better watch out or he'll have me to answer to.'

'I will. Oh, by the way, Hope, Faith and I are going to the pub at the end of Victory Walk on Saturday. Why don't you join us?'

'I'll see what shift I'm on and see you at home if I'm free,' Rose promised then disappeared out of the door.

Back in Victory Walk, Daisy went up to her room where she stood staring over the back yard to the rooftops of the terraces of East London beyond, those that had survived the Blitz. Dusk was just descending and pulling the curtains before blackout started, she couldn't help comparing her cluttered bedroom with the cosy room and private bathroom that Rose had. And she had it all to herself whilst Daisy still had to share with Clover when she came home, which meant most of her things were still taking up room in the wardrobe. She thought again of the recruitment posters she'd seen and wondered what accommodation the Land Army girls were given. She shook her head – a year ago she'd hated the very idea of joining the Land Army, but she'd grown up a lot since then, she realized.

Throwing herself down on her bed, her thoughts turned to Freddy. Whilst it had been lovely to see him and feel his arms around her, it had left her even more impatient for the time they could be together again. Would this wretched war never end? Unable to settle, she got up and paced the room, then, needing something constructive to do to stop her wandering thoughts, she took her best blouse from the wardrobe and started to pin the strip of lace she'd taken from her mother's workbox to the collar. At least she'd have something pretty to wear when she went out at the weekend.

As she began to sew, her thoughts turned to work. She was dreading going in the next morning. If that Percy Plonker Pratt started laying down the law, she'd give him what for. She would go down to the platforms as was her custom whether he liked it or not. After all, she could always walk out. Employers were crying out for workers or she could join up. Then she remembered she'd promised Mr Rathbone she'd look after things at Manor House tube station. And a promise made was a promise to be honoured, her mother always said.

* * *

Tightly gripping her small bag and a copy of Hugo's *German in 3 Months* which had become her bible these past few weeks, Clover slid into the back of the sleek black car that had drawn up outside the convalescent home. This one, however, was driven by a uniformed chauffeur and there was a glass partition between them. It was only once she was seated that she realized there was an officer in the front. He was puffing on a pipe and studying a sheaf of papers, but he never once looked up.

There was very little traffic as they made their way through countryside, where tall trees looked as if they'd been painted in bright white paint and hedgerows glistened with pearls of frost, and through little towns where shopkeepers were raising their blinds, queues of hopeful folk already forming. After passing a station, its name signs removed, the car veered into a lane which, to her horror, was bordered by a tall eight-foot chain-linked fence topped with barbed wire. Heavens, where was she being taken, she wondered, her stomach churning.

They stopped in front of a pair of iron gates where an armed guard emerged from a sentry box, accompanied by a burly, stern-faced corporal in a red-peaked cap who checked their papers. He nodded to the guard to open the gates then waved them through.

The wheels crunched along a gravel drive until suddenly a mansion rose before them. With its turrets, gables and numerous big windows at the front, it was the grandest building Clover had ever seen. Goodness, and she'd thought the convalescent home was impressive. What a contrast to the camp in North Wales with its rows of Nissen huts.

She noticed people strolling around a lake surrounded by a large, grassed area then frowned; to one side of the grounds was a cluster of dreary looking wooden huts with pitched roofs and metal-framed windows. Each one was numbered and looked incongruous against their magnificent surroundings. What on earth was this place? She didn't have time to ponder, for the car was drawing to a halt by the grand entrance. Clover watched as the driver jumped out, saluting smartly as he held the front passenger door open. The officer, briefcase under his arm, disappeared through the heavy wooden door without a backward glance.

Clover climbed out, but before she could thank the driver, he was back in the car crunching off down the gravel driveway. Smoothing her uniform, she clutched her bag tighter and looked around. As she stood wondering whether to enter through the same door the officer had, a small group of women dressed in civilian clothes appeared.

'Come to join us, have you?' a chirpy voice called.

'Yes, I've been told I have to register,' Clover replied, relieved to see a friendly face. The girl's shiny hair was pinned in victory rolls, and she wished she'd taken the time to do more than clip hers up under her hat.

'I'll show you where you need to go. I'm Ann, by the way.'

'Clover,' she replied, following the little group into the spacious oak-panelled entrance hall with its high ceilings, across the tiled floor and up to an impressive desk. Various rooms opened off this reception area and Clover could see they were buzzing with activity. Visible through a pink marble archway was an ornate stairway leading up to more rooms beyond and Clover felt a frisson of excitement. Imagine if she were to have one of those. She could just imagine her mother's face.

'Sergeant Jones will explain everything,' Ann told her, bringing her back to the present as she indicated the tall woman in a crisp khaki uniform who was eyeing her closely. 'Good luck, and I'm sure we'll see you around.'

'Name?' the woman asked, her voice brisk as she ran a gold pen down the huge register before her. 'Pass?' Clover handed over the papers she'd been sent. 'I see you've already signed the Official Secrets Act so that will save time. No need to remind you the importance of that or how unpalatable a stretch in one of His Majesty's prisons would be.' Her round amber eyes, sharp as a hawk's, bore into Clover's, making her stand even straighter.

'I quite understand,' Clover replied, pleased her voice sounded firm.

'See that you do. I note you have been transferred from North Wales so until your things are sent on you will be billeted in the town. Here are the details.' She passed Clover a slip of paper. There went her dream of slumbering like a lady upstairs, then. 'We operate a twenty-four-hour shift system here, rotating every week, 8.00 a.m. to 4.00 p.m., 4.00 p.m. to midnight, midnight to 4.00 a.m. Your supervisor will advise which you're on. Transport is provided to and from the park. It runs in conjunction with the shifts and will pick you up and return you accordingly. Failure to adhere to its timetable will mean a long walk.' The woman gave a stiff smile. 'Leave your bag in the anteroom over there and Brown will show you where to go for your induction.' She snapped her fingers. 'Hut 6.'

'Yes, ma'am,' A young woman dressed in navy cardigan and skirt hurried over to the desk, collected the papers and waited while Clover deposited her bag. Then, before she had time to draw breath, marched at a quick pace, out of the wide door and across the grounds towards the dark wooden huts.

'Dark and cold in winter, dark and hot in summer,' she commented.

'So, what do you do here?' Clover asked, trying to make conversation.

'Loose lips,' the woman said, frowning. 'None of us talk about our jobs here, not even with those we work with.' She quickened her step, so that Clover was quite breathless by the time they reached Hut 6. Despite her recuperation, she was still suffering from the after-effects of her illness.

Inside the hut was gloomy, with curtains drawn tightly across the windows and the stale smell of tobacco hanging in the air. As they passed through double doors, she could hear the rumble of machinery, but before she had time to look around, she was being led into another room, where there were about a dozen desks, each with a typewriter on it.

She was introduced to a smartly dressed young woman whose red lips seemed to shine brightly in the gloom. Taking the papers, she turned to Clover and smiled.

'Good, you're here at last. I'm Mrs Speedwell, the supervisor, and your induction is about to begin.' She followed the woman through yet another door, this one marked Administration, and into an even darker room where ten women were seated around a large table on which stood another typewriter.

'Be seated and when I call the register, please raise your hand,' Mrs Speedwell told them.

Clover's heart sank. This was worse than being back at school. If she was going to be a glorified typist, why on earth had she wasted the last three weeks brushing up on her German?

CHAPTER TEN

Dawn was just breaking as Daisy ran down the steps to the station below. People who had taken shelter on the platforms overnight were now leaving up the escalator and she waved cheerfully to them. She was determined to see all was well before Pompous Pratt arrived. Hopefully she would be back in the office by then and he'd be none the wiser.

Even the smell of disinfectant being sprayed over the platforms during this, the coughing period, couldn't dampen her enthusiasm, for she'd missed seeing the friendly people who kept the cogs of Manor House Station turning. As the morning shift of transport workers greeted her enthusiastically, she felt she was back where she belonged.

'Morning, Daisy, we haven't seen you in a while,' Mrs Nicholls called as she oversaw her WVS team setting up the urns ready for those eager for their morning cup of tea.

'Been busy in the office,' she replied.

'Don't you let that new man boss you about. He's been throwing his weight about down here something chronic. Thank heavens he's only temporary, that's what I say.'

'Arrogant arse,' Alfie muttered, leaning on his broom

as he paused in his sweeping of the platform to offer his opinion.

'Mind your language!' Mrs Nicholls shouted.

'Sorry missus, but 'e is.'

Swallowing down a giggle, Daisy walked along the platform ensuring all the checks had been carried out, for safety was paramount, especially when so many people were sleeping near the tunnels. Of course, not so many were using the station overnight now that no bombs had fallen in London recently, but you could never be too careful. Satisfied, all was in order, she said goodbye to the staff and reluctantly made her way to the office which felt more like a prison these days.

'Where the hell have you been?' Mr Pratt barked, glaring from her to the pocket watch in his hand.

'I've been making sure all's in order down on the platforms. And I'm still early for my shift,' Daisy replied curtly, her earlier good mood evaporating.

'That's not your responsibility, Miss Harrison. You're employed to work in the office and that's where you'll stay. Disobey me again and I'll . . .' His voice petered out as he tried to think of some suitable threat.

'Ah, yes, I was looking through your application form and it seems your date of birth has some sort of smudge over it. If I'm not satisfied you're twenty-one – and your inability to carry out the simplest of instructions makes me wonder – then I need to request sight of your birth certificate.' As he stood there smirking, looking even more weasel-like if that were possible, Daisy's heart sank.

Determined not to let him see her discomfort, she meekly took her seat at her desk. Then she saw another stack of fresh paperwork and groaned.

'Not afraid of a bit of work, are you, Miss Harrison?'

'No, but once again, it appears mainly to be from other stations. This never happened when Mr Rathbone was here and . . .'

'But he isn't here, is he? And whilst I'm in charge, Miss Harrison, you'll do any work I see fit to give you.' Pulling his cap further down on his greasy hair, he strode from the office, leaving Daisy fuming. She did a good job, she knew that, but the fact remained that she still wasn't old enough to be employed by London Transport and Mr Rathbone would be in serious trouble if they found out.

Putting aside the tickets and invoices from the other stations, she began ploughing through her normal paperwork. Finally, she had no option other than to look at Mr Pratt's papers. How was she supposed to deal with them? He had given her no guidance whatsoever when she'd asked him about the first lot. In fact, he'd so delighted in trying to make her look a fool she'd put them in her desk out of the way. Retrieving them, she began comparing them with the others, then frowned when she saw they were from a different station altogether.

There was no way she could just leave them again, especially if it was going to be a regular occurrence. Just as she decided to go and ask the ticket manager to help, she saw Mr Pratt watching her from the doorway.

'Don't tell me you can't manage to sort a few tickets and invoices?' he said, his voice so condescending, Daisy felt a sudden urge to pick up the whole lot and lob them straight between those weaselly eyes of his. Taking a deep breath, she tried to explain.

'There's no point entering them in our ledger here because there's nothing to tally them against,' she exclaimed. 'Mr Rathbone always said . . .'

'But as I've said before, Mr Rathbone isn't here,' he interjected. He moved closer, standing so close the smell of his unwashed body made her feel quite ill. Then he moved in still closer but to her relief he reached up to the shelf above her head and took down a new ledger.

'You're very young . . .' He paused, letting his words sink in. 'And obviously inexperienced, so I'll make it easy for you. Just enter everything in here and I'll tally it later. Never let it be said that Mr Percy Pratt is anything other than fair. And make sure it's all in your neatest handwriting.'

Before she could reply he placed the new book on her desk and disappeared.

What a nauseating man he was. If it wasn't for Mr Rathbone, she'd put on her coat and walk out right now. She'd been hoping she would receive her call-up papers which would get her out of this mess, but of course, the transport network had to be kept running.

Daisy stared down at the shiny new ledger. It would certainly be easy just to enter everything, but if there was nothing to tally it with, what was the point? Still, if that was what Mr Pratt wanted, then she would have to do it. However, it didn't feel right.

* * *

'It just doesn't feel right,' Vera said, holding up the skirt she'd attempted to alter. 'That panel you cut doesn't sit straight.'

'Well, my hands are grubby so I can't look at it now,' Patty told her, knowing it would be Vera's stitching at fault for her sister had never been any good at needlework. 'Tell you what, I'll take it home and look at it this evening,' she offered, pushing a loose strand of chestnut hair back under her headscarf.

Wincing as she straightened up, she put her hand to her back. She'd been replenishing the shelves with fresh carrots and parsnips, and the icy draught that whistled through the shop had seeped right into her bones. All she wanted to do was go home and put her feet up.

'But I need it for tomorrow,' Vera moaned. 'I'm going with my new friends to the Red Cross centre where they're packing boxes of goods to send to the prisoners of war. You did say that if I was going to keep up with the wives of Arthur's business colleagues then I should join in their activities. And it was you who mentioned that article about revamping our clothes.'

Patty opened her mouth to say that she hadn't meant she would do all the alterations, then closed it again. She was just too tired to argue.

'Joy has promised to help too, so that's good. I can

show those ladies that we Potters are willing to do our bit for the war effort. We'll be packing boxes for POWs. Apparently, there's a specific way the items have to be packed, but if I find a better one, I shall let them know.'

'I'm sure you will, Vera. Now, if you give me that skirt, it's time I locked up. I need to get Robbie some of that rosehip syrup that's just gone on sale and there's sure to be a queue.'

'But what about my skirt? I need to be at the packing station for ten.'

'And I open up shop here at eight so that will give you plenty of time to come and collect it.'

'Well, if that's the best you can do . . .' Vera muttered, before flouncing out.

Really, her sister could be a right madam sometimes, Patty thought, shaking her head. Still, it must be hard for her to be without her family home. Quickly, she locked the door and headed for the chemist, where predictably there was a long queue. Although the wind was blowing a hooley and it was nearly dark, the women waiting were still eager to gossip.

'They say soap's going to be rationed to one tablet a month,' the woman in front of her said as she turned to see who had joined the queue.

'As they've just announced we have to bathe in only five inches of water, it ain't going to make much difference,' a voice further up the line shouted.

'Perhaps the idea's to stink Hitler into submission,' another woman cackled.

Needless, to say, from then on everyone asked for extra soap when it was their turn to be served. Patty couldn't help thinking that Robbie would be over the moon when she told him he could only have a shallow bath and must be careful with the soap.

CHAPTER ELEVEN

'Private Benson seems to be making good progress although obviously it's too early to give a prognosis on his sight at this stage, sister,' Dr Edwards told her.

'It's hard for him not being able to see what's going on around him. And of course, he's too far away from his home for any family to visit,' Rose replied. She waited while he updated the patient's notes then handed them to the trainee nurse to clip to the end of the bed.

As they moved towards her desk, the ward round now finished, they heard Effie give a squeal.

'Bit old for that sort of caper, aren't you, Sergeant Adams,' she berated the smirking man.

'I'm only as old as the pretty girl I'm looking at,' he quipped.

'Then perhaps you need something in your mouth to keep you quiet,' Effie told him, shaking a thermometer at him. 'Or if you don't keep those hands to yourself, I'll find somewhere else to put it.'

Catcalls and ribald remarks erupted causing Rose to shoot them a forbidding look. The men muttered but duly quietened down.

'Well, as we can see and hear, the other soldiers are making a good recovery,' Dr Edwards grinned.

'Luckily the girls can stand their ground and don't take any mischief from them,' Rose replied, raising her brow. 'Although I keep my eye on what's going on.'

'Yes, I saw,' he replied, his eyes twinkling. 'Of course, they can jest in daylight, but it's the night traumas that really plague them. Then, in their sleep, they relive the horrors they have seen. One can't even begin to imagine what they've suffered.'

'Yes, I agree we must make allowances, although it's hard on the other patients and night staff who have to try and calm them.'

'I've prescribed sedatives but who knows whether they'll help? I'm sure they'd prefer a stiff whisky, but regrettably the Board wouldn't agree to that. However, this is purely a temporary situation. As soon as the military hospital has beds for them, they'll be transferred. The Queen Alexandra has better facilities to deal with Private Benson's burns and they know better how to deal with night terrors. Of course, it'll be therapeutic for the others to be with their colleagues, if they can bring themselves to talk about their experiences it might help.' Rose nodded, transfer to the military hospital would be beneficial for all concerned. While she had every sympathy for the men, she had to admit it would be a relief when her ward returned to some semblance of normality.

'Now, as to the other patients,' Dr Edwards continued. 'I'm a little concerned about Mr Rathbone's leg. It's not healing as quickly as I would have expected. Keep an eye on it, if you would. Other than that, things seem to be pretty much in order, which of course, I would expect from an efficiently run ward like yours.' He glanced down the ward then grinned. 'Although I notice at least two of our soldiers have already slipped away to the dayroom.'

'For a crafty smoke, no doubt,' she sighed.

'Who can blame them after all they've been through? Still, as I said, it's only a temporary measure so perhaps we should turn a blind eye. Best you don't tell Matron I said that, though,' he said, looking almost boyish. 'Which reminds me, she says can you drop by her office when you come off duty?' He turned to go, then hesitated. 'It's been a hectic time and we've all been working flat out, and don't think I haven't noticed you doing more than your share of night shifts. If you feel like a little light relief, there's a new Arthur Askey film showing at the Odeon at the end of the week. I've heard it's hilarious.'

'Thank you, but I doubt I'll have any time off for a while.'

'Well, the offer is open, all work and no play, et cetera.' He shrugged philosophically, then turning on his heel, strode from the ward, stethoscope swinging against his white coat.

Although her shift should have finished at 2.00 p.m., a new admission delayed her as somehow, yet another bed had to be wedged in.

'Blimey, it's like playing sardines in here,' Susan muttered as she squeezed in to help Effie smooth out the clean sheets.

'Which will make it more difficult to dodge those

men's 'ands. Like blinkin' octopuses they are,' Effie groaned.

'Livens up the shift, though,' Susan laughed.

'Don't let sister hear you say that,' Effie warned her.

'X-rays show Mr Roberts has a broken ankle,' Rose said, making them jump as she appeared beside them. 'Apparently, he slipped on the ice at Ridley Road Market. Ah, I think I hear him coming now,' she added, as a squeaking trolley was pushed into the ward.

It was another two hours before Rose felt she could leave and, glancing at the clock, she realized it would be too late to meet up with the others for a drink but she was so tired she didn't really feel like socializing anyway.

'Ah, come in, Sister Harrison,' Matron called, when she put her head around the door. 'I trust everything is going smoothly on the men's ward despite our extra patients? It shouldn't be long before those soldiers are transferred which will make life easier, for we're filled beyond capacity, yet still have to look after our own, as it were. Although, of course, it's a privilege to nurse those who have served their country, there's no denying it taxes our endurance. Have you encountered any problems?' she asked, studying Rose carefully.

'No, Matron,' Rose replied.

'Good, because I'd like you to take the next two days off, no . . .' she held up her hand as Rose opened her mouth to protest, 'I insist. You've been working long hours, including extra night shifts and, quite frankly, are looking exhausted. You'll be of no use to anyone if you collapse on the ward. I mean, what sort of example would that be to your staff? Staff Nurse Robbins is quite capable of coping in your absence.'

'Yes, Matron,' Rose replied, stifling a yawn because it was true, she was *out on her feet*, as her mother would say.

'Oh, and, sister,' Matron added as Rose turned to go. 'I'm here should you wish to discuss anything, private or professional. A problem shared, et cetera.'

Goodness, that woman really was a witch, Rose thought as she made her way up to her room. She always seemed to know when something was troubling her. However, despite the long shifts, she couldn't deny her meeting with Mrs Sutherland was what most preyed on her mind.

***

'You mean I haven't got to wash at all now?' Robbie cried, his eyes lighting up.

'What I mean, young man, is we're going to have to be careful with the soap from now on,' Patty told him.

'Well, I'm happy to donate my ration in aid of the war effort,' he told her self-righteously before turning back to his food.

Patty smiled, then looked round the table. Meals might be scratch affairs these days, but she felt a warm glow when she was with her family, or at least those who were home.

'Any plans for tonight, love?' she asked Bert. 'Only I've promised to take a look at Vera's skirt. It seems that panel I put in isn't hanging properly.'

'She takes advantage of your good nature,' he told her, shaking his head. 'I've no fire-fighting duties so I'll catch up on the news. Any post today?' he asked.

'None at all,' Patty told him. They exchanged worried looks. Every day was a day too many since they'd heard from Peter and their greatest fear was that he'd been posted overseas, possibly to North Africa.

'How about you, Daisy? You've been quiet this evening. Everything all right at work?' Patty eyed her shrewdly.

'No, not really. That stand-in manager, Pratt, is throwing his weight around and he's giving me work from other stations too.'

'Well, I suppose everyone has to pitch in now that staff shortages are hitting. I know it's affecting the factory, especially with the women joining up,' Bert said.

'I wish my papers would come through,' Daisy sighed.

'Surely yours is a reserved occupation?' he frowned.

'And Mr Rathbone is relying on you,' Patty chipped in. 'I couldn't bear it if another of my children left home.'

Daisy opened her mouth to protest that she was no longer a child, then remembered her promise to Mr Rathbone and began collecting up their dirty dishes instead.

'That was a tasty drop of stew,' Bert told Patty,

hastily mopping up the last of the gravy with a crust of bread.

'It's always better on the second day,' Patty told him, stifling a yawn.

'You stay in the warm, Ma, and see to Auntie's skirt. I'll take these through to the back kitchen and wash up,' Daisy offered, eager to escape talk about work.

'And you can dry the dishes, Robbie, but not till you've had your rosehip syrup,' Patty told him, taking the bottle from her bag.

'Aw, must I, Ma?' he groaned, giving her a pained look.

'Yes, you must – on both counts.'

As soon as the table was cleared and wiped, Patty spread out Vera's skirt, then grimaced. No wonder the panel didn't lie flat, her sister hadn't pressed the seams. Honestly, she thought, putting the iron on the range to heat. While she was waiting, she caught sight of her hands and taking a dollop of Vaseline from the pot, began rubbing it in. The movement was strangely soothing, and she realized with a pang that it had been a long time since she'd made even a few moments to look after herself.

'I could do with some of that,' Daisy said, appearing at her side. 'I don't know what they're putting in those soap suds these days, but they don't cut through the grease like they used to.'

'You're telling me,' Patty replied. 'Look at the state of my hands. I'm going to make sure I rub them with Vaseline every day from now on. Now, move yourself while I spread this blanket over the table so I can iron your auntie's skirt. Then I'll make a hot drink and join Father for the news bulletin.'

'He's listening to that chap with the plummy voice. You know, that Lord Haw-Haw? Can't think why he bothers.'

'It's because he wants to get another account of the war other than the BBC's and the newspapers,' Patty told her. She didn't add that he also listened keenly to the names of recently captured prisoners of war and messages from prisoners to their loved ones, hoping he didn't hear Peter's name mentioned. It was the not knowing where or how he was that was so unsettling and she kept her fingers crossed they would receive a letter from him soon. Was it any wonder her face had as many wrinkles as her sister's skirt?

Spitting on the iron to make sure it was hot enough, she began smoothing down the seams.

'By the way, Mrs Pryor stopped me in the street earlier,' she told Daisy. 'Apparently, she just happened to be looking out of the window the other morning and saw you in some man's arms. Reckons he was wearing a blue uniform. I told her she must have been mistaken. That was right, our Daisy, or else you'd have said summat, wouldn't you?'

Daisy cursed. The people of Victory Walk might be friendly, but there was no denying they were as nosey as heck.

'Actually, she was right, Ma. There I was walking to work, careful of the icy pavements when Freddy popped up right beside me. I nearly fell into his arms in surprise.'

'Did you, indeed. Well, you should have invited him in for a cuppa.'

'I couldn't. He was with some of his navy pals and said it was a flying visit. And it certainly was that. I mean, I'm used to him appearing out of the blue but this time it was one kiss then he was gone, just like that.' She clicked her fingers. 'He told me he was being posted and couldn't tell me where but felt he had to see me first. It fair unsettled me and I don't know what to make of it,' she cried.

Patty put her arms around her daughter and pulled her close. Every day they heard about supply ships being attacked by those U-boats. It was high time someone finally put paid to that power crazy German lunatic.

'You go and put on your best blouse then go for that drink with Hope and Faith, it'll cheer you up. No more than two, mind, you don't want to be spending tomorrow with a bad head,' she cautioned.

* * *

The main bar of the pub was noisy with revellers and filled with smoke by the time the three girls arrived.

'Rose is hoping to join us later,' Daisy told them as they spotted people vacating a table at the far end. 'What's everyone having?'

'Port and lemon for me,' Faith replied, smiling across at a tall fellow leaning against the bar then slowly lowering herself onto the velvet covered stool and crossing her legs provocatively. 'God, I've missed all this,' she exclaimed, staring around the room.

'Lemonade for me, I'm on the early shift tomorrow,' Hope said.

'No point in coming out if you're not having a decent drink,' Faith told her.

'It's just nice to be out,' she replied as Daisy went to order their drinks.

'Yes, but you can come out anytime you like. I have to stay at home with Artie. Still, if I get lucky tonight, I'll see if Martin's mother will babysit again.'

'Get lucky? But you're married,' Hope frowned.

'Might just as well not be. Having a husband away in the navy is no fun, I can tell you. Don't know why I got married in the first place.'

'You got married because you were pregnant and . . .' Hope began.

'All right, keep your voice down, don't want to cramp my style, do we?' she whispered, giving a little wave to the man at the bar.

'Really, Faith,' Hope began but her sister was paying too much attention to the tall man to notice.

Hope felt relieved when she saw Daisy returning, carefully balancing three glasses as she wove her way through the crowded bar, deftly avoiding any friendly punter who tried to waylay her. If only she had that confidence, Hope thought.

The evening was a welcome diversion from the working week and thankfully there were no interruptions from air raid sirens as they sipped their drinks and caught up on their news.

'Rose still hasn't appeared, so I guess she's been held up,' Daisy said when their glasses were empty.

'I'll get us another drink,' Faith said, hopping down and tightening the new sash around her waist before wiggling over to the bar, where she was greeted enthusiastically by the man she'd been sharing smiles with.

'I know hers was only a marriage of convenience, but I wish she'd remember she's Martin's wife,' Hope sighed. 'Oh, it's too embarrassing to watch,' she added, turning back to Daisy. 'I love that lace on your blouse, by the way. Have you heard from Freddy?'

'He paid me a lightning visit then just like that he was gone,' Daisy said, clicking her fingers. 'But that's war for you. How about your fellow, Ian, isn't it?'

'He was working long hours and now he's visiting his children who've gone to stay in Dorset, so I've barely seen him lately.' Hope sighed. On the one hand she really needed to talk things out with him, but on the other, she dreaded his answer. 'Still, work keeps me busy. How's things at the tube station?'

'You don't want to know,' Daisy replied, letting out a long sigh. 'I'm beginning to think I'm wasting my time there. In fact . . .' she leaned closer to Hope and lowered her voice. 'Between you and me, I'm tempted not to wait for my call-up papers to arrive. I fancy joining the Land Army. Being out in the fresh air rather than stuck underground all day really appeals.'

'I can't see Auntie Patty liking that idea, Daisy. It would give you some freedom, though.'

'Exactly, I knew you'd understand. Still, as I've promised Mr Rathbone I'll look after things it probably won't come to anything, so keep it to yourself, eh?'

'Of course,' Hope agreed. 'Well, it's been good catching up but I'm on the early shift tomorrow, so I'd better be heading home.'

'I'll walk back with you,' Daisy told her. 'I don't think your dear sister will notice we've gone,' she added, inclining her head to where Faith was now standing closer to the man and laughing up into his face.

CHAPTER TWELVE

After sitting through an hour's talk Clover's head was spinning. Mrs Speedwell talked at the speed her name suggested as she took them through their work pattern.

'You will be working one of three different shifts on a rotating twenty-four-hour basis which changes weekly,' she continued. 'The schedule is posted every Monday on the notice board. There is just one address you may give for your family and close friends to communicate with you. That is Box III c/o The Foreign Office. I reiterate, it is the only one you may give out regardless of where you're billeted, and there are marked boxes in the main house for you to post and collect. Any questions?'

Clover stared around, but it seemed everyone was as shell-shocked as she.

'Now, it is vital, however busy you are, that you always take your allocated meal break. On your way out, you will see the toilet block nearby whilst the canteen facilities are situated just outside the Park gates. The shifts are long and arduous so I cannot impress upon you how important it is that you keep yourselves well fed. Nutrition powers the brain, after all, does it not?' The supervisor looked at them in such a way that they all found themselves nodding in agreement.

'Right, before I go on to explain the vital work you are about to embark on in the machine room, I must impress upon you the importance of keeping it to yourselves. And I do mean yourself. There must be no discussion of anything seen or heard here, not even with the person you're sitting next to. Any queries you direct to me. You have all signed the OSA and know the penalty. Any hint to anyone of what we're doing here will be treated with extreme gravity. I do not say that lightly – the death sentence could be imposed. You must understand that any breach might not only hinder the important war work we're doing, but it could also endanger the lives of our brave military personnel.'

Clover frowned, wondering again what on earth she had got herself into. It all seemed very complex for the clerical work Major Westwood had mentioned. And since when did that entail using a machine? Nor had there been any talk of using the German she'd spent weeks studying. As for sending her mother a post box number for her to reply to her letters? Well, she was going to be less than impressed with that.

'Is that chair so comfortable that you don't wish to join us, Miss Harrison?' Mrs Speedwell's voice penetrated her thoughts, jolting her back to the present.

Looking up, she saw the others were now gathered around the machine on the table and jumping up quickly she went to join them.

'Now, you will have noticed that each hut has a

different number. This denotes the different work each team performs and although you must never discuss your work, you will all be operating as a team.'

'Don't get that,' the dark-haired woman next to Clover murmured.

'I agree it does sound somewhat contradictory; however, you'll soon see what I mean,' the supervisor smiled. 'Now, with the help of this machine here, which is a copy of the one they use in Germany called Enigma, you're going to crack their codes for the war effort.'

There was a stunned silence as, for the first time, the importance of what they were to embark on hit them.

'Oh, don't think you're going to be cracking important codes all day long. A lot of the time, maybe the majority even, the work you're doing will be routine, dare I say even mundane? The long shifts will leave you feeling exhausted, but on those rare days you do manage to make a breakthrough you will feel exhilarated, knowing you have truly done something to help end the war. I said earlier you would be working as a team and that applies to the whole camp, for your messages will then be passed on to the next hut, where they will be examined to see where and if they fit into the larger picture. We might be playing a small part in the war effort, but it is a vital one, you may depend on that.'

'I wish she'd hurry up and get on with it,' the dark-haired woman muttered. 'I'm hungry.'

'I hear you, Wilson,' the supervisor said, 'but if it's all the same to you, I'd like to explain how this machine works before we break for lunch.' She waited whilst the woman nodded. Having been too nervous to eat any breakfast, Clover's stomach was protesting too. However, as Mrs Speedwell began explaining the intricacies of the Enigma machine, she found herself enthralled and a shiver of excitement tingled her spine.

***

Having slept fitfully, Rose bundled herself into her warmest clothes, packed a bag, then deciding a brisk walk might help blow away the cobwebs, set off over Hackney Downs. The air was fresh and, apart from a couple of people walking their dogs, the common was deserted. Even the trees were devoid of foliage and the low, straggly hedges looked as forlorn as she felt. Conversely, the bombed-out houses on the edge of town already had buddleia and chickweed sprouting from the ruins.

Her footsteps crunched in time to her marching thoughts as she tried to digest what Mrs Sutherland had told her about Philip. She couldn't understand it. Perhaps Matron was right, and she did need time off after all.

'Hello, love, this is a nice surprise,' Patty cried, looking up from the pastry she was rolling. 'You've timed it right 'cos I managed to get a little bit of brisket yesterday and made a stew for one dinner then I'm turning the leftovers into a pie for tonight. Sort of cook once, eat twice to save time and fuel. Of course

104

it'll be packed out with vegetables, but the leftover gravy'll make it tasty. I'll just finish crimping the edges then I'll make us a cuppa.' As Rose threw down her bag and slumped into a chair, she looked up and frowned. 'You're looking peaky, pet. Busy time at the hospital?'

'It's been hectic. A couple of the repatriated soldiers have serious injuries but those with minor ones are happy to be back in Blighty and are lively during the day to say the least. However, some suffer night terrors which disrupt the whole ward so it'll be better all round when Queen Alexandra's has space to accommodate them.'

'Those poor men,' Patty sighed. 'What they've been through doesn't bear thinking about. Oh, I do wish we'd hear from our Peter.'

'I'm sure he'll write when he can,' Rose assured her.

'Yes, of course, he will,' Patty said. 'Anyway, Daisy says Mr Rathbone's been admitted to your ward. How is he?'

'Unfortunately, his fracture is taking time to knit so he's likely to be in hospital for some time. And now we're getting the inevitable winter falls, both from the ice and the blackout. Despite being so busy, though, Matron's insisted I take a couple of days off.'

'Well, she knows best I'm sure,' Patty said, putting the pie on the side then wiping her hands before spooning tea into the pot. 'It's used leaves, I'm afraid, but what's new, eh? Well, those leaves ain't, that's for sure,' she chuckled. 'Anyhow, our Rose, you look like you've lost a bob and found a tanner, so why don't you tell me what's up while we've got the house to ourselves for a change?' She sank into the chair beside her eldest daughter and smiled encouragingly.

Rose sipped her tea before speaking.

'I bumped into Mrs Sutherland recently and she told me Philip is now affianced to someone more suitable than me. She looked positively gleeful, Ma.'

'And have you heard from Philip himself?' Patty asked, staring anxiously at her daughter.

'No,' she sighed. 'Mrs Sutherland said she presumed he'd written to me with his wonderful news.'

'The old cow!' Patty exclaimed, unknowingly, echoing Daisy's words. 'But you know, our Rose, that doesn't sound like the behaviour of the Philip we met last Christmas. Both your father and I were impressed with his good manners – and the way he made time for young Robbie? Well, that showed consideration. And you said he was a gentleman when you went to Canterbury. He was, wasn't he?' she asked, scrutinizing her daughter's face closely.

'Of course he was, Ma. We came home with an understanding about our future. At least, I thought we had.'

'Well, it sounds like there's been some misunderstanding or mischief along the way, intentional or otherwise. You need to get to the bottom of it, and quickly by the sound of it. Have you written to him?'

'It's not my place to, is it? I mean, he hasn't replied to my earlier letter, let alone written to me about his new woman.'

'*Alleged* new woman, Rose. You've only got Mrs

106

Sutherland's word that he has one. And, although we haven't heard from our Peter, we still write to him. None of us know what's happening to our men in this war, Rose, and that's a fact. Write to Philip, tell him you met his mother and see what he has to say for himself.'

'What you say makes sense, Ma,' Rose replied.

Knowing her daughter had to think things through for herself, Patty changed the subject.

'It's a shame you didn't get to go out with Daisy and Faith. You should all arrange another get together; it would do you good to have a night out. Now, while you're here, I'd like your opinion. When I was adapting a skirt for your Auntie Vera, it occurred to me that I've let myself go a bit.'

'No, you . . .' Rose began to say, then realized it was true. Her mother did look a bit, well, scruffy was the word that sprang to mind.

'I have and that's a fact,' Pattie insisted. 'I've been very busy in the greengrocer's where it's like an icehouse, so I just wear an old cardi over my overalls, and then it hardly seems worth changing to clean the house when I get home. But I've been knitting socks for soldiers, or sewing for others, so I thought it was time I did something for me. Does that sound selfish?'

'No, Ma,' Rose smiled; anyone less selfish than her mother she'd yet to meet. Then a thought struck her. 'Pa hasn't said anything, has he?'

'Heavens, no. He'd only notice if his dinner wasn't put in front of him. That's not the point, though. Take a gander at this article,' she said, passing her the now well-thumbed copy of the *Woman's Own*. 'It's what I used for your Aunt Vera's skirt.'

'There are some really good ideas here, Ma. What were you thinking of doing?'

'Well, I really like the idea of sewing a collar onto my best dress and adding a belt or sash. I do still have a waist, after all.'

'Which is more than you can say for our dear Auntie Vera,' Rose chuckled, and although Patty shot her a reproving look, she couldn't help feeling just a tad smug. 'Why don't you get your dress and we can have a go at revamping it now?'

'Good idea,' Patty replied, pleased to see her daughter looking brighter. Her little distraction ploy had worked.

***

The Red Cross centre in Hackney was a hive of activity as Vera and her youngest daughter, Joy, were being shown how to pack the boxes that were to be sent to prisoners of war. Joy was happily humming along to 'Danny Boy' which was playing on the programme *Music While You Work* on the wireless.

'This is so much better than being cooped up in the flat,' she told her mother as she dutifully filled her box the way she'd been shown.

'I agree,' Vera replied, pleased to see her daughter happy at last. In truth, she'd been miserable since they'd had to move into the two rooms above Arthur's work. Apart from her shifts serving hot drinks for the WRVS, she'd hardly ventured out, saying she had no friends around here. 'However, I don't know why they don't just pack everything in as it comes to hand. It would be much quicker.'

'I'm sorry, Mrs Potter, but that just won't do,' the woman in charge told her, appearing at her side. She was tiny, with dark hair and beady eyes that missed nothing. This, along with the red apron she always wore, had earned her the nickname of Robin. 'It's essential you follow my instructions as space in these boxes is at a premium.' To Vera's horror, she then proceeded to remove everything already packed.

'But it takes longer that way!'

'Maybe initially, but we have perfected a method of getting the maximum number of items in neatly and securely, so they don't roll around in transit. It is important that each POW receives the same as his colleague – hence our list here,' the woman said, stabbing the piece of paper given to each volunteer. 'Try again, dear, and when you've managed to fit each item in, I'll show you how we tie up our boxes.'

Vera glared and muttered under her breath, but fell silent when Robin stopped by Joy, exclaiming in delight. 'Oh, well done, dear! That is a splendidly packed box. Perhaps you could follow your daughter's example, Mrs Potter?'

As Vera bristled with indignation, her neighbours stifled their smiles. Since the woman had moved to the area, she'd been trying to tell them all how things should be done and, quite frankly, they'd had enough. Her charming daughter, on the other hand, lived up to her name and was a joy to have around.

They watched as the girl deftly packed corned beef, cocoa, condensed milk, margarine and cheese without needing to consult the list, before adding the knitted socks and scarf. Her voice as she sang was pure as a lark's and brightened their morning.

'Ah, that's a bit better, Mrs Potter,' Robin said as she popped up beside her again. 'Just a wee adjustment to the tins here and everything will fit snugly in, ready for the next stage, which I always think of as putting everything to bed. We take some shavings from this box here then pack it between the items as it's important they don't move around when being shipped.'

'Yes, you said,' Vera muttered, conscious her neighbours were watching.

'Ah, you remembered, well done, Mrs Potter. Next, we take a lid, place it on top and tie securely with string. Now it can go in that packing crate and you're ready to start on the next one.' The woman almost hopped as she went off to answer someone's query.

'This is good fun, isn't it?' Joy cried. 'Can you imagine the men's faces when they open the boxes we've helped pack? I'm coming here every morning I'm not on duty at the mobile canteen.' The other volunteers smiled, for her enthusiasm was infectious.

'You've done very well, especially for a first time. I do hope you'll become regulars as we rely on our volunteers enormously,' Robin told them as they stood sipping hot drinks during their break.

'We will, won't we, Ma,' Joy told her.

'Of course,' Vera agreed, her equanimity restored.

'We must do our bit for the war effort, must we not?' she replied, turning to her neighbours.

'That's splendid,' Robin said, beaming widely. 'We also hold fund-raising concerts, and I couldn't help hearing you singing earlier, Joy – I may call you Joy?'

'Oh yes, please do.'

'Well, you might like to speak to Jane Bayliss over there, I'm sure she'll sign you up,' she told Joy, indicating the smart lady with bright copper curls who had just come into the room. 'In fact, I believe she's one of your neighbours is she not?'

'Oh yes, I recognize her, don't you, Ma?' Joy replied.

'Yes, I do. She works for my husband,' Vera announced grandly.

'Well, that's splendid,' Robin beamed, then hopped over to speak to the woman concerned.

CHAPTER THIRTEEN

It was late morning and Hope and Kitty, having returned from taking a woman with suspected appendicitis to Homerton Hospital, were having a much-needed break when the station supervisor appeared.

'Can I have a quick word please, Hope?' she asked.

Fighting down her frustration for she was enjoying her hard-earned hot drink, Hope nodded and followed the woman into her office, where to her surprise Ian MacLeod was waiting.

'Oh, hello,' she said, taken by surprise, 'Long time no see.'

'Hello, Hope, good to see you again,' he murmured, his eyes lighting up as he turned towards her.

'Right, well pleasantries over, let's get down to business. Queen Alexandra can now accommodate four of the more able-bodied soldiers. As you know, our hospital here has been run off its feet so that will no doubt come as a relief to them. I would like you both to carry out the transfer. I know you aren't rostered together,' she said as Hope opened her mouth, 'but I feel it would be in the patients' best interest and, as the soldiers might need assistance getting in and out of the ambulance, I suggest you drive, Hope. Here are your instructions,' she said, passing a sheet of paper to

MacLeod. As they turned to leave, she whispered to Hope. 'Here's your opportunity.'

Suddenly nervous in his presence, Hope forgot to declutch as they turned out of the yard.

'Haven't forgot what I taught you already, have you?' Ian tutted.

'Of course not!' she snapped, cross with herself for almost stalling the engine.

She had so many questions spinning around in her mind, but now she felt wrongfooted, and before she could sort out her emotions, they were pulling up at the hospital. The soldiers were waiting in wheelchairs, bundled up in their thick army coats against the cold, and orderlies helped them into the back of the ambulance.

Spirits were high on the journey, but Hope knew the route from their previous trips, and while she concentrated on avoiding the potholes and debris that still littered parts of the road, Ian MacLeod happily joined in with the men's banter. Realizing the ride back would be quiet without any patients to transport, she tried to formulate the questions she wanted to ask. After Sonia Strang's statement she needed to know what had prompted his transfer to their ambulance station as well as finding out how his children were settling in Dorset.

However, on the return journey, the atmosphere between them hung as heavy as winter smog.

'How have you been?' he finally asked. 'Did you miss me?'

'We've been extremely busy,' she replied tersely, then

could have bitten off her tongue. What was the matter with her? He sounded as if he was being conciliatory.

'Yes, I'm sure the soldiers kept you occupied,' he replied.

'What do you mean by that?' she snapped, the vehicle jolting as they hit a bump.

'Just that you probably haven't been staying at home every night,' he muttered and lapsed into silence. 'And I think you'd better slow down a bit, there seems to be a lot of rubble around.'

Defiantly, she continued at the same speed, ignoring his protests as they flipped over bumps and veered around potholes.

'Why don't you let me drive?' he suggested.

'No need,' she told him.

However, as dusk began to fall, she switched on the vehicle's lights and had to slow down as she picked her way in the pinprick of beam they afforded.

'So, how have you been,' Ian asked, turning to face her at last. This was her opportunity, she thought, knowing if she didn't ask him the question which plagued her, she might not get another opportunity.

'Busy as always. How about you? Have your children settled into their new home?'

'It's been unsettling for them to have to move again, and I long for the day I can have them back with me.'

'So will you all go back to where you used to live before?'

'I wouldn't think so. Why?' he asked, turning to face her.

'Well, I don't really know much about you. You've

never said why you actually moved here, for instance,' she murmured.

'Surely it's the present that's important? I've missed you and thought about you a lot, Hope.' He waited, then when she didn't respond, continued. 'Being an only parent now, it's important that I see the children settled. Of course, in time, and with the right woman,' he said, looking directly at her, 'I'd like to make a real home for them again.' Although she could feel him watching her, she kept staring ahead.

'Well, that's natural,' she murmured.

'Anyway, I've asked Sonia Strang to roster us together so I can spend as much time with you as I can between my job and any visit that I'm able make to see my children.'

They were fast approaching their depot now and Hope had to concentrate. He still intended coming back then, she thought, her spirits rising.

However, it was only as she lay in her bed that night that she realized he hadn't completely answered her question about his transfer.

* * *

Clover's head was spinning like a whirling dervish and it was only mid-afternoon. Temperatures in the hut had plummeted and the stuffy atmosphere from the closed windows, combined with the constant thrum of machinery somewhere behind their room, was giving her a headache. The typewriter like machines they were to operate had looked simple enough until Mrs

Speedwell explained they were turned to a new setting each day depending on what the cryptographers thought the Germans were using. After the briefest of breaks for a meal when the bangers had lived up to their name, having burst their skins, providing them with little or no filling, they had returned to their seats for another lesson. This time on decoding.

'Lawks, me head's fit to burst,' the dark-haired woman, Clover now knew to be Sally, moaned sometime later.

'Right, that's it for today,' Mrs Speedwell, announced, looking at her watch. 'The bus into town will be leaving in ten minutes. Get a good night's sleep and be back here at eight sharp. Tomorrow we'll try decoding some actual messages.'

'Phew, slave driver or what,' Sally muttered to Clover as they filed from the room and made their way outside, where they stood breathing in the cold but fresh air. 'Where are you billeted?'

'I'm not sure, I left my bag with the address in up at the main house. Shall I meet you at the bus stop?'

'Actually, I've got myself a lift into town where I've been promised a decent meal at the local hostelry, and then who knows?' she chuckled, giving Clover a wink.

The ride into Bletchley was bumpy but mercifully quick, the passengers too tired to make conversation. As she'd requested, the driver called out when they reached her stop on the High Street. 'Red Brick hostel, is it?' he grinned. 'Big house just up there, you can't miss it,' he told her, gesturing to a side road. 'Good luck,' he added, before roaring off in a cloud of fumes.

Clover hurried along the pavement. After such a long day, she couldn't wait to settle into her room and put her feet up. She stopped outside the biggest house in the street but couldn't see any name plate. Still, it was large and red so she rang the bell.

'Hang about!' a voice called, and moments later the door was opened by a woman of about forty. With her bottle-blonde hair and low-cut top, she was what her mother would term blowsy, Clover thought.

'My name's Miss Harrison and I'm looking for this hotel,' she explained, holding out the slip the sergeant had given her earlier.

'Hotel, eh? Well, yer better come in before that blooming warden bleats about the blackout. And keep yer voice down, do. We're a *hostel*, OK? I'm Ruby, known as Booby Ruby for obvious reasons,' she grinned, sticking out her chest so her breasts almost spilled out of her top.

'But . . .' Clover began, stepping into a long, green and dimly lit hallway that she couldn't help thinking would pose no threat to the blackout.

'Look, 'tis simple, see. Thems up at the Park pays for us to put up thems that work there. And as you're allowed to billet more in a hostel, that's what this is, get it?' She winked. 'More guests, more dosh,' she chuckled, rubbing her fingers together, before staring at Clover's bag. 'Ain't got much luggage for one who's staying, 'as yer?'

'The rest of my things are being sent on from my last billet in North Wales,' she explained.

'Well, I'd have them sent to the Park if you ain't

117

goin' to be in, 'cos you don't know what the rest are like. Everyone's out to make a pretty penny,' she grinned. 'Now, I'll show you round and explain the rules. This is the kitchen.' She pushed open the door to a large green square room with a table that looked clean enough, and green painted cupboards on the walls. Now, I knows you all work weird hours up at the Park, so once you've handed over your ration book, you can help yourself to cereal and toast for breakfast. There's a hot meal provided noon and six sharp. First come, first served. When it's gone it's gone, so's it's in your own interest to be prompt.'

Clover followed her up a creaky staircase where the carpet was so threadbare the boards were clearly visible. 'Bathroom's through there. Your days for a bath is Tuesday and Friday. I leaves it to you what times suit, and if you want to change your day it's up to you to sort it with the others. The five-inch line is there for a reason, so no cheating and make sure you leave the bath clean. There's an outdoor facility in the yard if the bathroom's busy.

'Right, your room's up on the next floor,' the woman said, puffing as they came to another staircase. 'No. 5 it is. Keys in door and if yous got any sense you'll use it. The main door's always on the latch as we has people carrying out trades at all times, if you get my meaning. And the gents do love a girl in uniform so you're goin' to come in for a lot of attention, you lucky girl.'

'Thank you,' Clover replied, trying not to shudder.

'OK, dearie, once you've settled in, come down for dinner, but don't forget – no coupons, no chow.'

Clover thanked the woman, then pushed open the door to room 5. Although the green-painted room looked clean, it was certainly shabby, and she couldn't help thinking of the comfortable establishment she'd left – was it really only that morning?

Turning the key in the lock, she sank onto the bed, the springs groaning in protest. Clover could have groaned with it. What kind of billet was this? Still, she was too tired to think much about it. Sighing she lay back on the green flowery eiderdown and closed her eyes. It had been a long day and every bone in her body was aching in protest, for she hadn't exerted so much energy in a long time. However, she'd been sent to Bletchley to help with the war effort and that was what she was going to do.

She was so tired she drifted off to sleep immediately and didn't hear the rattle of her doorknob as somebody tried turning it.

CHAPTER FOURTEEN

Hope woke full of resolve. She was cross with herself for not insisting Ian answer her question on the journey back from the military hospital, especially as he seemed to be trying to be amenable. However, it was all right him saying he'd arranged for them to be rostered together, but there were always so many people milling around the ambulance depot that privacy couldn't be guaranteed so as she wasn't on shift until that afternoon, she would go and see him right now. It was only as she was pulling on her overalls that she realized she had no idea where he lived. Sonia Strang would know, although whether the supervisor would divulge personal information was another matter. Still, it was worth a try.

Running down the stairs, pulling on her coat as she went, she heard voices coming from the hallway. Then her aunt appeared, Ian in her wake.

'Oh, there you are Hope, you have a visitor,' she said, beaming at her before picking up the kettle, and taking it out to the back kitchen.

'Forgive me for barging in like this,' Ian said, producing half a dozen daffodils from behind his back. 'I'm afraid they've been blown around a bit in the breeze, but my landlady let me pick them from her garden. Their brightness makes me think of spring and new beginnings'

'Thank you, they're beautiful,' Hope said. 'I didn't know you were in lodgings?'

'No point in paying the rent on a house when I'm hardly there. Look, Hope, after our awkward conversation in the ambulance, I was hoping we could try again. Or have I blown it?' he asked, when she didn't reply.

'I guess I was as much to blame,' she sighed. 'There's always such a gap between us seeing each other and then, when we do, we never have time to finish our discussions.' Or get answers to my questions, she thought. Impatiently, she pushed a lock of blonde hair back out of her eyes, wishing she'd taken more time with her appearance.

'Oh, daffodils – harbingers of spring, I always think,' Patty said, reappearing and placing the full kettle on the range. 'Hard to believe it's less than a month until Easter, though goodness only knows where we'll find any chocolate eggs for Robbie this year.'

Hope shook her head. They weren't even halfway through March and already her aunt was fussing about the next occasion they could celebrate. No doubt she'd be planning their festive menu next.

'Shall I put these flowers in water?' Patty asked, taking a vase from the cupboard. 'We don't stand on ceremony here, Mr MacLeod, so why don't you take the weight off your feet? The kettle won't take long to boil and can I offer you a hot drink?'

'Thank you, but please call me Ian,' he began as Hope interjected.

'Actually, Auntie, if you don't mind, Ian and I were just going for a walk. We have some things we need to discuss.' Snatching up her gas mask and gloves, she smiled at Patty.

'I suppose you want to talk about work after collecting those soldiers. Mind you put your hat on, the sun might be shining but there's still a nip in the air.'

'See you later, Auntie,' Hope said, ushering Ian from the room.

'I wouldn't have minded a hot drink,' he said, once they were outside.

'Sorry about that. My aunt is lovely, but when she gets talking it's hard to escape. Anyway, I know a nice little café opposite Ridley Road Market, we can get a hot drink there.'

'As you had your coat on when I arrived, I'm guessing you were off to browse the latest fashions,' he grinned.

'Well, as you can see, its only haute couture for us ladies of Victory Walk,' she joked, pointing to the overalls she wore for work.

Pleased to be easy in each other's company again, they wandered down the high street, heading south until they reached the entrance to Ridley Road. The market was smaller than it had once been, with fewer stalls and not many people browsing. Although there was less on offer, costs had risen sharply making the hoarding of precious coupons even more vital. Not for the first time, Hope wished the ambulance society would provide uniforms for its workers. Although

Sonia Strang had hinted that they might be forth-coming, at this rate the war would be over before that happened.

'It's over there,' she told him as they waited for a bus heading towards Liverpool Street to pass.

The atmosphere inside the café was cheerful, with small tables covered in bright gingham cloths and pictures of sunflowers adorning the walls. A chirpy woman, face flushed from the heat of the kitchen, came over and directed them to a table at the back of the room.

'Sorry all the window seats are taken,' she murmured.

'This will be fine,' Hope smiled. It would be easier to speak back here, away from the other customers.

'We have tea or that essence that passes for coffee these days. Teacakes or ginger cake.' The woman waited; notepad poised.

'Just tea for me,' Hope said.

'Make that a pot for two,' Ian told her.

An awkward silence fell as they sat looking at each other across the table and Hope began to fidget. She stared absent-mindedly at the other diners, watched the two waitresses delivering their orders, perplexed that the comfortable atmosphere between them should have changed. Yet wasn't that what had happened in the ambulance? Determined to break the silence she turned back to face him.

'So, you've . . .' she began.

'You seem to . . .' he started. They both broke off and laughed.

'Ladies first.'

'I was just going to say that I didn't know you'd moved. I thought you said you weren't going to move again.'

'I meant I didn't intend moving districts again, and I still don't, as long as the children settle in Dorset, that is.'

'Here we are, dearies, a pot of tea, milk and a small pot of sugar. I'm afraid we can't run to much of that these days,' the waitress said, unloading the tray onto their table then disappearing.

'Do you take milk and sugar?' she asked, realizing how little she knew about him.

'Milk only,' he replied, raising his brows as she took out a brown paper bag and poured the sugar into it before proceeding to pour their tea.

'If Auntie Patty's thinking of Easter already, she'll be wanting all the sugar she can get for her baking, and the cost will be factored into our bill so it's not stealing,' she told him, discreetly placing the bag back in her pocket. 'Now, where were we?' she frowned, determined to get some answers once and for all. 'What prompted your move to our ambulance depot? Was it a house move or did you ask for a transfer for another reason.'

He stared at her for a long moment, took a sip of his drink, then sighed.

'I can see the rumour wheel has been turning. If you must know, a couple of the ambulance workers who were men who'd served in the Great War, didn't relish the idea of working with someone they considered to be a conscientious objector, irrespective of the fact my work as an engineer is deemed vital to the war effort and therefore regarded as a reserved occupation. Believe me, Hope, my input is of far greater value to the country than if I signed up. However, since I don't like to brag about it, people get the wrong idea and then, like Chinese whispers, rumours spread.'

'But why don't you just tell people the truth?' she asked. He let out a long sigh.

'My work is sensitive. Besides, people will believe what they want. They see a tall, healthy man and assume he should be in uniform. Joining the ambulance service was my way of helping at home and I thought people would understand that.'

'I see.' She frowned, trying to take everything in.

'Do you, Hope?' He turned his penetrating gaze upon her, and she could see her answers mattered to him.

'I think so. Do many people know the truth?'

'Sonia, of course. Jimmy did and he understood my predicament. For what it's worth I valued his opinion.' They were silent for a few moments, remembering their brave friend who'd sacrificed his life saving others in a fire the previous year. She took a sip of her tea, hoping to swallow down the lump in her throat. She knew so many men who were away fighting for their country, not least Faith's husband Martin, her cousin Peter, Daisy and Rose's followers, it was hard to believe a job at home could be deemed more important. And yet, if Jimmy, who'd been a principled man, had known and not condemned, who was she to argue?

'I can see you're conflicted,' he said quietly, his look veiled.

'If your work is as important to the country as you say, then who am I to question?' she replied.

'And you'll still go out with me?' he asked, hope lighting up his eyes.

'I will,' she told him, smiling at last.

'The trouble is that between my job and my shifts at the LAAS I have little free time, but as I said before, so that we can spend as much as possible with each other, I asked Sonia for us to be rostered together and of course, I intend to travel to Dorset whenever possible, although train passes are getting harder to come by. However, children are resilient and I'm hoping they'll soon make new friends and settle. So, what do you say, Hope, can you put up with our limited time together until I'm free to offer you more?'

His blue eyes were heavy with emotion, and she felt herself empathizing with his predicament. She knew he cared for his children and felt his responsibility keenly. Characteristics to be admired, and, she had to admit, if they were rostered together, at least she'd see him regularly at work. This war wouldn't last for ever and, in the meantime, surely, she could wait until he had more time to be with her.

'Yes, Ian, I can,' she told him then blushed, her fingers tingling as he reached across the table and squeezed them.

'You've made me very happy,' he told her and the look in his eye let her know he meant it.

* * *

126

Daisy didn't enjoy going to work these days and if it hadn't been for her promise, she would have joined up. She couldn't wait for Mr Rathbone to return. Rose had told her mother his leg would take some time to heal, so she couldn't help wishing the hateful Mr Pratt would be transferred somewhere else. Arriving at Manor House Station that morning she smiled at the weary groups of people who were making their tired way up to the exit. Having spent the night sleeping on the platforms, they were only too eager to get out into the fresh air and she wished she could join them, especially as she was meant to stay cooped up in the office all day. However, the strong sense of duty Mr Rathbone had instilled in her meant she needed to ensure all was running as it should be. By the time the dreaded Pratt turned up, she would be back at her desk and hopefully he'd be none the wiser.

She sniffed the air, surprised to find there was no smell of disinfectant. Regulations stated the station should be cleansed at this time of day, which was known as the coughing hour. Then she noticed a group of children lurking by the entrance to the tunnel. Not only could this be dangerous as the first train was due, but it was also strictly against London Transport policy. Frowning, she looked around for a member of staff on the early shift, but when she couldn't see any, hurried over to warn them.

'Everything all right here?' she asked, giving them a bright smile.

'Yeah, why shouldn't it be?' a grimy looking lad

with lanky hair scowled. He looked to be about ten years old and was clearly the ringleader.

'Maybe you don't realize, but the first train will be coming through in a few moments.'

'Yeah, we know,' he replied, looking at her belligerently.

'Well, you'd better scarper, then,' she said, addressing them all in the brisk, no-nonsense manner she sometimes adopted with Robbie, her younger brother. 'Come on, before I call the manager,' she added, clapping her hands for good measure.

Shrugging, they ran off, leaving a young girl struggling behind. She was wearing a calliper and Daisy's heart went out to her as she tried in vain to keep up.

'Is your ma here,' she called. The girl shrugged.

'Nah, gone to work, ain't she.'

'Is anyone waiting at home for you?' Daisy asked. Before the girl could answer, a young lad dashed over, grabbed her by the hand and yanked her away.

'How many times have I told you to keep away from that gang? They're no' but trouble.'

Satisfied she was being cared for, Daisy walked along the platform until she found Alfie, who was sweeping the platform as if his life depended upon it.

'Stinks down 'ere summat chronic,' he told her, coughing for good measure.

'Where is everyone and why hasn't the station been disinfected?' she asked.

'Cutbacks, ain't it. That arrogant ars . . . well, yer know who I means,' he grunted, staring warily at Mrs

Nicholls who was setting up her tea wagon further down the platform.

'What cutbacks, Alfie?' she asked.

'Cutbacks on staff, cutbacks on safety. Yer name it.'

'He's cut my hours, so I don't know how I'm going to pay the rent. He'll be cutting back on the trains soon.' Wilf joined in. 'Who does he think he is, ordering us around? Army reject!' he spat. 'Not like us who served in the Great War.'

'But there haven't been any orders from the Transport Board to cut back on anything!' Daisy protested. 'In fact, their latest instruction is to be more vigilant as they're running extra trains to transport the forces.'

'Well, maybe nobody told 'im. All I knows is I got to do the work of two people now. And wiv me bad back an' all,' Alfie moaned, leaning heavily on his broom.

'Leave this with me, gentlemen, I'll find out what's going on,' Daisy told them, making her way over to the WRVS wagon.

'I suppose you've come to speak to me about that egotistical, pompous excuse for a man,' Mrs Nicholls cried before Daisy could open her mouth. 'He's only threatened to have us moved upstairs onto the pavement. I mean, what good is that to anyone wanting a hot drink before they leave for work, or in the evening come to that?'

'I don't know what's going on, Mrs Nicholls, but I intend finding out. The station hasn't been disinfected and there was a group of children playing by the entrance to the tunnel, just now.'

'Been the same all week. He sacked old Reg when he queried it. There's not enough staff down here as it is, what with the young men away. Anyway, I thought you weren't allowed on the platform? Mr Pratt told us that in no uncertain terms. Said we're to tell him if we see you,' Sylvie Simms declared as she began pouring tea from the urn for a customer.

'It's the safety aspect I worry about,' Mrs Nicholls interjected. 'All those unwashed bodies and no disin-fectant, asking for trouble that is,' she cried, puffing out her chest.

'Children playing around by the tunnel concerns me, Mrs Nicholls. Do you think you can keep your eye on them?'

'I'll do my best, Daisy, but I've a tea wagon to run. Anyhow, looks like we've got unwanted company. I'll keep him occupied whilst you scoot.'

'Yes, as if we'd sneak on you,' Sylvie told Daisy.

Following the women's look, Daisy saw Pratt arriving on the platform.

'Thanks, Mrs Nicholls, Sylvie,' she murmured, turning on her heel. As she hurried to her office, she heard Mrs Nicholl's strident shout.

'Mr Pratt! I need your invaluable advice over here immediately, please,' she called just as the first train of the day whooshed into the station.

Back at her desk, Daisy ignored the new pile of paperwork that had arrived overnight as she pondered what to do.

This was too serious to ignore yet she had no authority to speak to the Transport Board. Not that they would believe the word of a clerk over that of a manager. Besides, if they found out she was underage, Mr Rathbone would be in trouble. Perhaps she should speak to him . . . yet it wouldn't be fair to worry the man when he was in hospital. She was still fretting when Mr Pratt appeared, looming threateningly over her desk.

'I hear you've been disobeying my orders again. I've told you before you've no business to be down on the platform, you're a clerk and a mere female one at that. I would remind you again that I'm in charge here. Luckily, I have my spies who keep me informed on which members of staff ignore my orders. So, what have you to say for yourself?' He leaned in closer so that she could smell his stinking breath. Clearly, he hadn't washed recently, either. Rising to her feet, she stood facing him.

'Well, *my* spies tell me you've been making safety cuts.'

'Pff, safety cuts,' he scoffed. 'And what business is it of yours anyway. I am the manager here and will run this station how I see fit,' he hissed.

'It concerns me that children were running around the entrance to the tunnel when the first train—' she began.

'And it concerns me Miss-Holier-than-thou Harrison that you've been taken on by a trusted member of staff when you're obviously underage. Lying to the Transport Board is a serious offence, so who's in the wrong here?'

Daisy's heart sank. If she admitted her true age, she'd get Mr Rathbone in trouble.

'I can see by your face we understand each other,

Miss Harrison.' He gave that weasel-like smirk that made her sick to her stomach. She swore blind if he had whiskers they'd be twitching. 'You keep shtum and so will I – otherwise we know who will come off worse, don't we?'

CHAPTER FIFTEEN

Clover felt like a bag of nerves when she arrived at Hut 6, which seemed even dingier and stuffier than the previous day. Although excited about the work ahead, her experience at the hostel earlier had left her shaken. With her stomach grumbling in protest at the lack of food, she joined the others in the queue at the back of the hut, where they waited to claim their seats as soon as the night shift vacated them. It had been impressed upon them during their induction that the machines were never to be switched off, and each changeover was to be carried out quickly and quietly with no disruption.

'What a night!' Sally grinned at her and raised her brows. 'They were a lively crowd to say the least, especially those lovely men on leave. You'll have to come with me next time. How about your night, digs OK?' There was no time to answer as the women in front of them were rising from their seats. With weary smiles, they collected their things and, without a word, were gone.

'I'll tell you later,' Clover promised quickly, looking down at her machine as the supervisor glanced their way.

'Good morning, everyone. As the first shift of the new day, it's your job to change the settings as guessed by the cryptographers. I'll pass round the piece of paper showing these and you'll then turn the rotors on top of your machine to match them. Only when you've done this will you pass the slip to your neighbour. Remember, you do not speak or discuss anything. Any queries, see me.'

After she'd managed to do as asked, and with excitement overtaking her hunger pangs, Clover glanced down at the German keyboard, took up the first message and tried to remember what she'd been told the previous day. Letters always grouped in fives; press first coded letter on keyboard; decoded letter will light up on lamp board. Letter never same as one pressed first. Make note of new letter and continue with next, keeping in groups of five until whole message decoded. She was so engrossed in trying to make sense of a message, she hardly heard when Sally hissed across at her.

'Looks like you can't make head nor tail of this one either.'

'We can only hope that the cryptographers have got it right, so don't be disheartened if your work so far has made no sense. Rome wasn't built in a day and alas, the Germans won't be defeated overnight either. However, rest assured everything you do overall will be contributing to the war effort and who knows? That next message could be the one that makes sense,' Mrs Speedwell told them, looking pointedly at Sally.

Clover picked up the next message with renewed energy. How wonderful it would be if she managed to decode one. As they'd been shown, she neatly wrote down the new letters on the squared paper provided, careful to keep them in the blocks of five. Nothing resembled any German word she had studied so religiously whilst she'd been recuperating, nor any English one come to that. After a while, her spirits began to fall, her energy dwindled and the constant thrum of machinery from the room behind along with the clattering of their machines threatened to give her a headache. She was useless at this. Perhaps she should ask to be transferred back to Wales. She missed Marigold and it would be so nice to see her again. She was just wondering how her friend was faring, when Mrs Speedwell's voice cut into her thoughts.

'Right, ladies, those of you in the front row may now take a thirty-minute break. Remember what I said about using it to refuel. Your energy levels are bound to be flagging by now.'

'Not half,' Sally muttered as they made their way outside then stood blinking like owls in the midday sun. 'That canteen is so noisy and the food's not up to much so let's go to the café in Hut 2, have tea, cake and a catch up. Then you can tell me how you got on in your billet.'

Ignoring her grumbling stomach, Clover tagged along, breathing in gulps of fresh air as they walked. If only the other women didn't smoke. With no ventilation in the room, it just spiralled into the air where it hung over them like a grey pall.

'Coo, he's got some energy,' Sally cried, pointing to the athletic figure of a man who was jogging around the lake. 'First male I've seen here all morning, although if rumour is to be believed, he's not interested in we ladies,' she sighed. Clover wondered how she knew these things when they'd arrived at the same time. 'Apparently there are some good-looking airmen up at the house, though, so we can scout that out later.'

When they were seated at a table by the window, with a pot of tea and two pitiful slices of indiscriminate cake between them, Sally turned to Clover.

'So, how's the hotel – or should I say hostel?'

'You know about that?' Clover asked, warming her hands by stirring the tea in the pot. She'd just taken a bite of her cake when Sally, having paused to light a cigarette, continued.

'Talk of the pub, my old darling. Jeremy reckons it's the local knocking-shop, with the landlady being the principal knocker, if you get my meaning and—' She came to a halt as Clover started choking, spraying crumbs all over the table. 'Blimey, I thought that sponge looked bad. Anyhow, as I was saying, she registers to accommodate newcomers to the Park. Only women, mind, and the younger the better, then tries to persuade them to swap their profession, if you get my meaning. I understand a couple of the girls have done a few shifts alongside their job at the Park. Let's hope they didn't have loose lips, one way or the other,' she hooted, drawing attention from the adjoining table of women keen to share the joke.

'Tell me you're teasing?' Clover begged, pushing her plate away, her appetite completely gone.

'Come on, give. You were as white as a sheet when

you arrived here this morning, so what was your experience of the place?' she asked, eying Clover steadily over the rim of her cup.

'Well, I haven't had anything to eat since yesterday. The hostel was clean, if somewhat shabby and in dire need of a lick of paint. However, I was so tired I fell asleep as soon as I'd been shown to my room and missed dinner.'

'So, you didn't encounter any strange men?' Sally asked, looking disappointed as she lit up another cigarette then blew a perfect smoke ring into the air between them.

'I locked my door and didn't surface until first light. I never actually saw anyone, but . . .'

'Yes?' Sally asked eagerly.'

'Well, it sounds stupid, but when I left my room, I felt as if I was being watched.'

'You probably *were* being watched, my old darling. If I were you, I'd get out sharpish. Unless you fancy making a bit on the side,' she grinned, getting to her feet before Clover could answer. 'Look, we'll talk about this later. Now, I must visit the facilities, if you can call that archaic block anything like a facility. Not much choice when you're desperate, though. See you back in the prison hut.'

Clover watched her weave her way between the tables, crowded now with a mixture of military and civilians, again nearly all female, and most smoking, she noted. What was she to do? She really didn't want to return to the hostel. She'd ask to be transferred to another billet. They were bound to have others on offer.

137

She glanced at the clock on the wall which showed she only had five minutes left of her break. With Mrs Speedwell's warning about punctuality ringing in her ears, she knew she didn't dare risk being late back. She would have to go up to the house on her next break.

Music was playing and everyone was celebrating, although Clover knew not what, as a glass of something fizzy was placed in her hand.

'This is better than going back to that hostel, isn't it?' Sally cried, raising her voice to be heard over the hubbub. Clover nodded, wondering how she'd managed to be persuaded to come here rather than seeing about another billet, for she'd still have to go back to her room, wouldn't she? 'Well must circulate, my old darling.'

As Sally made her way over to a good-looking man, wearing the blue of the RAF and a cheeky grin, Clover looked around the low-beamed bar, thronged with servicemen and women clearly out to have a good time. A fire burned cheerfully in the grate, and it seemed rationing wasn't a problem this evening as plates of cold meats, cheeses and bread were being passed around. Feeling absolutely ravenous and remembering Peter warning her against drinking on an empty stomach, she helped herself to some of the offerings along with a napkin. She wondered how her brother and the rest of her family were. She'd better write and let her mother know her address, although what she'd make of a box number, goodness only knows. There again, she could imagine her face if she saw Ruby and the hostel.

Reminded of her problem, she decided to spend one more night at the hostel and then speak to the sergeant about finding alternative accommodation tomorrow. At least it was only around the corner from this inviting hostelry on the main street. In the meantime, she'd join in the fun.

'Hello, you're one of Ruby's girls, aren't yer?' Clover looked up to see a man of middle years, conspicuous by his shabby dress and unwashed hair, leering at her through yellowing teeth.

***

Hope was humming as she arrived early for her shift. She'd been rostered with Ian for the past few days and, as the depot hadn't been busy, they'd spent the time together maintaining the ambulances. Their relationship had resumed its former easygoing nature and was no longer strained. Although his principal role was as instructor/driver, their depot hadn't taken on any new recruits for some time, so he'd been showing her what needed doing to keep the vehicles in top running order. With all the potholes and rough roads they'd been driving over, the tyres had taken a hammering, most needing patching or changing. She still had much to learn but he was an enthusiastic teacher, his bright blue eyes shining with enthusiasm as he explained things.

Although it was early, the depot was buzzing when she walked in.

'Grab yerself a cuppa, the Super wants to see us all in the office pronto,' Kitty told her.

'Perhaps more soldiers are being repatriated,' Hope responded, remembering her uncle Bert talking about it the previous evening. Of course, she knew he was hoping Peter might be amongst them. Wouldn't it be wonderful if she could go home with news like that, just as long as her cousin wasn't badly injured, of course. He and Auntie Patty had been so kind taking her in after their home had been bombed, treating her the same as Daisy and Robbie. It was a beautiful spring morning, so a trip out with Ian would be pleasant, especially if they were helping to bring soldiers home again, she thought smiling widely as Ian appeared beside her.

Although he returned her smile, Hope could tell it was forced. She was about to ask if all was well with his children, when the supervisor's voice rang out.

'Right, gather round everyone. I have some exciting news.'

'We're getting a pay rise,' someone shouted.

Sonia Strang smiled. 'Sadly not. However, as of next week, the LAAS daily shift pattern is changing, and you will be required to work 24 hours on and 24 hours off. In their infinite wisdom, the powers that be have decided this will be a more efficient way of working. In line with the other depots, you will be rostered from 09.00 until 09.00.' She waited while a buzz of surprise and in some cases, indignation, rippled around the room, before holding up her hand. 'I shall be drawing up the new rosters and appreciate this will affect some of you more than others.'

Was it her imagination or did the supervisor stare

directly at her, Hope wondered, taking a sip of her tea.

'Obviously, this will mean you having meals whilst you're on duty, so the kitchen is to be extended, and a cook employed. You will, of course, be required to provide your coupons for the meals you have. If you prefer, you can bring in your own soup and sandwiches. Now, as for sleeping arrangements . . . We have limited facilities available so you'll be bunking three or four to a room, depending on what the shift entails.' As whistles and catcalls filled the room, she held up her hand.

'Naturally, it will be girls in one section and boys in another.'

'Boo, spoilsport,' someone called. 'Just when I thought the job was getting interesting.'

'As you're almost entirely a female brigade, that shouldn't pose any problem,' Sonia continued. 'Now for the news you have all been waiting for: your new uniforms will be arriving soon.'

As a cheer went up, Hope turned to Ian, surprised to see was looking stricken.

'Don't you like the idea? I suppose it will take some getting used to, but it means we'll get whole days off which we can spend together . . . what's wrong,' she asked, when he shook his head.

'You don't understand, Hope. There's no way I'll be able to manage the new shifts. Between my work commitment and the children, I just about manage to juggle shifts here as it is. And that's only with Sonia Strang's help. The LAAS need to be able to rely on their ambulance staff turning up. Supposing I'm in the middle of a job or get stuck in Dorset? You know how unreliable the trains are these days.'

'What will you do?' she asked, her spirits sinking.

'I shall have no option other than to resign.'

'Couldn't you ask them to reduce your working hours?' she implored, looking at him appealingly.

'I wish I could but that isn't an option, Hope,' he sighed. 'I wish I could explain how vital my work is to the war effort so you could understand, but I'm afraid I can't,' he said, his expression bleak as he turned away from her

'Where are you going?'

'To speak with Sonia Strang before she starts drawing up the new rosters,' he told her tersely, then marched over to her office. Hope blinked back the tears that pricked her eyelids. Why hadn't she thought before she spoke?

'Trouble in paradise?' Kitty asked, coming over and taking Hope's arm. 'Let's go outside then yer can tell me about it in private. Good news about our uniforms, though, isn't it? It'll save on coupons. Think of the new clothes we can get.'

Outside, under the cover of the bonnet of their vehicle, Hope explained Ian's reaction to the change in shift pattern. Expecting Kitty to sympathize, she looked up sharply when her friend remained quiet.

'Maybe it's for the best,' she said eventually.

'What do you mean?'

'Well, let's be honest, he's a bit old for yer, ain't he? And he comes with a ready-made family and all the problems that entails. He's so serious, too. Then, of course, there's all those rumours about why he didn't sign up.'

'He's explained about that. His job is just as vital as enlisting.'

'Mmm. No smoke without fire, I reckon. Yer a bit naive on the male front, Hope. Could it be yer've been a tad too trusting?'

Hope stared at her friend in horror. Had she really been too trusting? If only dear Jimmy was still alive so she could discuss this with him. He was the only one who had really known Ian, after all.

CHAPTER SIXTEEN

'There wasn't any frost inside my bedroom window this morning,' Daisy said, helping herself to a bowl of porridge from the pot on the range then joining Hope and Patty at the breakfast table. 'Where's Robbie?'

'Cleaning out the rabbit hutch before school, much to his disgust,' Patty laughed. 'Let's hope spring is here at last and it's not long until Easter so I'd better see what baking ingredients I can scrape together. Hope has kindly donated some sugar which will be useful for the cake.'

'It's only what Ian and I didn't use in our tea at the café,' she replied, a frown clouding her face. Before Patty could say anything, Robbie burst into the kitchen, grinning gleefully.

'Yeah, Easter eggs! I hope this year's bigger than last year's 'cos I've grown lots,' he announced, puffing out his chest.

'You'll be getting nothing if you don't go and wash those filthy hands,' Patty told him.

'It's going to be a busy day at the depot getting everything sorted for the new shift regime, so I don't know what time I'll be home,' Hope murmured, jumping to her feet and snatching up her coat.

'Twenty-four-hour shifts are going to take a bit of getting used to, aren't they?' Daisy asked.

'Yes, and they're not going to work for some. See you later,' she muttered, putting her gas mask over her shoulder and leaving before any more could be said.

'I'll leave a covered plate of dinner in the range if you're late,' Patty called after her.

'Trouble?' Daisy asked, quirking a brow.

'I understand Ian MacLeod has a lot of commitments,' Patty sighed.

'So he won't be able to manage the new shifts, then?' Daisy tucked into her breakfast and gulped down her drink. 'I'm sure Hope will work it out.'

'At the moment, I'm more concerned about where we'll get an egg from for our Robbie. Chocolate is even scarcer than last year, and he only got one then because of Rose and Philip.

'Has Rose written to Philip, do you know?'

'I don't think so, and she hasn't heard from him either. But then we're all waiting for letters these days,' Patty sighed. 'Seems the whole lot of us could do with cheering up, so let's make Easter a real celebration. We can have a party – invite Vera and her family and, who knows, perhaps Clover will get some leave to come home.' Patty's eyes gleamed with excitement.

'I'll leave you to your planning, Ma,' Daisy smiled as she took her dishes through to the back kitchen. 'You should see the state that boy's left the sink in. Well, it's time I was on my way too,' she sighed. She was just reaching for her coat when the letterbox rattled and there was a thud on the mat.

145

'Looks like it's your lucky day, Ma,' she cried excitedly, hurrying back into the kitchen and handing Patty a pile of envelopes.

'Oh my, *all* these are from Peter! They must have been held up just like your father said. He might put on a brave face, but it's knowing our Peter survived Dunkirk that keeps him going, you know. Ooh, this envelope's in Clover's handwriting. Well, the greengrocer's will just have to wait until I've had a good read,' she told Daisy, pouring herself another cup of tea from the pot. Daisy chuckled – nothing would stand in the way of Ma reading the much-awaited post from her offspring.

'Well, I'll be jiggered!' Patty exclaimed. 'If we want to write back to our Clover we have to use a Box Number care of the Foreign Office! Whatever next? I knew that girl wasn't just doing plain old clerical work.'

'She did say it was special clerical work,' Daisy pointed out. 'And I do clerical work too remember, more's the pity. I'd better get a scuttle on, or Pratt-features will have something else to moan about.'

'You really shouldn't call him that,' Patty chided, then seeing her daughter's woebegone expression sighed and put down the letter. 'Things not getting any better, love?'

'No, Ma. In fact, they're worse. That man's making so many cutbacks there's going to be trouble, I just know it.'

'In that case, perhaps you ought to speak to someone in authority or quit and come and work with me at the greengrocer's. It's becoming busier now the meat ration's tighter than ever. Everyone's using more vegetables to make their meals stretch and of course potatoes are in demand thanks to Lord Woolton and his pie. It would be nice to have some company too.' She looked hopefully at her daughter.

Daisy sighed and snatched up her gas mask. She couldn't deny things had been almost unbearable at Manor House Station since the arrival of Mr Percy Pratt, and the idea of doing something else was tempting. However, she would be shirking her responsibility if she just walked away having promised Mr Rathbone that she'd look after things. If only she could speak to him about the cuts. Perhaps when he moved into the nursing home at the end of Victory Walk he'd be strong enough for her to run her concerns by him. The fact that the odious Pratt knew they'd both lied on her application form hung over her like a black cloud. If it was just for herself, she'd let him know she didn't give two figs who he told, but she couldn't land Mr Rathbone in it, could she?

'Sorry, Ma?' Realizing her mother was speaking, she came back to the present.

'I was saying that Clover doesn't really tell us anything about her job or where she's living, which is disappointing I must say. Just says the women she's working with are nice.'

'Perhaps her mail gets censored like Peter's?' Daisy suggested.

'And she won't be allowed any leave for three

months,' Patty said with a grimace, thinking of her hopes for a family celebration at Easter. 'Let's see what our Peter has to say. Gracious, the first one was sent over five months ago.'

'You'll have to tell me all the news tonight, Ma, or I'll be late for work.'

As soon as the fresh air hit her, Daisy's thoughts crystalized. She was banging her head against a brick wall with Mr Pratt, so why bother? It was time she did something for herself. She would go and see Mr Rathbone, but first she intended making enquiries about doing the war work she now really wanted to do.

The station was quiet by the time she arrived, and the usual departing crowds looked anxious. Daisy's heart began pounding and she willed the down escalator to move quicker. Again, there was no smell of disinfectant, she noticed.

'Thank goodness you're here, Daisy!' Mrs Nicholls cried, hurrying over as soon as she reached the platform.

'Whatever's wrong? And why does everyone seem agitated. Is everything ready for the first train?'

'We think a young girl's still in the tunnel. You know, the one with the calliper on her leg? She followed the lads in there but didn't come out with them.'

'What! How long ago? And where are those boys?' Daisy cried, her stomach turning over as she stared around.

'They reappeared about twenty minutes ago. Alfie

and Wilf went over to speak to them but nearly got knocked over themselves in the gang's haste to get away,' Sylvie Symms interjected. 'They were laughing, thinking it funny she couldn't keep up with them. That poor girl . . .'

'Is Mr Pratt aware?' Daisy asked, interrupting her diatribe.

'Ain't even here. Too early for him, ain't it?' Alfie muttered, shuffling over. 'Wouldn't 'ave 'appened if them safety checks were still being done.'

'The first train's almost due,' Daisy said, frowning up at the big platform clock. 'Have you phoned ahead and stopped it, Wilf?'

'Ain't got no authority to, and it's more than me job's worth.'

'For crying out loud! There's a girl's life at stake here! Make that call right now, Wilf! Give them my name if they ask, but you must get the power turned off and the train stopped this instant!' she shouted and hurried towards the tunnel.

'Where are you goi—' Alfie began but his words were swallowed up by the pounding of her feet as she ran like she'd never run before. Her sole thought was to find that little girl who must be scared out of her wits.

It was dark and smelly in the tunnel and Daisy shuddered as something ran over her foot. How she wished she'd thought to pick up a lantern or torch. She went to call the little girl's name then realized she didn't know it. What to do? Keep calm and carry on, wasn't that the wartime motto?

149

Heart in her mouth and trusting Wilf had managed to stop the train, she inched her way deeper into the darkness, calling out at intervals. Then, just when she thought it was futile to continue, she heard the faintest of sounds, like a little mewing. She stopped and listened. Nothing. Perhaps someone had brought their cat down to shelter for the night and it had run off. She called again, louder this time. Then she heard an answering whimper.

'Hello, it's Daisy,' she called. 'Where are you, love?' Silence. Perhaps desperation and her imagination had conjured up the noise. But no, this time she definitely caught the sound of sobbing and miraculously it sounded nearer. Creeping ahead, trying to track where it was coming from, she almost tripped over some sort of obstacle. This time there was a squeal.

'Ouch! That's me you just kicked.' As Daisy bent down, she could just make out the girl's eyes shining up at her. 'I'm scared, miss! Me calliper's got caught and I can't move,' she whimpered, her entire body shuddering.

'Here, put this round you,' Daisy said, shrugging out of her coat and placing it over the girl. 'Now, stay still and I'll see if I can free you,' Daisy told her, carefully feeling her way along the girl's leg, satisfied it wasn't broken. The calliper was obviously caught in something rough, but she couldn't make out what it was, and no amount of jiggling would free it.

'Am I goin' to be squashed by the train?' the girl asked, shaking and shuddering.

'Of course not. The men have stopped all the trains,'

Daisy told her, sincerely hoping it was true. And once again no amount of wriggling and jiggling would free the leg brace. Then, just when she thought she would have to leave the girl and go for help, she heard men's voices and the squeaky sound of a trolley on the rails. Two figures appeared, lanterns swinging from their hands.

'Over here! Her calliper's trapped,' she called. The next moment, strong arms were helping Daisy to her feet, but shock took over and she found herself swaying, unable to stand.

''Tis all right, Miss Daisy. We'll take over now,' she heard someone say. Then she was being lifted into the air and carried through the tunnel.

'The girl . . .' she began.

'Will be fine, thanks to you. Now, let's get you out of here,' the voice murmured.

The next thing she knew she was being placed on a platform seat and covered by a blanket. Mrs Nicholls hovered, encouraging her to take a sip from the cup she was proffering.

'Hot sweet tea, it's the best thing for shock,' the woman crooned. 'Gave me a fright, you haring off like that into the tunnel. Thank heaven Wilf got them to stop the train.'

'What about the girl?'

'They're just wheeling her out now, the Lord be praised. There's an ambulance waiting ready to take her to Homerton Hospital. And if you don't mind me saying, you should go and be checked over yourself.'

'No need,' Daisy replied, feeling warmth seeping into her insides.

'I would agree with my mother,' replied the tall man in uniform, who'd carried her. 'Best not to take any chances.'

'Thank you for your concern and for coming to my aid, but I'm fine, really,' Daisy assured him.

'Ooh, look, the police are questioning Pompous Pratt! I hope they throw the book at him. I told Alfie and Wilf they must explain about the safety cuts he's imposed,' Sylvie told her, shaking her white curls importantly

'As for you, young lady, you deserve a medal,' Mrs Nicholls said. 'I dread to think what would have happened if—'

'I'm fine thank you, Mrs Nicholls,' Daisy cut in quickly. 'And I'm relieved the little girl is too. All I want to do is go home and get warm,' she sighed.

'My son Jack here will give you a lift,' Mrs Nicholls told her.

'I'd be honoured to, as long as you don't think you should stay. The police might want to speak to you,' he said.

'Couldn't face it. I just want to get out of here.'

His dark, shiny car was parked right outside the entrance.

'Being an officer has some advantages, especially with petrol being rationed now,' he told her, seeing her surprised expression as he helped her inside. 'Now, where to, my lady?' he asked, bowing as he closed the door.

As the car purred along, Daisy's mind began whirling. Surely this was her opportunity whilst the recruiting office was open.

***

Rose was supervising the TPRs on the men's ward. As usual, they were busy, the departing soldiers having been replaced by local patients. Mr Rathbone was due to be discharged into the care of the district nurses, which would free up a bed, however, she was waiting for Dr Edwards to examine him first, and he was late.

'Have you heard about the hoo-ha down at the Manor Station, sister?' Effie asked, hurrying past with a bedpan.

'A young girl got stuck in the tunnel and had to be rescued,' Susan added as she made her way to the bed opposite. 'Dr Edwards is there an' the police an all.'

Which explained why Dr Edwards was late visiting Mr Rathbone, Rose thought. The poor man was raring to be discharged so she'd better explain the delay. It was only as she was making her way to his bedside that it hit her. Manor House Station was where Daisy worked. Surely it wouldn't have been her? She very much hoped her sister had been safely tucked away in her office out of harm's way. No doubt Dr Edwards would furnish her with more details when he arrived. If only he'd hurry up!

'Good morning, Mr Rathbone, it's a big day for you, isn't it?' she said, giving him a bright smile.

'I was excited, sister, but then I heard what the nurse just said about a girl being stuck in the tunnel. That's the station I manage, you see, so I can't help worrying.'

'Now, Mr Rathbone, it won't do your blood pressure any good getting het up like this,' she told him, lifting his arm onto the covers and feeling his pulse. 'That's why Dr Edwards is late for his ward round. Don't worry, we'll ask him for an update as soon as he arrives.'

'If he doesn't get a move on, I'm sure those two youngsters will find out first,' he replied, gesturing to the end of the ward where Effie and Susan were chatting to the patients as they rolled bandages. 'What they don't know is nobody's business.'

Rose hid a smile. It was true they did have a habit of finding out what went on before anyone else, but they were hard-working girls with the makings of good nurses.

'Ah, here's your wife. Good morning, Mrs Rathbone. The doctor's running a bit late, I'm afraid.'

'I know. He's seeing to a young lass who got trapped in the tunnel at your station,' she said, turning to her husband. 'I saw that lovely girl from the ambulances, Hope, she's called. They'd just brought that poor lass in. Trapped by her calliper she was. The boys she was with scarpered when she got caught up. Young hoodlums, they should be shot!'

'Easy now, Poll,' Mr Rathbone soothed.

'You take a seat Mrs Rathbone, and I'll ask an orderly to bring you a nice cup of tea,' Rose told her, pulling up a chair for the woman. 'I'm sure Dr Edwards won't be long now.'

Hurrying back down the ward, her shoes clicking as she went, Rose let out a sigh of relief. Obviously, Daisy hadn't been involved after all.

CHAPTER SEVENTEEN

The oily man leaned in closer, his bad breath making Clover recoil in disgust. She took a step backwards, only to find herself trapped against the wall. She looked beyond him, wondering how she could feel so alone in a room full of people. However, everyone seemed to be intent on having fun and didn't seem to notice her predicament.

'Cat got yer tongue, darlin'? Saw yer this morning coming out of yer bedroom, all dressed up in yer swanky uniform. Sleep in it, do yer?' he asked, his eyes gleaming with excitement. 'Charge extra for that, does yer?'

'Ah, there you are, Clover. Flight Lieutenant Ramsay is looking for you.' A hand came out and pulled her past the odious man.

'Oi, that's my foot yer treadin' on,' he yelped.

'You shouldn't get in the way then, should you?' her rescuer replied giving a tinkling laugh. 'I think you must be in the wrong place; the pigsty is out the back.'

As the man glowered, the woman gave another tinkling laugh and turned back to Clover. Only then did she recognize the girl with the shiny hair pinned in victory rolls she'd met the day she'd arrived at the Park.

'Ann, I can't thank you enough for rescuing me from that . . .'

'Slimy toad? Must have crawled out from the ghastly hostel around the corner. The landlord here usually chucks old toads out, but this one must have slid by him when his back was turned. Here,' she said, taking two glasses of fizz from a passing waiter and handing one to Clover. 'Cheers.' They clinked glasses and Clover took a much-needed gulp of her drink.

'At least it's quietened down now everyone's eating,' Ann continued. 'Not by yourself, are you?' she asked, gazing curiously at Clover with violet-coloured eyes.

'No, I came with Sally. We work together in Hut— well, at the Park,' she amended quickly, remembering she mustn't discuss exactly where she worked or what she did. 'She persuaded me to come.'

'And promptly left you for a handsome man in uniform, no doubt. Can't blame her for letting down her hair after a day at the madhouse.'

'You said something about a Flight Lieutenant wanting to see me.'

'Just an excuse, darling. Roly's my brother and he's over there somewhere,' she said, waving her hand in the general direction of a party of airmen who were having some kind of competition to see who could cram the most sausage rolls into their mouths at once. 'Heathens!' Her tinkling laugh rang out once more. 'But you can't blame them for letting off steam when they could be shot down tomorrow.'

'Are they based near here, then?' Clover asked.

'RAF Cranfield is just down the road,' Ann replied,

whipping a cheese-topped cracker from a young man brandishing a loaded tray. 'Hazard of living by oneself, can't be bothered cooking,' she grinned. 'Look, there's a free table over there.' She indicated to a couple who were leaving, and they quickly moved to take their place. 'That's better,' she sighed, rubbing her feet. 'These new shoes are killing me! Well, they're a couple of years old, but I've hardly worn them – and now I remember why,' she laughed. Clover stared at the shiny Mary Janes and then down at her own serviceable lace-ups.

'Did you get them in Bletchley?'

'Good grief, no. Have you seen what's for sale in this darling little town of Bletchley? You wouldn't believe the offerings the one and only clothes shop stocks. My darling grandmother would turn her nose up at the lot. Are you billeted around here?'

'At the same hostel as slimy toad by the sound of it,' Clover groaned. 'One night there was enough. I was going to see about being moved but I was invited to the party here and . . .'

'It sounded like fun after a hard day's graft?'

'Don't get me wrong, I'm happy working, but knowing what I do now, I cannot go back to that hostel.' As she took another sip of her drink, she noticed Ann eying her speculatively.

'As it happens, I'm looking for someone to share. The house is on the edge of the town and the Park bus stops there.

'Really?' Clover gasped, hardly able to believe her luck. 'That would be wonderful.'

'I take it your things are at the hostel?'

'Some of them, but I daren't go back.' Clover shuddered at the thought of bumping into the slimy toad again.

'Don't worry, it's almost closing time,' Ann said, putting her fingers to her mouth and whistling. Seeing Clover's astonished look, she grinned. 'Came in most handy on the marriage circuit, darling.'

Before Clover could ask what she meant, the group of airmen they'd been watching earlier materialized beside them.

'Roly, this is Clover who's working at the Park, and she needs your assistance. Clover, this is my baby brother,' she said, laughing up at the tall man towering over her. 'She's been billeted in that ghastly hostel round the corner.'

'Not Booby Ruby's?' he grinned, and his mates all whistled.

'The same. Now, I want you to carry out your one act of chivalry this year and rescue this poor girl's things. We'll see you back at the house. Key?' she asked looking at Clover and holding out her hand.

Quickly Clover searched her bag then handed it over, saying, 'It's room 5. My bag is in the wardrobe, and I didn't unpack.'

'Consider it done,' Roly said, perfecting a bow then making his way through the crowds, followed by his pals.

'Thank you, Ann, but won't they get into trouble?' she asked anxiously.

'Would you argue with that bunch of brawny men?

Right, one more drink and then we'll hit the road,' Ann said, and Clover couldn't help thinking that for a pint-sized figure she had a mighty capacity.

'I'm still drinking this one,' she replied, recalling she had to go to work the next day.

'You're probably right. What shift are you on?' she asked, getting to her feet and leading the way outside.

'Eight till four.' Clover replied, trying not to reel as the cold air hit her.

'Poor you. I'm doing four till twelve so will get a leisurely lie-in.'

'Is it me, or is this road even more winding than usual?' Ann asked, sometime later as they made their way past the Post Office, library, butcher's and clothes shop, in which, despite the meagre light from their covered torches, Clover could make out that their offerings were every bit as dismal as her friend had said.

Finally, on the edge of town Ann clicked open a wrought-iron gate and led the way towards the door of a magnificent house, which seemed to tower way above them, disappearing into the darkness. Goodness, Clover thought, her spirits rising. Talk about going from seedy to the sublime.

***

'I agree, Patty. A party at Easter would lift our spirits and goodness knows we need it with the way this war's dragging on. That were a nice bit of hash,' Bert said, moving his dish to one side. 'Now, let's see these letters that have come at last.' Although he said it in a matter-of-fact way, Patty could see the excitement in his eyes as she slid them across the table.

'You haven't eaten much, love,' she said, frowning at Daisy, who was toying with her food.

'I'll have it,' Robbie said, looking gleeful as his sister pushed her plate across the table.

'Then you'll have extra energy and can do the dishes,' Patty told him.

'Aww, that's not fair,' he groaned.

'I've just two words to say to you,' she replied. 'Easter egg.'

'All right,' he sighed, gobbling down the food then collecting up the plates.

'Hope you're not going down with something, Daisy. That flu's doing the rounds again.'

'I'm just tired, Ma,' she told her. In truth, she was trying to pluck up the courage to tell them she'd been to the enrolment office and enlisted. Wanting to keep her parents in a good mood, she hadn't told them about the events at the station that morning. Time enough for that later, when Hope got home. By then Daisy would have imparted her news about enlisting and, knowing how unhappy she'd been at work recently, hopefully they would have accepted it. The heat from the range was making her sleepy and she was just dozing off when a loud knocking on the front door made her jump.

'Whoever can that be at this time of night?' Patty asked, automatically glancing at the clock.

'I'll find out,' Bert said, pushing the mail to one side and getting to his feet.

They heard the low rumble of voices and then he returned followed by two men, one a police officer, the other in the uniform of the London Transport Board.

'These gentlemen wish to speak to you, Daisy,' he said, frowning.

'I hope you've not been up to no good, our Daisy,' Patty said, looking alarmed.

'On the contrary, Mrs Harrison. Your daughter is a heroine and to be congratulated. Allow us to introduce ourselves. I'm Mr Crawford, London Transport Board Inspector, and this is Chief Inspector Lawley. We should like to ask Miss Harrison some questions.'

'Can I offer you gentlemen a hot drink?' Patty asked, remembering her manners.

'Thank you, but no. We need to get our reports finished this evening. Now, Miss Harrison, congratulations again. Your brave action this morning undoubtedly saved that young girl. However, it was unfortunate that you left the station before we could speak with you,' the Chief Inspector said, giving Daisy a stern look.

'But you wasn't here at lunchtime when I came home,' Patty interjected, only to see her husband shake his head.

'Let Daisy answer the questions, love.'

'The young girl, Betty Brown, is making a good recovery, and all the gang have been caught and cautioned. I think I can safely say they now see the error of their ways,' Chief Inspector Lawley told her. 'What we have to establish is if the staff at the station were in any way negligent.'

'To that end, I need to ask you some very serious questions and I would appreciate your candid response.' Mr Crawford told Daisy.

'My Daisy always tells the truth,' Patty huffed.

'I'm sure she does, and just to be clear, your daughter is in no way to blame,' he continued. 'Now, Miss Harrison, as we've already established, we've been making enquiries into the circumstances leading up to and during this incident. As you're aware, the London Transport Board has strict safety procedures in place. Can you tell us if, in your opinion, any of these have been bypassed or cut in any way recently?'

As Daisy related the changes that had been made since Mr Pratt's arrival, both men looked grave.

'Well, that corroborates what we've already been told, so I think we can now finish those reports and submit them. There will be a thorough investigation of Manor House Station. We must ensure an incident like this can never happen again,' Mr Crawford said. 'Thank you for your frank and honest answers, Miss Harrison, you have been most helpful and may I congratulate you once again on your brave actions today? I am sure the Transport Board will wish to recognize them in some way, but in the meantime, I trust we'll see you at your desk again in the morning.'

Daisy swallowed, mumbling something about being exhausted. The thought of returning to the station, let alone the underground, filled her with horror. She looked up to see the Chief Inspector watching her closely.

'I also would like to applaud your actions, Miss

Harrison,' he said. 'And you might be interested to hear that Mr Pratt is being questioned at the police station, so you're unlikely to see him when you turn up for work tomorrow. As for you, young man,' he said, turning to Robbie and ruffling his hair, 'you have a sister to be proud of.'

'She can be a right pain at times, though. I think I'm going to be a policeman when I grow up then I can wear a smart uniform like yours. Do you blow a whistle?' he asked, making them all laugh.

'I think we need a pot of tea,' Patty said, once Bert had returned from seeing them out. 'Well, our Daisy, and to think you sat there all through dinner and never said anything. No wonder you weren't hungry!'

As she poured water onto the leaves in the pot, Bert sank into his chair and eyed Daisy keenly.

'Why do I get the feeling there's more to this than you've said? And if you left work this morning, why weren't you here when your mother came home at lunchtime?'

'Maybe she went to see Mr Rathbone. Is that it, our Daisy?' Patty asked, recalling their earlier conversation.

'No, Ma, I didn't.' She took a deep breath. 'The truth is that for some time now I've been dissatisfied with my job at the station.'

'And that Mr Pratt hasn't helped,' Patty cried.

'That's true,' she agreed. 'But it's more than that. I want – no, *need* – to be doing more for the war effort, so . . .' She paused then took a deep breath. 'I've enlisted with the Land Army. That's where I went after I left the station this morning,' she continued, ignoring her

164

mother's gasp. 'I've been accepted, and subject to passing a medical, which is tomorrow, I then wait to hear where I'll be sent for my training.'

'How long till you hear?' Patty asked, her stomach sinking at the thought of her last daughter leaving home.

'Within the next week or so and then it might be a few weeks until I'm placed on a training farm.'

'Coo, so you'll be leaving home too. Tonight's more exciting than the shows on the radio!' Robbie cried.

'Well, your excitement is about to be curtailed, young man,' his father told him. 'No arguments, you've got school tomorrow.'

They'd just settled down to listen to the news when they heard the front door open.

'Rose, whatever are you doing here at this time of night? Is everything all right?' her mother asked.

'Well, that's a lovely greeting I'm sure,' Rose replied, taking off her coat and sinking onto the chair next to her sister. 'I heard about the accident at the station and wanted to make sure you were all right, Daisy. The young girl, Betty Brown, was admitted to the children's ward, and I went to see how she was. She told me about an angel called Daisy who had saved her from being squashed by a train moments before it roared into the station.'

'Well, it wasn't quite like that!' Daisy chuckled. 'How is she?'

'Going to be fine. Dr Edwards managed to straighten out her leg and even signed her plaster, so now he's her hero.'

'He sounds nice,' Patty said, placing a cup of tea on the table in front of her.

'Oh, and Daisy, Mr Rathbone's been discharged into the care of the home at the end of the road if you want to go and see him.' Daisy nodded; indeed she did. There were some things she still needed to clear up, for she meant it when she said she had no intention of ever going back to Manor House Station.

'Is he recovering well?'

'He's better than he's been since his accident.'

'We had three letters from our Peter today, although they were hopelessly out of date, he was fine when he wrote so we must be grateful for that,' Bert piped up.

'Oh yes, and a letter from our Clover, not that she said much other than she won't get leave for three months. It means she won't be able to come to the Easter party we're thinking of having. How about you, our Rose, will you be having time off then?'

'Before we go into that, Patty, I think Daisy should tell Rose her news,' Bert prompted.

'She's joined the Land Army and is leaving home!' Robbie shouted excitedly from the top of the stairs.

'Robbie, get back to bed,' Patty shouted. 'Talking of which, I take it you're staying the night, Rose? It's much too late to walk back over Hackney Downs. You take Clover's bed and then you and Daisy can have a proper catch up.'

Patty sipped her tea, her thoughts awry. Peter was already away, goodness knows where in the army, Clover was at this BP place and now Daisy had joined the Land Army. She knew her daughter had been unhappy at Manor House but never in her wildest dreams had she thought her youngest daughter was thinking of leaving home. Of course, she was proud she wanted to do her bit, and goodness knows the country needed all the food that could be produced, but the fact remained another of her children was leaving home.

And with the way the war was dragging on, who knew when she'd be back?

CHAPTER EIGHTEEN

'It sounds as if you've had an eventful day, one way and another. Are you feeling all right, Daisy?' Rose asked once they were tucked up in bed.

'Yes, thank you, Sister Harrison,' Daisy giggled, for having told her parents about enlisting, the cloud that had hung over her all day had miraculously lifted. Now she was tingling with excitement and raring to get started on her new adventure.

'Do you want to talk about the incident or would you rather not?'

'Not. I'd prefer to forget it to be honest, although I'm pleased Betty is safe. The thought of spending any more time underground makes me feel ill, and I have no intention of ever returning to the station. I'll pop and see Mr Rathbone. That's only right as he's still officially the manager, and the inspector from the London Transport Board is likely to contact him. Other than that, if I don't hear another thing about the place, it will be too soon.'

'Things got that bad, then?'

'Yes. But looking on the good side, it propelled me into doing what I've been thinking about for ages. Oh, Rose, I'm so excited! As long as I pass my medical, I'll be out in the fresh air instead of cooped up underground all day. I'll be growing vegetables to feed the nation and then I'll feel I'm really contributing to the war effort.'

'Just think of all that dirt and grime under your nails,' Rose teased.

'I'll have to write and let Freddy know my new address,' Daisy continued, seemingly not hearing. 'Not that I've heard from him since his surprise visit. How about you, Rose. Did you write to Philip?' There was a long pause and Daisy turned over to face her sister, just able to make out her expression despite the blackout curtains. 'You don't have to discuss it if you don't want to.'

'No, it's all right. I was thinking of last Easter when Philip managed to find that chocolate egg for Robbie. We were so happy when we were last together, I find it hard to believe he's found someone else.'

'You only have Mrs Sutherland's word for that – and from what you've said, she's not your biggest fan.'

'True, but then I haven't heard from him.'

'That doesn't mean he hasn't written to you. One of Peter's letters was dated more than five months ago and who knows how many go completely astray? As Ma said, we don't know where our boys are or what they're having to put up with.'

'You're right, Daisy, I really should write to him, then at least I'd know.' She let out a sigh. 'But what would I say. *Your mother tells me you've found someone else. Is it true?* That would just make me sound like a schoolgirl, surely?'

'But at least you'd know. Anyway, what's this Dr Edwards like? It sounds as if he looked after little Betty well today, and I've noticed how often he seems to crop up in your conversations.'

'Dr Edwards is a lovely man. Kind and caring with the patients, pleasant and helpful with the staff.'

'Including you?'

'Don't go getting any ideas, Daisy. Now, I'm on duty in the morning so let's get some sleep,' she said, turning over to face the wall.

'Good night, big sister,' Daisy replied.

Rose lay staring at the wall. Daisy's teasing had stabbed her conscience. While Dr Edwards had indeed been helpful, he was becoming increasingly attentive, his invitations more frequent and, although she'd told him about Philip, she couldn't deny his interest had helped massage her bruised ego after that horrible meeting with Mrs Sutherland. Had he really met someone else? Perhaps she shouldn't write to him; a girl had her pride, after all. However, when she finally closed her eyes, it was an image of a smiling Philip, handsome in his RAF uniform, that materialized. Keep safe, my darling, she whispered into the darkness, for in her heart she knew she still loved him more than life itself.

Daisy lay staring up at the ceiling. It had been an eventful day and her mind was still whirring. Although she enjoyed the luxury of being in the bedroom by herself whilst Clover was away, it was comforting having company, especially tonight. When her eyelids finally grew heavy and she closed her eyes, it was to

170

dream of lush green fields, wide-open spaces and a handsome man in blue running towards her.

* * *

It was all systems go at the ambulance depot. They'd had fun mucking in together to rearrange the sleeping quarters which could now accommodate them for their new twenty-four-hour shifts. Then they'd helped to move the equipment in the small kitchen area, ready for it to be adapted to cater for cooked meals, although nobody knew who was to cook these yet. Now, just when they'd taken a break, sinking thankfully onto their chairs with hot drinks, there was a delivery of large boxes which the supervisor was directing into her office.

'Bet it's the new uniforms,' Kitty sang, jiggling up and down, spilling tea all down herself in the process.

'Right, everyone, listen up.' Sonia Strang's voice rang out and an expectant hush descended. 'As I'm sure you've guessed, the boxes containing the new uniforms have arrived, so as you've had such an easy time of it recently . . .' she stopped as jeers and whistles rang out. Holding up her hand, to silence them, she waited for hush to descend. 'At least you've not had time to get bored. Now, I propose sorting everything out into the relevant categories before distribution and then . . .' She paused, the air raid siren's wail screaming out making them all jump.

'Bloody Moaning Minnie, I bet it's another ruddy false alarm,' Geraldine cried.

'We can't afford to take any chances, in case it's a real raid, so the new uniforms will have to wait,' Sonia told them. 'Everyone check your vehicle is ready for action should you get called out, then take shelter in the basement. Geraldine and Ivy, carry out the usual inspection to ensure the building is clear. I take it those rostered for fire duty have ensured all the buckets are filled with sand?'

Finally, satisfied the depot was prepared for any emergency, she let them go. They'd only just settled down on their makeshift seats when they heard the thunderous roar of aircraft overhead and the deafening ack-ack of anti-aircraft guns. Fearfully, they all looked at each other and held their breath.

'Blimey, that were a lot,' Ivy muttered, when at last it went quiet.

'Yes, but some other buggers are copping it today, poor things,' Kitty muttered.

Hope nodded, and whilst she was sorry for whoever the Nazis were targeting, she felt relieved that her family were safe. As the all-clear sounded, they brushed themselves down and made their way back outside to check their vehicles were secure and ready for action.

'Right, everyone, as you were. That was a nuisance, but we must be thankful it wasn't the real thing. However tempted, we mustn't ignore the siren, or we might not be here to help those who need it,' Sonia Strang told them sternly. 'Now, Geraldine and Kitty, get yourselves to this address right away.' She held out a piece of paper. 'Man with suspected appendicitis needs to be ferried to Homerton Hospital. He's in a bad way, so step on it. Hope, you can help me sort out the uniforms in my office. Everyone else about your duties.'

'How come you always get the good jobs?' Kitty moaned good-naturedly as she pulled on her heavy coat.

'Must be my sweet nature,' Hope grinned, making her way towards the office.

'Right, Hope, we need to separate all these into their respective piles,' Sonia said, gesturing to the now opened boxes, from which their black contents were spilling. 'Packaging is so flimsy these days, isn't it?'

'My mother said they had to be careful how they pack the boxes for the POWs at the centre. Apparently, they wouldn't listen to her when she suggested a better way,' Hope grinned, recalling her ma's affronted expression as she recounted the episode.

'Paper is even more at a premium now, so we mustn't waste a scrap,' Sonia told her, taking a strip from the box and carefully folding it. 'Right, now put the jackets and trousers here on this table, then jumpers, shirts, and finally ties over there. From what I can see there is little difference in the sizing so everyone will have to make any necessary adjustments themselves. Whilst you're doing that, I'll sort the badges and work out where they'll need to be sewn.'

They worked in companiable silence for a few minutes. As Hope sorted the clothing into piles, she realized she would have to shorten the trousers and take in the jacket, or they would hang on her diminutive frame, and she'd end up looking like the scarecrow she'd seen once. Still, at least she would now have some clothing coupons to take to Ridley Road Market. She was just imagining the material she might buy when she realized Sonia was speaking.

'I was asking if you'd seen Ian MacLeod recently?' Sonia repeated, watching Hope closely.

'No, I haven't,' Hope shrugged.

'This change has come at a bad time for him. Do I take it you haven't seen him outside the station?'

'No, I haven't, and he knows where I live,' Hope replied, fighting down her disappointment that he hadn't called at Victory Walk.

'He does have a lot on his plate, trying to juggle his engineering work with ensuring his children are settled in their new home,' Sonia told her with a frown.

Well, if he's so good at juggling, why doesn't he juggle enough time to see me, Hope thought, fighting down her indignation.

'Look, Hope, from what I now know of him, he is an honest, hardworking chap trying to do his best for both his country and family, so don't be too hard on him, eh? I refused to accept his resignation and have granted him temporary leave until such time as he can resume his duties and integrate into the new shifts. Now, this conversation is just between the two of us. When they say walls have ears, they're not just referring to wars and spies, you know,' she grinned. 'Let's pray this war will be over soon and we can all get back to normal. Well, at least as normal as it will ever be for some of us again.'

Hope looked at her boss, but when she didn't elaborate, resumed her task.

'Right, I think we're pretty much done here, so go and call everyone in. You can supervise the distribution while I deal with the inevitable queries.'

It was twenty minutes, and much hilarity as to the sizing later, before everyone had equipped themselves with one of everything.

'Large uniform and rationing ain't a match made in heaven,' Ivy sighed, frowning as she held out her jacket. 'You could get two of me in here.'

'With the right man that could be fun,' Kitty giggled.

'I'm sure your dressmaking skills are up to the task, Ivy,' Sonia replied, ignoring Kitty's comment. 'Now listen carefully while I tell you where your badges are to be sewn, for it's important they're placed correctly. The Ambulance Service Badge goes at the top of your sleeve like so,' she said, demonstrating on herself. 'Then your Civil Defence Insignia on your left top pocket, with the London Badge below that. Any questions?'

'Yeah, what if we can't sew?' Kitty muttered.

'Then you learn and fast,' Sonia told her. 'Now, you all go off shift shortly so that will give you twenty-four hours in which to get everything sorted. Next time I see you, it will be to carry out a full inspection.'

As mutters and groans resounded, Sonia grinned and held up her hand.

'You are the lucky ones. Having got your uniforms first, you have a head start on your compatriots on the next shift.'

'She's all heart,' Kitty muttered as they made their

way outside. 'I was thinking of going down to the club for a bevy with the boys. Care to join me?'

'No, thanks. It's going to take me ages to sort out my uniform so I'd better head straight home.'

'All work and no fun will make Hope a dull girl,' Kitty sighed. 'You don't think Ian MacLeod is just sitting around too, do you?' With a knowing look, she swaggered off down the road. As Hope watched her go, she couldn't help wondering if Kitty was right. She had no idea what Ian got up to so maybe it was time to go and have some fun, she thought, turning for home.

At least the weather was warming up, she noticed, as she waited to cross the busy main road. She'd not gone far when she heard her name being called.

'Joy, what are you doing here?' she asked as her sister caught her up.

'I've just been to see an old school friend and was going home, not that I'm in any hurry to return to that poky flat,' Joy said, grimacing. 'Couldn't swing a cat even if we had one. Have you just finished work?' she asked, eyeing Hope's bag.

'Yes, and we've got our new uniforms at last. Well, that's the good news, the bad is, I've got to adapt it to fit and then sew on the badges. At least I've got the next twenty-four hours off,' she said, brightening.

'Have you got time for a cuppa? The café opposite the market is still open and we can have a good old catch up. It's ages since we've seen one another, and I've got so much to tell you.'

Hope looked at her sister's animated expression and thought she had never looked so pretty. Her eyes were shining, blonde hair bouncy despite the privations they were enduring, and she wanted to know her sister's secret. Even though she moaned about the tiny flat in Hackney, she was clearly having a great time.

'Good idea,' she agreed.

No sooner had they been served with their pot of tea and the last scone to share, than Joy began regaling Hope with stories of her time at the Red Cross centre. 'It's such fun being with others. We sing along to *Music While You Work* or *Workers' Playtime* in the afternoons. And it's so rewarding thinking of the prisoners of war who will be receiving the boxes we pack.

'But the best thing of all is the fund-raising concert that Jane Bayliss is arranging. She's really pretty, with copper curls, and has so much energy. She went to see Myra Hess at the National Gallery. Apparently, Myra plays Mozart Concertos on the piano and Jane found it so uplifting it's given her inspiration for our concert. It's funny, she's really friendly, yet for some reason Ma can't stand her. She goes all bristly whenever Jane comes over to chat about the concert, saying I shouldn't mix with the likes of her, which is strange because she speaks really nicely, and Ma usually encourages us to mix with people like that. I don't care though, because I'm going to have a starring role!' she gushed.

Before Hope could reply she'd taken a quick sip of her drink and was off again.

'I'm going to sing "Don't Sit Under the Apple Tree", and "Lili Marlene", which is a song also known as "The Young Sentry". It was written as a poem in the first World War by a soldier to his girlfriend. Oh, Hope, it's so moving. I really trust I can do it justice.' She looked uncertain for a moment, biting her lip in the way Hope remembered.

'Of course you will. You've the voice of an angel, remember?'

'And you've the croak of a frog,' her sister giggled. 'Well, at least that's what Pa always said. Anyway, I'm hoping it will lead on to better things as I can't wait to leave Hackney – it's such a dump, despite what mother says. Imagine singing at the National Gallery?' Hope smiled and shook her head. She'd forgotten how pie in the sky her sister could be.

'Seriously, Hope, you should come along to the rehearsals, they're such a scream. Or are you too busy seeing that Ian chap? He sounds a bit too serious and not much fun from what I hear.'

'It's true that he takes his responsibilities seriously, but there is a lighter side to him too,' Hope said defensively.

'Blimey, I should hope so, else why on earth would you go out with him? No, in my book, life's for living, specially with this darn war on. You should let your hair down a bit, sis,'

That was the second time in the last hour she'd been told to have some fun. Kitty was right, she shouldn't be sitting at home each evening. She wasn't interested in chasing blokes like her friend, though, especially as the available ones these days seemed to be those not eligible for war service for whatever reason. Watching Joy rehearse could be just the tonic she needed. It would

178

be good to spend time with her sister, for now she realized just how much she'd missed her since moving into Victory Walk with Aunt Patty and Uncle Bert.

'All right, Joy, I will. Oh . . .'

'What's up, you look like you've seen a ghost.'

'Our Faith's just come in and she's with another bloke.'

'Blimey, she's just walked right by us and never even noticed.'

CHAPTER NINETEEN

'Daisy, my dear girl, what is to be done with you?'
Mr Rathbone asked, shaking his head. He was sitting
in a comfortable chair, his plastered leg on a stool.
Although they were the only occupants of the bright
lounge in the nursing home, he lowered his voice. 'I
have already had a visit from Mr Crawford, Inspector
of the London Transport Board who had much to tell
me about the staff and their actions at Manor House
Station, especially you. Now, you've been sitting there
some twenty minutes or so recounting events of the
other day and yet not once did you mention your
involvement.'

Daisy's eyes widened in alarm. Had he found out
about the entries in the ledger and was she to be held
accountable, even though she'd just been doing as
instructed?

'I realize it must have been traumatic, but you're a
real heroine, going after that little girl like that, with
no thought to your own safety. Mr Crawford couldn't
praise you highly enough, and I too am very proud of
you, Miss Daisy Harrison.'

'It's what anyone would have done,' she replied, relief
washing over her.

'No, Daisy, it is what *you* did. I cannot believe

Mr Pratt made safety cuts that endangered life, as well as banning the disinfecting of the platforms first thing in the morning. That's entirely against the Transport Board's regulations as you well know. They've been carrying out investigations and speaking to members of staff, none of whom have anything complimentary to say about Mr Pratt, yet they can't praise you highly enough. When I think of all the years I spent building up the Manor House Station's reputation, well, it doesn't bear thinking about. Of course, Mr Pratt has been dismissed and will no doubt be prosecuted and Mr Crawford has assured me that my job will be waiting when I'm ready to return. I was thinking, Daisy, and Mr Crawford agrees, that you should act as stand-in manager in my absence.'

Daisy looked at his animated expression and felt her heart sink. 'That's very kind of you, Mr Rathbone, but you should know that Mr Pratt insisted I stay in the office every day and enter things in a new ledger. There were invoices and tickets from . . .'

'Other stations. Don't worry, the Transport Board are well aware of his deceptions. It turns out it's not the first time he's tried to defraud them, and like I say, he is to be prosecuted. I have no doubt if it wasn't for the war he would have been gone long since.'

'But what about me? I made those entries,' Daisy cried.

'Under his instruction. Don't worry, Daisy, in no way are you implicated. So, what do you say to my proposal?'

'Not replacing me, I hope?' They looked up in surprise as a shadow loomed above them. Having been so focussed on their conversation, they hadn't heard the woman enter the room.

'Gosh, Poll, you fair made me jump,' Mr Rathbone cried, looking at his wife in alarm.

'Seems I need to keep you on your toes, crafty old devil,' she chuckled. 'Hello, Daisy, it's good to see you and I understand congratulations are in order.' As she eased herself into an easy chair beside them, Daisy's heart began to pound. Surely, she hadn't heard about her enlisting in the Land Army?

'Hello, Mrs Rathbone, isn't it nice to see our patient recovering so well?' she smiled, playing for time for she'd been about to tell her boss she was leaving.

'It certainly is, and it's nice to see you looking so well after your ordeal the other morning. You are quite the heroine you know, and I understand the *Hackney Gazette* is to run a piece on the incident. Although Alfie and Wilf went to the rescue, it was Jack, Mrs Nicholls son, who cut her free. Have they spoken to you yet?'

'No,' Daisy replied, suppressing a shudder. She really didn't want to feature in the local paper. The sooner she could forget the incident and move on with her life the better.

'You're very modest, my dear,' Mr Rathbone smiled. 'However, Mr Crawford mentioned some kind of reward.'

'Goodness me no, I don't want anything!' Daisy protested.

'Don't look a gift horse, as they say,' Mrs Rathbone interjected. 'There must be something you'd like, especially with all the privations we are suffering.'

'Well, if anyone could find a chocolate Easter egg for my young brother, that would be a load off my mother's mind. She can't find one for love nor money,' Daisy told them, remembering her ma's agitation at the thought of letting Robbie down.

'Chocolate? Goodness me, whatever is that?' Mrs Rathbone sighed.

'Actually, Mr Rathbone, there's something you should know,' Daisy burst out. 'For some time now I've been feeling I need to do more for the war effort.' Sensing him watching her intently, she paused, took a deep breath and gathered her thoughts. No need for him to know how unhappy she'd been recently.

'Go on,' he encouraged.

'I've had enough of being cooped up underground and after the other day, well, I just don't feel I can go back. So . . . I have enlisted in the Land Army.'

'Well, good for you, girl!' Mrs Rathbone cried. 'If I were a few years younger, I'd join up myself. Can't think of anything more satisfying than growing food for the nation, and goodness knows we need it.'

'You're sure about this?' Mr Rathbone asked, looking crestfallen. 'You could have quite a career with the Transport Board, you know.'

'Until the men return from war and reclaim their jobs,' Mrs Rathbone pointed out.

Daisy shook her head. 'I've written out my letter of resignation,' she said, passing him an envelope.

'Which I will accept most reluctantly,' he told her. 'And if things don't work out as you hope, then you must come and see me.'

'Good morning,' the Home Superintendent called, striding into the room in her crisp uniform, polished shoes squeaking on the floor. 'Everything all right, Mr Rathbone, you've settled in well, I hope?'

'Yes, thank you, Fiona,' he replied. 'Everyone has been most welcoming.'

'Good, good. I'll get Peggy to organize some elevenses for you all.'

'Thank you, but not for me. I really must be going as I have an appointment,' Daisy told her, rising to her feet. She hadn't realized the time until Fiona had said elevenses – and there was no way she was going to risk being late for her medical.

* * *

In Bletchley, Clover waited in line for the graveyard shift to vacate their chairs. Looking at their exhausted faces, she could only imagine what it must be like to work through the night in this claustrophobic hut, shuttered with blackout blinds and smothered by palls of cigarette smoke. And yet the thought that she might crack a German code and help turn the tide of the war sent tingles of excitement through her. Taking her place, she stifled a yawn and waited for the sheet showing the day's settings the cryptographers had selected.

She wasn't used to late nights these days, and by the

time Roly had turned up with her bag and Ann had shown her to her new room, which compared to the one at the hostel, was comfort personified, it had been two o'clock in the morning. She still couldn't believe her luck to have found another billet so easily, and with such a nice person.

'Psst, wake up,' a voice hissed, jogging her back to the present.

'Sorry,' she murmured, taking the paper from Sally.

'Where did you disappear to last night?' Sally asked, her eyes wide with curiosity. 'I searched high and low for you.'

'Having abandoned me as soon as we arrived at The Eight Bells,' Clover muttered.

'Is there a problem with the settings?' Mrs Speedwell asked, appearing beside her.

'No, Mrs Speedwell,' Clover replied.

'Then I must once again remind you that the only time we speak on shift is if there is a query or you have cracked a code,' she rebuked, her disapproving look encompassing them both.

'Ha ha, serve her right if we crack loads of them. We'll catch up at break,' Sally muttered, turning back to her machine and leaving Clover to adjust the rotors on top of hers. Then she remembered she had to check to make sure the set-up was correct or, heaven forbid, she'd be wasting the next few hours. Three wheels set to A, type out keyboard alphabet. Hallelujah, it corresponded letter for letter so now she could start.

She took the first paper left by the previous worker,

determined to prove her worth. Yet, no matter how hard she studied each group of five letters, nothing she recognized materialized. After cramming herself with Hugo's German for the past few weeks, surely she should recognize something? Or was she just dense? Perhaps she should apply a little lateral thinking as Mrs Speedwell had suggested at their induction. Look past the five letter clusters, try names of people, places, dates. Finally, just when her eyes were burning, her head throbbing from intensely concentrating for so long, she was told it was time for her break. Grabbing her coat, she followed the others outside.

'Thank goodness for that,' Sally cried, blinking as they emerged into the brightness of a spring day. She stopped abruptly on the gravel path to light a cigarette only for Clover to bump into her. 'Steady on, I could have burnt myself there.'

'Sorry, but it takes a minute to adjust after the gloom inside.'

'Never mind,' Sally grinned, linking arms. 'Let's enjoy this sunshine, weak though it is. Look, there's the NAAFI kiosk, let's grab a hot drink instead of going to the canteen. We can walk round the lake and you can tell me where you disappeared to last night.'

'As I remember, Sally, it was you who disappeared shortly after we arrived at the pub. Not that it matters.'

'Ah yes, I remember now. Got caught by a dashing airman – literally, if you get my meaning. What a night.' She chuckled, giving Clover a salacious wink.

'Anyway, what about you? How did you get on at the hostel?'

'I didn't go back,' she said. By now they'd reached the queue for refreshments and Clover took a perverse delight in watching Sally's curiosity almost burst over as they waited to be served. Where she came from, friends looked out for each other, didn't abandon them. Still, there were lots of other people she could pal up with, she thought, looking around at the various groups of people, some in uniform like her, others wearing civilian clothes.

'Well?' Sally asked when they'd finally purchased their drinks, a two-finger KitKat between them, and were strolling by the lakeside. Clover took a sip of her drink then watched the antics of the ducks, wishing she had some crumbs to feed them, before answering.

'It was an interesting evening. I met some lovely new people.'

'Yes, but what about the hostel? Did you sleep there or did one of those lovely new people whisk you away to their pad?'

'That is *exactly* what happened,' Clover replied, hiding a smile.

'So, tell me all,' Sally cried, all agog. 'Who was he? And are you seeing him again?'

'Well, firstly, Roly and his chums retrieved my bag from the hostel. Then his sister, Ann, offered me a room in the house she's renting. No billet for her.' Clover smiled and took another sip of her drink. 'Goodness, someone's swimming in the lake. They must be freezing.'

'Some of the boffins are renowned for it, whatever the weather,' Sally said. 'Anyway, carry on, where is this house?'

'It's on the edge of town, but don't ask me what it's like because it was dark when we arrived, and I only glimpsed the inside before I was shown to my room, which is delightful, I have to say.'

'So, you've landed on your feet, then. Hang on, did you say Roly and Ann, short for Roland and Annelise? He's in the RAF? She's a former debutante?'

'Perhaps,' Clover shrugged. 'Gracious, look our break is up. We'd better hurry back or we'll be in trouble.' Ignoring Sally's frustration and still peeved at the way her so-called friend had glossed over abandoning her the previous evening, she headed towards Hut 6.

'She's in with Dilly Knox and his harem of women,' Sally puffed as she caught her up. 'Her father is some bigwig in Whitehall, probably friends with one of the Deputy Directors, Denniston or Travis. I mean, you have to ask yourself what a debutante could possibly have to offer Bletchley. Well, apart from the obvious, I guess,' she smirked.

'I thought we weren't meant to talk about what went on here?' Clover frowned, but Sally just laughed and tapped the side of her nose with her finger.

Glad to be back at her seat, Clover tried to concentrate. She hadn't liked the tone of Sally's conversation, for Ann and Roly had shown her nothing but kindness, rescuing her from that horrid hostel and offering her a room. Ann had even given her a key to the house as their differing shift patterns meant it would be the weekend before their paths crossed again. Still, that would give her time to settle in and write a letter to Marigold. She did miss her friend and couldn't wait to pen all her news, or as much of it as she was permitted.

CHAPTER TWENTY

'*There is a green hill far away, Outside a city wall,*' Patty trilled as she lifted down the old scales that had been her mother's. She wasn't a religious person as such, but it was comforting singing the old hymns and remembering days cooking in the old kitchen of her childhood home. Thankfully, this one was warmer, she thought, glancing fondly at the range, but with rationing, the amount of ingredients on offer was about the same. '*Where our dear Lord was crucified . . .*' Her carefully hoarded store of currants and sugar meant she had just enough to make hot cross buns for the immediate family, along with a very light fruit cake for the party. There would be no marzipan simnel cake this year and numbers would be smaller for their party as Peter was away, serving goodness knows where. '*He died to save us all . . .*'

It was no good, she'd have to sing something more uplifting. Her excitement at having received letters from her older son had waned when she'd realized how out of date they were. 'Keep safe, my love,' she murmured.

Determinedly, she began singing *Amazing Grace, how sweet the sound,* her thoughts returning to numbers for the party. Rose would be on duty although she'd promised to pop in during the afternoon and Clover was away at this BP place. That left her, Bert, Daisy – who'd passed her medical but assured them that her papers wouldn't come through for a couple of weeks yet – and Robbie, of course. Poor boy, he was going to be so disappointed, for although she'd searched everywhere for an Easter egg, there were none to be had. Chocolate was at a premium these days. Hope would be home, although she'd refused to invite that nice Mr MacLeod, saying he would probably be away seeing his children.

Carefully she spooned the flour into the cream enamel weighing pan with its chipped edge, then placed the shiny weights on the other side until they balanced. She loved using her own mother's tried and tested recipes which were committed to her memory, although it might be prudent to write them down now life was so precarious. Luckily there had been no more bombing of London, although there had been numerous nuisance false alarms with the sirens stirring up panic until the all-clear sounded. When she'd suggested ignoring them, Bert had made her promise she would always take shelter – though if Hitler dared interrupt her baking session today, she might be tempted, for she could ill afford to waste all these lovely ingredients.

She inhaled the fragrance of spice and dried fruit and sighed, remembering last year when the girls had helped stir the mix. A knock on the back door roused her from her reverie and she looked up to see her sister easing her ample frame into the room. Trust her to appear when she was cooking, Patty thought.

'Something smells good,' Vera said, sniffing the air appreciatively.

'Baking for our Easter party,' Patty told her. 'Have you found out if Faith and Artie are coming?'

'It seems Faith prefers to spend the time with her in-laws rather than her own mother,' Vera sniffed. 'Somehow that woman has managed to get a joint and is providing them with a roast and all the trimmings along with a blinkin' simnel cake for afters. I mean, how on earth did she manage that?'

Patty had her own idea on the subject but kept quiet and continued mixing.

'So, it will be you, Arthur and Joy then?'

'No, Patty, it will be just Joy and me.'

Patty looked up but seeing her sister's pursed lips, covered the mixing bowl and put the kettle to boil. The rest of the baking would have to wait. A cup of tea was clearly needed.

'Well, I'll be having a leaving party for our Daisy when she gets a departure date, so I'll expect you all to be there to give her a right family send-off.'

***

Excitement crackled in the air at Victory Walk that Sunday as the family gathered round the table for breakfast. Only Robbie was quiet as he sat morosely spooning up his porridge.

'Come on, young man, it's Easter Sunday,' Patty cajoled.

'Yeah, and the only bunny I've seen is Snuffles,' he mumbled.

192

'And what other rabbit would you expect to see at your age? Now, take the dishes out to the back kitchen, while I finish my tea, there's a good boy.'

With much hurrumphing and clattering of crockery, he did as he was told, and Patty and Daisy went into action. When he returned there was a parcel wrapped in newspaper waiting at his place.

'Ooh, what's this?' he cried, his eyes lighting up in delight. Without waiting for an answer, he tore at the paper.

'Steady on, lad, we need to reuse that,' Bert chided.

'Sorry, Pa,' he murmured, his smile fading as he caught sight of the burgundy wool.

'I know it's April now, but the wind is still chill, so a balaclava and gloves will keep you warm,' Patty told him, trying to keep a straight face.

'Well, son, what do you say to your mother? She's been sitting up each night after you've gone to bed, knitting like crazy to get those finished for you.'

'Come on, let's not tease him any longer,' Patty cried, watching as Daisy reached under the table and presented him with her gift.

'Happy Easter from us all,' she said, ruffling his hair.

'Cor, a chocolate egg!' he cried, beaming from ear to ear. 'And it's bigger than last year's an' all. Wait till Ricky sees this, he'll be so jealous.'

'Well, I trust you're going to share it with him, Robbie. And you can thank your sister for that. It was her reward from the London Transport Board for rescuing that young girl,' Patty told him.

'Thanks, Daisy. You ain't so bad for a sister, really.'

'I should think not, young man. Not many sisters would choose something for their brother instead of themselves. We're all really proud of you, Daisy,' Patty said, handing her a small parcel. 'It's not much but they might come in handy for your new job.'

'Thanks, Ma,' Daisy cried, holding up the green scarf and fingerless gloves. 'These will be so useful for working outside.'

'Hope made all the tassels for the scarf.'

'It was fun, once you'd shown me how, Auntie,' Hope smiled. 'Although I will miss you when you go, Daisy.'

'We all will.' Patty smiled tightly, for she still hadn't come to terms with the fact her youngest daughter would soon be leaving home. 'Right, I must get on or lunch will be late,' she added, getting to her feet. 'I could only get sausages, I'm afraid, but I've saved a couple of eggs to whip up a batter for a nice toad-in-the-hole. I've some onion to add too.'

'Yummy,' Robbie murmured, hardly able to tear his eyes away from his egg.

'What can I do to help?' Hope asked.

'You and Daisy can peel the potatoes, carrots and parsnips, then Robbie can take the scrapings out for Snuffles.'

'Can I go and show Ricky my egg first?'

'Go on, then, but don't eat it all and spoil your lunch. And don't forget to put on your coat.' She chuckled as he ran off, pleased they hadn't had to disappoint him after all.

'I think there's a drop of sherry left for us to make a toast later,' Bert said, pushing aside the copy of the *Sunday Express*. 'The Commandos have destroyed the main Nazi U-boat base in St Nazaire and the RAF have resumed bombing of Lubeck. They're using the new Stirling and Halifax heavy bombers, and with their improved navigation, these are proving very effective. If they carry on making progress like this, we might just win this war.'

'And soon, I hope, before any more of our troops lose their lives.' Patty sighed, crossing her fingers that Peter would stay safe, before turning her attention to preparing the lunch. As she whisked the batter, though, she couldn't help wondering when her family would be all together again. Empty spaces at the table on occasions like this really tugged at the heartstrings.

As the girls came through from the back kitchen, arms laden with vegetables, Patty pushed her thoughts aside and pinned on a bright smile. Glum thoughts had no place at a celebration.

'I'll get Joy to run through her songs when she arrives,' Hope told Daisy. 'She has an amazing voice, and I can see why Jane Bayliss is going to give her the leading role in the concert.'

'How exciting, we must go and see it,' she replied. 'Singing will be just the thing to get our festivities going. Gosh, these parsnips are woody, Ma.'

'I know; it's the end of the season for roots, and all we've got left in the shop. I wish I could grow some vegetables out the back, but that Anderson shelter takes up all the room and blocks out the light. Still, I mustn't grumble, it kept us safe from all those bombs. But I think I'll look out those seeds I got from the recent swop, anyway, see if I can get some to germinate.'

'Do you think the Luftwaffe have finished bombing London now?' Hope asked.

'Don't count on it,' Bert said, coming through with the bottle of sherry and placing it on the table. 'London might be experiencing false alarms at the moment, but those enemy planes are on their way somewhere, so make sure you always take cover when the siren sounds.'

'It's very nerve-wracking being out in the ambulance when the siren sounds.'

'It mut be, but you do a fine job, our Hope. Rose was telling me how the man you helped when he'd cut his hand on shrapnel was singing your praises.'

'That does make it worthwhile,' Hope admitted. 'Well, that's the potatoes peeled. What's next, Auntie?' she asked, placing the saucepan onto the range, then gasping as a draught of cold air hit her in the back.

'Well, this is a fine how's your father, and on Easter Sunday too!' Vera exclaimed, bustling through the back door as quickly as her bulk would allow. 'Ah, sherry. A big glass, please, Bert,' she added, collapsing onto the nearest chair.

'Forgive Ma, she's just had a shock,' Joy explained, following her in and shutting the door behind her.

'It's Martin. His ship's been attacked, and he's been reported as missing. We went to see our Faith and Artie to take them a little something for Easter and the telegram came whilst we were there.'

'Oh no, poor Martin and poor Faith! She must be devastated,' Bert said, pouring a sherry and handing her the glass.

'That's what I don't understand,' Vera said, puzzled. 'She said it would save having to worry about when he was going to turn up next!'

'Probably the shock, it takes people in different ways. What about his parents.'

'Devastated. His mother didn't stop crying all the time we were there and that started Artie blubbing. Oh, you should have heard the noise. Ta, Bert,' she said, handing him her empty glass and staring at him hopefully until he refilled it. 'It would be terrible news anytime, but to receive that telegram on Easter Sunday, it don't seem right.'

'No,' Patty murmured sympathetically and wondered what Rose would say when she heard. 'Shall I delay our midday meal whilst you recover?'

'No, no, I'll manage to eat a little something,' Vera said, giving a martyred look before downing the sherry in one go. Daisy, Hope and Joy exchanged looks then disappeared upstairs.

'Is Faith really all right?' Hope asked her sister when they were sprawled on her bed.

'Hard to say. She seemed quite unemotional, but you know what she's like.' They nodded – Faith had always been self-contained and a law unto herself. 'I expect the shock will hit her later when it sinks in.'

'And people who've gone missing do turn up,' Daisy told her, remembering a neighbour's joyous news about her son.

'It's Ma I'm more worried about. She and Da have either been arguing or giving each other the silent treatment. I've been putting in more shifts at the Red Cross to get away from the flat and practising for the concert, of course. The strange thing is, Ma clams up whenever I mention it,' she sighed.

'Food, girls!' Patty's voice sounded up the stairs.

'Mmm, something smells nice, Auntie,' Joy said as they took their places at the table. 'Oh, where's Mum?' A loud snore from behind made them turn and they saw Vera, out for the count, slouched in an easy chair.

'Ooh, someone been at the sherry?' Rose chuckled as she breezed into the room. 'All was quiet on the ward, so I got away early,' she explained, kissing her mother's cheek. 'What's happened?'

Patty quickly explained as she dished up an extra serving.

'Poor Faith and Artie,' Rose murmured.

'Don't you mean poor Martin?' Patty frowned.

'Poor all of us,' Bert muttered, holding up the empty sherry bottle. 'Come on, we mustn't let this good food go to waste. Our starving won't help Martin, will it? Of course we'll say a prayer for him at the table,' he added, seeing his wife frown.

Later, when Vera had slept off her excess, Joy helped her into her coat.

'You're sure you don't want Bert to see you home?' Patty asked.

'We'll be fine, Auntie, the fresh air will sober Ma up – and besides, Uncle Bert's on fire-watching duty this evening. Sorry if we put a damper on your day, but that was a lovely meal.'

'You're welcome, although I'm sorry we didn't get to hear you sing. It wasn't appropriate today though, was it? I gather things are a bit difficult at home, so let me know if you need any help with anything,' she whispered as she saw them out. If it wasn't one thing it was another, she thought, leaning against the door. Poor Martin! Although Rose had been shocked, she didn't seem unduly upset, assuring her she'd got over any feelings she'd had for him long since.

That evening, as they gathered around the table waiting for the news on the wireless, Bert reached out and took Patty's hand.

'That news about Martin's shaken you up more than you let on, hasn't it, girl?' She looked at him in surprise. It wasn't like him to notice such things. She let out a long sigh.

'Yes, it's such a terrible thing to happen and I know he's not, or wasn't,' she corrected herself, 'Artie's father, but he was a good man stepping in to save Faith's reputation. I think they had the makings of a nice little family.'

'I know. All these casualties of war, such unnecessary loss of life,' he sighed. 'It's made me wonder where Peter is and what he's doing.'

Patty squeezed his hand, knowing full well that he meant that he was praying their son was safe. And soon Daisy would be going away too. At least the training farm near Exeter would be safe. Now she needed to plan her leaving party, see what rations she could get hold of; and if Bert could get hold of some more sherry. It was going to be a bittersweet day, but as she'd told Vera, she wanted all the family present so they could send her off in style.

CHAPTER TWENTY-ONE

It was Rose's half-day and, after a busy morning, she was enjoying a few moments break with a cup of tea and an egg and cress sandwich in the hospital canteen when a shadow fell across the table. Glancing up she saw Dr Edwards trying to juggle a precariously balanced tray and, reaching out, she managed to catch a fork before it fell to the floor.

'Will you take pity on me and share your table?' he asked, giving his lopsided grin although it didn't quite reach his eyes.

'As it's you, Dr Edwards,' she smiled, pulling out a chair for him before he dropped anything else. She waited until he'd settled and was stirring his coffee before asking if everything was all right. He frowned down at his plate of rapidly congealing stew then pushed it away before replying.

'I know it's a little way off, but I wonder if you'd do me the honour of accompanying me to the May Ball? I have it on great authority that the music will be first-class, the food superb – well, as superb as rations will allow. I know it's still a few weeks away, but I've taken the liberty of checking the rotas and see you'll be free that evening, so what do you say?'

'That's very kind of you Dr Edwards but—'

'You never use my first name,' he sighed. 'I know Teddy Edwards isn't exactly sophisticated but . . .'

'It's not that,' she began. 'It's just not professional to . . .'

'But I'm not asking you to be professional, Rose,' he said impatiently. 'I'm inviting you, as a friend, to accompany me to a ball at the Town Hall. A few hours of fun and laughter away from the serious business our hospital work entails and the grim reality of war.'

'I know, and I do admire your work and professional manner but . . .'

'No more buts!' he burst out, his expression so sombre the hustle and bustle of the noise around them receded. 'I've been weighing up my future, Rose, and your answer today has made up my mind. For a while now, I've been asking you out, either for dinner or to see a film and you've turned me down every time. That's your prerogative, of course, and I don't hold it against you. However, I cannot go on seeing you on the ward each day. As things are quiet on the home front, I'm enlisting with the Royal Army Medical Corps where my skills can help those who are wounded on the frontline. I have already spoken with Matron and shall leave tomorrow. It's been good knowing you, Rose, and I wish you every good luck for your future,' he said, holding out his hand.

'You can't just leave . . .' she began, but his determined expression prevented her from continuing. Instead, she took his hand. 'Good luck, Teddy,' she murmured, then watched as he rose to his feet and strode from the canteen.

Well, that was a shock. But surely his work at Homerton Hospital was important? And what did he mean by he couldn't continue seeing her on the ward each day? They worked well together and had always acted professionally. Had it really mattered that much that she couldn't call him by his first name? Obviously, he must have anticipated her refusal to go to the ball with him if he'd already spoken with Matron, had already enlisted. Should she have told him that she'd been wavering about accepting his invitations recently? She liked and admired him enormously, and his obvious admiration had been balm to her battered ego after her meeting with Mrs Sutherland. Deep down, though, she'd known that not hearing from Philip was not a good enough reason to go out with him.

'May I sit here, Sister Harrison?'

She looked up from the table for the second time that lunchtime to see Matron staring down at her.

'Of course, Matron,' she replied, trying to pull herself together.

'A fine man, Dr Edwards. He will be sorely missed,' she said, stirring her cup of tea thoughtfully. 'If it's of any consolation, you did the right thing not accepting his attentions.' Rose looked at the woman in astonishment. It wasn't the first time she'd known what Rose was thinking.

'And no, I'm no witch. I just have years of experience caring for staff. And care I do. It was obvious from the first time Dr Edwards set eyes on you that he was smitten, but when those feelings aren't reciprocated then it's not meant to be. You would have been cheating him if you'd gone out with him. Now he's free to find someone who will truly return his feelings. As you already have, I believe?' Shrewd eyes twinkling, she rose to her feet. 'Don't let pride stand in your way, Rose. Be brave, find out the truth. None of us knows what's around the corner, especially these days. Now, go and enjoy your afternoon off and, for heaven's sake, if you haven't written that letter already, then hurry up and do so.'

Not for the first time Rose thought that despite her protestation, Matron must at least be a wise woman, although she didn't know she had already written to Philip. Once again, her heart sank, for that was a while ago and she still hadn't heard back from him.

***

Joy sang along to the *Music While You Work* programme that was playing on the wireless, making the volunteers smile as they packed the goods into boxes for the prisoners of war. They found her sunny nature uplifting and felt for her each time her mother reprimanded her for some minor demeanour.

'Why don't you sing us one of the songs you're doing for the concert?' Mary the woman beside her suggested.

'Well, I will, as long as it's all right,' Joy replied, looking down the table at Jane Bayliss.

'You carry on, Joy, it will do your voice good to practise, and everyone can let us know what they think of it. That's all right, isn't it, Robin?' she asked the supervisor.

'Of course, as long as it doesn't slow down the packing.'

The wireless was switched off and Joy began singing, 'Don't Sit Under The Apple Tree'. She was word perfect and as her voice rose to the rafters, everyone began singing along.

'That was really good, Joy. All you need is some red lipstick and your hair done in curls like that Patty of the Andrews Sisters,' Mary said admiringly. 'You sing well and who knows, if you look the part, you might even get into ENSA.'

'What's that?' Joy asked, frowning.

'It stands for Entertainments National Service Association, a group set up to entertain the armed forces,' Jane Bayliss told her. 'They travel all around the country, so it's not something you need to concern yourself about, Joy. But you're right, Mary, we do need to make sure she looks the part for the concert.'

'There's nothing wrong with how she looks now,' Vera snapped. 'My Joy's a good girl; pure and natural, she is, and doesn't need any tarting up. She's not all fur coat and no knickers like some I could mention.'

There was a stunned silence as Jane stood by her station gaping like a stranded fish.

'Come along, ladies, back to your packing. Think of all those poor boys waiting for a nice cup of cocoa to drink or a pair of warm socks to wear,' Robin encouraged, her nut-brown eyes surveying them all. 'I think we'll have the wireless back on, if you don't mind, Joy.

Not that your song wasn't beautiful, because it was, but perhaps it would be better to rehearse when we've finished our work,' she added diplomatically.

'I've never been so embarrassed,' Joy hissed at her mother as she resumed boxing up the items.

'Well, you just stay away from that woman,' Vera ordered. 'I won't have you mixing with the likes of her.'

'Mrs Potter, could I have a word, please?' Robin asked, appearing by Vera's side. She might be small in stature, but her presence was immense and even Vera knew not to argue with her.

'Of course, I would be pleased to offer you the benefit of my expertise,' Vera replied, raising hr voice so everyone could hear above the music. She'd let them all know who was in charge.

'Perhaps we could go into the kitchen?' the supervisor suggested, gesturing for Vera to lead the way before patting Jane's arm reassuringly as she passed her.

'We'll continue our task now, Joy,' Jane whispered, 'but perhaps you could join me for a cuppa when the shift finishes. There's something I'd like to discuss with you.'

'Yes, of course,' she replied, her heart sinking. Was she going to lose her place in the concert because of her mother?

'Well, that told her,' Vera said in a loud voice as, head held high, she marched back to her place. However, she was noticeably quiet for the rest of the afternoon.

* * *

'You really mean you'll take me to one of Myra Hess's concerts at the National Gallery?' Joy gasped; her eyes wide as she stared at Jane Bayliss in the little kitchen behind the hall.

'Think of it as a lesson in performance. I've mentioned before that I've seen a Myra Hess recital and as well as being a gifted pianist, she has such presence – you can learn a lot from her. Mary is right, entertaining is about so much more than just the singing or playing of an instrument, although they are important too, of course. We want our concert to raise much-needed funds for the Red Cross and the way to do that is to give the audience a night to re-member, one they'll recommend all their friends must see.'

'Heavens,' Joy gulped, leaning back against the cup-board.

'I should take a sip of that tea if I were you,' Jane laughed. 'Now, you don't volunteer here tomorrow, do you?'

'No, I don't, but Ma does.'

'Good,' Jane replied, her eyes glinting. 'The concerts are held at lunchtime, but we have to get there early for there are always long queues. However, we'll be back here late afternoon.'

'But don't you work tomorrow?' Joy asked.

'Leave that for me to arrange. Your father is going to be proud as punch when I tell him.' She grinned, then took a sip of her tea.

'But he'll tell mother.'

'Believe me, he won't,' Jane told her.

* * *

'God, I need a cuppa,' Vera cried as she pushed open the back door and settled her bulk thankfully onto the chair nearest the range.

Patty stifled a sigh. Whilst she had every sympathy for her sister's temporary living arrangements, she couldn't help wishing she wouldn't call in every day and interrupt her routine. With all the queuing and privations this continuing war caused, everything took so much longer. Telling herself to be more sympathetic, she put the kettle to boil.

'Faith said you'd been to see her. How did you find her?' Vera asked. Patty paused. She'd offered her sympathy and any help her niece might need but had been shocked at the girl's lack of emotion. Of course, it would serve no purpose to tell Vera that.

'Detached is probably the best way to describe her, but then it must have been a huge shock hearing that Martin's ship was torpedoed and that he's missing, presumed drowned.' She continued, rubbing fat into the flour for the pie crust she was making. Whilst it was true that Faith had always been aloof, surely, Patty thought, she shouldn't react so impassively to devastating news like that. There again, perhaps she was putting on a brave face while hoping he would be found.

'And would you believe that today she's wondering whether she'll get a widow's pension. I have no idea how these things work, so told her to contact the Ministry of Defence. She's always been self-contained but I'm blowed if I can reach her.' Vera shook her head.

'Well, they say time's a great healer and of course

208

she has young Artie to keep her busy.' As the kettle began to sing, she shook the flour off her hands to make the tea.

'Except Martin's mother, whilst obviously devastated herself, is fussing around them both while Faith sits there lapping up the attention like a martyr. I don't know, Patty, what with her, and our Joy hanging on that Jane Bayliss' every word, I feel as if I'm invisible.' Trying not to smile at the thought of her forceful sister not being seen, Patty poured their drinks then returned to her pie, bringing the pastry together.

While she had every sympathy, she had worries enough of her own. She knew Daisy was growing up and had a sensible head on her shoulders, yet she couldn't help wondering how she would fare without her family. She hadn't experienced life away from home before and Exeter was such a long way from Victory Walk. Then just that morning her boss had paid an unexpected visit to the greengrocer's with news of his own to impart. Realizing her sister was still talking, she shook her head and tried to concentrate.

'And when I mention it to Arthur, he won't have a word said against her. Not that he's ever home now. Hours on my Jack Jones I spend, alone in that box of a flat and the council still can't say when our house will be repaired.'

'But Joy said Mrs Bayliss was really friendly and . . .'

'Mrs Bayliss, my foot!' she spluttered. 'She's no more married than the Pope. And her being "really friendly" is the problem, don't you see? And I don't just mean with our Joy, either.'

Patty could feel the beginnings of a headache creeping across her temples as she tried to focus on lining the pie plate.

'Well, I'd better be getting home whilst I still have a family to go home to. At least, I hope I do. This war work's giving some women ideas above their station.' She sniffed and let out a long sigh.

'I'm sure you're worrying unnecessarily,' Patty reassured her. The idea that Arthur would look at another woman was ridiculous, surely?

'And I don't suppose they'll find poor Martin's body down in the briny now either,' Vera continued, determined to have her moan. 'Still, at least you know your Daisy will be safe when she goes to Devon, what with it being the back of beyond. Right, I need to see what offerings they've got left in the baker's, if any. Now the government's announced the baking of white bread has been banned, goodness only knows what we'll be eating.'

'Bert says its grains like barley and oatmeal grown in the UK that will be used, so at least we'll know where it comes from, although I dare say it'll make for a heavier loaf – and pastry too,' she added, looking ruefully at her pie. With her having to be ever more inventive with the fillings, it was often only the crust that filled them up and made their meals palatable. 'Don't forget Daisy's leaving party on Saturday, will you? I'm expecting a full family turn out to send her on her way with everyone's good wishes ringing in her ears.'

'We'll all be there, don't you worry,' Vera assured her as she let herself out.

As the door closed behind her, Patty put the pie on the side to cook later and poured herself another cup of tea. If she could only sit and rest in peace for half an hour, she was sure this headache would pass. Whilst there hadn't been any actual raids recently, all the false alarms and enemy aircraft flying overhead were both noisy and unsettling. At least it had been half day at the greengrocer's, although Mr Moreton visiting and telling her he was selling up was another problem. Bert's job as foreman at the Sutherlands' factory was reasonably paid, but everything was so expensive these days and they had become increasingly reliant on the extra money she brought in. Thinking of the Sutherlands reminded her that she must ask Rose if she'd heard from Philip. Mrs Sutherland was an out and out snob, and she didn't trust the woman not to be trying to cause trouble. Rubbing her throbbing temples to ease the tension, she grabbed a pencil and paper. She really needed to prepare everything for Daisy's party . . .

Their meal that evening was a quiet affair, Patty's mind still swimming with everything she needed to prepare for the party. At two minutes to nine exactly, Bert switched on the wireless.

'Time for the news, love,' he told her, and she duly put down her notepad and listened as it was announced.

'In recognition of the valiant defence of the island by the brave people of Malta, King George VI, in a handwritten letter to the governor, has announced the award of the George Cross to the Island Fortress of

Malta to bear witness to a heroism and devotion that will long be famous in history.

'Lieutenant General Sir William Dobbie, the Governor of Malta, replied. "By God's help Malta will not weaken but will endure until victory is won."'

'That's all well and good, but let's hope the people of Malta can hold out and that our boys continue to fight off the constant attacks,' Bert murmured.

'And that Peter, if he's there, or wherever he is, stays safe,' Patty prayed.

CHAPTER TWENTY-TWO

The little front room in Victory Walk was packed to capacity with family and friends all wanting to celebrate Daisy's new job and to wish her 'bon voyage' as Vera put it.

'You must be so excited, Daisy,' Joy said.

'Yeah, think of the freedom. Although you could have picked an outfit with more men. I mean, the Land Army is nearly all women, isn't it?' Faith muttered, helping herself to a savoury tart from one of the plates set out on the table, then pulling a face. 'What on earth's in these things?'

'Fish paste,' Robbie told her. 'Smelly stuff gets in everything. I'm having a jam one, it's safer.'

'You be thankful you've got summat to eat at all, my lad,' Bert told him. 'Now, everyone, grab yourselves a glass – sherry for the adults, lemonade for you lucky young 'uns, and we'll give a toast to our Daisy and wish her well in her new venture.' He waited until they all had a drink in their hands then raised his glass towards his daughter.

'To Daisy, yer ma and me's right proud of yer, so here's to your new job. Stay healthy, mind the mud and come safely home again. Oh, and behave yourself,' he added, wagging his finger at her and making everyone laugh.

'To Daisy!' they cried and as she looked at all the familiar faces surrounding her, she felt tears begin to well. Blinking rapidly, she forced a smile.

'Thank you, everyone, especially you, Ma, for putting on such a spread.' She turned and raised her glass to her mother. 'I know it's not easy feeding everyone these days, which is why I'm going to help feed the nation.'

As a rousing cheer sounded, Joy began to sing what had become one of the most popular songs of the war.

We'll meet again
Don't know where
Don't know when.
But I know we'll meet again some sunny day.

Then, as everyone joined in, their voices almost raising the roof of their little front room in Victory Walk, Daisy didn't know whether to laugh or cry.

***

Despite her bottle-green jumper and brown corduroy breeches, Daisy shivered as she clambered from the bus that had taken her from Exeter Station and dropped her at the end of what appeared to be a muddy track. She hadn't been able to see where exactly it was as the names on the sign had either been scratched out or the posts chopped down entirely. As she stood there clutching her bag, she was joined by two others, also dressed in Land Army uniform.

'My goodness me, the noise on that bus was

horrendous! If I got dug in the ribs by one more shopping basket or squalled at by another toddler, it would be too soon.' The fair-haired girl shuddered, then extended her hand. 'Merryn Dyer from Cornwall, but known as Merry,' she said in a soft burr.

'And I'm Dorothy Todd, known as Dotty,' said the second girl, 'and I agree, whoever put us on the market bus should be shot.'

'Daisy Harrison from the East End of London.'

'Oh, you do speak funny, my lovers,' Merry smiled.

'So do you,' Dotty replied, grinning back. 'I was living in Surrey but . . .' she began then stopped as a battered and muddied truck pulled up alongside them. A serious-looking man with mop of sandy hair poked his head out of the open window.

''Arris,' he said. 'Mr Penfold's put me in charge of yer lot. Now hop in,' he ordered.

'How do you know who we are?' Merry asked.

'Uniforms. Come on, haven't got all day.' His slow drawl was similar to how everyone she'd heard on the bus spoke, and Daisy guessed it must be peculiar to Devon.

Leaving them to put their bags in the back of the vehicle, and climb on board, he pulled away almost before they'd had a chance to scramble up. As they were jolted and bumped over numerous potholes in the muddy track, conversation became impossible. Instead, Daisy stared around at the passing countryside, where the tall trees were already in leaf and a maze of straggling hedges enclosed the greenest of fields in which cows and sheep grazed. In the distance she glimpsed a

215

mass of mauve sloping hills, the like of which she'd never seen before. Suddenly a long, pink building loomed in front of them, topped with thatch and two enormous chimneys and faced with small, square windows.

As the truck juddered to a halt, Daisy felt a thrill shoot through her. What a wonderful place to stay.

'This looks fantastic,' she cried as they jumped down and retrieved their bags.

'That it be,' he agreed. 'Yer'll find yer hostel up yonder.' Before they could reply, he'd sped off, mud spraying in his wake.

'Mr Charming, he is not,' Daisy declared. 'Well, we'd better see what delights await us.'

'I can see why they issued us with rubber boots,' Dotty said, grimacing as she trod in something which smelled decidedly worse than mud. 'Heavens, this stinky stuff is everywhere.'

Finally, they came to another long building, but this one had a crooked roof and looked like a row of barns all squashed together. Behind that a cluster of farm buildings were visible. As they stood looking around a cluster of clucking fowls appeared seemingly from nowhere and began pecking at their feet.

'Shoo, go away!' Dotty cried, flapping her hands but the chickens just clucked louder.

'New, are we, dearies?' a voice called. In the doorway they saw a plump, grey-haired woman in a coarse brown smock trying not to laugh. 'They'll not hurt yer. Thems could be yer dinner come next month, so it'll be in yer interest to feed 'em up good and proper. Now, come in and I'll show yer to yer dorm. I'm Mrs Rattery, the warden here. Good name, eh?' she chuckled, leading them down a long passageway, which was dusty and draughty, before throwing open a rickety door. 'This be yer billet for the next six weeks whilst yer does yer training. The three beds far end haven't been taken yet. The bathroom and lavvy's back down where yer came in. Yers all fends for yerselves, then breakfast is served at eight in the morning and supper at six, both in the farmhouse kitchen.'

'Oh good, eight o'clock is a reasonable time to get up,' Dotty replied.

'No, dearie,' Mrs Rattery said, raising her brows. 'You'll have milked the cows and swilled out the sheds before yer eats and 'Arris expects all the day's farm work finished before yer gets supper. Now, I'll be in the scullery when yers unpacked.'

Daisy stared down the room and counted ten camp beds evenly spaced with a rickety cupboard between each. There was also a table with a cracked, flowery ewer with matching jug, above which was placed a fly-spotted mirror. At the far end was a window but it was covered with cardboard and blackout curtains, and they couldn't see what it looked out onto.

'It's hardly the Ritz,' Dotty sighed.

'More like the Rotz,' Merry muttered. 'Best we bag our beds,' she suggested, putting her bag on the one nearest that was yet to be made up. It was furthest from the window, through which a gale seemed to be howling. Daisy chose the one next to her then realized she was dying to go to the toilet.

'I'm going to find the lavvy, as Mrs Rattery called it.'

The others followed and they made their way back along the passageway until they found the narrow bathroom, which had a solitary bath, the statutory five-inch line drawn around the inside, one lavatory and a tiny sink squeezed into the corner.

'Blimey, how many of us have to share this?'

'That be for the ten of yer,' Mrs Rattery said, appearing beside them. 'One bath a week each, but a word to the wise . . .' She paused and tapped her nose. 'The old boiler can only cope with hot water for a couple, so unless yer quick yer ends up sharing. Now, I'll show you the dairy.'

'Oh good, I'm parched,' Dotty cried.

'Dairy's where yer'll learn to make butter and cream, specially our golden clotted,' the woman told them, shaking her head in despair. 'Course, afore yer can do that yer has to milk the cows. 'Arris will show you how to do that later, but as we has to use the milk while it's fresh yer need to know where all the para-phernalia is.'

'But I thought we were going to be growing vege-tables?' Daisy frowned.

'My lass, but yer be keen. Don't worry, yer'll be doing that after mornin' milking's done.'

'You mean the cows are milked more than once a day?' Dotty asked.

'Oh ar, twice at least. I'll show you the milking parlour first bein' as how yer so keen,' she said, leading the way across the yard, seemingly heedless of the cow muck beneath her feet. How could she stand the smell? Daisy wondered, grimacing.

'Now this be where yer sits to milk the beasts,' she said, pointing to a couple of three-legged stools, 'and this be what yer squirt the milk into.' As she held up a tin pail, Daisy was convinced she was joking.

'Oh yes, and how do you get it from the cow into that pail?' she asked.

'Why, yer squeezes its udders, of course.' The woman frowned and shook her head. 'Theys them things hanging between their legs.'

'Do you think she's having us on?' Dotty whispered.

'Yer'll sees in exactly one hour 'cos Dolly, Buttercup and the others don't like to be kept waiting,' the woman replied. The girls looked at each other in dismay. There was obviously nothing wrong with the woman's hearing and they had a horrible feeling she wasn't joking at all. And just how many cows were there?

'Dearie me, look at the state of yers,' Mrs Rattery exclaimed as Daisy, Merry and Dotty staggered wearily into the farmhouse in time for supper.

'Didn't realize them cows would be so huge and heavy,' Daisy mumbled, removing lengths of straw from her hair. 'Or stink,' she added, wrinkling her nose.

'Or that we'd have to squeeze the dangly bits under them,' Dotty cried, wiping a mud-streaked hand over her face, then grimacing at the smell. 'Never even saw a cow in Surrey, let alone touched one.'

'Yer don't sound posh like that other girl we had

here from up country, Dotty,' Mrs Rattery replied, taking a towel from a peg and handing it to them.

'It was the people I were in service to that were posh,' Dotty replied. 'Lord Cranford shut up the big house and went to Canada when the war started. Didn't want me, of course, even though I'd been . . . nice to him.' She sniffed and curled her lip. 'I went to live with my aunt in London, got work in the munitions factory, but couldn't stand it, so here I am.'

'Best get yerselves cleaned up afore 'Arris comes in to eat. He's the farm manager and strict but will see you get a good all-round training. Tomorrow yer must use the water in the trough outside the milking parlour when you've done. I'm surprised he didn't tell yer.'

'He was too busy snorting at our attempts at milking,' Merry laughed.

'Ah well, not to worry, it'll come easier tomorrow.'

'We thought we'd be growing food for the nation,' Daisy replied, sharing horrified looks with the others at the thought of repeating the ordeal they'd just been through.

'And yer will tomorrow; after yer seen to the cows,' 'Arris told them, striding across the flagstones, heedless of his mud-caked boots, and helping himself to the savoury-smelling broth that was simmering on the range. He snatched up a hunk of crusty bread, the likes of which Daisy hadn't seen since before the war started, then disappeared into the room beyond without another word.

Daisy just had time to notice that the range was far

bigger than her ma's and had been polished with black lead until it shone, before she heard the babble of voices and footsteps approaching.

'Ah, here's t'others,' the warden said, lifting the huge soup pot from the range and placing it at the head of the rustic table that ran the length of the room. She took bowls from the high dresser that was stacked with earthenware crockery and set them on the table alongside a platter of bread and a dish of glistening golden butter that made Daisy's mouth water. She was just thinking how hungry she was, when a group of girls wearing the same green and brown uniforms appeared, stamped the mud from their boots, then trudged wearily into the room and sank onto their chairs.

'Right, girls, this be Daisy, Dotty and Merry,' the woman announced as she began ladling thick broth into the waiting bowls. ''Tis rabbit stew. Help yerselves to bread. That's all there is until miller's been, mind, so make sure yer all gets a piece.'

As the fragrant aroma filled the room, Daisy's stomach rumbled loudly making them all laugh. She hadn't eaten anything since the paste sandwich Patty had packed for her to have on the train, and she tucked in ravenously. The kitchen fell silent apart from the clunk of spoons against pottery.

As Mrs Rattery collected up their bowls, Daisy sat back in her seat replete and happy that if the woman's cooking was every bit as good as her mother's, then her time here wouldn't be so bad after all. But then clean dishes were placed on the table and the warden reappeared brandishing a steaming pudding dripping with ruby red jam. Seeing their astonished looks, she smiled then produced a huge jug of creamy custard.

'This be why yer milk them cows,' she grinned. 'Be worth the effort, eh? 'Arris might be strict, but he makes sure you gets good grub.'

They tucked into the delicious pudding and, as energy levels revived, the girls became quite chatty, so that by the end of the meal Daisy had all but forgotten the nightmare of the milking parlour as she got to know the others. It seemed the early starts and long hours working outside in all weathers hadn't dampened their spirits. The main grouse seemed to be the cold, almost primitive conditions, in the hostel.

'If you don't know someone before you share a bath with them, by the time you've got rid of all your dirt, which incidentally gets in the unlikeliest of crevices, you are definitely bosom buddies,' Mandy, who seemed to be their leader, chortled.

'And, unless you want an audience, don't pull back the blackout blind. The branches on the big oak behind overlook the dorm and there's always some dirty bugger up there gawping in while you're dressing.'

'Also, whatever you do, unless you want your head blown off by the wind, don't open the window in there either. The cardboard's there for a reason.'

'That's why we stay here in the farmhouse until the range dies down or we can't keep our eyes open any longer.'

'Luckily, you've missed the snow. Trying to dig up frost-encrusted cabbages and caulis is a killer.'

'But of course, the warden being a terrific cook, turns them into tasty meals,' Mrs Rattery chuckled, placing a huge teapot covered in a bright knitted cosy on the table. 'Now, girls, by the time you've washed the dishes, this tea'll be brewed.'

'Okey dokey, Mrs R. I know it's my turn to dry and, Anna, it's yours to wash,' Mandy replied. 'Make the most of it, D, D and M, 'cos you'll have your names added to the rota tomorrow, and be warned, it's brassicas in the scullery,' she grimaced, disappearing through another door with Anna.

As their fellow workers filled them in on life on the farm, Daisy gathered that, despite their moans and all coming from different parts of the country, they got on well and were happy here.

'Avoid the fumbling gropes of the local farmhands employed to teach us the rudiments of farming and you'll be fine. Mind you, the handsome airmen who come to the dances in Exeter are another matter,' Mandy hooted.

Any trepidation Daisy might have had about leaving home disappeared. Quitting Manor House Station and joining the Land Army had been the right decision. Now she could really do her bit to contribute to the war effort – and hopefully have a bit of fun too. However, her affections were still with Freddy, so getting involved with any of the servicemen was not on her agenda.

CHAPTER TWENTY-THREE

'You won't believe where I've been or who I saw!' Joy cried, when her sister let her into the house in Victory Walk the following day. 'Honestly, Hope, you should have seen her. She looked magnificent and played like a dream. I wish I could learn to play the piano.'

'Who are you talking about?' Hope asked, then listened intently as Joy told her about her visit to the National Gallery to hear Myra Hess perform a Mozart piano concert. 'To think she plays nearly every day and for free too. She says she likes to cheer up everyday folk in these extraordinary times. We had to queue for ages, but then you'd expect that, wouldn't you?'

'It sounds fantastic but why should Mrs Bayliss take you?'

'So that I can learn how to present myself to an audience. I need to have presence for the Red Cross concert. And she says for me to call her Jane. It's a secret, of course, for Mother would have kittens.'

'And you've no room for any of those in that tiny flat,' Hope giggled, then frowned as her sister sighed. 'What's up?'

'I wish I could come and live here! We're all on top of each other in that pokey flat and I'm fed up with making do with that lumpy old sofa for my bed each night. I've forgotten what it's like to have a bedroom, even one to share. Mother snaps at me all the time, then nags Father so he hardly ever comes home before midnight. She was really rude to Jane Bayliss at the Red Cross centre yesterday. Everybody is so nice there and it was embarrassing.'

'Hmm, she can be a bit forthright, can't she? Oh, Auntie Patty's home,' Hope murmured as they heard the click of the front door. 'Don't mention staying here, Joy, she hasn't been herself this past day or so. She says it's a headache, but I think something's worrying her. I'm back on shift in the morning but I'm hoping to have a word with her before I leave.'

'Hello, girls. Cor, what a day. If I had a penny for every time I've been asked why there are still no oranges, I'd be a rich woman. Honestly, don't people know there's a flipping war on?'

'Sit down, Auntie, I'll make you a nice cuppa,' Hope told her, exchanging looks with Joy.

'It's nice to see you, dear. Have you been to see Faith and Artie?' Patty asked Joy as she sank into a chair with a sigh. 'Only I wondered how she's feeling now.'

'I saw her first thing this morning, but she didn't have much to say. Artie's a right little bundle of laughs, though. Anyway, guess who else I've been to see?' she continued, then proceeded to tell Patty about the concert.

'And you said Mrs Bayliss took you?' Patty said, her frown deepening.

'Yes, she's in charge of the fund-raising concert. Anyway, I've been perfecting my Patty pout – ooh, I'm

225

going to be a Patty like you, Auntie,' she giggled. 'I've got to curl my hair for the concert too. Can you show me how to do it?' She looked at her aunt eagerly, but she just shook her head.

'Another time, Joy. I'm going to have a rest before I get the supper,' Patty told her, closing her eyes.

'Don't worry, Auntie Patty,' Hope told her. 'I've made a cottage pie although it's mostly vegetables. Still, I've done your trick and made a tasty meat gravy so hopefully nobody will notice.' But Patty was dead to the world and didn't hear.

'Let's go up to my room so we don't disturb her,' Hope suggested. 'I've got to get everything ready for my shift tomorrow anyway. These twenty-four hours on then off take some getting used to.'

'How do you manage for food?'

'They've brought in a cook, but she takes some getting used to as well,' Hope grimaced.

'Can't be worse than Mother's cooking,' Joy muttered, then brightened. 'Anyway, guess where else Jane Bayliss is taking me? Only the American Eagle Club on Charing Cross Road!'

'Whatever are you going there for?'

'To learn more tricks of the trade. Honestly, Hope, until today I never realized just how green I am.'

'Well, just you be careful, little sis.'

'Are you joking? I intend finding out what living is really about.'

Clover looked up from the letter she was writing as Ann came gliding into the room in the most beautiful

226

sapphire dress, a sumptuous fur stole draped elegantly around her shoulders.

'You look wonderful. Who's the lucky fellow?'

'Charlie, and he's taking me for dinner at Claridge's. Afterwards we're going dancing. Apparently, he's found a darling little club right under a café that stays open all night, serves wonderful cocktails and has a swing band. Luckily Mother's out of town so if he plays his cards right, we might end up in her suite for a nightcap or three.' She chuckled, giving a saucy wink. 'Luckily, it's the weekend and Dilly doesn't need me although we're all having to do more now that he's working from home most days.'

'Is Charlie driving you back in time for your next shift?'

'Golly, no,' she hooted. 'One should never show reliance on a guy, or before you can blink they'll have a ring on your finger and a brood of brats in your belly to continue their lineage. You remember that, Clover. No, he can drive me there, then I'll catch the dawn milk train back to Bletchley. It's a shame you're on the graveyard shift or you could come with me.'

'I'm sure Charlie would love me playing gooseberry. Besides, I'm hardly dressed for dining and dancing,' she laughed, glancing down at her plain ATS uniform with its stout, black lace-up shoes. Neither was there anything suitable in her bag of clothes which had been forwarded from North Wales. 'Working overnight is a bit of a killer but at least I caught up with some chores today.'

'You certainly live the high life, old thing. You really

227

should let loose, have some fun . . .' She stopped as a horn tooted outside. 'There he is. Try and crack loads of codes whilst I'm away,' she trilled before disappearing in a cloud of Chanel No 5.

Although they never discussed their actual work, she'd learned that Ann was indeed one of Dilly Knox's harem, but far from being the air-headed debutante Sally had suggested, she was one of the 'brains' the man specially selected for his team. She was friendly, but their differing shifts meant they were like ships that passed in the night, only sharing a quick cuppa or drink in the pub when they ran into each other. And while she'd always be grateful to Ann for saving her from the seedy hostel she'd first been billeted in, she missed the closeness and confidences she'd shared with Marigold.

Quickly she finished the letter to her dear friend, put it in her bag ready to post when she got to the Park, then sat back in the comfortable velvet-covered armchair. She'd really landed on her feet, she thought, staring around the high-ceilinged room with its decorative cornices and marble fireplace. The bay window with its primrose-coloured drapes looked out over the garden which, although not large, was planted with narrow-leafed sundrops and bright scarlet poppies bordered by majestic lupins. Not that she'd known their names until she'd asked Ann. How her mother would love it! It wouldn't be long until Clover qualified for some leave and thoughts of her family made her realize how much she missed them – although she didn't miss sharing a room with Daisy. She still couldn't believe her sister had joined the Land Army and was training on a farm in Devon.

As the clock chimed the half hour, she gave a yelp. She'd miss the bus if she didn't hurry. Lateness and letting people down were never acceptable.

Even at this late hour, the bus was full of workers heading to the Park. She smiled, remembering how she'd heard customers in the local store speculating that they must all be agricultural workers growing crops for the country. Well, they were helping the country, just in a different way.

As the bus trundled through the gates to the Park, which was thronging with activity despite the late hour, Clover thought again how strange it was that all these people who either worked in the mansion or one of the numerous surrounding huts didn't actually know what each other did because talking about work was forbidden and, conscious of the penalties of the Official Secrets Act, everybody abided by it.

Clover felt the sense of exigency as soon as she entered Hut 6. There was no sign of Sally, which was not altogether surprising as she loathed the graveyard shift and Clover couldn't help thinking that if she carried on like this, she'd be back making components for airplanes at the Hawker Siddeley factory she'd been keen to escape from, but there was no time for pondering, as she took her seat.

'Your attention, ladies, please.' Mrs Speedwell's voice was measured but Clover caught the underlying sense of urgency. 'Intelligence has received word of impending raids on some of our cities so today we are to begin by changing the settings on our machines.' Everyone stared at each other in surprise at this variation, for usually everything followed the same pattern.

'Wait until you receive the sheet showing what they should be, then pass it on and continue working in the usual way. You will be vigilant as always, but today you are to pay particular attention to anything that might look like, or could be, the name of a city. If you have any doubts, then do not hesitate to see me. I cannot impress upon you enough the importance of this.'

Hearing the gravity of the supervisor's voice, Clover swallowed hard. Would today be the day she actually cracked a code? Taking the sheet, she changed the settings on her machine then picked up the first message from the basket which, as usual, was piled high.

For hours she worked solidly at the machine, trying to sort each block of five letter gibberish into groups of German words. The thrum of machines and rustle of papers receded into the background as she tried to make sense of the letters. She hardly noticed the stuffy, close atmosphere, was even oblivious to the cigarette smoke that swirled around her. Finally, as her head began to throb and her eyes itched, she thought she saw something emerge. She blinked then stared again, and then at the next block of five characters. There was no doubt about it, they definitely formed the letters of an English town! With her heart thumping, she rose to her feet. Then, ignoring the curious looks of her fellow workers, she handed the message to Mrs Speedwell.

***

Daisy watched as the sun rose above the moors, bathing everything in a blush pink. Standing in such beautiful surroundings, it was hard to believe there was a war taking place. She breathed deeply of the fresh air which was welcome after the noxious smells of the cowshed she'd just mucked out and swilled down. How she loved the feeling of space and freedom here on the farm after the sooty environs of the underground. The work was hard and varied, as they were expected to turn their hand to anything asked of them, but she fell into bed each night exhausted but satisfied that she was at last doing her bit for the country.

If only Freddy could see her now, she thought, grimacing at her mud-encrusted hands. Not for the first time she wondered where he was and what he was doing. Her mother had promised to forward any letters, but it was ages since she'd heard from him.

'Come on, Daisy Daydream!' Merry called. 'We've got a briefing from his nibs before breakfast. I'm starving, so hurry up, do.'

'Right now, this being a training farm we has cows, chickens, horses and sheep that all need looking after,' 'Arris told them a minute later. He was wearing faded brown cord trousers and a plaid shirt that had seen better days, and his boots were caked in do-do as Merry called it.

'Is that all?' Dotty muttered.

'No, that is not all, miss,' he grunted. 'We has acres of planted fields needing hoeing so the weeds don't choke the vegetables, stones to be picked up so the veg

231

can grow, grain the country is crying out for to make its bread, fences that need mending, stone walls that needs rebuilding – and then there's the rats that need keeping down.'

'What do you mean, keeping down?' Daisy frowned, feeling sick at the thought of having to stop them from jumping over the fences.

'I mean yer has to kill them,' he replied, eyeing them each in turn. 'Either that or they climbs up yer breeches and bites yer. Still, yer can go and get yer breakfast now,' he said, grinning at their ashen faces.

'Like I fancy eating anything after that,' Daisy groaned.

'Perhaps he was just trying to scare us,' Dotty sighed.

However, as they took their places at the farmhouse table, the others who'd arrived the previous week, soon enlightened them.

'There's hundreds of them in the barns, out in the fields, every bloomin' where. Love the grain, they do. Best you tie string round the bottom of your breeches to stop the varmints biting your bits,' Eileen told them gleefully as she spread marmalade liberally on her bread.

'Right, 'ere yer are,' Mrs Rattery said, placing bowls of porridge in front of the late arrivals. 'Eat up, yer've got a long day of working in the fields ahead.'

Suddenly Merry burst out laughing and the others all turned to look at her.

'Sorry, Mrs Rattery, I've just realized why you said you were aptly named.'

* * *

'I never thought hoeing would be this back-breaking,' Dotty muttered, grimacing as she tried to straighten up.

'Or that a field could have so many weeds,' Daisy sighed. It was nearly noon and they'd been bent over, working their way three abreast down the seemingly never-ending field of cabbages. To think she'd always picked one off the shelf at the greengrocer's without a thought as to how it got there. She was just wondering how her mother was when she heard the tinkle of a bell. Looking up, she saw Mrs Rattery riding a bicycle and waving to them.

''ere we goes,' the warden said when, moments later, she placed a basket covered with a checked towel on the ground. 'Noonsies. Yer gets a twenty-minute break,' she explained. 'Luckily the miller came early so I bin able to bake.'

Daisy's mouth watered and her stomach gave a growl as the aroma of freshly baked bread wafted her way. 'There's slices of ham from last year's pig we smoked up the chimney, home-pickled onions, and me speciality chutney. Oh, and a jar of cold tea each. That should keep yer goin' till supper,' she told them. 'Bring the basket back when yer comes or there'll be no noonsies tomorrow. Oh, and 'Arris said be sure to milk the cows when yer finished here. Then I'm to teach yer to make cream.'

'What, all before supper?' Daisy gasped. 'It takes ages to walk everywhere round here.'

'Didn't 'Arris tell yer about bicycles in yon barn yer can use? Yer'll get around much quicker if yer does,' the woman told them, then with a wave she disappeared back down the lane.

'Slave labour or what?' Dotty groaned as they collapsed onto the ground and tucked into their food.

'The bikes should make getting around faster,' Merry commented, through a mouthful of bread. 'Bet 'Arris forgot to tell us on purpose.'

'I haven't ridden one for years, but I'm game to give it a go,' Daisy replied.

'Be better than trying to mount one of *them*, anyhow,' Dotty cried, gesturing to the field beyond where four very large horses grazed.

CHAPTER TWENTY-FOUR

'Who's up for the dance in Exeter on Saturday night?' Mandy asked at the supper table that night. 'Rumour hath it there will be American GIs as well as airmen and military from the local bases attending.'

'Then you know you can count me in, Mandy Moo,' the dark-haired Eileen declared. 'I've only got one pair of nylons left so I'll be at my friendliest,' she smiled. 'Bugger bare legs for patriotism. Who wants to look like they've got sausages for pins? That's not going to turn on any chap.'

'I've been practising my new look and I'm almost out of Yardley Renegade lipstick,' Sarah said. She'd shaken her hair out of its plait and her honey-blonde tresses fell in waves around her shoulders. Daisy thought she looked glamorous despite the unflattering harsh bottle-green of her jumper.

'You'll have to be nice to the GIs then, won't you?' Eileen chuckled. 'Last time they came loaded with Hershey bars, which they call candy, and cola as well as nylons – although they made us take part in a dance competition before they dished any out.'

'Come on, let's go back to our room and see what makeup we've got between us,' Mandy suggested. 'How about you, D, D and M? Are you up for a bit of fun?' she asked, turning to Daisy, Dotty and Merry.

'Can we just leave the farm, then?' Daisy asked.

'We finish work at four on Saturdays and are free until Monday morning so we can make a weekend of it.'

'It does sound like fun,' Merry told them.

'And who's goin' to milk the cows on Sunday mornin', then?' The girls let out a groan as the dark shadow of 'Arris appeared in the doorway. 'Mr Penfold, the owner, put me in charge of yer lot to run his farm, remember. Yer has responsibilities.'

'As if you ever let us forget,' Mandy mumbled. 'We are allowed a day off a week, you know.'

'But not all at the same time. Two of you need to be on the farm to see to the animals, you know the rules.' As he stood there looking challengingly at them, a heavy silence fell. Being new, Daisy knew what she had to do.

'I'll stay behind and milk the cows,' she volunteered.

'Me too,' Merry agreed.

'No, that won't work. Can't have two rookies let loose in the parlour. One of you others will have to be here to supervise.' As he stood, hands on hips, staring at them, the room was filled with another awkward silence.

'No volunteers? In that case, I'll have to choose.' He paused and looked at each of them in turn. 'Bearing in mind these two made a right Horlicks of the milking again earlier, then couldn't even churn it to cream, they'll need someone who has at least half an idea of what they're doing to supervise. So . . . I volunteer you,' he said, pointing to Mandy. You can have Monday off instead.'

'But I've made arrangements!'

'Then you'll have to unarrange them, won't you? As for you three rookies . . .' He stared pointedly at Daisy, Dotty and Merry. 'Yer three can draw straws to see who stays behind. No need for more than needed to miss yer dance. Now yer can't say I'm not a fair man, can yer?'

As Mandy glared daggers at them, Daisy and Merry exchanged looks. The last thing they wanted to do was make an enemy of the girl who clearly thought herself in charge of them, and yet clearly, 'Arris was in charge and they had to do as they were told.

The man held out three pieces of straw and Daisy, Dotty and Merry had no choice but to select one each.

* * *

'Just our blooming luck to have to spend our weekend down in the cellar turning cheeses and washing down all the racks whilst the others have fun,' Mandy moaned. 'I mean, I don't know about you, weekends used to mean a nice lie in, breakfast in bed . . . blimey, what's that?' she gasped as they felt vibrations beneath them. Then the ceiling began shaking, the racks vibrated making the huge rounds of cheddar wobble precariously.

The two girls stared at each other in horror as, right before their eyes, the heavy cheeses began dropping to the floor.

'Let's get out of here,' Daisy screamed, running up the stone steps as fast as her legs could carry her.

Outside the ground was trembling and their eyes widened in alarm at the deafening roar.

Looking up they then saw a dark cloud of bomber planes thundering above them, before disappearing over the fields.

'There's loads of them and they're heading for Exeter!' Mandy muttered, staring in horror at Daisy.

***

Eating with the family was usually Patty's favourite time of day, but this evening she had little appetite, toying with the food on her plate. Letting out a deep sigh, she pushed it away only for Robbie to pounce on it gleefully.

'Manners, Robbie,' Bert admonished.

'Can't let good food go to waste,' the boy mumbled through a mouth full of mince and carrots. 'Finished,' he said, moments later as he scraped his plate clean. 'It's still daylight so can I go out to play with Ricky? We found an old pram base with the wheels still on earlier.'

'I hope you haven't been rooting around those bombed-out houses, Robbie, you know they could collapse at any time,' Patty said.

'Right, son, your mother's tired, so clear the table and wash up, then you can go out to play. And we mean what we say about not playing in those buildings.'

As Robbie took their things through to the back

238

kitchen and Patty poured fresh tea, Bert returned to the *Daily Express*. Sighing and muttering as he sipped his drink, he waited until Robbie had taken himself out to play, then carefully folded his newspaper and turned to Patty.

'Right, love, you've been out of sorts for some time, so now we're by ourselves will you tell me what's wrong? Worrying about that sister of yours again, are you?' As he looked tenderly at her, she felt like a dam had burst and her pent-up emotions came flooding out.

'It's not her, although she does seem to have a lot on her mind at the moment. No, it's Mr Moreton, he came to see me at work.'

'Really? I thought he was too old to come into the shop now?'

'That's exactly it, Bert. Because he's old, he's decided to sell up. Apparently, he's had an offer for the shop, although he doesn't think the owner intends keeping it as a greengrocer's, so I'll be out of a job come the end of June.'

'Oh, that's a blow. I know you love working there.'

'It's not the job I'll miss so much as the money. Everything's so expensive now.'

'The day I can't provide for my family, it'll be a rum do,' Bert replied, sitting up straighter in his seat. 'I'll ask Mr Sutherland if I can do more hours. He's always moaning he's short-staffed now that so many women have joined up.'

'But you already work long hours, and what with the fire watching . . .'

'There's not so much to do on the fire-watching side

239

now the Luftwaffe are leaving London alone, though we still have to be vigilant, mind. So, you can stop worrying your pretty head, my dear, we'll manage,' he insisted, patting her hand. They sat like that for a few moments, Patty drawing comfort from his support, then he glanced at the clock. 'It's time to turn on the wireless for the news.'

As Patty picked up her cup, her disquiet returned, and her head felt as if someone was playing a set of drums inside it. It was only when Bert switched off the set, she realized she hadn't heard one word the broadcaster had said.

'All these blinkin' raids!' Bert burst out. 'The Luftwaffe might be leaving London alone, but they seem hell-bent on destroying our other cities. They've gone and bombed Norwich and York, now. All those poor people killed and injured. Where next?' He shook his head. 'No doubt they'll give more details in the papers. I just pray our Peter's safe.'

The drumsticks beat harder in Patty's head as that feeling of dread surfaced once again. She looked over at Bert, but he was lost in thought himself, looking quite morose. As he let out a long sigh Patty couldn't help wondering if it was just Peter he was fretting about, or if her losing her job was worrying him more than he'd let on. Not for the first time she wished this war over and her family, which seemed to be spreading even wider, was safely back at Victory Walk, home where they belonged.

***

Although her shift had long finished, Clover, along with many of her colleagues, realizing the urgency of the situation, volunteered to stay on. The next team arrived and, having been briefed, were squashed onto any seat with every available machine being pressed into use. Consequently, the hut was soon like a bubbling cauldron of perspiration mixed with desperation. Along with the ever-present smell of tobacco and clank of machinery, it wasn't long before Clover felt the beginnings of a headache creeping over her temples.

Everyone was filled with a sense of trepidation, that the next slip they picked up could contain the name of yet another city Hitler had in his sights, or the codename for the mission. Anything that could be considered of use was to be handed to the supervisor for passing on to the next appropriate section, whatever that was, for she had no way of knowing. Neither did she have any way of knowing whether the decoded paper she'd passed to Mrs Speedwell had been what she thought, for the woman had glanced at it then promptly disappeared into the room behind them without saying a word, leaving her to continue with the next slip in her basket.

Although it played on her mind, she knew it was no good tackling her supervisor. Questions were forbidden and all she'd be told was, that if what she had seen was correct, it was only part of a larger picture of which she had no knowledge. Everything was kept separate for security and she must continue with her job.

However, although she was dog-tired the niggle persisted; then, when she thought she could take no more, Mrs Speedwell clapped her hands and told them all to go home.

'Your dedication has been appreciated and anything and everything of any note passed on. You may now leave, knowing you have done your best for your country. Some of you have gone many hours without eating, so I suggest you fuel up then get some much-deserved sleep. I will see you all tomorrow.'

As they all filed silently and wearily from the hut, any notion that they were indispensable was soon quashed as their places were taken by the next shift. Clover's yearning to see her family was growing by the minute. How she wished she could jump on the next train from Bletchley to Euston then make her way home to their little terraced house in Victory Walk. But then her mother would naturally be full of questions about what she did here, and what could she tell her? She wasn't stupid and fobbing her off with talk of clerical work, special or not was out of the question. Yet the desire to check all was well was growing stronger by the minute.

Although she was bone weary and desperate for her bed, the need for a strong cup of coffee or what passed for it these days, was greater. Heeding Mrs Speedwell's advice, she joined the queue in the canteen.

Having downed the mug of chicory coffee and with her brain clicking on again, that niggle recurred, this time even stronger. It was no good, her leave was due and although she knew it would be frowned upon, she was going to take it.

***

Daisy's head was spinning as she lay sprawled on the ground, covered in muck and goodness knows what else. She could even taste it, she thought, spitting out a mouthful of mud in a most unladylike manner. She ached all over and was convinced that underneath her clothes she was black and blue. A tall, dark shape loomed over her.

'Freddy?' she murmured. But the only response was the lowing of disgruntled cattle. Her spirits plummeted but at least she was alive, she realized, fighting back the tears as she struggled to her feet. Then she saw Bluebell staring at her with doe-like eyes and the memory of her huge bulk shoving Daisy out of the way surfaced.

'Why you . . .!' she shouted, raising her fist, but the cow just gave an insolent moo.

''Aving a spot of bother, are yer?' 'Arris asked, appearing in the doorway of the milking parlour.

'No,' she muttered. Being the only Land Girls left on the farm meant she and Mandy had to milk all the cows by themselves, and it seemed Bluebell enjoyed taking advantage of her inexperience, nudging her with her huge bulk when she'd grasped her udders. She waited for the man to say something sarcastic, but he just looked bleak and shook his head.

'Come up to the farmhouse when yer've finished milking. I've a message from Mr Penfold.'

'Can't you tell me what it is now?' Daisy asked. Having waited seemingly ages for news after they heard about the recent Exeter bombing, her nerves were shot away and she couldn't take any more suspense.

'Not with them cows bellowing like crazy. Strains their guts when the milkin's late.' Before Daisy could reply, he turned on his heel and strode back across the farmyard.

'What was that all about? Is there any news. And what's happened to you?' Mandy asked anxiously, appearing from the other stall and seeing the state of Daisy's clothes.

'It seems Mr Penfold's sent a message, but 'Arris won't pass it on until the cows are all milked.'

'Well, we'd better get on, the suspense of wondering if everyone's all right is killing me.'

Daisy was shattered and the strain of waiting for news about their friends was getting to her as well. Righting the three-legged milking stool, she returned to her task, daring the mooing beast to do anything other than behave.

Finally, with the cows returned to their field, the two girls trudged wearily over to the farmhouse.

'Come in and sit down,' Mrs Rattery greeted them, placing two bowls of broth in front of them. 'And before yer says anything, yer've got to eat whether yer thinks yer hungry or not. When yer've finished – and only then, mind – we'll talk.'

Knowing it would be no good arguing with the warden, the two girls nodded and took their places, only too aware of the empty seats around them. Anxious to hear what the warden had to say, they ate their broth as fast as they dared, although it could have been mud for all they noticed.

'Right,' Mrs Rattery said as soon as they'd pushed

their empty bowls away. 'Mr Penfold has ascertained from the commanding officer at the local Wyvern Barracks that some of his men had offered to accompany our Land Girls to the city centre after the dance. Unfortunately, it seems likely they were in the vicinity of the cathedral when the bombs fell, badly damaging it. He's promised to let us know as soon as he has any definite news, but says we should prepare ourselves for the worst . . .' Her voice broke as tears trickled down her cheeks.

'Maybe they went somewhere else,' Daisy cried as she recalled the grumbling about having to miss the dance.

'Yes, perhaps they went window shopping,' Mandy added hopefully.

'Look, girls, you need to understand there has been huge damage to the city centre as well as the Green, so . . . we mustn't . . . don't yer get yer hopes up.' She shook her head.

Daisy and Mandy exchanged stricken looks.

CHAPTER TWENTY-FIVE

The canteen at the ambulance station was busy as Hope took her place in the queue.

'Hello, stranger, how are you?' Hearing her name, Hope looked up from the dish of stew she'd helped herself to and did a double take when she saw Ian MacLeod standing behind the table, wielding a tea towel.

'Wh-what are you doing here,' she stammered, taking in the white apron that barely covered his front.

'Working,' he chuckled. 'Mrs Evans isn't well, so I volunteered to help out in the canteen.'

'You mean you cooked this?' she asked, gesturing to the stew and vegetables.

'Guilty as charged. Look, I've nearly finished up here, so may I join you for a cup of our amazing tea?'

'Well, yes, I suppose so,' she agreed, before making her way over to where Kitty was grinning.

'Sight for sore eyes, eh?' she asked as Hope pulled out a chair beside her.

'You could have warned me he was here,' Hope murmured.

'What, and spoil seeing that look on your boat race? After moping about these past few weeks, you lit up like a firework when you saw him, so put a smile on your dial and be nice to him.'

'But you said I should play hard to get and . . .'

'I said you need to lighten up, grab your fun where you can. Go on, give the poor chap a chance. Oops, time I wasn't here,' she added, jumping to her feet as Ian approached.

'No need to leave on my account,' he said, pulling out the chair opposite Hope.

'Nah, you're all right. Got to finish cleaning our ambulance,' she told him, then with a last grin at Hope, collected up her things and disappeared. He smiled at Hope, and she smiled hesitantly back. Kitty was incorrigible but maybe she should hear what he had to say.

'This stew's tasty,' she remarked.

'Glad you approve m'lady.'

'You mean you really did make it?' she gasped. 'I had no idea you could cook.'

'No reason why you should. Sonia asked me to call by her office as she had a proposition to discuss.'

'Oh?'

'Although the kids have finally settled in Dorset, I'm still too busy with my engineering work to commit to the twenty-four-hour shift pattern. However, I do now have time to be a "Jack of all" or "Ian of all" as she called it. I've agreed to help out with anything that needs doing around here as and when I can. Sonia's agreed I can resume my regular duties when I'm able, which at the rate things are going will be when this war finally finishes,' he sighed. 'Anyway, it's all been a bit hectic but worth it to know the children are safe.'

Although Hope nodded, she'd noticed the use of the supervisor's first name and wondered just how friendly they'd become. She hadn't realized he'd spoken again until he coughed to catch her attention.

'I was saying that I've really missed you. I see your shift finishes tomorrow morning and wondered if you'd like to catch up properly, maybe over lunch at that nice little caff near the market?'

'I'm sorry, but my sister's calling round. She's singing in a concert to raise funds for the Red Cross, and I promised to help her adapt one of her dresses.' Although it was true, she knew Joy wouldn't mind if she made it another day. However, she didn't want Ian thinking she'd just been sitting around waiting for him to turn up. Although Kitty seemed to have changed her tune, Hope still thought it was important to let men know you had your own life. Then she looked up and saw the disappointed look in his eyes and her heart flipped.

'I'll be free in the afternoon, though.'

'I'll call for you then,' he said, his face lighting up.

* * *

Hope was singing as she let herself into the little house in Victory Walk the next morning. However, one look at her aunt and uncle's faces let her know something was badly wrong. They were sitting at the kitchen table, mugs of cold tea and a pile of unopened post in front of them.

'What's happened?' she asked, dropping her bag and gas mask onto a chair then hurrying over to her aunt's side.

'The Germans have bombed Exeter,' Bert told her, his

expression grim. 'We heard it on the wireless. They said the damage is heavy and lots of people have been killed. I wanted to go to the factory, telephone the numbers we've been given for the Land Army and the Ministry of Agriculture to find out if our Daisy's all right, but Patty's in such a state I daren't leave her by herself.'

'Of course not,' Hope told him, putting her arm around her aunt and holding the trembling woman close. 'You go now and I'll look after her.'

He nodded, patted his wife's shoulder then hurried from the room. It was clear Patty was in shock, so Hope made a fresh pot of tea then added precious sugar from their store. If this wasn't an emergency, then she didn't know what was. 'I knew those headaches were telling me something,' Patty muttered.

***

Impatiently, Clover willed the London-bound train to go faster. Having worked nonstop for the past few days, all she wanted was to close her eyes and snatch some sleep before she reached home. However, the carriage was hot and noisy with servicemen smoking cigarettes and chewing gum. They tried turning on the charm, teasing her when she showed no interest. However, she was so exhausted she hardly noticed, for it had taken two days of pleading before she'd finally been granted leave.

Mrs Speedwell had been brusque, informing her that as their department was under extreme pressure all leave was cancelled, and it was only after she'd cited a family emergency that the woman had finally given in, begrudgingly granting her a one-day pass, which meant that, allowing for the inevitable delay to the trains, she would be lucky to have time for even a cup of tea at home before travelling back again. However, now, she was away from the Park, Clover wondered if she hadn't overreacted. To her mind the message she'd partially decoded had been clear enough, but suppose she'd made a mistake? Although, they weren't meant to use any information gleaned for personal use, many a Wren endeavoured to find out where their boyfriend's ship was so they could track them. Thankfully, she'd had time to write a letter home so would be expected. She'd have to play it by ear when she arrived, though, for having signed the OSA she didn't dare reveal what her work entailed.

Knowing her mother, she would be bustling around cooking one of her delicious stews or pies, and Clover's mouth watered in anticipation. The food at the Park might be plentiful but the quality left much to be desired. Thankfully, the soldiers left at the next station, replaced by a handful of civilians. As the train pulled away again, she sat back in her seat and tried to relax.

Clover had just begun to unwind when she felt eyes boring into her and, looking up, she caught the man opposite staring at her with a glazed look. She heard his ragged breathing then realized he was fondling himself through his trousers. Seeing her watching, he gave a smirk then blatantly opened his fly. Clover saw red.

'You should be ashamed of yourself, you pathetic

excuse of a man!' she burst out. 'And you can put that pitiful specimen away right this minute. I've seen bigger winkles on the fish stall in the market!'

The man flushed as red as the signal they were stopped at. Fumbling with his trousers, he jumped to his feet and fled from the compartment. There was a loud guffaw from the middle-aged woman sitting in the corner seat.

'Good for you, girl. Dirty old bugger! It's the uniform that does it, turns them on seeing a female wearing one.'

'Then it's a shame he doesn't don one himself and serve his country,' Clover retorted.

'Don't think the services would want the likes of that,' the woman replied. 'Ah, here we go,' she added as the train gave a lurch and started up again.

Moments later they were pulling into Euston Station and, nodding goodbye to the woman, Clover jumped onto the platform. Hardly noticing her surroundings, she pushed her way through the throng of people, anxious to get home as quickly as she could.

'Hi. Ma, it's me!' Clover called, letting herself into their little house in Victory Walk. It was good to be home no matter how briefly, she thought, even though, unusually, she couldn't detect the aroma of any baking or even dinner cooking.

Bursting through the door, she stopped dead at the sight of the dismal faces that greeted her.

'So, it's true then,' she said, without thinking. 'Has Exeter been badly hit?'

'How could you possibly know about that?' Patty

251

asked, rousing from her stupor to stare at Clover in disbelief. 'And what are you doing here?'

'People were talking about the latest bombings on the train,' she added, crossing her fingers behind her back, but her mother was too distraught to notice. 'I had leave owing and sent a letter the other day letting you know I was coming,' Clover replied quickly.

'Yes, look, Auntie, one of these letters is from Clover,' Hope said, flicking through the little pile of post on the table. 'I'll make some more tea,' she added, jumping to her feet as Clover bent to kiss Patty.

'Where's Pa?' Clover asked. 'Surely he hasn't gone to work at a time like this?'

'He's gone to the factory to use their telephone. Daisy left us contact numbers. Oh, I do hope she's all right!' Patty burst out. 'You don't expect this kind of thing to happen in the West Country, do you?'

'No, you don't,' Hope murmured, thinking how Ian's sister had taken his children to Dorset, believing they'd be safer there than in the East End. She wondered if he'd heard the news.

'Hitler is targeting our major cities; they're calling them the Baedeker raids,' Clover said without thinking.

'You seem to know a lot about all this, our Clover,' Patty remarked, staring at her through red, puffy eyes.

'I follow the new bulletins,' she replied. She really was going to have to watch what she said for her mother was no fool. However, right now her mother was too wrapped up in her misery to notice.

'Oh, where is Bert? Why is he taking so long?' Patty wailed, wringing her hands in her lap.

'Drink your tea, Auntie, and try not to fret. Uncle will be back as soon as he's found out something,' Hope told her.

'Supposing it's bad news?'

'But it could be good,' Clover told her. 'I see you've got bread. I'll make us something to eat.'

'I couldn't manage a thing,' Patty protested.

'You need to keep up your strength, Ma. Even if this brown-coloured bread is hard as heck,' Clover said. She wasn't hungry either, but if she kept busy, she couldn't put her foot in it.

They were attempting to nibble the inevitable paste sarnies and making inane conversation, all the while willing Bert to return with news, when Robbie burst through the door.

'We've been let off school early 'cos there's been more bombs dropped down the West Country and sir says he's got to check our fire precautions in case it happens again here,' he announced gleefully. Oblivious to the fact he was adding to his mother's misery, he stared at the plates of half-eaten food. 'I'm starving,' he announced. 'Oh, hello, Clover,' he said, noticing his big sister for the first time as he helped himself. 'Not ponky paste again!' he sighed.

'You should think yourself lucky to get that,' Patty snapped.

'What's up with everyone?' he asked, frowning as he took in their glum faces.

'Those bombs that were dropped hit Exeter and father's gone to check Daisy's all right,' Clover told him.

'But she's working on a farm, isn't she? Everyone knows they don't put the farms in the city. They put them out in the country.'

'Oh, Robbie,' Patty cried, ignoring his protests as she pulled him tight. 'Of course, that makes sense.'

'Course, I makes sense,' he replied, through a mouthful of bread. 'You forget I go to big school now.' He grinned, puffing out his chest. 'Can I go and play with Ricky?'

'When you've fed Snuffles,' Patty told him, the colour beginning to return to her cheeks. 'Why didn't we think of that?' she asked as he skipped outside.

A knock on the front door made them jump.

'Bert took his key – you don't think . . .' Patty began, her hand going to her heart as her voice trailed off.

'I'll see who it is,' Hope said, jumping to her feet then starting in surprise when she saw Ian on the doorstep.

'Oh, it's you. I'd forgotten you were coming,' she exclaimed.

'You certainly know how to make a man feel wanted,' he replied, looking put out. 'If it's not convenient, I can always go away again.'

'Sorry, Ian. We've just heard about the bombing of Exeter and Auntie and Uncle are worried sick about Daisy.'

'Of course, she's doing her Land Girl training there, isn't she?'

'Uncle's gone to the factory to use their telephone to see if he can find out anything because our public one's been out of action for weeks now. Still, as Robbie said, they don't put farms in the middle of cities, do they?'

'That's true. As long as she was on the farm at the time. Sorry, I shouldn't have said that,' he muttered, wincing as Hope gasped. 'Look, you obviously won't want to go out for afternoon tea now, and I need to make some enquiries of my own, so shall I call back later, or tomorrow even?' he asked, taking her hand and giving it a squeeze.

'Tomorrow would probably be better,' she admitted for she really couldn't think of anything other than Daisy at the moment. He nodded, gave her hand another squeeze.

'Try not to worry,' he murmured, before hurrying away.

She'd only just settled herself back on her chair when there was another knock on the door. This time it was Joy, and she was carrying a large bag.

'Guess what?' she cried. 'Old Mrs Hatchard who helps at the Red Cross remembered she had some cocktail dresses packed away in her loft. She used to wear them to dances after the Great War. Anyway, when she heard that Jane Bayliss was looking for material for the concert, she offered to let her have them. Look, Auntie, aren't they gorgeous?' she gushed, shaking out a satin dress in emerald green and then one in black velvet.

'Oh Joy, I'd forgotten you were coming round,' Hope cried.

'I know I said this morning, but I had to wait until Mrs Hatchard arrived for her shift,' she told them. 'You will help me alter them, won't you, Auntie?' Joy asked, looking beseechingly at Patty. Then she noticed her aunt's pale face and red-rimmed eyes and frowned. 'Is everything all right?'

'We hope so, Joy. That ruddy Hitler's gone and dropped some of his flaming bombs near where Daisy's training, and we're waiting to hear she's all right.'

'Oh crikey, and there's me bleating on about dresses! You should have stopped me.'

'That's all right, Joy, you weren't to know. Anyhow, now Robbie's kind of reassured us, so why don't you show us more of those lovely dresses? It will help take our mind off things while we wait for your uncle to come back and confirm that our Daisy is safe,' Patty suggested, making a supreme effort to smile. If she didn't have something else to focus on until Bert appeared, she'd go mad.

'Looks like we'll need more tea,' Clover said, returning from the back kitchen where she'd been washing up. 'Hello, Joy, it's good to see you. Going to be the star turn at the concert, I hear.'

'Hello, Clover, long time no see. Don't know about the star turn but it is exciting, although Mother doesn't approve. Still, I'm grown up now, so there's not much she can do about it.'

'I wouldn't be too sure about that, young lady,' Patty interjected. 'Now, as I said, it'll be good to keep busy, so let's take a proper look at these dresses.'

'Ooh yes, and you know how I want to look, Auntie, like Patty from the Andrews Sisters or perhaps Phyllis

Dixey. Now she really is something.' Joy gave a giggle that had Patty looking at her suspiciously. 'I just need to look glamorous,' she added quickly.

'Well, there's glamorous and then there's glamorous,' Patty replied, remembering how her niece had suggested she cut the neck of one of her tops lower. 'And we have to remember you're still quite young,' she added, ignoring Joy's pout. 'What happened to that blue cotton blouse of yours we updated?'

'That's all right for afternoons, Auntie, but I need something more alluring to captivate the audience at the concert.'

'Do you indeed?' Patty tutted. 'These dresses must have been expensive,' she added, feeling the material and studying the cut with a critical eye. 'So it would be criminal to mess about with them too much. We'll just adapt them to fit you. And looking at them, this Mrs Hatchard probably had a similar build to yours in her day. Although she must have been taller.'

'Actually, she's still quite stylish now that she's old,' Joy admitted.

Engrossed in their work, they lost track of time and jumped when the front door slammed. As Bert walked wearily into the room, they looked at him expectantly.

'It took ages, but I finally got through to the Ministry of Agriculture. Then they had to go away and make enquiries, which took even longer. However, they finally confirmed that the farm Daisy is training at wasn't hit by any of the blasts.'

'Thank heavens,' Patty murmured, her hand going to her heart.

257

'That's not all, love. When they managed to speak to Mr Penfold who owns the farm, he told them some of the Land Army girls had gone into Exeter for the Saturday night dance and hadn't returned that weekend.'

'Oh, merciful heavens!' Patty murmured, slumping back in her seat. 'And Daisy? Was she one of them?'

'He didn't know any names. Told them he needed to check with the warden. As soon as they have any definite news they'll telephone the factory. Mr Sutherland has promised to keep us informed. He said I was in no fit state to work and to come home and get some rest,' he added, looking exhausted as he sank into his chair.

'I'll make us some more tea,' Clover said, but Patty didn't respond. She was too busy berating herself.

What kind of mother was she that she could even think of looking at dress alterations when her youngest daughter could be lying injured or worse somewhere?

CHAPTER TWENTY-SIX

Rose hurried through the main doors of Homerton Hospital, anxious to get home as quickly as she could. Although it had been busy on the ward, as soon as the message from Clover regarding Daisy had been passed to her, she'd pleaded a family emergency and handed responsibility for the ward over to the capable staff nurse. She hoped to catch Clover on her way out but could see no sign of her. Making her way as fast as she could through streets thronging with people out enjoying the afternoon sunshine, she didn't notice the tall figure in front of her until they collided.

'Sorry,' she gasped. 'Oh, Mr Sutherland, I'm afraid I'm in a hurry to get home and wasn't watching where I was going.'

'Good afternoon, Miss Harrison – or I believe I should say Sister Harrison. Philip wrote about your promotion,' he added, seeing her surprise. 'Anyhow, I'm sure you've got more important things on your mind at the moment. I've just come from Victory Walk, as it happens. The Ministry of Agriculture telephoned the factory with news about your sister, and I promised to pass on the message.'

'Is Daisy safe?' she asked, staring at him anxiously.

'They are almost certain she was one of the Land

Girls tasked with looking after the animals, which means she would have been on the farm when the others went into the city. Regrettably, the outlook for them is bleak as they would undoubtedly have been caught up in that terrible bombing. One just hopes they had time to get to a shelter. However, speculation never helped anyone. Confirmation is being sought, and I've promised your parents I'll let them know as soon as I hear anything further, although your father insists that he'll be back at work tomorrow.'

'Thank you, Mr Sutherland. It's kind of you to go to so much trouble.'

'It's the least I can do. This terrible war is tearing enough families apart as it is, and frankly, it makes a change to pass on, if not confirmed good news, then at least hopeful information.' He smiled but Rose noticed the deep lines around his eyes and guessed he was under strain too. 'Still, we have that splendid news about Philip to cheer us, do we not?'

'You and Mrs Sutherland must be very happy.' Rose's heart felt like stone as she forced herself to utter the polite response. 'Has he set a date for the wedding yet?' she added, unable to resist asking, yet dreading to hear that he had.

'Well, I'm sure he would have written to you about that, my dear,' he replied, giving her a puzzled look.

'I haven't heard from him for a while,' she sighed. 'It was Mrs Sutherland who told me about the Earl of Edmonton's daughter.'

'Ah yes. Charming girl, in the WAAF with Charlotte. She brought her home when they were last on leave.'

'Is that when Philip met her?' Rose asked.

'I don't think they've ever met. Philip hasn't been home in ages as you know. No, I was referring to his promotion. Hope I haven't put my foot in it,' he added, seeing her expression. 'Knowing my son he was probably waiting to tell you in person, so I'd be obliged if you could pretend you don't know when he does impart his news. I'm afraid I already spend too much time in the doghouse at home, if you get my meaning. Anyhow, I won't keep you any longer, you must be eager to see your family.'

Adrenaline pumping through her, Rose continued on her way, her thoughts racing as fast as her footsteps. Relief flooded through her that Daisy was almost certainly safe. She knew enough about the red tape governing the 'powers that be' to know they wouldn't have intimated her sister was all right without some pretty strong evidence, although until they received official confirmation, they couldn't be a hundred per cent sure. She could only guess at the anguish her parents had been through and was pleased that Clover had been able to get a pass home. She crossed the road, oblivious to the bus that was turning the corner.

'Careful, love,' a voice called. She nodded her thanks, but her mind was still on Philip. So he wasn't – how had Mrs Sutherland phrased it? – affianced to the Earl of Edmonton's daughter after all. It seemed her mother's suspicions that the woman had been meddling were correct. Her spirits soared to the white fluffy clouds above and she could have yelled out loud in delight. Thank heavens she'd written to him after all, she thought, as she let herself into the family home.

'Rose!' her mother cried, jumping to her feet and throwing her arms around her. 'Clover said she'd leave a message at the hospital on her way to the station. We've been that worried about our Daisy, but Mr Sutherland called in . . .'

'I know, Ma,' Rose interjected, cuddling her mother close. 'I bumped into him on my way home and he told me the news. Goodness, when did you last eat, you're all bones?'

'Well then, I'll suit those new utility clothes they're selling now. They're close-fitting with not an inch of spare material to them,' Patty replied, giddy with the relief of knowing her youngest daughter was almost certainly safe. Although, truthfully, she would only rest easy when she knew for sure. 'I'd best get some food on the go. Your father's out in the yard helping Robbie mend Snuffle's cage. That rabbit considers himself a right Houdini and no mistake. With Clover on her way back to BP and Hope out for afternoon tea with Ian MacLeod, there'll only be the four of us. Of course, neither of them would leave here until Mr Sutherland called and told us he thought our Daisy was on the farm when the bombs fell. I know she hasn't been a Land Girl for long, but they're bound to grant her leave to come home now, aren't they?' she asked, looking hopefully at Rose.

'I don't know, Ma, we'll just have to hope so. Now, you sit down again and I'll rustle up something to eat. You need to take care after the nasty shock you've had.'

'Yes, Sister Harrison,' Patty quipped, but did as she'd

been told for in truth, she was still feeling a bit shaky. 'Fancy you bumping into Mr Sutherland like that.'

'It was fortunate, though, Ma, because apart from the news about Daisy, he told me Philip has never even *met* the Earl of Edmonton's daughter. Apparently, she's a WAAF friend of Charlotte.'

'And Mrs La-di-da fancies a titled daughter-in-law, no doubt. I told you she was trying to cause trouble, didn't I?'

'Yes, Ma, you did, and I'm so pleased I wrote that letter to Philip.'

'I said he was a decent young man who would never treat you shabbily. You shouldn't always take people at face value, our Rose. With a mother-in-law like you'll have in Mrs Sutherland, you'll need to be on your guard.'

But Rose couldn't give a fig about a silly old woman like Philip's mother because Philip *hadn't* met someone else. He was still hers. They might not be engaged but they did have an understanding, and although it was some time ago, memories of that time they'd spent together in Canterbury still had the power to send tingles down her spine. All she needed now was to hear from him, receive definite confirmation that Daisy was safe, then she'd truly be happy.

CHAPTER TWENTY-SEVEN

'Listen up, Mandy and Daisy, Mr Penfold has received telephone calls from both the Ministry of Agriculture and the Land Army enquiring about your welfare,' Mrs Rattery told them. 'I was able to confirm both of yers was on the farm when the bombs went off, so at least they know yer safe, and will relay that information to yer families. As for the others, there's been reports of so many casualties, we still have to wait and see,' she said, her eyes misting.

'But did they say anything about sending replacements? I can't run this place with just two if the others don't come back,' 'Arris said, coming through from the other room where he'd been having his supper. Daisy and Mandy stared at him in dismay, wondering how he could be so callous.

'Obviously, I hopes they're all right,' he said quickly, 'but this is a training farm, with girls coming and going all the time. Them animals still needs looking after whatever 'appens and luckily yer two are contracted here until the end of yer training,' he muttered.

'We'll worry about getting new girls if and when we need to,' the warden told him firmly. 'In the meantime, Mr Penfold has offered the use of his telephone if either of yer girls wish to contact yer families.'

'Good idea,' Mandy said, brightening slightly.

'We don't have a telephone at home,' Daisy said, thinking how nice it would have been to hear her ma's voice or, even better, Freddy's. That image of him looming over her, false or otherwise, had made her remember how much she missed him and how long it was since she'd heard from him. Even knowing it was usual these days for letters to take an age to get through, if they arrived at all, did little to pacify her.

'Well, then, Daisy, they'll be that worried, perhaps yer best sends them a telegram,' Mrs Rattery suggested.

'Ma'll have kittens if she sees the telegram boy on her doorstep. She'll think something's happened to Peter, my brother. He's in the army, you see. I'll write a letter tonight.'

'Well, yer'd both better go and get on with yer call and letter and I'll clear up here. Then I suggest we all get an early night. God knows, I'm tired and there'll be the milkin' to do first thing. I know we can rely on yer girls to help us until we hear about the others. Then, hopefully, the old Aggy will send us more helpers if need be. It might seem heartless to yer town girls for us to be thinking like that, but the ways of the country have to be practical by necessity. It don't mean we don't have feelings, though. I always gets quite fond of me girls.' Her voice broke, and she turned quickly away.

Daisy would have loved nothing better than to go home and see her parents rather than write to them, especially as she wasn't sure she'd feel like staying on at the farm if the worst had happened to the others.

But whatever the case was, even if she wanted to leave, she couldn't until she'd finished her training. Besides, it wouldn't be fair to walk away and leave Mrs Rattery and 'Arris in the lurch. Once again it seemed that, through no fault of her own, people were relying on her to stay in her job.

* * *

'Alone at last,' Ian sighed.

Hope stared around the busy café filled with people enjoying their afternoon tea, while the waitresses scurried between tables balancing trays to the background hiss of the coffee machine.

'If this is your idea of being alone then you have very funny ones, Ian MacLeod,' she chuckled, then looked mortified. However, their laughter released the pent-up tension of the past few days, so that by the time the waitress came to take their order, they were relaxed and ready for their refreshment.

'Any more news of Daisy?' Ian asked. Hope shook her head.

'Uncle went into work as usual, but we hadn't heard anything further by the time I left. Luckily, Joy is keeping Auntie busy adapting an evening dress for the concert. It's so gorgeous, I'm almost tempted to offer to do a song myself,' she told him, picking up the pot and pouring their tea.

'You sing?' Ian asked.

'I'd be good in the chorus,' she replied. 'The cats' chorus, that is.'

266

'Surely not?'

'Yep, Joy was head of the queue when singing voices were dished out and I was the last. Anyway, you can hear for yourself when you come to the concert at the weekend. It's going to be such fun, first the cinema then the concert in the evening.'

'I'm afraid I won't be here, Hope. I've managed to get an emergency pass and leave for Dorset first thing in the morning,' he said quietly.

Hope stared at him in dismay, their cups of tea and shared teacake with its scraping of margarine cooling on the table before them.

'You mean you're going tomorrow?' Hope frowned as she focussed on the steamed-up window behind him to stop her disappointment from showing.

'I have to, Hope. I know the children are safe, but Devon is the next county along, and those bombs going off in Exeter have shaken me. Oh, I know it's nothing like the scare you've all had about Daisy, and I sincerely hope Mr and Mrs Harrison receive the confirmation of her safety very soon. It's hard to explain the responsibility you feel as a parent, but the need to physically see my children is gnawing away at me. My boss has granted me two days leave provided I make up the time at the weekend, and Sonia has been understanding, although your colleagues at the depot might not be so amenable when they don't get a decent hot meal.'

He smiled and reached across to take her hand, but she ignored him. All she heard was Sonia, Sonia, Sonia. He'd obviously had the time to go and see her before thinking about Hope. That they got on well, she knew, and Sonia was nearer his age, so perhaps he'd be better suited going out with her. It struck her that it wasn't the first time she'd had these thoughts. Finally, she looked directly at him only to discover he was watching her intently, a puzzled expression on his face.

'I know it's a lot to ask, especially when we already have plans to go to see a film before going on to the concert, but could you be patient for just a while longer?'

'You mean you want me to stay indoors on my days off?' she cried.

'No, of course not, Hope. I'm not that mean. You are very attractive and, frankly, I never cease to be amazed that you should even want to go out with me.'

'Except you never seem to be here long enough for us to actually *go* anywhere. Well, after the Red Cross concert there is to be a dance in the hall. Kitty tells me it will be attended by men from the forces, including GIs, so you needn't worry I'll be lonely. If you think about me at all, that is!' she cried, getting to her feet so hastily her chair almost toppled over. Then, heedless of the stares from the customers at the other tables and the bewildered proprietress, she fled outside.

'Hope!' She heard Ian's shout, his footsteps hurrying after her, but resolutely ignored him.

Determined to lose him, and using the shoppers in the market, and the workers leaving the local factory after their shift as cover, she threaded her way through the crowds, running on until she reached the sanctuary of the Downs. Did he really think she had nothing better to do than wait around, ready for when he was available? Except he wasn't like that was he, her conscience nagged. Ignoring the misshapen trees and craters caused by the bombing where chickweed and purple buddleia now sprouted as if in defiance, she threw herself down onto the grass and stared up at the clouds scudding across the sky. When she was younger, she used to imagine the shapes were dogs, or sheep, once even a dragon with a pointy tail, but she had no enthusiasm for such games today.

As her temper cooled, she realized she'd over-reacted and she began to feel ashamed of her outburst. Was it really surprising that, after the bombings, a father should want to see his children? And would she think so much of him if he didn't? Goodness only knows, the news about her sister had upset her enough.

But it wasn't that he'd deferred their trip to the cinema that had upset her. It was the fact that Sonia Strang had entered their conversation once again. To be fair, he was a good worker so was it really unreasonable that, as station manager, she tried to accommodate his irregular hours? The clouds were thickening now and as she watched they formed into the shape of a monster – all it needed were green eyes, she thought, realizing now that the cause of her outburst had been jealousy. She had been that monster with the green eyes, she realized, shame washing over her. It was she who'd been unreasonable, and it was time she started behaving in a more mature way.

She needed to find Ian and apologize for her behaviour. Jumping to her feet she began retracing her steps.

She couldn't let him go to Dorset with bad feeling between them. Especially as these days nobody knew where or when the next bomb would fall. Then she saw his rangy figure loping towards her and her heart flipped.

'Oh, Ian, I'm so sorry . . .' she began

'Hope, I'm sorry . . .'

Laughing nervously, they both came to a halt and stood there looking uncertain.

'Ladies first,' he said, his clear blue eyes staring solemnly into hers.

'I just wanted to say I'm sorry for my outburst, it was unforgivable,' she murmured, shame washing over her again. 'Of course, you must go and see your children. We can go to the cinema another time – that is, if you still want to. And I really don't mind staying in until you get back.' Her words all came out in a rush and, apart from the rustling of leaves, there was silence as she stood waiting for him to answer. He shook his head then sat down on the grass, patting the space beside him.

'But that's just it, Hope,' he began when she was seated next to him, 'I don't want you not to go out and have fun when I'm away. You're young and should be enjoying yourself,' he declared, plucking blades of grass and twisting them together.

'Too young for you?' she couldn't resist asking. He frowned and shook his head.

'Surely it's more the fact I'm too old for you?'

'You mean you're more Sonia's age?' That monster on her shoulder just wouldn't be silenced.

'Well, yes, I am, but I'm not going out with her, am I?' he replied.

'Perhaps you would prefer to – after all, you're always talking about her,' she retorted, any pretence of being calm and mature disappearing. To her surprise, he burst out laughing.

'Is that what this is all about? Honestly, Hope, I admit I admire Sonia for the splendid job she does overseeing everything at the depot, but it's you I love, you idiot.'

'Oh!' she squeaked, trying to digest everything he'd said. 'You – you love me?'

He took her hand, then looked earnestly at her.

'Yes, I do. I thought you realized that? And when this damn war is over, I'm hoping we might get together properly. However, life is too precarious and uncertain to make concrete plans at the moment, especially with the children away, so if you're prepared to put up with my family commitments and long working hours, Hope Potter, you would make me a very happy fellow.'

'Now I know you don't have any other love interest than your children, who I'm dying to really get to know better, I'd be happy to accept, Ian MacLeod.'

'Then please take this as a token of my future intent,' he said, lifting her left hand and placing the grass he'd plaited into a ring onto her finger.

As his lips came down on hers, she felt warm and fuzzy, that green-eyed monster having finally disappeared. Now she knew where she stood, she could put up with only seeing him when his commitments allowed. The news about Daisy had made her realize how fragile life could be. And when this dreadful war was finally over, they would have the rest of their lives to spend together, to make a home. She'd be the best mother to his children and, hopefully, they'd have a couple of their own. Her mind buzzed in time to the beating of her heart as she pictured it all . . . In the meantime, though, their engagement would be their secret.

CHAPTER TWENTY-EIGHT

Patty looked around her neat kitchen and sighed with satisfaction. Since Bert had come home with the news that Daisy was definitely safe, she'd felt full of pent-up energy and this morning had given the downstairs a good clean and tidy. She'd even got round to opening the post which had lain on the table these past few days. One letter was for Daisy which she would forward to Devon, although she was still harbouring the hope that, after the terrible bombings, she would be able to come home for a few days. The other was from Mr Moreton, telling her the sale of the shop had been finalized earlier than anticipated. He thanked her for her loyal services, told her she was no longer required to go into the shop, but mercifully had paid her until the end of next month. Obviously, she'd need to look for a new job, but this morning Joy was coming round for the final fitting of the dress she was to wear for the concert.

She was just putting the kettle to boil when the back door opened and in came Vera followed by Joy. As Patty smiled in welcome, she couldn't help noticing her sister was looking drawn and that her blouse and skirt were loose on her.

'I hope this new dress you're making for our Joy is respectable,' she greeted Patty.

'And good morning to you too, Vera,' Patty replied. 'And you, Joy,' she added, noticing the set of her niece's lips. 'Kettle won't be long so make yourselves comfortable.'

'Terrible thing about those bombs. Who'd have thought your Daisy would be in danger down in the West Country. We were pleased to hear that she's safe, though,' Vera added. 'Mind you, Arthur says nowhere is safe now. Apparently, Hitler's bombing our major cities in retaliation for us bombing his. Course, I couldn't ask any questions because he was straight off out after his tea again. Hardly see him these days. And when he's in all he talks about is this blessed war, if he talks at all, that is.' She sniffed.

'I expect he's busy,' Patty said. 'Let's look at your dress, while we're waiting for the kettle,' she suggested, shooting her niece a sympathetic look. Carefully removing it from the paper she'd covered it in, she spread it out on the table, marvelling again at the sumptuous material.

'Just as I thought – that neck's too low!' Vera snapped.

'I agree it is at the moment,' Patty replied. 'However, as the dress was too long for today's look, I've cut some lace from the bottom flounce and turned it into a modesty panel. Inserted like so,' she said, carefully tucking it inside the neckline, 'it does what is intended and looks quite charming, even if I do say so myself.'

'Gosh, Auntie, you're a genius!' Joy told her, beaming delightedly. 'Phyllis Dixey eat your heart out.'

'Now I know you're happy, I'll just finish off sewing

it into the neckline. Oh, there's the kettle – perhaps one of you could make the tea.'

While Joy poured water into the teapot, Patty threaded her needle.

'How long will it take to finish that? Only we've got to be at the Red Cross centre by noon. A large consignment of tins and commodities have arrived and Robin wants them packing into boxes today, although she says the number of socks and scarves she's receiving have dwindled.'

'I must admit, what with hearing about Daisy and the shop closing, I haven't been very productive myself. However, as soon as I've finished Joy's dress, I'll pick up my needles and get knitting again,' Patty promised.

'You can always come and help pack boxes if you've got time on your hands,' Vera suggested. 'We need more volunteers now that some think it's more important to prepare for their show than help out.'

'Oh, Ma, you know we're only putting in extra rehearsals until after the concert. Mrs Bayliss says . . .'

'Mrs Bayliss!' Vera scoffed. 'As I've said before, she's no more married than you are. And the way she acts around men, well it's . . .' She sniffed, her voice trailing off as if she thought better of what she'd intended saying.

'Well, the concert will raise much-needed funds for the Red Cross,' Joy told her, and Patty thought no one could argue with that. Her niece had grown in confidence and was coming out of her shell. With her blonde hair gleaming and eyes shining, she looked charming. Patty couldn't wait to see her all dressed up and, modesty panel or not, knew she would look stunning.

'So do you know what the greengrocer's is going to be?' Vera asked when, dress finished and admired, they were sipping their drinks.

'Mr Moreton never said in his letter. He's paid me until the end of next month so at least that will give me time to look around.'

'I suppose you'll look for more shop work,' Vera said. Hearing her condescending tone, Patty felt herself rebel.

'Not necessarily. I might look for something more worthwhile. Hope was saying they needed someone at the depot to cook decent hot meals. Apparently, the one they had was useless so poor Ian MacLeod has been filling in, but he has work commitments.'

'Funny way of carrying on if you ask me. I thought he drove the ambulances in his spare time?'

'I gather the change in shifts was an issue. Anyway, I do enough cooking here, I'm not sure I'd want to take on any more.'

'You could do dressmaking, Auntie. You've made a lovely job of my dress and those adaptations you did on Ma's clothes looked very professional.'

'Not that your father noticed.' Vera sniffed again, and Patty was tempted to ask if she needed a hand-kerchief, but seeing her sister's expression, refrained.

'I'm sure Arthur did notice. He always seems atten-tive,' she said instead.

'Yes, but who to?' Vera snapped. 'Anyway, it's time

we were off. Duty calls,' she said, gathering up her bag before Patty could comment.

'Thank you for altering that outfit, Auntie. I think you'd make a wonderful dressmaker,' Joy said, kissing her cheek.

'And I think you'll make a wonderful singer at the concert. We'll see you both on Saturday,' she told them as Vera bustled out of the back door.

While Patty cleared away their tea things, she couldn't help wondering what was up with her sister. Clearly, there was something very wrong and yet, although she made enough barbed remarks about Arthur, she clearly didn't want to discuss the situation. Oh well, there wasn't anything she could do. All couples went through their bad patches and matters between husband and wife were private, unless they wished to share anything.

Besides, Patty had her own problem. She might have been paid until the end of next month, but she still needed to find another job. Robbie had gone through his school shoes, and she'd already let down his trousers as much as she could. Scarcity of fabric and materials in general had pushed up the prices of everything. In the meantime, perhaps she would volunteer at the Red Cross centre. It would be good to do something worthwhile as well as mix with other people. She missed the chatter of her customers and the feeling of being useful outside the home. The extra vegetables had come in handy too, she thought, mentally assessing what she had in the larder for dinner and wondering if she'd have to go out to the shops.

Kitchen clean again, she'd just settled down with her knitting needles, when the rattle of the letterbox announced the arrival of the lunchtime post and Patty hurried to see what had been delivered. Her spirits rose when she saw the envelope addressed in Daisy's neat handwriting and she hurried back to the living room to read it.

The letter had obviously been written in a hurry and whilst it was a relief to know Daisy was safe, it was evident that until they knew what had happened to the other Land Girls, she had responsibilities to help with the chores on the farm and wouldn't be coming home any time soon. Still, at least her girl was unhurt, Patty thought, saying a prayer for the others. The effects of this war were devastating. Surely, it couldn't last much longer? But then they'd been saying that for nearly three years now.

She'd just picked up her knitting again when there was a knock at the door. Sighing, she went to answer it, then gasped and nearly fainted when she saw the telegram boy standing on the step.

***

'Are you sure you're up to going to the concert, love?' Bert asked, putting down his paper and looking anxiously at Patty.

She sat back in her chair, knitting resting on her knee.

'Yes, Bert. I can't deny it was a huge shock getting that telegram the other day. Being a prisoner of war is

278

bad, but at least we know our Peter is alive, even if he is in some Godforsaken country.'

'Well, Italy is in the Mediterranean so we can only hope he's getting some decent sunshine as well as being looked after. Anyhow, as long as you're all right.'

'It was a bit much coming straight after that scare about Daisy – and we still don't know if the other Land Girls have been found.'

'It's not looking good,' Bert sighed. 'The report here said that over one hundred and fifty deaths have been reported so far and there are bound to be more.'

'Bloody, bloody war!' Patty cried, dashing a tear from her eye. She hadn't cried since she'd received the telegram, and she was blowed if she'd give Hitler that satisfaction now.

'Are you swearing, Ma?' Robbie asked, eyes wide with disbelief.

'I'm ashamed to say I am, Robbie. Take no notice of me, it's this war getting to me. And wipe your feet on the mat, I've just cleaned that floor.'

'Ricky says the Eyeties are good at painting and stuff so maybe Peter will come back a famous artist or sculptor or something then he won't have to be in the army anymore. I'm starving, what's for tea?'

'As it's Saturday we're having a treat. How does Welsh Rarebit sound?' Patty said, getting to her feet. 'We'll be eating early as we're going to see Joy sing in the concert, so you go and wash – properly, mind, none of yer lick and promise stuff.'

'Only doing my duty for the country by saving on

279

soap,' Robbie quipped, then seeing his father's expression, quickly vanished into the back kitchen.

'It will do us good to get dressed up,' Patty said as she began cutting bread from the dark-grain loaf. 'I haven't been out since . . .'

'Fiona came to your rescue after she saw the telegram boy cycling away.'

'Yes,' she sighed. 'I might grumble about the nosiness of the neighbours round here sometimes, but there's no denying I was pleased she was looking out of the window of the nursing home just then. She said she was coming here anyway to ask me to let Daisy know Mr Rathbone has been sent home. He'll always have a slight limp but at least he can get around without crutches now.'

'Some good news at last.' Bert smiled. 'Let's hope the tide is turning,' he added before disappearing behind his newspaper again.

CHAPTER TWENTY-NINE

The hall was bustling when they arrived, everyone dressed in their smartest outfits, keen to support a good cause.

'Coo-ee, over here!' Patty peered through the fug of cigarette smoke to see Vera waving her programme at them. She began making her way towards her, only to be stopped by people enquiring after Peter.

'I see the *Homerton Herald* has done its job,' Bert whispered as finally they settled into their seats next to Vera and Arthur in the front row.

'Hope sends her love and says she's hoping to finish her shift early so she can come along,' Patty told Vera as the lights were dimmed and an expectant hush fell.

An elegant lady, her auburn hair swept up in a French pleat, and wearing an emerald floor-length sheath dress welcomed them. She went on to explain that as the concert was to raise funds for the Red Cross, they needn't feel any donation was too large to be appreciated. After waiting for the ensuing laughter to die down she went on to introduce the first act, a juggler, who was followed by the local primary school children singing 'A Song for Maytime', accompanied on the piano by their teacher. After a comedy skit, Joy was introduced, and as the strains of 'Don't Sit Under the Apple Tree' rose to the rafters, everybody joined in.

'That's my darling Joy! Doesn't she look lovely?' Vera cried.

She certainly did and Patty couldn't help feeling proud that the dress she'd adapted for her niece fitted so well. Then Jane Bayliss took to the stage.

'The next song is called "Lili Marlene" and it was originally written by a young soldier as a poem to his girlfriend. Ladies and Gentlemen, please give another big hand to our very talented vocalist, Joy Potter.'

Joy smiled, waited until the applause had died down then began to sing. She put everything she had into the song, and as the haunting lyrics filled the room you could have heard a pin drop. When she finally drew to a close there was silence followed by deafening applause. As a cry of encore rang out, Jane Bayliss rejoined Joy on the stage.

'Isn't she marvellous?' Bert asked, turning to Arthur.

'Absolutely amazing,' he replied, but to Bert's consternation he was staring in wonder at Jane Baylisss and not at his daughter.

Whilst refreshments were being served and raffle tickets sold, Vera was in her element with many people stopping to congratulate her on Joy's performance. Patty was sipping her tea, listening to the compliments, when she felt a tap on her arm.

'You have a very talented niece, Mrs Harrison. She is literally a joy to have working with us. Forgive me,' she added, seeing Patty frown. 'I'm known as Robin and run the operation here for the Red Cross parcels.'

'Nice to meet you, Robin, and please call me Patty.'

'Well, Patty, I understand your son is a prisoner of war. You have my every sympathy, and believe you me, I know how you feel. However, at times like these I feel to actually be doing something helps. Oh, I'm not suggesting you join us packing boxes – although we do need all the helpers we can get and you'd be most welcome. I was thinking more along the lines of letting you know the process for sending parcels and letters to your son – Peter, isn't it?'

'Yes, it is. We understand he's in a camp in Italy.'

'Well, things do get sent there, but there are rules and regulations. However, by adhering to them, you are ensuring he has the best chance of receiving the things you send.'

'Thank you. My sister volunteers at the centre and seems to know everything,' Patty told her, inclining her head to where Vera was now holding court.

'Ah yes, Vera – she does like to share her knowledge.' The woman's nut-brown eyes twinkled. 'If you'd like to call by when you have a moment, I'd be happy to go through my list with you so that you can get things dispatched quickly.'

'Why thank you, Robin, I'd appreciate that. I'll call in on Monday morning.'

'I'll see you then. Now I must circulate. People have been so generous both with their time and their donations. It's most gratifying.' With one last smile, she slipped away only to be waylaid by a crowd of well-wishers.

'Well, that was a nice evening, and didn't our Joy do well? She's becoming quite the young lady,' Patty said, tucking her arm through Bert's as they strolled through the streets of Dalston and turned into Victory Walk. Bert, lost in thought, muttered something non-committal.

'It's a shame Hope couldn't join us; she must have been on a call out. Still, I'm seeing Robin on Monday. She runs the Red Cross centre and has offered to tell me exactly what we can send to Peter.' Feeling the tears well up at the thought of her elder son, she dashed them angrily away. She would *not* cry. 'I'll feel better when I'm doing something for him. Did you hear me, Bert?'

'What? Oh yes, of course,' he mumbled, his mind on Arthur. He just couldn't get the image of the way he'd been staring at Jane Bayliss out of his mind. He'd looked infatuated with the woman. 'Where's young Robbie got to?' he asked to cover his lack of attention.

'He and Ricky got bored so left after their lemonade and biscuit. He promised to be home before it got dark, which, thinking about it, gives him plenty of leeway,' she laughed, staring up at the evening sky which was streaked with crimson and orange. 'Let's hope this fine weather is an omen for better things to come,' she added, crossing her fingers and sending her love winging across the sea. *Stay safe and come home soon, son,* she whispered.

* * *

Music While You Work was playing on the wireless as Patty entered the Red Cross centre on Monday morning. It was busy with volunteers packing tins and knitted garments into boxes.

'Coo-ee, over here!' Vera called when she caught sight of her.

'Hello, Auntie Patty,' Joy called and waved.

'Morning, Joy and congratulations again on such a super performance on Saturday. You looked stunning and sang beautifully. I was very proud of you.' Her niece beamed.

'I've come to see Robin,' Patty explained.

'No need to bother her,' Vera scoffed. 'I know as much as she does and have a better way of packing.'

'Except you have to take everything out and repack them,' Joy trilled.

'Ah, Patty, how nice you could come,' Robin said suddenly appearing beside them. 'I know you offered to help, Vera, but the packing of personal items for a relative is slightly different, so if you'll excuse us, I'll just explain how everything needs to be done,' the woman said, neatly guiding Patty into her tiny and very cluttered office. Catching sight of her sister's outraged expression, Patty had to smother a grin. She really couldn't stand being left out of things.

'Do take a seat,' the woman said, indicating the chair by a desk snowed under with piles of papers that threatened to topple over. 'Forgive the mess – there are always more important things to attend to than filing. Now, here is a list of items you're permitted to send to your son. It's wise to adhere to this as all boxes will be checked at the Next-of-Kin Processing Centre in Finsbury Park, before being rewrapped and transported across Europe. There they will be checked and censored by the Italians before being sent on to the appropriate camp.'

'Goodness, I had no idea it was such a complicated process. Let me write all this down,' Patty said, searching in her bag for a pencil.

There was a knock at the door, but before Robin could answer, Vera appeared.

'Oh, you needn't write anything down,' she said, seeing Patty furiously scribbling. 'There's nothing I can't tell you.'

'Thank you, Vera, but as we've already established the packing of next-of-kin parcels is slightly different to what we do here, so if there's nothing else?' She quirked her brow then waited.

'Er, no. It's just that I know you're so busy and . . .'

'Must get on,' Robin interjected. 'Thank you, Vera. We won't be much longer.'

Knowing she was beaten, Vera stalked out of the office, and Patty could only marvel at the way the tiny woman handled her forceful sister.

'Now, where were we?' Robin asked. 'Ah yes, you may send four parcels to a next of kin per year, although you can write as often as you like. However, letters must be sent separately, have no enclosures and cover no more than two sides of notepaper. These too will be censored for any sensitive information. Also enclosed will be the *Prisoner of War* magazine, supplied by the Red Cross. I'll show you a copy if I can find one,' she

286

added, scrabbling through the pile of papers that teetered even more precariously. 'Ah, here it is,' she said triumphantly. Patty couldn't help thinking it would be quicker in the long run if everything was tidied away, but Robin was already on to the next thing.

'You can get extra coupons to buy clothes to send. Pyjamas are especially needed, along with undergarments, bootlaces and pencils. Now, unless you have any questions, I'll let you get on as I'm sure you'll want to pack and send Peter a parcel as soon as possible.'

'Indeed, I do,' Patty said, jumping to her feet. 'Thank you for all your help, I'm most grateful. You were right when you said I'd feel better knowing I was doing something to help Peter.'

'You are most welcome – and don't hesitate to ask if you need any further help.'

'Thank you.' Patty smiled, got to her feet then hesitated. 'Erm, I was wondering if I could do something for you in return? The shop I was working in has just been sold and I've been let go, leaving me with plenty of time on my hands, so I could come back and sort out your papers if that would help.'

'How kind, but I couldn't possibly impose and, regrettably, there is no funding to pay any sort of wage.' Although Robin protested, Patty had seen her eyes light up at the prospect.

'I would be pleased to do it and certainly wouldn't want payment.'

'Well, if you're sure, then thank you. Just one thing,' she said as Patty finally made to leave. 'Your sister is very . . . er . . . enthusiastic and likes to know everything that goes on here. However, some of these papers contain names and addresses, that kind of thing and . . .'

'Don't worry, Robin. My lips are sealed,' Patty assured her.

'Actually, I wanted to check that everything's all right with your sister. Vera's always been excitable but recently, well, she seems to get agitated very quickly. She was quite rude to poor Jane Bayliss recently. Working closely with people, you get to know their personalities quite well, and I wondered if there might be something wrong at home perhaps?'

'I know she's finding it difficult living in that tiny flat for such a long time. The authorities have so many properties to repair, it's taking longer than she thought.'

'I can understand that would be frustrating, but I can't help thinking it goes deeper than that. Perhaps I'm imagining things . . .' Robin sighed. 'Anyway, I just thought I'd mention it in case we can help in any way.'

'That's kind, and I'll let you know if I hear anything.'

'Good. No doubt she's agog to hear what we've been discussing, so if you want to use the back door, then feel free,' she offered, gesturing to the exit sign beside her desk.

As Patty hurried home to fill in the forms for extra clothing coupons for Peter, she couldn't help thinking Robin was probably right about her sister. She'd discuss it with Bert when he came home from work, see if Arthur had said anything.

* * *

Joy was walking down Victory Walk when she bumped into Hope coming the other way.

'Hey, stranger,' she called.

'I'm so sorry I didn't make it to your concert, but we were called out to a medical emergency. Auntie told me you were the hit of the evening, well done you.'

'Thank you, but everyone else was good too, and we raised a fair amount for the Red Cross which is the main thing. I just popped in to see Auntie and give her a candy bar as a little thank you for altering my dress.'

'Candy bar?' Hope asked.

'That's chocolate to you, English girl,' Joy chuckled. 'You want to get yourself a GI boyfriend, they have supplies of nylons, lipstick and candy, and are happy to share, if you get my meaning,' she winked.

'And you're friendly with these GIs, I take it.'

'Of course, silly. There are lots of them at the American Eagle Club and I go there quite often, now. Look, I can't stop, I'm meeting Jane. She's got a new song for me to rehearse. She thinks I'll soon be good enough to sing at the club! It's so exciting, Eagle Club one day, and then . . . who knows!' She gave another chuckle. 'See you, sis.'

'Joy . . .' Hope began but her sister was already tottering down the road in a tight skirt and a pair of high heels she'd never seen before. Hope frowned. Until recently her little sister wouldn't have said boo to a goose, now she was mixing with American soldiers. She didn't want to be a killjoy, but she was worried

Joy might be getting out of her depth. Perhaps she should pay a visit to her mother and see if she had noticed any change in her sister's behaviour, and if she knew where she was spending her free time. Although recently her mother had seemed preoccupied, with not much time for anyone else.

CHAPTER THIRTY

The ambulance crews stood in horrified silence as their supervisor briefed them for their next job.

'Although there have been no bombings recently, the hot summer weather and traffic vibration has caused more unexploded bombs to go off,' Sonia Strang told them. 'This time, an entire block of flats on the outskirts of Homerton has been demolished and casualties are high. The Bomb Disposal Crew, the sappers, have been deployed to check for any more explosives. To help you identify them, their army trucks are canvas-covered, with distinctive red-painted mudguards and the men wear denims, not their khaki uniforms, to dig out the bombs.

'Now, it's my duty to warn you that although your services are badly needed, the risk to life is high and you are under no obligation. Anyone wishing to leave may do so now.' She paused, but they were all dedicated to helping others and nobody moved.

As she went on to give details of location and responsibilities, Hope felt her heart sink. Would there ever be an end to the consequences of this infernal war, she wondered, feeling in her pocket for the little purse where she kept the grass ring Ian had given her, and which she always kept on her, in order to feel close to him. Her heart flopped as she recalled the last time a bomb had exploded, causing the damage to his sister's house which led to her taking his children to Dorset. Was he there now?

'Right, everyone. Remember, do everything the authorities ask of you. They will have assessed the situation and you risking your own lives will help no one. This is not going to be an easy mission, but as I said, your services are badly needed. Good luck, everyone.'

Hope jumped into the driving seat, pleased she was rostered with Kitty. For all her exuberance, the girl was dedicated to her job and they worked well together.

'Crikey, fancy going to bed then waking up to find your home collapsed on top of you?' she muttered as Hope double declutched and followed the leading ambulance out of the depot, then turned into the street out of town. 'Or even not waking up at all.'

Expert now at avoiding the potholes, Hope put her foot down, studiously ignoring the crowds heading for the underground on their way to work, who stared curiously as the fleet of ambulances screamed by. She did glimpse one woman grabbing hold of her collar and guessed she wouldn't release it until she saw a dog, in the unlikely hope that the old wife's tale would help save the victims.

However, all such thoughts faded as they neared the edge of Homerton and saw dark plumes of smoke rising into the air minutes before they arrived at the scene of the disaster.

'Blimey, the whole row's gone, and them houses over there have been damaged as well!' Kitty gasped, her eyes wide with horror as they stared around at the vast mounds of burning rubble that had once been a large block of flats. 'No bugger could survive this, surely?'

Further along they spotted the sappers in blue carefully digging down into the debris. Where should she go? Hope wondered.

However, an ARP approached, signalling them to drive to the far end of the street, where casualties were being tended to by the army and other helpers. Men were frantically searching through the blackened rubble and already a row of bodies had been laid out in what had once been their gardens. Fighting down the nausea that threatened to engulf her, Hope jumped from the vehicle and, trying not to breathe in the noxious fumes, pulled out medical supplies from the back and hurried over to help.

* * *

At Homerton Hospital, Matron had also been alerted to the emergency and was briefing her senior staff.

'I know you're all tired after the recent flu epidemic, but I'm afraid this unexploded bomb disaster has been classed as a category A incident, and all leave is cancelled for the foreseeable future. Although, of course, in the interest of safety you must ensure all your staff break for their meals.'

This resulted in general muttering – while the principle

was sound, putting it into practice when everyone was working flat out, was a different matter.

'I'm sure I don't have to remind you that the body needs fuel to function, and fainting nurses help no one,' the woman continued, her strident tones leading to dutiful silence. 'Now, I know everyone was disappointed that the May Ball had to be cancelled owing to the outbreak. However, you may tell your staff it is to be rescheduled for the autumn. They're going to need some encouragement to get through the next few days. Right, the first casualties are being transported here as we speak and the accident and emergency staff are already waiting, so please go and brief your team to be prepared to deal with severe burns and the effects of smoke inhalation, amongst other things.'

Rose strode briskly down the corridor with its ever-present smell of disinfectant, thinking that with Philip away she hadn't really minded missing the ball. Did she dare to hope he might be home in the autumn? She would have liked to see her cousin Joy sing at the concert, though. However, responsibilities sometimes meant sacrifices.

Reaching the ward, all personal thoughts were pushed aside as her staff gathered round to hear what she had to say. From their expressions, it was apparent the grapevine had already been working overtime.

'So, it's going to be like when we had all of them soldiers here,' Susan the trainee chirped, as Rose explained they were likely to be dealing with burns.

'Not exactly, Susan,' Rose replied, remembering the

294

merriment and mayhem that had ensued on the ward. 'Obviously, until the casualties have been assessed, we won't know exactly what injuries they have. However, we'll be dealing with the effects of smoke inhalation, broken bones and bad burns, so please make sure the supply of bandages, lint, antiseptic and appropriate ointments are ready. I'll check the oxygen equipment and medicine cabinet.'

'See, I said it would be like when those soldiers arrived,' Susan whispered to Effie.

'Then we'd better make sure all the beds are ready,' the nurse replied.

'Two more things,' Rose continued. 'All leave is cancelled until further notice. However,' she hurried on as the expected mutterings began, 'the May Ball has only been deferred and will now be held in the autumn.'

'Ooh, goody. I can wear a gold dress and go as goddess of the harvest,' Susan squeaked excitedly.

'You sound more like the harvest mouse,' Effie quipped as they made their way to the store cupboard to check they had sufficient supplies of everything.

Rose smiled at their resilience, knowing they'd step up to the plate as soon as the first new patients were wheeled in.

***

Glad to be home again after queuing for nearly two hours for a loaf of bread and what the butcher had claimed were ribs of beef but, as usual these days, turned out to be bone with little meat, Patty poured a cup of the weak tea that also passed for normal these days. With rationing even tighter, the leaves had to be mashed at least three if not four times to make them last the week. Although with Rose and Hope both working flat out after that terrible explosion, she hadn't seen either of them, and the need for making pots of tea and plates of sandwiches had diminished. What she wouldn't give for a good blether and a pot of strong tea with her family gathered around her, she thought.

It had been some days since the blast, yet according to the news bulletin, the Civil Defence Rescue Parties were still working their way painstakingly through the rubble looking for bodies, alive or otherwise, and the death toll was expected to rise further. Their job was being made more difficult by hot spots of fire breaking out, and her heart went out to both the families affected as well as all the services involved in the rescue and recovery. Her own troubles paled into insignificance by comparison.

Sighing, she sat back in her chair, enjoying the silence of an empty house for once. The past few weeks had been hectic. She'd been sorting papers in Robin's office at the Red Cross centre most mornings, queuing to purchase the items she could send to Peter and knitting the socks she was assured he needed so desperately. To think she'd anticipated having time on her hands when she'd finished at the greengrocer's! Now, though, finance dictated she must get a job. She was still asking herself where the time had gone, when she heard the rattle of the letterbox and the thud of post landing on the mat.

There were letters from both her girls, and she settled back in her chair, eager to read their news.

Dear Ma and Pa,

Hope you are both well.

I have finished my training but owing to the tragic deaths of the other Land Girls I've been asked to stay on at the farm here in Devon.

Obviously, I have no choice but to agree, and Mrs Rattery, the warden, looks after us well and we get the most amazing puddings with clotted cream and custard (although her cooking isn't as good as yours, Ma). I'm getting quite adept at milking the cows which is where the cream and butter come from, in case you didn't know. The climate is milder here in the West Country, although wet, and I've already been harvesting all manner of vegetables. I wish you could see the fields with their lush red earth, Ma. They spread as far as the eye can see and you'd love it.

I should get leave to come home at the end of the summer. By then I'll know where my next posting will be to.

Love to you all, Daisy Doodles xxxx

Patty smiled at the reference to her old nickname, recalling how they'd called her that from the first time she'd picked up a crayon and doodled on any scrap of paper she could find. She had difficulty imagining her smartly dressed daughter getting her hands dirty in the fields or milking a cow, for that matter. Still, she was working in the fresh air, which was what she wanted. It was tremendously sad about those poor Land Girls though, and Patty could only send up a prayer of thanks that her daughter had drawn the short straw that day.

She lifted her cup, grimacing at the skin that had formed on the surface, then opened the letter with its official postmark, from Clover.

Dear Ma and Pa,

Hope you are both well. All good, if some-what hectic here. We have been put on special duties, with all leave home cancelled for the foreseeable.

The good news is that Marigold has been transferred and is now working at the Park alongside me. We are just off to grab some dinner from the canteen – for what it's worth. Honestly, Ma, the food here isn't a patch on yours.

Will write when I have news about my next leave. Perhaps I could bring Marigold home with me?

Love

Clover x

Clover's letter perplexed her. She was pleased her daughter was well but couldn't understand why a clerical job would require leave to be cancelled, even a special clerical job. And why did she refer to the Park her office was in with a capital letter. Surely a park was just a park? Still, it was good her friend Marigold had joined her. Although Clover had never said anything, Patty had the feeling the girl was special to her, and she never mentioned any of the handsome soldiers they'd seen at the convalescent home.

Sighing, she put the letters on the side ready for Bert to read when he came back, then catching sight of the *Hackney Gazette*, decided it really was time she looked for another job. They were nearing the end of June already and she'd just been too busy to do anything about it before.

She was busy scanning the vacancy column when the back door slammed and Robbie came thundering into the room, throwing his bag and gas mask down on the mat. She tried not to wince when she saw the state of his shoes. Although Robbie hated shopping, it was a chore she couldn't put off any longer.

'Had a good day, love?' she asked.

'What, at school?' he scoffed. 'They've found some more bodies in that block of flats, though,' he said through a mouthful of biscuit crumbs.

'Where did you get that?' Patty asked.

'Ricky's gran came with some baking. Right, I'm off, he's waiting outside.'

'Pick up your bag and mask first – and mind you don't get your clothes dirty. I've got enough washing to do as it is,' she called after him.

She sighed, then turned back to the paper only to be interrupted by the front door closing and Bert arriving home from work.

'Hello, love, have you had a good day?' she asked, ringing a possible job vacancy. There was silence and she looked up to see him frowning.

'What's wrong?' she asked.

'You know you asked me to speak with Arthur and I kept on forgetting? See what was wrong with your Vera?' he began, not looking at her.

'Yes, she's not been herself for ages, moaning even more than usual. I've had to shut myself away in the office at the Red Cross centre to avoid her or I'd never get anything done. Have you seen Arthur, then?'

He turned away, taking so long hanging his jacket and hat on the peg that Patty wanted to scream.

'Well?'

'Yes. I caught up with him on my way home from work. He was hurrying along to the Social Club. All dressed up and reeking of some fancy cologne. He didn't want to talk at first but then thought better of it and invited me for a drink. That's why I'm late.'

Patty didn't like to say she'd been so preoccupied scanning the advertisements she hadn't noticed.

'Well? What did he say?' she asked.

'It's as I thought, love. He's infatuated with that woman who introduced Joy at the concert. I had my suspicions then. You know Arthur's always had an eye for a good-looking woman. This one works with him, though, so they have plenty of opportunity to . . . well, er, talk and that,' he said, easing himself into his chair.

'You're not telling me you condone his behaviour, Bert Harrison?' Patty exclaimed.

'No, of course not,' he cried, looking affronted. 'Although you have to admit your Vera has let herself go and she's forever sniping at the poor man.'

'Poor man?' Patty nearly exploded. 'It's my poor sister who sits alone in that cramped flat night after night while he's out entertaining another woman! It all makes sense now. Vera's been saying for months that he's hardly ever home, other than for his meals. I hope you told him to stop seeing this woman, Bert. She must know he's married.'

'Look, love, I agree Arthur is behaving shamefully, but perhaps it'll all blow over. He's just behaving like an infatuated schoolboy.'

'But we can't just sit here and do nothing!'

'Neither can we interfere, love. Let's face it, nobody knows what goes on inside a marriage other than the two people involved – even family,' he added when Patty opened her mouth to protest. 'Like I say, hopefully, it'll blow over. In the meantime, why don't you suggest Vera looks after herself again. She always used to be smart.'

Patty thought for a moment. It was true, her sister had once taken a pride in her appearance and Patty understood it was hard to think about personal vanity with a war on, but Vera had recently lost weight, so what could be more natural than Patty suggesting she make her a new outfit? She'd seen some lovely check fabric on a stall in Ridley Road Market recently. The thing was, now she knew what was going on, should she say something or stick to the principle of least said?

'It's worth a try, Bert,' she replied. 'If Vera smartens herself up, perhaps Arthur will appreciate what he has at home.'

'Especially if she can try to be a bit sweeter too. Even you must admit that tongue of hers can be somewhat caustic.'

'You mean she should try using honey instead of vinegar?' Patty said, thinking that although she could help Vera smarten up, the rest would be up to her.

CHAPTER THIRTY-ONE

Patty finished clearing up the kitchen, made a pot of tea, and was just settling down next to Bert to listen to the evening news, when the front door slammed, making them jump.

'Who's that at this time?' she asked, getting to her feet as Hope burst through the door, tears streaming down her face. She was dirty and dishevelled, but it was her wide-eyed look that caught at Patty's heartstrings.

'It's ghastly, Auntie, and I just can't do this anymore!' she wailed, throwing herself into Patty's arms. Pulling her close, Patty made consoling noises then gently led her niece over to the armchair and put a cover over her trembling body.

'Pour a cup of that tea, Bert, and put lots of sugar in,' she instructed her husband, perching on the arm of the chair. Knowing it was best to let the grief out, Patty sat quietly, patting the girl's shoulder while she sobbed until she could cry no more. Finally, Hope gave a shudder and shook her head.

'Sorry,' she whispered. 'Everything just got on top of me. The sights, the smells, the screams of those people in agony . . . The hospital's overrun and there are so many patients on trolleys in the corridors – it's a nightmare.'

'Here, drink this,' Bert said, handing her a mug. 'I've put a nip of brandy in as well as sugar. It'll help calm your insides.'

Hope gave a wan smile, but her hands were shaking so much Patty had to help her.

'I can't begin to imagine what you've been through, love,' she murmured. 'It's a brave and courageous thing you've done, and many folk will be grateful for your help.'

'But that's just it, Auntie. They said we can't do any more. That nobody else could be alive now. All the authorities can do is damp down the hot spots and try and pull any remaining bodies from the rubble.' She swallowed hard and closed her eyes. 'I'll never forget those agonizing screams as long as I live.'

'But you saved lots of people and that's what you must think of,' Patty told her, gently smoothing back the hair which had fallen over her eyes. As the hot drink and brandy began to take effect, and Hope's eyelids fluttered, Patty gently led her upstairs and pulled back the bedcovers.

'But I'll make the sheets all dirty,' she protested.

'You get some rest, and we'll worry about that in the morning,' Patty told her. 'Just don't tell Robbie – you know he'll do anything to get out of washing,' she added, trying to lighten the moment, but Hope was already dead to the world.

**

The men's ward at Homerton was full to bursting with extra beds crammed into every corner. Perhaps Susan hadn't been wrong when she'd likened this to the time the soldiers had been repatriated, Rose thought, trying not to wince as the squeaking of trolley wheels heralded the arrival of yet another patient.

Nurses scuttled back and forth, carrying out routine TPRs and emptying bedpans while doctors examined the more seriously injured patients. As they'd feared, many had suffered crushed limbs as well as burns, and cages were provided to keep bedclothes from touching scorched flesh, while ointment was rubbed on to soothe more minor burns.

She'd been on duty virtually non-stop since the disaster, with barely the minimum respite for meals as instructed by Matron, and she was out on her feet. Still, as the man was offloaded onto a hastily assembled bed, she pasted on her professional smile and hurried to help.

Downstairs in the bustling reception area, a man in blue uniform was enquiring of the new receptionist how he could get a message to Sister Harrison.

'She's too busy to be interrupted now, sir,' the young girl told him. 'As you can see, we're snowed under dealing with a Class A emergency. If you leave a note for her, I can make sure she gets it when she comes off duty, although I couldn't say when that will be.'

As she smiled apologetically, and turned to deal with the next enquiry, the man was jostled by impatient people pushing up the queue. Seeing he was in the way, he turned towards the exit. It had taken so much longer to get across London than he'd anticipated, and then this emergency meant he'd had to wait ages to speak to the receptionist. Now his twenty-four-hour pass was nearly up. His driver was picking him up from outside the hospital and he didn't dare risk being late. He looked around, but saw nobody he recognized, then a glance at the clock on the wall showed him he barely had time to pen a note to the love of his life.

He cursed under his breath. This was the only opportunity he'd had to see her before his squadron was shipped out, and he'd blown it. Quickly taking pen and paper from his pocket, he scribbled a few words. Then, apologizing profusely, he pushed his way through the queue and asked the receptionist to ensure it was passed to Sister Harrison. Heart heavy and cursing this dratted war which meant he was being transferred yet again, he made his way outside to where his driver was waiting.

Upstairs in the men's ward, Rose thought she must be hallucinating as, thermometer in hand, she glanced out of the window and saw a tall man dressed in Air Force blue climbing into a waiting car. Surely that's Philip? she thought, her heart flipping. Then she shook her head. She'd been thinking of him so much, recently, she must have conjured up his image. Forcing herself back to the present, she checked the reading then turned to smile encouragingly at her patient. It really was time she went off duty. She'd be no good to anyone if she started seeing things.

***

Bert opened the front door the next morning to find a woman, smartly dressed in a black uniform, reaching for the knocker.

'Mr Harrison? Good morning,' she continued when he nodded. 'I'm Sonia Strang, supervisor at the local ambulance depot. I was worried about Hope and called to see how she is this morning. These past few days have been traumatic to say the least and I'd like to make sure she's all right.'

Bert shook his head. 'She was in a terrible state when she arrived home. The reports of the explosion and its aftermath have been horrific. Look, come in and I'll call my wife. Oh, there you are,' he added, turning round and finding Patty standing behind him. 'Forgive me, Miss Strang, I must leave, or I'll be late for work,' he told her.

'Hello, I'm Patty, Hope's aunt. She's just getting dressed but I really don't think she's fit enough to work today, especially after the trauma she's experienced, Miss Strang.'

'Nor would I expect her to be,' the woman replied. 'And please, call me Sonia. As I told your husband, I know Hope was very distressed when she left the depot, so I wanted to make sure she's all right this morning.'

'That's kind of you. Do come in – there's a brew in the pot if you'd like a cuppa while you wait?' Patty offered. 'Take a pew,' she said, indicating a chair at the table.

They discussed how the shifts at the depot were working out, rationing and the war in general, but by tacit consent avoided talking about the catastrophe.

'The hardest thing is finding someone to provide hot meals when Ian MacLeod can't cover. His work as an engineer means he's in demand by the government, but he still helps at the depot when he can,' Sonia told her.

'Auntie could do that. She's an excellent cook and does wonders with a few bones and a handful of beans,' Hope said, yawning as she came down the stairs.

'How are you?' Patty and Sonia asked at the same time.

'Better today. I'm sorry if I was a bit overwrought yesterday. Everything just caught up with me.'

'That's understandable. It was a harrowing experience, but you did an admirable job, and I insist you take the next couple of days off to fully recover,' Sonia told her. Expecting Hope to say she wouldn't be turning in again, Patty could only admire the resilience of youth, when she nodded in agreement.

'Well, now I've seen that you're all right, I must be getting back to the depot. Thank you for the tea, Patty. If you think you could bear cooking for a group of greedy gluttons, then do come and see me at the depot. We'd love to have you on board.'

'There you are, Auntie,' Hope cried delightedly. 'Your new job awaits.'

* * *

Did she really want a job cooking, Patty asked herself as she made her way through the main thoroughfare towards the Red Cross centre. The sun was shining and the thought of being cooped up in a steamy kitchen all day, then coming home to cook for her family, didn't fill her with joy. Still, it would be a job, and the scarcity of food meant the cost was going up all the time. She was still pondering when she let herself into the hubbub of the hall. Having finished sorting out Robin's office, she was to learn how to pack the boxes for prisoners of war, and was bracing herself for having to listen to Vera's expertise on the subject.

'Good morning, Patty,' Robin said, meeting her at the door, then leading her to a long table where a dark-haired woman was busy checking a pile of packaged food items. 'Pam here is going to show you the ropes.'

'It's easy when you know how,' the woman told her. 'Here's a list of things that need to go into each box. Follow how I pack them, and you'll be fine.'

'Oh, Patty doesn't need to bother with all that rigmarole,' Vera shouted down the long table. 'Come and stand with me and we'll get things done in half the time. We don't go in for the fancy bits here, not like some,' she added, glaring down the hall, where Jane Bayliss was working.

'Ah, Vera, a word in my office, if you please,' Robin said, from her doorway.

'I suppose she wants my expertise again,' Vera smirked.

'Is she really your sister?' Pam asked. 'Not much alike are you, apart from your beautiful chestnut hair.' Then the radio was turned on and any further talk was swallowed up by the music.

As Patty got into the rhythm of packing the boxes,

her thoughts turned to Peter. She wondered how long it would be before she heard from him. Robin said it could take up to three months for even a postcard to arrive as they were all censored first. How she hoped the parcel she had packed so lovingly for him wouldn't take that long to get there. In the meantime, all she could do was pack as many boxes as she could for other people's sons.

As the radio was switched off, signalling the end of the morning session, Jane Bayliss came up to Patty and said, 'Could we have a quick word outside?'

'Oh, er, yes of course,' she replied and followed her round the side of the building, wondering what the woman could want to speak to her about.

'First of all, may I thank you for making such a splendid job of Joy's dress? The way you adapted it to fit, yet kept the flowing lines, was a tribute to your skill. You must enjoy dressmaking?' she continued, her expression warm as she studied Patty with clear green eyes.

'Well, I wouldn't say it was dressmaking as such, more altering what we already had, but yes, I do enjoy doing it.'

'A little bird tells me you're looking for a job,' the woman continued. 'A friend of mine owns a smart lady's outfitters near here, and with material and new stock hard to come by, she's looking for someone really skilful to adapt clothes for her customers. If you're interested, I could put a word in.'

'Wh-why, thank you,' Patty stammered, taken aback both by the woman's offer and her friendly manner.

Could she really be out to wreck her sister's marriage, she wondered?

'What did that woman want?' Vera hissed as Patty went back to her place. She was all agog and had obviously been waiting for her sister.

'She was just being friendly,' Patty replied.

'Oh, yes, she's good at *that*. You want to watch her.'

'If you must know, she was being complimentary about the dress Joy was wearing at the show.' She thought it prudent not to mention the possible job offer, which Patty found more enticing than cooking. Still, the choice of two jobs in one day was quite exciting and both were better than the office jobs she'd seen in the paper.

'She's got her singing at a club now; did you know that?' Vera continued.

'Well, Joy does have a beautiful voice, Vera,' Patty replied.

'Yes, but she's also got her wearing lipstick, shoes with heels and nylon stockings,' she spluttered.

'Oh, Vera, Joy's growing up. It's natural she wants to experiment. Perhaps we should too,' she suggested, seizing the opportunity. 'Why don't we see what clothes we've got to adapt? I mean, you've lost so much weight recently you'd really suit the new utility look. It's designed to skim the hips then flare softly to the knee.'

'Why not?' Vera asked, a gleam in her eye. 'That would never suit Jane Bayliss, got hips like a hippo, she has.'

'Well, Hope's not working today, so why don't you

311

come home with me? We can all have a sandwich together, then go through some old clothes, see what we can revamp,' Patty suggested, ignoring her barb. 'Hope's had a distressing few days so we could take her to Ridley Road Market and browse the fabric stalls. We might even pick up a new lipstick to brighten ourselves up.'

Although what she was going to do about her sister's sharp tongue, she didn't know. Still, she had to start somewhere.

**

'I don't believe it!' Rose cried, throwing herself down on the bed in her little room and rereading the note she'd been passed as she came off duty.

It *had* been Philip she'd seen climbing into that car. To think he'd been downstairs waiting in reception while she'd been upstairs on the men's ward. Why hadn't someone come to tell her? The answer was obvious, of course. The hospital was snowed under with injured patients who'd survived the horrific blast, and worried relatives desperate to see they were all right. Staff had been working round the clock, snatching food and sleep whenever they could. In short, everyone's life had been given over to the catastrophe, their personal lives put on hold these past few days.

It just wasn't fair, she thought. Couldn't he have telephoned the switchboard? Though, even if he had, the emergency would have been given priority. Had he visited his parents, she wondered. The thought of Mrs

Sutherland's superior look if he'd seen her and not Rose would be too much to bear.

And now her beloved was being posted to God only knew where, with no indication of when she'd next see him. Would this bloody war never end?

As the tears streamed down her cheeks, she pulled the cover over her, too tired to undress, and fell into an exhausted sleep, where images of her tall, handsome pilot driving away from her, haunted her dreams. No matter how hard she tried to catch up with him, just as in real life, he always eluded her.

CHAPTER THIRTY-TWO

In the dim and stuffy atmosphere of Hut 6, Clover sat back in her chair and rubbed her eyes. They were stinging with tiredness and felt like pin pricks from the fierce concentration of the past few hours and the thick pall of cigarette smoke that hung overhead. Blinking hard, she looked at the next slip, letters separated into their blocks of five. Was that the bones of a message emerging? She was adept at checking for clues now, the latest instructions being to look for beginnings of names, rank, weather or any repetition. Trying to suppress the tingle of excitement she experienced on these occasions; she forced herself to focus.

Whilst there hadn't been any more of what they were calling the Baedeker raids, since Norwich had been bombed at the end of June, they had been warned to be especially alert for any 'code' words or city names. After Daisy's narrow escape when Exeter had been bombed back in May, Clover felt it was her duty to be even more vigilant, volunteering for overtime, despite all leave being cancelled

Yet, as often happened, despite her best endeavours, the start of the message didn't yield any further clues, leading instead down a blind alley. Sighing in frustration, she was reaching for the next slip when Mrs Speedwell clapped her hands to gain their attention.

'Right, ladies, that's it for today. Vacate your seats and leave your work for your colleagues.'

Clover rose thankfully to her feet, smiling wearily at the woman waiting to take her place before making her way outside. Gulping in great lungful's of fresh air, she marvelled at the brilliance of the afternoon sunshine and the colours of the leaves. It was always disorientating emerging from the gloom of the hut and, ignoring the hustle and bustle of people passing by, she took a few moments to adjust. Over the months she'd been at Bletchley, personnel numbers had increased dramatically, and buildings were popping up all over the Park in order to meet the ever-growing demand.

The ringing of a bell made her turn, and she grinned when she saw Marigold cycling towards her. What an absolute surprise it had been to find out her friend had been posted here, but then Marigold was bilingual, after all. Life had certainly looked up since her arrival, and her idea for them to hire bikes to get around was fantastic. It saved having to wait for the bus and gave them independence to explore the surrounding areas when they had any free time.

'Come along, slowcoach!' Marigold called. 'My head's swimming after being inside all day, let's see if there's any bread left in the shop and we can have tea al fresco.'

Having pooled their coupons, bagged the last of what was being termed 'The National Loaf', and a pot of fish paste, they were now picnicking in the garden of the house they rented with Ann. As soon as Clover had explained about her friend having been posted to the Park, Ann had invited Marigold to join them, and they now shared the spacious front room upstairs.

'There's enough here if you want to join us,' Clover told Ann as she flopped down on the grass beside them. 'Although this new bread leaves much to be desired. It's so grey and heavy and takes forever to chew.'

'Mr Simms told me that, by law, he now has to make it in his bakery one day then sell it the next,' Marigold informed them.

'Why on earth would he do that?' Ann asked, wrinkling her nose.

'Apparently, it cuts better and saves waste now they're not importing much grain. This so-called bread,' Marigold cried, throwing it down in disgust, 'is fortified with chalk to save us from getting rickets, would you believe?'

'Good grief. Thank heavens I'm going to Claridge's this weekend. At least the food there is still half-decent. I say, why don't you both come with me? We could go in Charlie's car. It will be a bit of a squeeze, but we'll have a laugh – and you'll get a darn good meal.'

'You mean you've been granted time off?' Clover asked. 'Ours has been suspended.'

'Same here,' Marigold sighed, 'and in this beautiful weather too.'

'Well, Dilly Knox doesn't believe in conforming even when he's working from home. His attitude is that if we work when we want, take time off to clear our heads, we're more productive. Of course, he knows full well our conscience won't allow us to shirk when duty calls, and we often work well into the night, long after our shifts finish. Anyhow, Mummy is dining with Clemmie, and Winston is bound to be too busy to join them, so we'll be free to enjoy ourselves.'

'You mean Winston Churchill, the Prime Minister?' Marigold asked, her eyes widening.

'The same. Oh, don't be put off by his manner. He values the work we do here. When he visited the Park last September, he spoke to everyone, even praised the codebreakers for their silence as well as their work. He relies heavily on Park intelligence to guide his public policy.'

'Should we be talking about work like this? You know, what with the OSA?' Marigold asked, staring over her shoulder.

'Oh, piffle,' Ann scoffed, waving her hand in the air. 'For a start, there's nobody else in the garden and we haven't exactly discussed anything those Nazis would be interested in. Although Dilly reckons Hitler would be mad as heck if he realized how many of their messages we manage to decipher. Serves him right for underestimating the English minds. Bletchley has the top intelligence linguists and cryptanalysts here. No offence, Clover, but that Sally you called an airhead has turned out to be a whizz since she was transferred to us and Dilly can't talk

317

highly enough of her. It goes to show you can't judge a book, et cetera.' So *that's* where Sally had disappeared to, Clover thought, but Ann was still talking.

'We'll help win this war or damn well die in the process.'

Clover shuddered and Marigold patted her hand and changed the subject.

'Talking of not judging a book . . .' she said. 'Margaret lent me a copy of *Gone with the Wind* as it's being discussed at the book club next week. Anyone fancy coming along with me?'

'Aha, if that Margaret is Wren Winslow, then you must be working on the Italian Job,' Ann cried gleefully. 'No wonder you were transferred to the Park.'

'But I never said . . .'

'Don't worry, Marigold, it's Ann's little game. She likes to work out which hut everyone's in without actually asking them,' Clover told her.

'Yes, don't mind me. It hones my powers of deduction. Dilly believes we achieve more by discussing and pooling our work, and I'm convinced he's right. Many's the clue we've solved that way. Luckily, we work in our own room and only answer to him, so no one's any the wiser. Well, pity you can't join me for a slap-up meal at Claridge's – but I'm sure you'll enjoy having the house to yourselves,' Ann, laughed, giving them a knowing look.

***

After her last regular shift at the Red Cross before starting her new job the following week, Patty had walked home to have lunch with Vera.

'How on earth am I meant to cut this slab of concrete into sandwiches?' Vera cried, slamming the loaf down on the table.

'Bert almost choked on his tea last night, ours was that hard,' Patty sighed. 'I can't believe they have to sell us day-old bread with goodness knows what in, just so we don't waste a measly crumb. Pam was telling me this morning that in France they bake their bread two or three times a day. Although I don't suppose that happens now that their rationing is worse than ours, by all accounts.'

'This sodding war's got a lot to answer for,' Vera replied. 'I've lost my house and have to live in this poky box. It might be above Arthur's business, but none of his colleagues ever talk to me. Load of snobs they are, think they're something they're not. Arthur's out most of the time, his excuse being he's giving Joy and me more space. Well, we all know where he spends his time, don't we?'

Not sure how to answer, Patty quirked a brow, but without pausing for breath, Vera continued.

'The council say there's no point in me hassling them as they won't be able to help until they've rehoused all those people made homeless by that bomb going off. I don't know, Patty. I'm losing my family as well as my home,' she wailed. 'You've got Hope living with you, for which I'm grateful, but she's so busy I hardly ever see her. Joy is forever down at that wretched club and Faith is acting all secret. I met her on my way to the market earlier and she was dressed up to the nines.

When I asked where Artie was, she said he had a cold and was at home with Martin's mother. Her voice was all squeaky and she wouldn't look at me. With our Faith, that's a sure sign she's lying. If I didn't know better, I'd say she was meeting some fellow. And Martin's body still at the bottom of the sea.'

'It's been a difficult time for her but I'm sure you're imagining things . . .' Patty began.

'Well, why else was she reeking of posh scent?' she asked, shaking her finger at Patty. 'I know my daughter. She needs the admiration of a fellow, always has.'

'Maybe she just fancied dressing up and getting out of the house. Bringing up a little one is demanding,' Patty pointed out.

She had enough to think about without taking on more of her sister's problems. Having only that morning secured the job at 'Elizabeth's', the smart lady's outfitters set back from Hackney High Street, she had a hundred and one things to sort out before she started next Monday.

'Anyhow, talking of being tarted up, what are you doing all dressed up like a dog's dinner?' Vera asked, staring at the matching top and skirt Patty had spent the past evenings remodelling for today.

'I had an interview before my shift at the Red Cross and I've been offered a new job,' Patty told her proudly, but as she went on to explain further, her sister's lips began to curl.

'You can't work there!' she exploded. 'That's where all the wives round here go to update their wardrobes, including that Jane Bayliss, I shouldn't wonder.'

'Well, the money's good and I'm starting next week,' Patty told her firmly. 'And talking of dressing up, I thought you were going to smarten yourself up? What happened to that black and white skirt I made for you.'

'Doesn't seem worth the effort,' her sister mumbled, staring down at her old grey dress.

'Now listen here, Vera Potter. I haven't spent the last few weeks revamping your clothes and listening to you moaning about Arthur not paying you any attention, for you to let yourself go. You've lost weight and could look every bit as good as Jane Bayliss, so stop carping and do something about it! Dress up, do your hair, put on some lipstick and give her a run for her money.' Then, leaving Vera gaping like a stranded fish, she picked up her bag, put her gas mask over her arm and hurried from the room.

Patty had almost reached Victory Walk before her anger cooled. Perhaps she shouldn't have been so sharp, but really, her sister had become even more selfish and self-obsessed than usual lately. If Vera wanted to keep Arthur, then it was up to her to make an effort and fight for him. Patty had her own family to look after and worry about, as well as her new job.

Although she was excited and welcomed the challenge, it entailed working longer hours than she had at the greengrocer's, and whilst the extra money would be welcome, it would take planning to ensure she could fit everything in. Perhaps, if she started giving Robbie some pocket money, she could encourage him to do a few extra chores around the house. His penchant for sweets would be a good inducement.

She let herself in, picked up the mail from the mat, then hurried through to the kitchen to make herself a cup of tea. With her indignation about the National Loaf followed by her tales of woe, Vera had quite forgotten about lunch and Patty was parched.

Waiting for the kettle to boil, she flicked through the post, her heart flipping when she saw the long-awaited postcard from Peter. It just gave the date as May 1942:

Dear Ma and Pa,
Just to let you know the worst has happened and I am a prisoner of war at PRIGIONE di GUERRA (Campo) PG66. I am well but – the next few words had been blanked out – *would welcome a Red Cross parcel. Some of the others have received warm socks and tea which are appreciated.*
Hope you are all well. Missing you.
Peter

Oh, my poor darling, Patty thought, hoping her next-of-kin parcel would soon arrive with him. She had some green wool left and would start knitting another pair of socks straight after supper. At least she knew he was safe or had been in May.

Determined to push away all melancholy thought, she picked up the envelope, smiling when she saw it addressed in Daisy's neat handwriting.

Dear Ma and Pa,
Hope you are well.

I have finished my training and extra time here in Devon. Now the new Land Army Girls have settled in and more or less know what they're doing, I am being posted to a farm in Suffolk to help harvest the crops.

The good news is that, at last, I have been given my promised forty-eight-hour pass to come home and will be with you sometime on Friday. Can't wait to see you.

Love Daisy xxx

How lovely it would be to see her daughter, Patty thought, her spirits rising as she picked up her tea.

Then she looked at the letter again and nearly sent her cup flying. Friday? Why, that was tomorrow, and she had nothing ready!

She'd have to make a shopping list, she thought, finding a pencil to write on the back of the envelope. Goodness only knows how long she'd have to queue or what would be on offer when she eventually reached the counter.

'Hello, love,' Patty had been so lost in thought she hadn't heard her husband come home.

'Is it that time already?' she spluttered, staring at the clock on the wall in disbelief. 'I'm afraid tea will be late. We've had a postcard from Peter who needs more socks, a letter from Daisy, who's coming home tomorrow and oh, Bert, I've nothing ready! Suppose they don't have anything nice left in the butcher's or—'

'Calm down, love. It's our Daisy coming, not the Queen. Now sit yourself down and I'll make us a fresh pot of tea. I can see by the state of that one that it's stone cold.' He nodded towards her cup where a skin had formed.

'You'll need to pour more water on the leaves,' she told him.

'Righto,' he said, the news of Daisy coming home clearly having put him in a cheerful mood. 'How did your interview go?'

'Goodness, I'd quite forgotten in all the excitement. I've got the job and start on Monday. Robbie's going to have to do a few more things around here, but now I'll be earning more, I thought we could give him a bit of pocket money so he can . . .'

They were interrupted by the slamming of the door.

'Steady on, son,' Bert said as Robbie burst into the room.

'This blooming war just gets worse and worse!' he exploded. 'Mr Johns in the shop told us they're putting sweets on ration. He was teasing us, wasn't he?'

CHAPTER THIRTY-THREE

The bus lurched as the driver tried to avoid the potholes and craters in the road, and Daisy clutched the paper bag tighter, feeling sick to her stomach. Although the bombings had taken place months ago now, it was the first time she'd left the farm since, and the devastation in Exeter city was worse than she had imagined. Then, as they took a detour by the bombed cathedral and Daisy saw where her new friends had perished, she couldn't stop the tears from welling. To think, if she hadn't drawn that short straw, she would have been blown up too.

'Criminal, isn't it, all this damage?' the woman behind her muttered as they alighted at the railway station. 'To think there were almost two hundred killed and that's just the bodies they found. Goodness only knows how many more are still buried under all that rubble.' Daisy shuddered, recalling the prayers they'd said and the cross they'd placed in the top meadow at the farm in memory of the poor Land Girls.

Although Daisy was lucky enough to squeeze into a corner a seat, the train was crowded with both service personnel and civilians, and it kept stopping and starting, with trees and fields giving way to buildings as they approached London. It was much later than planned by the time she eventually reached Dalston and, knowing her mother would be worried, she hurried down the main street, but before she could turn into Victory Walk, she was waylaid by Hope and Joy.

'Hey, stranger, long time no see,' they called in unison. 'We're going for a cuppa at the café – why don't you join us and we can catch up on all the news.'

'I'd love to, but Ma's expecting me and I'm already late,' Daisy explained.

'Then come to the Eagle Club with us later instead,' Hope suggested. 'It's not far and Joy's singing there tonight. It's ages since we saw you.'

'Why not?' Daisy replied, her spirits rising at the thought of a night out with her cousins. They arranged to meet up later, and no sooner had she turned into Victory Walk than their front door was thrown open before she'd even reached it.

'There you are, our Daisy!' Patty cried, throwing her arms around her daughter.

'Careful, Ma, you'll crush my present,' she laughed, handing her the somewhat crumpled offering. 'Whortle-berries from the moors of Devon,' she announced proudly. 'Oh, it's good to be home,' she added, throwing her bags down and staring round the living room. 'Something smells good too.'

'That'll be the lamb stew. I managed to get a bit of scrag end but had to eke it out with veg and pearl barley. Oh, and I made some spiced biscuits too, so we'll have a brew and catch up before your father gets home.'

'Sorry I'm late, Ma, those flippin' trains stop and start

without giving any reason, and it took me four hours longer to get here than it should have,' she said as she made her way to the kitchen and flopped onto a chair.

'Well, you're here now and looking brown as a berry. Which reminds me, what on earth are whortleberries?' Patty asked, peeking inside the bag.

'They're also known as windberries or bilberries and they make a lovely pie,' she replied. 'I would have brought some of the clotted cream the West Country's renowned for – it's all thick and gorgeous and Mrs Rattery, the warden, taught us how to scald the milk to make it. It reduces the waste, you see, and . . . sorry, I got a bit carried away there. Anyway, I would have brought some with me, but Mrs Rattery said the heat on the train would sour it.'

'Well, it was a nice thought, and I'll see if we've got enough flour left to knock up some pastry. You know we've got to use this national flour now?' she said, placing a steaming cup on the table in front of Daisy.

'Yes, the farms are supplying all the grain they can grow. It's a different life in the country, Ma, you'd love it.'

'I'm sure I would, but regrettably I'm too old to enlist as a Land Girl. Besides, I've got a new job as a seamstress in a nice little shop off Hackney High Street,' she announced proudly, slipping into the seat beside her daughter. 'And I can do some of the alterations from home, which will be handy.'

'Good for you; it'll beat standing in that draughty old greengrocer's. Has any post come for me?'

'No, dear. Why?'

'I haven't heard from Freddy since his surprise visit, and I rather hoped he might have sent a letter here,' she explained, letting out a long sigh.

'The post's all over the place these days. We finally had a postcard from Peter, and it took months to get here. I'm sure you'll hear from Freddy soon. Make sure you give me your new address and I'll forward anything on.'

'Thanks, Ma. So how is Peter, did he say?' Daisy asked but before Patty could reply, the door burst open, and Robbie ran in, making a beeline for the plate of biscuits.

'Well, who's this tall, young man?' Daisy teased before Patty could reprimand him.

'It's me, Robbie, stupid,' he laughed.

'So, it is, and still hungry as a horse, I see,' she chuckled as he snatched a biscuit and popped it into his mouth whole.

'Robbie!' Patty snapped.

'Well, we only get treats when someone comes home,' he grumbled, disappearing outside again. Then, before Patty could settle down and resume their chat, the shutting of the front door announced Bert's arrival.

'We'll have a good catch up after supper,' she told Daisy.

'Oh, I met up with Hope and Joy on the way here and promised to go to the Eagle Club with them. Apparently, Joy sings there now.'

Patty nodded, fighting down the disappointment of

not spending the evening catching up with her daughter. She'd missed her so much, yet Patty couldn't begrudge her the chance of an evening out after all she'd been through, could she?

***

The American Eagle Club was situated on Charing Cross Road and had the Stars and Stripes flags flying over the entrance. Joy, obviously popular, was warmly greeted by many of the smartly dressed servicemen the moment they arrived.

'Swell to see you, Joy. Let me get you and your pals a drink.'

'Hey, Joy, light of my life, won't you introduce me to your beautiful friends?'

'What are you singing for us tonight, sweetheart?'

Daisy watched as her cousin, obviously at ease in these surroundings, laughed and returned their banter as she followed them to the bar.

'I think we should celebrate with champagne cocktails as my cousin here has just returned from the West Country,' she announced grandly, and Daisy could only marvel at the way she had grown in confidence. She'd styled her hair and was wearing a bright red lipstick and, although she was dressed in her best blue top and skirt, Daisy felt quite frumpy by comparison.

'Bit different from the coffee you usually serve to us, sweetheart,' a thickset, dark-haired man, smart in his RAF uniform chuckled.

'That's when I waitress during the day, Brad,' Joy

replied, slapping his arm playfully. 'If you want me to sing, my vocals need lubricating.'

'A special champagne cocktail for the lady and her friends.' Brad winked at the barman, then showed them to a table, pulling out a chair for Joy.

To Daisy's relief, when she gingerly sipped the drink put before her, she found it was mainly lemonade and she could only detect the faintest hint of what she thought might be champagne. The paper umbrella balanced on the side of the glass was studded with a glossy cherry, the like of which she'd never seen before.

'That's a maraschino, ma'am,' the fair-haired chap opposite her murmured, his eyes twinkling.

'Oh, thanks. Is this where you spend your free time?' she asked.

'It's the most congenial place in London, ma'am. Home to all allied servicemen, and charming gals too,' he grinned, taking a sip of his beer. 'The name's Koi, by the way.'

'Daisy.'

'Cute, just like the flower. Koi means panther so I reckon Mom must have had aspirations for me, though I doubt I live up to them,' he chuckled. Daisy looked at the others, but they were busy either chatting or being chatted up by the American servicemen.

'My chap's in the navy,' Daisy told him, so he didn't get any ideas. 'Though I have no idea where he or his ship is.'

'Gee, this war's tough, isn't it? My gal's in the WRENS, last heard of on some godforsaken island off Scotland. Takes far too long to get to on my time off so . . .' He shrugged, just as the music started up.

'Give us a song then, Joy,' Brad demanded. She smiled coyly, and it was only when she shrugged off her cardigan that Daisy saw she was wearing a top cut so low it showed a fair amount of cleavage.

'Surely she's not going to stand up in front of all those men looking like that?' she whispered to Hope, thinking her aunt would have a fit if she knew. But as the cries and whistles increased, Joy smiled demurely then went to stand over by the piano.

As the strains of 'Don't Sit Under the Apple Tree' began, the room fell silent, but when she began singing 'Boogie Woogie Bugle Boy', the men went mad, cheering, clapping and singing along.

'She's good, isn't she?' Daisy said as Hope pulled her chair closer.

'Fantastic. I can hardly believe that's my sister up there. Of course, Ma doesn't know she dresses like that when she sings and she's not too happy about her waitressing here during the day.'

'How is Auntie Vera?' Daisy asked, but Hope pulled a face.

'Look can you keep a secret' she asked. 'I'll just burst if I don't tell someone.'

'Of course, what is it?' Daisy asked.

'Ian and I are to be married.'

'Why, that's wonderful!' she cried, and her cousin flushed with happiness. 'I'm so happy for you.' And she was – yet that made her think even more about Freddy and wish he would write.

'Thanks,' Hope continued, oblivious to her thoughts. 'It won't be until after the war finishes and I've got to know his children well, but we can begin making plans; that's if I ever get to see him. He's always working and since that bomb raid in Exeter has been down in Dorset a lot,' she sighed. 'Oh, but you know all about that, don't you? Was it very bad?'

'In a word, yes. Some of my colleagues were killed, which is why I had to stay longer in Devon than planned. But under the circumstances I was very lucky, and now I'm off to Suffolk tomorrow, which reminds me, I'd better be going. I've hardly seen Ma and Pa,' she said, stifling a yawn as her long day's travelling caught up with her.

'I need to go as well. I'm on shift first thing in the morning,' Hope replied getting to her feet, just as the strains of 'Danny Boy' began.

'Allow me to escort you ladies home,' Koi said, rising too.

'Oh, there's no need,' Daisy began.

'There's every need, ma'am. My mom raised me to always take care of ladies.'

'Perhaps we should wait until Joy's finished singing?' Daisy pointed out, still worried about her cousin's appearance.

'Don't you fret, sweetheart,' Koi told her. 'Brad will look out for her. He has strict instructions from Mrs Bayliss, and it'd be more than his life's worth to upset her.'

***

'Well, this weekend didn't turn out the way I hoped,' Patty grumbled as the door closed behind Daisy.

'I can't deny it would have been nice to see more of our girl, but you can't blame her for wanting to have a night out. It sounds like she had a rum time of it during that bombing.'

'Yes, but then to accept a lift to Suffolk with a bunch of American GI's . . . Oh Bert, you do think she'll be safe, don't you?'

'Stop fussing, Patty, it'll be a lot easier for her going by car than train. If Jane Bayliss can vouch for them, then that's fine by me.'

'Bert Harrison, how come you're an authority on Jane Bayliss all of a sudden?' she asked, staring at him in astonishment.

'You asked me to speak to Arthur again, didn't you?'

'Yes, but you never said you had, though,' Patty replied, frowning as she mashed up the left-over stew to make a shepherd's pie for their evening meal.

'I haven't had a chance, love. I only spoke to him on Friday and our Daisy was here when I got in. Then you weren't happy when she went out in the evening.'

'Well, she'd only just arrived home,' Patty sighed. 'Oh, I don't blame her for wanting an evening out. Forget it, I was just disappointed, that's all. Anyway, why should this Jane Bayliss be trusted?'

'For a start, her part-time job with Arthur involves her having to keep certain aspects of their work secret. Arthur couldn't even tell *me* what. Also, she thinks Joy's very talented and wants to help further her singing career. She's trying to arrange an interview with ENSA – you know, the Entertainment National Service Association. Obviously, with Joy being so young, she had to get Arthur's permission, and she couldn't speak to Vera, could she? Anyway, being a singer herself, Janie's known and respected at the Eagle Club and has asked a couple of the lads to take Joy under their wing, as it were.'

'You mean this Brad and Koi that Daisy is travelling to Suffolk with?'

'Yes. They're on a base near the farm Daisy will be working at.'

'Oh, I see. Well, I feel much better now.'

'I'm pleased to hear it,' Bert grunted. 'This war might be horrific, but you have to admit our girls are experiencing things they wouldn't have had the opportunity to before.'

He was right, Patty thought, the girls were mixing with new people and travelling to exciting new places.

'Now, it's time to listen to the news bulletin,' he said, switching on the wireless.

'At El Alamein the British Army has beaten back the great German offensive. For the first time they have struck back against General Rommel's attacks with fresh troops and new equipment,' said the newsreader.

'Praise be, the tide seems to be changing,' Bert murmured.

* * *

Tired after a long gruelling day, Rose threw herself down on the bed in her room. However, her mind refused to be still, the events of the day whirring round and round like a carousel. She let out a long sigh. Despite their best efforts a man had died of pneumonia. It didn't matter how old a patient was, it was always sad not to be able to save them. She'd stayed holding his hand until he finally passed and then had been caught up in settling a new patient who'd been admitted with a grumbling appendix. Now, hours after she should have come off shift, it was too late for her to go home to Victory Walk and see Daisy.

A knock on the door made her jump. What now? she thought, for she really was much too exhausted to deal with any emergency. However, seeing a letter had been slipped under her door, she realized she'd been too tired to check her pigeonhole. Then she saw the handwriting and her heart flipped. Tearing open the envelope, she quickly scanned the contents then let out a cry – Philip was coming home!

Her heart beat faster as she reread the note. He'd be home next month and had some exciting news to share with her. Could she make sure she was off duty then, as having missed her last time he couldn't bear not to see her again.

Could she? Nothing would stop her from seeing him this time. The middle of August couldn't come soon enough, and tiredness forgotten, she snatched up her notepaper and penned a reply.

CHAPTER THIRTY-FOUR

The sun was shining brightly as Rose sauntered through the Strand, stopping when she saw the smart sign, gold lettering and cream background denoting the Lyons Corner House.

Going inside, she paused, taking in the bustling dining room with its crystal chandeliers, gleaming brass fittings and polished wooden counters piled high with sumptuous pies, cakes and biscuits. She had never been here before and seeing the smartly dressed waitresses in their black and white uniforms trimmed with pearl buttons, she felt pleased she was wearing the purple crepe dress her mother had helped her repurpose from an old, flared summer dress she'd found in her wardrobe. It had been inspired by an article in the *Ladies' Home Journal* entitled 'Fashions with Dual Personality' and she felt every bit as glamorous as the girl in the magazine.

A sudden movement caught her eye and there he was, tall and handsome in his RAF uniform, waving to catch her attention. Her heart fluttered as she made her way to join him.

'Philip!' she cried as he bent to kiss her cheek.

'Rose, dearest, I can't tell you how much I've longed for today,' he said, pulling out a chair for her at the beautifully laid table. 'I've taken the liberty of ordering the full afternoon tea, so I hope you've brought a good appetite with you,' he added, his gaze never leaving hers.

'I've haven't seen this much food in ages,' Rose exclaimed as a young girl placed the heavy tray on the table before them, unloading a silver stand, each tier piled high with cakes, scones, and dainty sandwiches, followed by a silver teapot, dainty crockery and napkins.

'I'm reliably informed Joe Lyons always manages to keep his tearooms well stocked even though there's a war on,' Philip grinned, eyeing the food hungrily. 'Thanks, Nippy,' he said, and the waitress beamed.

'I haven't heard that name before!' Rose told him, selecting a sandwich as he proffered the stand.

'All the Lyons' waitresses are called Nippies,' he told her. 'Have been for some time. They used to be called Gladys, but in 1925 Lyons decided to hold a staff competition to find a more suitable name. Nippy was chosen because of the way they nip about.'

'They're certainly busy nipping between the tables,' Rose observed. 'And they seem well organized too,' she added, thinking of the way some of her nurses flitted from bed to bed on the ward.

'Lyons actually runs a training school,' Philip told her, helping himself to a scone which had plump fruit in.

'Robbie would love it here,' she sighed.

'We'll ask a Sally to bag up some treats for him on our way out – they're the ladies dressed in blue who

337

serve on the counter,' he added, seeing her bemused look. 'Now, that's quite enough of an education for today. Tell me what you've been up to. You're looking quite delightful today, if I might say so.'

'You may,' she told him, smoothing down the bolero edged with the lilac ribbon she'd found on Ridley Road Market.

'And how are your family?' he enquired when she'd finished reciting an anecdote about life on the ward.

'Ma and Pa are fine. They've had a postcard from Peter who's a POW in Italy. Ma helps out at the Red Cross centre packing boxes for them.' He nodded sympathetically but didn't interrupt. 'Daisy's gone to harvest crops in Suffolk and Clover's bringing her friend Marigold home for the weekend.'

Philip looked thoughtful for a moment. 'I've heard life in the Park is more relaxed than in the outside world.'

'How do you know where Clover is? I don't recall telling you.'

'It's a small world these days,' he shrugged.

'And what about you? You've hardly talked about what you've been up to?'

'What can I say, other than we're trying to shoot down the Nazi bastards before they shoot us.'

'Sounds terrifying. And what do the braids I see on your lower sleeve signify?' she asked, when it was clear he wasn't going to mention his promotion.

'Why, ma'am,' he saluted, 'you are now looking at Flight Lieutenant Sutherland, although I have to admit

I'll be pleased when this goddamn war is over.' His expression sobered and for a moment he was lost in thought. Then he brightened and pointed to their empty plates.

'Now, if I can't tempt you to any more delights, I suggest we go for a stroll. There's a great little club just round the corner from here where the music is pacey and guaranteed to get you dancing.'

'That was delicious, thank you, and I couldn't possibly eat another morsel.'

Having queued at the counter to purchase some treats for Robbie, they made their way outside, surprised to find the sun was already sinking. How long had they been chatting? Rose wondered.

'One good thing about driving for pleasure being banned, is that the streets are much quieter,' Philip said, proffering his arm.

'I could do without having to cart this thing around, though,' Rose added, gesturing to her gas mask. 'It quite spoils the line of one's outfit,' she quipped, mimicking the high-class tones of the ladies who'd been seated at the next table.

'Indeed,' he laughed. 'Oh Rose, I've really missed you,' he told her, pulling her closer.

'It's such a lovely evening, if it wasn't for those damaged buildings and the barrage balloons, you wouldn't know there was a war on, would you?' she said.

She felt him stiffen and turned in time to catch a bleak expression cloud his eyes. However, it was gone in a flash.

'The night is young and we shall have fun,' he quipped but her instincts told her something was troubling him. However, before she could say anything, he turned into a side road then led the way inside a tall building where a uniformed doorman tipped his hat and waved them through to a private lounge.

Rose found herself in a room thronging with a mixture of civilians and service personnel, all intent on having a good time: some were drinking and chatting, others dancing to the band. Gingerly, Rose clutched her handbag, hoping Robbie's biscuits and cakes wouldn't get squashed. The poor lad had been so upset when sweet rationing had been introduced, she could just imagine his eyes lighting up when he saw the treats.

'You can give your bag to the attendant over there,' Philip said, gesturing towards a hatch through which she could see rows of jackets and bags. 'Whilst you do that, I'll get us a drink. Fancy a glass of champagne to celebrate?'

'What are we celebrating?' she asked, her eyes sparkling.

'Being together,' he replied, raising his voice as a saxophone began playing the intro for the singer behind the microphone.

By the time the strains of "You Made Me Love You" were belting out, and Rose had relieved herself of her bag and gas mask, Philip had returned with two coupes of fizzing liquid.

'Here's to us,' he murmured as they clinked glasses.

'To us,' she agreed.

He began to say something, but the tune had changed to a waltz and, putting down their glasses, he pulled her into his arms, and they began moving to the beat. As his arms tightened around her, she felt her heart fluttering. It felt so good to be close to him again.

'Darling Rose, I dream of us being together like this for all time,' he murmured, kissing the top of her head and sending tingles down her spine.

'Me too. Let's make the most of the time we have together. How long are you home for?' she asked. He didn't answer; just pulled her closer so she could hardly breathe. Then he let out a long sigh. 'We fly out first thing in the morning.'

Her heart flopped, but as she stared up at him in dismay, his lips came down on hers, kissing her long and hard; stirring up feelings she'd never experienced before.

* * *

It was a cheerful journey as Brad and Koi drove towards East Anglia, and Daisy drank in the scenery, the flat plains of Suffolk such a contrast to the steep moors and craggy tors of Devon. They dropped her outside the hostel, which was situated in the village of Great Bradley, where she was billeted with other Land Girls. They were friendly, but they were all moved from farm to farm around the area as required and it seemed to Daisy that no sooner had she got to know someone than they disappeared.

The golden days of autumn passed by in a haze of hard work. Her first task was potato picking and lifting the beets, but when the farmer discovered she could milk cows she was sent to the nearby Great Bradley Hall Farm. To her horror, they kept a ferocious bull called Brutus, housed in a separate building nearby, and she was tasked to look after it.

'I just can't go near it,' she told a young, dark-haired man who was watching her curiously.

'I talk no English,' he muttered, shaking his head.

'He's Mateo, one of the Italian POWs,' another Land Girl told her. 'They'll help, but you have to mime what you want them to do. Like this.' She picked up a brush, pretending to groom her hair, then pointed to the bull.

'*Si*,' the man replied and took the brush from her.

'Thanks. I'm Daisy, by the way.'

'Jenny. The POWs live in that hut on the edge of the farm,' she said, pointing to a wooden building. 'They're very helpful, but we're forbidden to mix with them, so watch out when old Wilf's around. Thinks he's in with Lord W and likes to "inform him" of what goes on. In other words, he's a snitch.'

She broke off as a whistle sounded.

'Oh goody, lunchtime. Shall we eat under the oak over there?' she added, collecting two parcels wrapped in greaseproof paper from the huge basket on the trestle table and handing one to Daisy. 'Pays to get in quick here,' she added, laughing as the others came running across from the next field.

The days passed by pleasantly and with Mateo's help

she eventually plucked up enough courage to start caring for the bull. One day, he even helped her lead it out to the field until the beast turned and bellowed, which had her hurtling for the gate. She was leaning against the fence, trying to catch her breath, when she saw Wilf watching her through narrowed eyes.

* * *

It was just on two months since Patty had started at Elizabeth's, and she was enjoying the challenge of her new job. Having a good eye for what suited people, she had quickly become popular with customers wanting to have their old outfits revamped. Her only bugbear was her sister, who, living so close, constantly called in to the shop.

'I'm happy to help you, Vera, and I quite understand that your old clothes are too loose now you've lost weight, but I'm paid to do a job here so will have to charge you,' Patty said, when she appeared with yet another dress she wanted adapting.

'I'm your sister,' Vera cried.

'And I have a job to do. Look,' she said, peering around to make sure no customers were waiting, 'bring your dress round to Victory Walk and I'll do it at home. I won't have to charge if I do it in my own time and we can have a nice cuppa and—'

'Really!' muttered Vera, snatching up her bag and marching from the shop.

'Was that Mrs Potter I just saw leaving?' asked Mrs Wise, the proprietor, emerging from the storeroom in a cloud of the eau de parfum she sprayed throughout the premises. 'I don't mean to be funny, Mrs Harrison, but she does come in here rather regularly without actually purchasing anything. Personally, I pride myself on never letting a client leave empty-handed,' she added, her smile not reaching her eyes.

'I believe she's losing weight, Mrs Wise, and keeping an eye on the latest styles to encourage herself.'

'I see. Well, in that case it will be interesting to see if she actually decides to make a purchase. Now, about those alterations for Mrs Jamieson . . .'

'I have them right here, Mrs Wise,' Patty said, taking the two-piece from the table behind.

'Oh good. Be a poppet and pop them round to her on your way home, will you? You can bring the money in with you in the morning.'

'But . . .' Patty began, knowing the customer lived nowhere near her route home.

'Good, good. You know, Mrs Harrison, if you carry on like this, you'll pass your three month's trial period.'

***

'And if I carry on like this, I'll be a nervous wreck,' Patty told Bert as she relayed the events of her day over dinner. 'There's hardly enough time in the day as it is, without having to deliver people's alterations.'

'Hmm. She does seem to demand rather a lot of you,' he agreed.

'Coo-ee!'

'As does someone else,' he muttered as Vera appeared.

'I've brought that dress for you to alter. Oh, you're eating,' she said, eyeing their plates hopefully. 'Don't let me interrupt,' she added, sinking onto the chair beside her sister.

'There's a spam fritter left,' Patty offered.

'Ooh, goodie, I'm starving,' Robbie cried. 'Tell you what, I'll go halves with you, Auntie,' he offered.

'That's my boy,' Bert murmured, picking up his newspaper to hide his grin. 'And when you've finished, you can go and do the dishes for your Ma.'

'That's a swizz. What's the point of earning pocket money when you can't get any sweets?'

'Think of the good it's doing your teeth,' Bert chuckled.

'Will you be long, Patty?' Vera asked. 'Only I need this dress adapting by Saturday. Arthur's taking me to see our Joy sing at the Eagle Club and I need to look my best,' she announced proudly.

Bert lowered his paper and exchanged a knowing look with Patty.

Although Patty was pleased things seemed to be improving for her sister, she couldn't help worrying how she was going to fit everything in. When Clover and Marigold had visited, they'd prepared the evening meal for her, and it had been such a help. As well as being charming, Marigold had proved to be a proficient cook, doing wonders with their rations. If only she had help on a regular basis, life would be so much easier.

When Vera left, Bert turned on the wireless, saying, 'Time for the important news.'

'A U-boat has sunk the transport ship *Laconia* with many Italian prisoners killed.

'The German offensive on Stalingrad continues with hand-to-hand fighting in the city.'

Patty sighed as she picked up her knitting. Would there never be any end to all this fighting?

CHAPTER THIRTY-FIVE

As the ambulance crews gathered round, Sonia Strang held up her hand for silence.

'What now?' Kitty muttered. 'Hope there's not another disaster – I'm blooming knackered.'

Knowing her colleague had been out partying with GIs, Hope hid a smile. The bright lipstick she was wearing, and the Hershey bar tucked in her pocket being a give-away, even if she wasn't yawning every ten seconds or so.

'Right then, everyone!' The supervisor's strident tones rang out, commanding instant hush. 'I have some good news to impart, which makes a change, I know. In recognition of our sterling work for the war effort, November 15th has been declared Civil Defence Day by the King.'

'Does that mean we'll get a day's holiday?' Kitty asked, suddenly alert.

'Even better, Kitty, there is to be a march through the streets of London, culminating in a special service at St Paul's Cathedral which will be attended by our King and Queen. We have been one of the depots chosen to represent our service, which is a huge honour, so it will be best bib and tucker and smart marching.'

'Can't say I've ever marched before,' Geraldine remarked.

'Which is why we will need to spend the next few weeks practising. Don't worry,' she added, 'this will be carried out during work time when, hopefully, the station will continue to be quiet. Now, I know I can rely on you to do our depot and the entire ambulance service proud. Recognizing how important our presentation will be, I've tasked MacLeod with licking you into shape, as it were. He's had experience of such matters and, having spoken with his bosses, barring any emergency, he has been granted leave from his job until after the ceremony. He will be back at the depot later today, and I know I can rely on you to give him your full cooperation. Any questions?'

'Well, that's a turn up for the books,' Kitty said as they made their way outside to check their vehicles over. 'You could have said Ian was coming back?'

'Hmm,' Hope murmured, opening the bonnet and disappearing under it. Not having heard from him since that afternoon on the Downs, she hadn't known herself. That didn't stop her heart from flipping at the thought of seeing him again though.

'You could have told me,' Hope cried as soon as he walked through the gates. She'd spent the rest of the morning in the misty murk, tinkering with the engine, so she'd catch him as soon as he arrived.

'Nice to see you too,' he replied. 'Don't look at me like that, Hope. I suppose you're referring to the march. Well, I only found out I'd been granted leave last night and then it was too late to come and see you. I also had a job to finish before I was released this morning.'

'Released? You make it sound like a prison.'

'Believe you me, it feels like it at times. Anyhow, I'm hoping we can spend some time together over the next two weeks. Unless you've already made other plans, of course?' he said, eyeing her quizzically.

'I'll try and fit you into my busy social calendar,' she grinned, her spirits soaring.

'Unless you've changed your mind, I thought we might go to the West End, visit a few jewellers.'

'Why?' she asked, puzzled.

'I can hardly ask for your hand in marriage without a decent ring to put on your finger, can I?' he grinned.

'Oh yes,' she cried, her hand automatically feeling for the purse in her pocket, her eyes shining.

'I'd like nothing better than to kiss those lovely lips of yours right now, Hope Potter, however, I'm mindful we have an audience.' He nodded towards the little group watching them intently from the doorway. 'Come on, I promised Sonia I'd start the training at lunchtime.'

'Yes, sir,' she said, saluting, and promptly began marching towards the others.

* * *

The bull stamped his hoof and let out a loud bellow, causing Daisy to step smartly backwards. 'Come on, Brutus, I thought we were friends?' she murmured.

'Yer wanted up at the Hall straight away, Miss Harrison,' Wilf announced, looking smug.

'Me? Up at the Hall. Why?'

'Must be something bad. They don't call Land Girls up there for nowt.'

She hadn't really done anything wrong had she? Daisy pondered as she duly hurried up to the grand old building situated two miles or so from the farm. Although it was misty and damp, she was perspiring by the time she reached the entrance. Back door or front? And should she ask to use the convenience so she could tidy herself up?

As she stood dithering on the driveway, the oak door opened, and a silver-haired woman, neatly attired in a tweed jacket, matching skirt and pristine white blouse beckoned to her.

'Miss Harrison? I'm Mrs Alice Newman. Come in,' she invited, leading the way down a hallway and into a small room which had been set up as an office. 'Of course, back in the day they would have a maid to answer the door.' Smiling, she gestured for Daisy to take a seat. 'I hope you've settled in well at the hostel?'

'Yes, thank you, Mrs Newman,' Daisy replied, perching nervously on the edge of the chair. If she was going to be told off, she wished the woman would get on with it.

'Alice, please, and perhaps I might call you Daisy? It's so much friendlier, don't you think?' Before Daisy could reply, the woman continued. 'Now, you're probably wondering who I am and why you've been summoned here?'

'What have I done wrong?' Daisy asked, impatient to find out.

'Let me introduce myself properly and then we'll discuss the issue. I'm village registrar for the Women's Land Army and, as such, have responsibility for the girls at the hostel at Great Bradley along with others in the surrounding areas. It's my job to ensure all the girls are looked after, carry out their duties efficiently and basically do as they are asked.'

'You mean you liaise between the Land Army and the farms?'

'And the Ministry of Agriculture. It's no exaggeration to say we're all involved in ensuring we produce enough food to feed the country. When a matter is brought to my attention, I find the best way to deal with it is to speak to the person concerned for there are usually two sides to it.'

'So, what have I done?' Daisy persisted.

'Mr Meddler is, how can I say, Lord W's lookout and, as such, reports back anything he thinks his lordship should know. Now, Daisy, I understand you have been put in charge of Brutus, his prize bull?'

'Yes, I wasn't sure of him at first, he's so ferocious, but he's all right when he gets to know you and Mateo showed me how to gain his confidence.'

'Mateo being an Italian POW working on the farm?' the woman asked, glancing at her notebook.

'Ah, I see the problem. We're not meant to speak to them, are we? Well, I think that's so wrong! My brother is a POW, and I would hope he's being shown some kindness and compassion by the Italians there.' She came to a halt, aware she shouldn't have spoken out like that.

'For what it's worth, I agree with you, Daisy,' Alice

told her. 'However, the rules are there as much for the safety of you girls as anything else. The problem I have is that Lord W's bull is what keeps this place going financially. Brutus is hired out to other farms for them to use on their cows, if you get my meaning. Naturally, his lordship wants someone Brutus likes to be in charge of him. He has watched you at work and thought you were that person, until Mr Meddler . . .'

'Meddled?' Daisy supplied.

'Precisely – and with an exaggerated account, by the sounds of it. Now, if I can reassure Lord W his judgement was correct, then there is no need for further action. However, you must promise to stay working here instead of moving on.'

'Oh, I will.'

'Good, then problem solved,' she said, ticking a page in her notebook. 'And is everything else all right? No other worries?'

'None you can help with,' Daisy murmured with a sigh.

'Try me, I don't only help with difficulties on the farm you know.'

'Well, you see, my boyfriend is in the Royal Navy and when I heard on the news about the Allied landings in North Africa, and that there had been numerous casualties, I got this terrible feeling like I've never had before. I just know he's been hurt, but I don't know how to find out. We're not married, and I don't know what ship he's on or anything and . . .'

'I understand,' Alice replied, quietly. 'Write down his details, name, rank, and anything else you know.' She tore out a sheet from her notebook and handed it to Daisy with a pencil.

'Thank you, but I'm not quite sure what good it will do,' Daisy said, handing it back.

'You never know. The Forces have what we call the War Line. It's a bit like a grapevine except we deal in facts and not Chinese whispers.' She grinned. 'It's amazing what we can find out on that. Although, I'm not promising anything.'

'It's just that I have this strong sense something's wrong.'

'Intuition, a hunch, call it what you will, it's always better to act on it, I find. Now, I really must be getting on,' she said, rising to her feet. 'Go back to the farm and I'll reassure Lord W you're the right girl for his precious Brutus. In the meantime, I'll make enquiries and contact you when and if I find out anything.'

'Thank you so much, Alice. I really didn't know who to turn to.'

'Chin up, and remember the Land Army are relying on girls like you to keep our nation fed.'

As Daisy made her way back to the farm, her thoughts were all over the place. On the one hand she felt better for having discussed the news report with Alice, yet on the other, she still knew in her heart that something had happened to Freddy.

* * *

Rose stifled a yawn as she came off duty. As usual it had been a long shift and, although it was only four

353

o'clock in the afternoon she was out on her feet. Of course, her night out might have had something to do with how she was feeling, for it was the early hours of the morning when Philip had dropped her off outside her room, whispering, 'What I wouldn't give to come inside with you.' Well, she would have given anything for him to as well.

'Hello, Rose.' Shaken out of thoughts, she looked up to see Hope hovering in reception.

'Hope, how are you?'

'Waiting for a patient to be discharged. We just brought a woman in who's in labour, so it's not worth returning to the depot only to come back again. Kitty's outside.'

'If it's Mr Sanderson you're taking home, he still needs to be checked by the doctor. I was just going to grab a coffee – why don't you join me. I'll let the receptionist know where we'll be.'

'So, how's tricks?' Rose asked, when they were seated with their drinks.

'Great. They're holding a Civil Defence Day and we're busy practising our marching. It was decreed by the King himself,' Hope said.

'Sounds exciting, tell me more,' Rose encouraged, sipping her coffee, then nodding as Hope relayed the details of their route through the streets of London to St Paul's Cathedral where there was to be a special thanksgiving service for the defence workers. 'Ian's in charge of training us,' she finished.

'Hence the sparkle in your eyes?'

'Yes, and we'll have some news to tell the family soon,' she gushed.

'Exciting. I can't wait to hear what, although I can guess. And how are your family?'

'Things seem to be improving between Ma and Pa. Joy says Pa is staying home more in the evenings and they're not so scratchy. She's waiting for her interview with ENSA, but Faith, well . . .' she shrugged. 'Thing is, I've seen her out with another man.'

'And did she look happy?'

'Yes, she did. Still, it's not right, is it? I mean they haven't even found Martin's body yet,' she sighed then picked up her mug.

'You realize they may never find it?' Rose said gently.

'I guess so. I just think Faith should still be mourning him, or at least hoping he will come home one day.'

'Perhaps she's just being realistic. It can't be easy bringing up a little one, even with Martin's parents helping.'

'You're probably right,' she sighed. 'Anyway, how was your date with Philip?'

'Fantastic,' Rose gushed.

'And when are you seeing him again?'

'I don't know. He left without mentioning it. He definitely had something on his mind, though.' She sighed, her doubts about how he truly felt about her surfacing again. When they were together, she was sure he loved her, but then, when he left without making further plans to meet, it left her questioning his true feelings.

'He must be sick of fighting. This war just drags on, doesn't it?' Hope said, thinking of the numerous times Ian was either delayed by a last-minute panic at his engineering works, or visiting his children. Each night she dreamed that the war was over, she and Ian were married, and they were all living in a little house as a proper family.

When Kitty called from the doorway that the patient was ready, Hope jumped to her feet.

'Don't worry. I bet Philip's writing to you as we speak,' she said. Rose nodded. Perhaps being overtired was sparking her doubts.

CHAPTER THIRTY-SIX

Despite the November day being damp and dismal, thousands of people turned out to watch Civil Defence workers from all over the country march through the streets of London. The crowds clapped and cheered as they made their way towards St Paul's Cathedral and the atmosphere was jovial as they forgot the cares of the war for a few hours.

Everywhere was a sea of colour, each group divided into chronological sequence, and carrying a banner to show where they were from. Men from the Anti-Aircraft division led the parade followed by the ARP Wardens, police and fire brigades, each wearing their different colour and style of uniform.

The Homerton Depot of the LAAS, impeccably dressed in black, were led by Sonia Strang, proudly brandishing their banner aloft.

'I didn't realize there'd be so many of us,' Hope murmured to Ian who was marching by her side.

'The King and Queen wanted to recognize the good job Defence Workers are doing for the Country,' he told her. 'Look, there they are, sheltering under that striped awning.' Then, as if as one, all crew members looked right and saluted, and the King saluted back.

The cathedral was lofty and grand, but the singing

soared to the roof as everyone rejoiced. Hope watched in awe as the King in uniform and the Queen wearing a blue suit with a diamond maple leaf brooch on her hat, walked past, so close she could almost have reached out and touched them.

'That was the best day of my life!' Hope declared later when they were celebrating with a glass of lemonade.

'Better than last Saturday?' Ian asked, pulling a hurt expression as he looked at the diamond sparkling on her finger.

'No, of course not, silly. It was wonderful trying to choose from all those different rings and even more wonderful when you placed this on my finger in Bushey Park,' she told him, smiling as she stroked the gold band. She would always keep the grass one in its little purse, though.

'I'm surprised you didn't scare the deer away with all that shrieking,' he grinned.

'Well, I was happy. Anyway, I thought that was a great suggestion of yours for us all to go out to dinner to celebrate. Ma's suggestion of a huge engagement party is not my idea of fun.'

'Nor mine. I'd rather have you all to myself any day, Hope Potter, soon to be Hope MacLeod,' he murmured, making suggestive expressions with his eyes.

'And when we're married you can, any day and every day, Ian MacLeod,' she promised, letting out a sigh of happiness.

***

In Suffolk, Daisy had been on tenterhooks, the days passing agonizingly slowly since her meeting with Alice Newman. Although she had carried out her work conscientiously on the farm and looked after Brutus to the best of her ability, she found herself jumping at the slightest noise and couldn't eat, so that the warden at the hostel had enquired if she was going down with something.

She was busy grooming Brutus, who now grudgingly tolerated her presence, when Wilf shouted that she was wanted up at the Hall.

'Best get up there sharp. It don't do to keep Mrs Newman waiting, though I can't think what she wants to see yer for,' he grumped, clearly put out that he hadn't been told. 'And get yerself back here sharpish an' all. 'Tis yer job to be looking after Brutus, not gadding about the estate.'

Trying not to laugh at his indignant expression, yet anxious to see if there was any news of her beloved Freddy, she began to run. The newspapers had been full of reports of the latest offensive in North Africa, but did not go into detail about any casualties, and her heart sank further every time she read another one. Yet, she couldn't stop herself from trying to analyse them, nor from listening to the bulletins on the wireless, even though afterwards, she always wished she hadn't.

Despite the cold weather, the front door was ajar when she arrived.

'Come in and shut the door behind you, Daisy,' Alice called, her voice carrying down the hallway.

She was sitting at the table in the office, studying what appeared to be a map.

'Ah, Daisy, how are you, dear?' she asked, squinting as she looked up. 'No, don't answer that. I can see you have been worrying. Well, I hope what I have to say will in some way help to alleviate your concerns. Sit down, dear. I have taken the liberty of making us some tea.'

Impatiently, Daisy watched as the woman carefully poured milk followed by the scalding liquid into the dainty china cups, passing one to her.

'Biscuit?' But as she proffered the plate. Daisy shook her head then could contain herself no longer.

'Is there any news?' she cried, her voice coming out like a high-pitched screech.

'Yes, Daisy, but do try to stay calm. Getting worked up will help nobody. Now, I have been able to ascertain from the War Line that your Frederick – Freddy – was indeed one of the casualties of those Allied Landings when his ship was sunk off the city of Algiers. He is alive, but unconscious and badly burned. At present he is being treated on a hospital ship in the Western Mediterranean, which will soon be heading for Gibraltar.'

'Oh, poor Freddy!'

'Indeed. But although his condition is serious, he has fared better than many of his colleagues, some of whom are . . . well, I'll spare you the details.'

'But I must go and see him!' Daisy cried, jumping to her feet.

'Sit down, my dear. I understand your concern but

remember, we are talking about Africa here. Look, I'll show you,' she added, turning the map around so Daisy could see. 'There are many hundreds of miles, not to mention the time it would take crossing the seas between England and there, even if you could get transport.'

'Oh,' Daisy muttered, slumping back in the chair. Without warning, hot tears began to course down her cheeks.

'There now, pull yourself together,' Alice said briskly, passing her a snowy white handkerchief edged in lace. 'Faint heart and all that. Now, you may think I'm not sympathetic, but believe you me, I am. My husband was missing for months before I could establish that he was a POW, so I know all too well the agony of heartbreak. What you need now is a plan of action.'

'But I wouldn't know where to begin,' Daisy cried. 'What can I do?'

'Stay calm for a start. From what I've gleaned, Freddy needs to be stabilized before he can travel. When he's fit enough, and no one can give any idea of when that might be, he will be shipped back to a hospital in England, most likely Queen Alexandra's, in London.'

'That's great, because then I can visit him,' Daisy cried, her spirits lifting for the first time in weeks.

'There is a fair way to go before we get to that stage,' Alice cautioned, studying Daisy intently. 'However, we shall think to the future positively. Now, Christmas will soon be upon us and as I see it you have two options. You can go home and spend the festivities with your family . . .'

'Much as I'd love to see them, I don't feel like celebrating. It will be noisy, and they'd ask questions,' she interjected, shuddering at the thought.

'I understand. The other option would be for you to stay here, continue looking after Brutus and carry out the essential tasks around the farm, like the milking, et cetera, which still needs to be done. Naturally, all the girls want to go home for the holidays, and they usually draw straws to see who stays behind.'

The mention of drawing straws reminded Daisy of Devon and she shuddered.

'My dear, the shock is setting in,' Alice said, picking up the teapot. Daisy watched as she poured the amber liquid into her empty cup, yet for the life of her she couldn't remember drinking the first one.

'Remaining on the farm will win you brownie points with Lord W. He's already impressed with the way Brutus has taken to you. And, of course, you will carry over your days of holiday which you can then use to visit Freddy. As and when that time comes,' she added, seeing Daisy's face light up at the prospect.

'Thank you so much, Alice.'

'You're welcome. And I'll pray for a happy outcome for you both. In the meantime, get back to your work and I'll keep my ear to the War Line, as it were. When and if I hear anything further, I will let you know. You should be aware, though, that these things all take time. Oh, and, Daisy, don't forget to write and let your parents know you won't be home for Christmas.'

Heart bursting that Freddy was alive, Daisy ran back

down the path, the words 'he's alive, he's alive, he's alive' pounding round her brain in time with her footsteps. She would write to her Ma and Pa of course, but she wouldn't tell them about Freddy until she had more news.

* * *

'Daisy won't be coming home for Christmas,' Patty told Bert as she scanned the letter that had just arrived. 'It seems she's entrusted with looking after a prize bull, would you believe?'

'Bring in a fair bit of income, those bulls,' Bert grunted, looking up from his paper.

'But you'd think she'd want to celebrate with us, especially as Clover has to work too. And what about our Rose? Will she be home?'

'She wasn't sure. Still, that's what this war does for you.'

'Surely it can't go on for much longer,' Patty sighed, picking up her knitting. 'It's nearly the end of 1942, for heaven's sake.'

'I wouldn't bank on it finishing any time soon, love. The papers are still full of news of casualties in North Africa, the Far East and at sea. Thank heavens our Peter's in Italy and out of the way.'

'I suppose I'll have to see what I can get from the butcher for our Christmas dinner. Although it would help if I knew who was going to be here to celebrate,' Patty sighed.

'Well, I'll be here,' Robbie said, looking up from the piece of paper he'd been scribbling on. 'Get as much food in as you like, I'll see it all gets eaten,' he added gleefully. 'Anyhow, I've finished writing my present list for Santa.'

He passed it to Bert whose eyebrows nearly disappeared beneath his hair.

'And where is Santa getting a bike from?' he asked.

'I don't know, Pa. You and Ma always told me he was magic, so I guess he'll know.'

'Will he, indeed,' Patty cried. 'In that case, he'll also know if you've cleaned your rabbit out, won't he?'

'All right, I'll go and do it,' he muttered. 'But *everybody's* getting a bike, you know,' he added, disappearing into the yard.

'Don't look so worried, love. I doubt anyone will be getting anything new the way all the metal and iron's been collected for the war effort.'

'True. Still, that doesn't answer my question about what we're going to do for Christmas?'

'If you ask me, I can't think of anything nicer than you and me putting our feet up beside the fire and relaxing. When was the last time we had time for ourselves without worrying about one of our darling offspring? Could be quite nice to cuddle up together, just you and me, don't you think?'

'You silly old thing,' tutted Patty, but feeling pleased, nevertheless.

'Guess what, it's snowing!' Robbie cried, appearing excitedly in the doorway. 'Father Christmas needn't worry about bringing me a bike, I'll need a sledge now.'

As he disappeared before Patty could tell him to put on his mittens, Bert turned to her, a big grin on his face.

'At least I can make him a sledge using an old wooden tray and some of that string you save.'

'And maybe we'll have a white Christmas,' Patty mused. 'That would make up for the lack of decorations.'

'We'll have a lovely time, never you fret, even if we have to eke out the fuel for the fire.'

'I'll bring those extra blankets in from the Nissan hut, being as how Hitler's gone quiet over here.'

'Thankfully, it's our troops who are gaining ground now. They're starting to push back the Japanese in Burma, Patty. They're saying the tide is turning at last, so fingers crossed that's true.'

Patty slipped her arm through Bert's, 'Ooh, listen . . . Carol singers at the door. Now that's got to be a good omen.'

'I couldn't agree more.' Bert kissed his wife's cheek, as the strains of *Silent Night* drifted in from Victory Walk.

CHAPTER THIRTY-SEVEN

Although it was Christmas Eve, there had been no let-up in the activity on the ward. Whilst admissions had reduced, Rose spent a considerable time consulting with the doctors as to which patients were well enough to send home. Nobody wanted to spend the festivities in hospital if they could avoid it, but sending a patient home too soon could result in dire consequences.

She had elected to work tonight so that the nurses could go to the party being held in the canteen. Keeping busy was the best thing, for she hadn't heard anything from Philip since he'd left.

'Are you sure you don't want to go, sister?' Susan asked. She was wearing a sprig of holly in her nurse's cap and her face was flushed with excitement. 'I can always come back upstairs after an hour or so. They're setting up a gramophone so we can dance.'

'That's very kind of you, but I'm sure the doctors would prefer to dance with a pretty young nurse like you,' Rose told her.

'We've done all the TPRs and settled the patients; is there anything else before we go?' Effie asked, as conscientious as ever.

'No, off you go and have fun,' Rose said, shooing them out of the door.

She looked around the ward, festooned with as many paper chains as the girls had been able to make from old newspapers, and sighed. She'd always loved Christmas, but this year she didn't feel like celebrating at all.

Perhaps she was getting old, she thought, taking another look around the ward before settling down to complete the paperwork that was an inevitable part of her job.

'Sister?' She looked up to see a porter beckoning to her from the doorway.

'What is it, Tibbs?' she asked. 'Is there some problem?'

'You could say that, sister. You're wanted in the staff room immediately. I've been told to stay here until you return.'

'Well, it's highly irregular.'

'Just passing on the message. Sounds urgent to me, so I'd get a shufty on.'

Seeing the man was adamant and knowing there could be an emergency of some sort, she hurried along the corridor, her heels clicking as she walked.

Pushing open the door, she saw the lights on the Christmas tree had been left on and was just thinking of rebuking someone, when a shape materialized out of the shadows.

'Oh!' she squeaked. The figure advanced and she was about to scream when she saw who it was. '*Philip?*' she gasped. 'Whatever are you doing here?' But she was talking to thin air.

'Rose?' Puzzled, she looked down to see him kneeling

on the floor and holding up something that sparkled in the lights from the tree.

'Rose, my beloved . . . Will you do me the honour of marrying me?' he asked. Struck dumb by surprise she could only stand there gaping, until he muttered.

'For Lord's sake please answer me, Rose, I'm getting cramp down here.'

He looked so unlike the capable, unflustered RAF officer Rose was used to, she had to fight down the temptation to giggle. Then she realized what he'd actually said, and her heart soared.

'Of course, I will!' she told him, watching as he got to his feet. Then, taking her hand, he slid the most beautiful sapphire ring onto her finger.

'In that case, my beautiful fiancée, there is only one thing left to do,' he said, holding a sprig of mistletoe above their heads. As his lips came down on hers, Rose sighed. Oh, she did love him – and she loved Christmas too.

'Well, this is exciting news,' Patty cried as Rose stood before her waving her left hand, while Philip held her other. 'I'm so happy for you both.'

'Thank you, Mrs Harrison. I promise I'll take great care of Rose. Although, when I met Mr Harrison earlier to ask for her hand formally, I was a nervous wreck waiting for him to grant his permission to wed.'

'It was an important decision, young man, and not one to be given lightly,' Bert told him.

'Well, at least it gave us time to get the vegetables peeled,' Patty laughed. 'As I'm sure you can understand, our Rose is very precious to us. Now, if you're going to be part of the family then you can at least call us by our first names.'

'I don't know about that,' Bert said, looking at Philip sternly. 'But I do know this calls for a celebration.' He smiled, brandishing a bottle of sherry before them.

'That would be lovely, and I've brought my own contribution to the party,' Philip told them, retrieving a bottle of wine from his coat pocket. 'Luckily our heavy coats have some uses.'

'Cooee, something smells good,' Vera said, sniffing the air appreciatively as she appeared through the back door, followed by Arthur and Joy. 'And we hear congratulations are in order.'

'How on earth . . .' Patty began.

'Sorry, Auntie. I found out when I went to Homerton to take a patient home. Then it sort of slipped out when I popped round to wish Ma and Pa a happy Christmas,' laughed Hope as she came down the stairs, having changed out of her uniform. 'Talk of the hospital it is, what with Rose being so popular.'

'I managed to get a leg of mutton off the butcher – hours I had to queue for it, mind, but I've turned it into mock goose so if we peel some more spuds and carrots, I'm sure we can feed everyone,' Patty – ever the hostess – said, ignoring Rose's groan.

'And we brought some shortbread and buns that nice Jane Bayliss made for us,' Vera told them, ignoring the surprised looks being shot her way.

'Well, it seems we have the makings of a feast,' Bert said, holding out a tray of glasses. 'But first of all, let's toast our newly engaged couple and wish them every future happiness.'

'To Rose and Philip.'

'Hear, hear, Rose and Philip.'

'And we must remember our dear Peter, Clover and Daisy, God bless them and bring them safely home soon.'

'And Father Christmas who brought me a spiffing sledge,' Robbie added. 'Can we hurry up and eat so I can play in the snow before it melts?'

As the laughter died down, Patty raised her glass.

'And here's to all our brave lads and lasses who are doing their utmost to win this war. Pray God it will be over soon, and we can all get back to normal – after all, we have a wedding to plan.'

'Or maybe even two,' added Vera, never one to be outdone.

So much for their quiet Christmas, Bert thought, and it looked like 1943 was going to be an eventful one too.

'Perhaps we'll all be together next year,' Patty murmured, for there was nothing more important than family, was there?

ACKNOWLEDGEMENTS

With sincere thanks to Kate and Teresa for their invaluable guidance.

Pern for his meticulous research and encouragement.

My writing buddies at BWC for their continued friendship and support which is so very much appreciated.

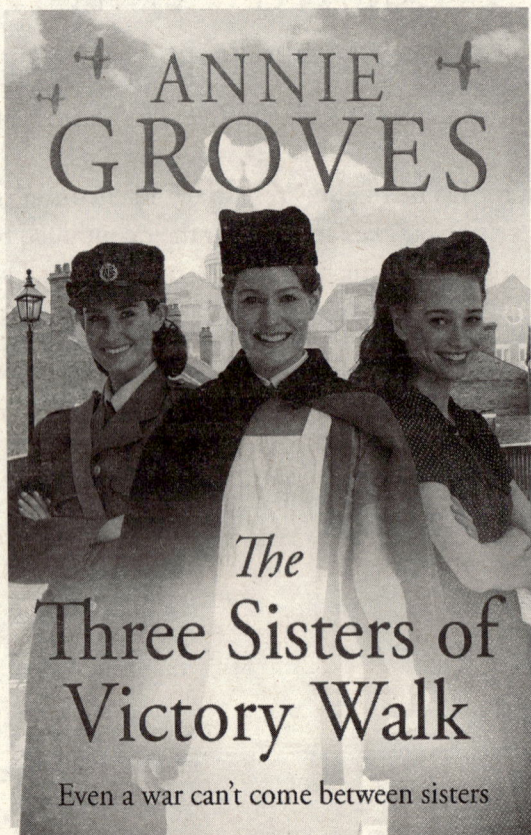

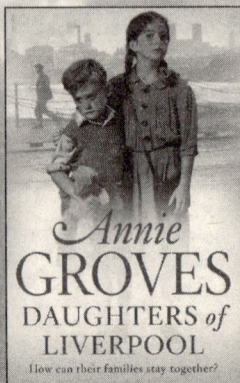

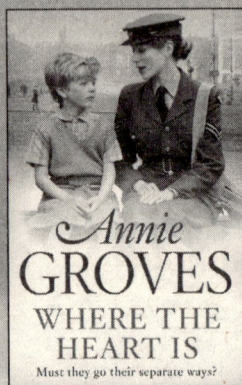

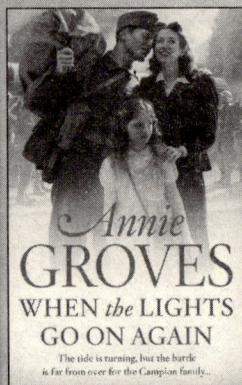

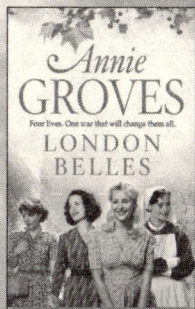

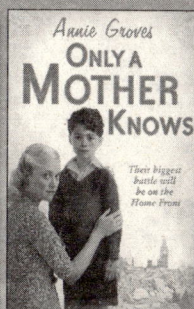

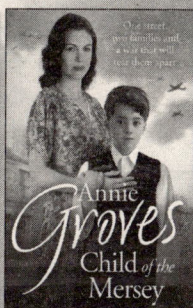

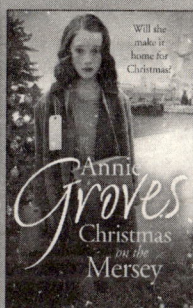